# BEDOUGALNN

## THE ART OF CHRONOSTASIS

A TIME TAILORS NOVEL

MORTICUS HOLTZ

ISBN 978-1-7393130-0-5 (paperback)
ISBN 978-1-7393130-1-2 (ebook)

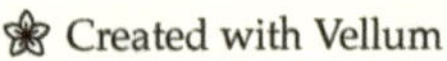

*For Humbug.*

*Thank you for your support, guidance, encouragement, and patience.*
*And not just during the creation of this book.*

# I

# THE MAN WITH THE RAVEN TATTOO

With a loud THUD! He hit the floor, but that would be eight days from now.

Dougal gazed out into the frosty early evening. The rain pounded like a psychotic jackhammer against the cold concrete pavement, as if it had forgotten how to make the traditional pitter-patter sound he had grown up with.

The trickles of water streamed down the windowpane, distorting everything outside into grotesque monsters. He played for a while, turning everything he looked at into objects and faces, or even objects with faces. *Strange,* he thought, *how easy it was to amuse himself, whilst also scaring himself a little with the images his mind created.*

As of this moment, he was picturing a werewolf staring at him from across the street, the shimmering streetlights becoming like piercing yellow eyes. Dougal chuckled out loud, before realising the streetlights were not yet lit. His brow furrowing as he squinted through the downpour, mustering his concentration as he stared a little harder, focusing his mind, but he could not recreate the image.

He slunk down off the windowsill, slipping into his oversized, comfortable red reading chair, and burying his head into the cushion. A moment later, he found himself sneaking a peek back through the glass to check if the werewolf was back. It was not.

He was just 23 years old when his parents died, and had moved into the apartment not long after. His mother being taken by cancer, and his father days later from a broken heart. Dougal had never thought such a thing possible, but what he witnessed had a profound effect on his life.

He gave up trying to find his one true love many years back, after suffering numerous failed relationships. Most of them ending with him being accused of not being in the present, or away with the fairies. How he would have chuckled, had he known both would turn out to be true.

These days it was just him and Bounce, his white and tan four-year-old English Bulldog. Someone had dumped him outside the local animal shelter when he was just four months old, and there had been an instant bond between them. After adopting him, he put the inheritance his parents left to him to good use, by becoming the shelter's largest benefactor. Purchasing the land, covering all medical and salary costs, and anything else they required.

Bounce got his name from the way his whole front end would lift off the floor when he barked and he was Dougal's best friend, by all accounts, his only friend, and he knew it. Had Dougal known how much Bounce was to infect him with affection, he may have adopted an aloof cat instead, although this scenario would have been unlikely in the extreme.

Dougal flicked on the television and skipped through the channels for a few seconds before flicking it off again. The same old inane trash, merely reconstituted and sold to an unwitting audience as something new. *Ha,* he thought, *I am 35 years old, and there is still nothing new in this world, no surprises.*

As he settled back into his chair, the harsh buzzing sound of the apartment's intercom pierced the room, and he leapt from his seat like the startled aloof cat he never got. Bounce let out a single deep bark and charged down the hallway to the front door.

The buzzer sounded again, followed by another impatient bark.

Dougal was not expecting any visitors, and he had no idea who would call at just gone six o'clock on a Wednesday evening. He pressed the intercom, wondering for a moment whether he had ordered pizza and simply forgotten.

"Hello."

After a slight pause, a crackled voice replied.

"It's me. We need to talk."

*Hmm, certainly not pizza,* he thought, *unless of course there was an issue with my choice of toppings.*

Now Dougal was not in the habit of buzzing random people into the building. But he was bored, had no plans, and as previously iterated, had no known friends, at least not ones that would turn up unannounced. *What was the worst that could happen?*

Dougal paused for a moment to think about that.

*Who could it be? What could they want?*

These would have been excellent questions to ask the voice on the other end of the intercom before pressing the door release.

The buzzer sounded again, jolting Dougal back into the present. He glanced down at an overexcited Bounce, raised his eyebrows, and with a smile that reflected his willing acceptance of fate, he pressed the button.

The click of the door opening crackled through the intercom. Bounce woofed again, pressing Dougal to open the front door of the apartment. But Dougal hesitated, stood there in only his grey lounge pants and Pixies t-shirt. *What am I doing,* he thought, *buzzing a stranger into the building? It could be anyone, or anything.*

For a second or two, he regretted pressing the door release. *Too late for that,* he thought, *just as long as it was not that bloody werewolf.* He chuckled and opened the door, keeping the chain on just in case.

Dougal peered through the crack into the foyer, as Bounce squeezed past his legs and pressed his snout against the gap, eager to see who came visiting. Stood before him was a dwarf.

Now I know what you are probably thinking, but stop, because this dwarf bore no resemblance to any other dwarf from popular fiction, not even if you squinted.

A friendly craggy face smiled at him, his long woolly white hair cascading down past his shoulders, and blending into his matching half braided beard. Perched upon his nose were a pair of small, round, gold-rimmed glasses, which were half buried into his voluminous white bushy eyebrows, perfectly framing his deep-set, piercing blue eyes. By all accounts, he looked not dissimilar to a miniature Santa minus the clothes. That's not to say he was naked.

For a moment Dougal thought he spotted something lurking in the visitor's beard, but dismissed the idea as preposterous.

A small weathered hand, which by the look of it had been around for many years, thrust forward through the gap grasping for his. He paused to grip it should he break it, but less than a second later, it almost lifted him off the floor with a shake that could have triggered an avalanche. Luckily, he lived in the inner part of the city, and there were no mountains, let alone snow.

"The names Graimel, and I am hoping you are, The Bedougalnn?" Graimel said, in a voice so deep it could be mistaken for a giant's whisper.

That is, of course, if giants were real.

"Nope. Sorry mate, you must have the wrong address. My name is Dougal, Dougal Malumont, and most definitely not *The* anything."

"Are you sure?"

"Quite, well, look, I hope you find the, er, Mr Bedougalnn is it, you're looking for."

"Cup of tea?" Graimel asked, always the optimist.

"No thank you! Could you let go of my hand, please?" Dougal said, in his most insistent, authoritative voice.

Now to most, this would have sounded like a snail apologising for getting in your way, after you narrowly avoided stepping on it. This was further evidenced by the fact, Graimel did not let go of his hand.

"Do you, by any chance, have a tattoo in the shape of a raven? On the back of your left shoulder, I believe?" Graimel asked, still gripping Dougal's hand a little tighter than necessary.

Dougal gulped, somewhat disturbed by the question. He tried to withdraw his hand in vain, trembling as a shiver ran down his spine.

"Err, yeah. Why?"

"Fantastic!" Graimel howled. "Then it is true, you are, Bedougalnn. I thought I might have the wrong door again. You should have seen the bewildered expression on the face of the last guy when he opened the door and saw no one there," Graimel said, with a beaming smile.

"How do you mean?"

"Well, I didn't know what number you lived at, so I have been going through them all," Graimel said, his smile seeming to inch a little wider.

"No, I mean, why would you not be there when they opened the door?"

"Oh, I see, for the same reason I knew you were Bedougalnn when you opened your door. Humans cannot see us magic folk, and you can. The rest, merely a formality."

"But I'm human, and what do you mean by magic folk?" Dougal said, digging for a fuller explanation.

"Yes, of course you are. Can't say more than that, not yet. Clever idea of your parents, subtly changing your name like that. Much more fitting for humans, I suppose. I can call you Dougal if you prefer?"

"Well, seeing as how that is my name, yes I would prefer that." Dougal snatched his hand into the safety of his apartment. "Now what do you know of my parents?"

Dougal heard a click from the foyer, followed by his neighbour's door closing.

"Got you as well, did they? Bloody annoying kids. I don't know how they manage to run off so fast," said John.

Not to be confused with John the window cleaner, he lived across town above the Nag's Head.

"Yeah," Dougal said, as John trundled down the stairs.

"Then Dougal it is," Graimel whispered, with a knowing wink, "but I don't think it's wise for us to discuss anything else with me on this side of the door."

Graimel waited for Dougal to say or do something. When he didn't, he spoke again.

"Well, are you going to invite me in?" Graimel asked, in a pleasant yet persistent tone, which clearly stated he was going nowhere.

"What do you think, Bounce? Should we let him in?"

Bounce bounced and barked his unmitigated approval, eager to meet the visitor and receive the gift he carried in his left hand.

"Seeing as Bounce thinks you're all right, yeah, okay, but no funny business." Dougal removed the chain and swung the door open. "I have a black belt in Jujutsu."

Dougal didn't even know what Jujutsu was, let alone have any skill in it, but tried his best to sound convincing.

Graimel stepped into the apartment, trying to look impressed with Dougal's boast, but failing miserably, and looking confused as he threw his long black trench coat on the floor. Of course, when I say long, this being a dwarf's trench coat meant it was only about 1m long.

"It's a martial art you know," Dougal said, assuming Graimel like himself did not know of Jujutsu. "I can hang that up for you if you like?"

"He wouldn't thank you for that; he'll be happy on the floor."

Dougal eyed him curiously. *What an absurd thing to say,* he thought, *did he just refer to his coat as He? Can a coat actually be happy? No, that is preposterous.* He peered at the coat on the floor, the folds and creases in the leather, appearing to form a wide grin, squeezing his eyes shut before looking again, the illusion still clear.

"That was him," Graimel said, as he followed Dougal into the living room.

"Oh, he's always like that." Dougal gestured for Graimel to take a seat. "Grumpy seems to be his default setting."

A warm burnt orange colour decorated the walls of the living room. Which were bare, except for a few sample poems by an unknown poet, and a photo of Bounce sat on Dougal's lap while he tried to drink coffee. All framed in a rich mahogany. On the mantle above the fireplace, a small naked pendulum clock ticked noisily away inside a glass dome, next to a photo of his parents holding hands and smiling. Most likely taken on their wedding day, and how he always remembered them.

Graimel sauntered over to the sofa, hoisted himself up, and sunk back into it, the plushness of the cushions almost absorbing him. Dougal slumped down into his favourite chair.

"My parents?" Dougal asked.

"Yes, and rightly so of course," Graimel said, his eyes darting between the window and the clock on the mantle. "The time is not right to tell you everything, but I can tell you a little."

"Well, even a little might get me closer to a point where I can trust you," Dougal said, hoping to hear something enlightening about his secretive parents.

"I knew your father for a long time, even before he met your mother. I cannot tell you how or under what circumstance, but he gave up a lot to be with her, and to have you. You are very much like him in fact, very much."

"Is that it? Is that all you can tell me? You could've guessed as much!" Dougal said, almost spitting his words out, frustration spewing from his throat.

"It was your father who told me about your tattoo, which, in truth, is a birthmark, I believe. Before he passed, he entrusted me to watch over you, and to keep your secret safe from all, including yourself."

"Secret? I don't have any secrets."

"Your true identity is your secret, a secret I have kept for 35 years, but it is time you understood who you really are. You're, Bedougalnn."

"Yeah, so you keep saying, but that means nothing to me. When are you going to explain all this?"

"It's complicated, but I will try. You're a Time Tailor Dougal, as am I. More specifically, you're a—"

"I'm a what?"

"Let me finish. More specifically, you're a Time Tailor known in the fae world as Bedougalnn. As Time Tailors, we can manipulate time, or at least moments in time. This is something I do knowingly, and excel at, I hasten to add. You, however, do not do it at all in fact, as you are not trained." Graimel glanced up at the clock on the mantle. "But we will come on to that. As you will—"

"Hang on! So is this one of those master and apprentice type scenarios I've read so much about? Where I am destined to take over from you, and save the world from a calamity," Dougal said, trying to keep a straight face, but failing miserably.

"You really must stop interrupting. No, not at all, well maybe the bit about saving the world, but it might not come to that," Graimel said, the seriousness in his voice erasing Dougal's stupid grin. "As you will know, assuming you received some formal education, tailors use weights to help keep the fabric they are working with in the correct place. We are kind of like those weights, but we help keep the fabric of time in place, so to speak."

This was partly true, but mostly codswallop.

"Are you following?"

"No, not really, but go on," Dougal said, wondering if a discussion with the pizza delivery guy about his choice of toppings would be stranger than this one.

"Now, you're probably wondering why I am here. Well, your time is being hunted, and I do not know to what end. But in my experience, when someone is hunting something, it is not because they want to give it a hug. What I do know, however, is the hourglass containing your sands of time, is running out, which is puzzling to say the least, since time for a Tailor is indefinite. And if the last grain of sand should fall, well, that would be bad, very bad."

Dougal paused for a moment, portraying an impression of someone deep in thought.

"Hang on, did you just say that time for a Tailor is indefinite? Does that mean I'm immortal, I will live forever? When was I going to find this out?"

Graimel shrugged.

"Hmm. You ask some good questions, but the question you should ask is. What is hunting you, and why? Although I'm glad you didn't, as I do not have answers, and until we do, I cannot risk letting you out of my sight."

After a moment of quiet reflection pondering over the seriousness of Graimel's comments, Dougal found his mind wandering. The captivating ebony staff in Graimel's left hand had drawn his attention. It was intricately engraved with strange markings and had an overwhelming presence. The handle was mounted with a raven's head, the eyes of which appeared to follow you.

"Would you like me to put your stick with your coat?"

"Stick?" Graimel scoffed. "Do you not know a staff when you see one? And not just any staff, either. Let me introduce you to Harg, my most trusted companion."

Graimel stamped his staff against the floor. As he did so, Dougal swore he saw the raven's head move, and its two iridescent green eyes light up. He shook his head and squeezed his eyes tight shut for a second. When he opened them, everything was as normal as it could be. As Graimel lent forward to slide Harg onto the table, a small unintelligible sound came from his beard.

"Yes, yes," he whispered into his beard. "I meant one of my most trusted companions."

Dougal shifted uncomfortably in his chair, regretting his decision to let this seemingly insane mumbling dwarf into his apartment.

With a sudden unexplained compulsion, his eyes darted across to the coat by the door, almost willing Graimel to pick it up and leave. The coat now appeared to look as grumpy as a teenager who had lost Wi-Fi midway through a game. Suffice to say, it also seemed to be more than a little annoyed with what Graimel said.

"Were you just talking to your beard?" Dougal asked.

"No, simply clearing my throat, a little parched, you see, that's all."

"Sorry, where are my manners? Can I get you a drink?"

"A nice cup of tea would be marvellous; we should have time for tea."

"Time?"

"Yes, I hope so, but all in good time."

A little bemused, Dougal nipped through to the kitchen to prepare the tea.

Bounce had greeted Graimel like an old friend. Like all dogs, he was incredibly intuitive, and it was this that put Dougal in the right frame of mind to trust, at least for the moment.

"We have a lot to discuss, I just need to find the right start point," Graimel called into the kitchen, "I only hope there is enough time."

*There we were, back to time,* Dougal thought.

Time was of the utmost of importance to Graimel. Not only was manipulating it part of his job, but he knew the consequences should the Bedougalnn's time expire. To say that would be bad was an understatement, and certainly far worse than breaking wind in a lift with your new boss, after eating three-day-old reheated prawn vindaloo and drinking stale beer. Something Dougal still denies to this day. So it was Graimel's responsibility to ensure this did not happen, the time expiring thing that is, he just hadn't figured out how yet.

But there is, of course, always time for a cup of tea. Everything waits for tea, even time.

# 2

# One Lump or Two

Bounce shuffled his way along the rug towards Harg, intermittently stopping to rest his head on the table, his jowls leaving huge wet smears of saliva as he glanced doe eyed between Harg and Graimel. In his eyes, Harg was a delicious-looking stick, and Dougal always gave him sticks, so taking this one should not be a problem. After all, why else would that polite man bring a stick, if not as a gift for him?

To be clear, this is exactly how bulldogs think, and I use the word think, lightly.

Dougal stepped back into the room and ambled over to the table, tea tray in hand. Bounce made his move and snatched up Harg, his mouth salivating like a waterfall in a monsoon as he shook him vigorously, flicking huge droplets of dog drool everywhere.

"One lump or two," Dougal asked, as a large drop of Bounce's slobber landed with a delicious plop into the cup of freshly poured tea he had just brought in.

"I guess it'll be one," Graimel said, cringing a little as Dougal placed the tray on the coffee table.

As he did so, he took a moment to ruminate over the faint-stained ring forever ingrained into the wood, where his former partner once put down their hot mug of cocoa, without using a coaster. Not the reason they separated; I hasten to add.

Dougal tried to snatch the staff, Harg, from Bounce, but he raced off, careering around the room.

Yes, bulldogs can race. However, bulldogs do not possess the best depth perception, or width perception for that matter, especially when they are hurtling around with a Harg sticking from either side of their mouth.

Bounce careened around the living room like the proverbial drunk in a drag race, knocking over and breaking everything of bulldog height.

"Bounce, Drop," Dougal said, the command falling on deaf ears, *nothing new there* he thought, "Bounce, Drop it!" Dougal pressed, but again there was not even a glimmer of acknowledgement from Bounce, "I am so sorry about this."

"It's no problem, Dougal. I am sure they are only playing... but just to be sure."

Graimel sprang to his feet, standing on the sofa in his absurdly clean shoes. He held out his left arm, and with an open hand, he commanded.

"Harg, back."

In that instant, Graimel's staff transformed into a raven, flew once around the room, and re-transformed back into a staff in Graimel's hand.

"Perhaps I should keep a hold of Harg for now." Graimel sat back down and picked up his cup of tea. "Right, where do I start? I guess it should be at the beginning, but, no. Get comfy, I will try to explain."

"Whoa, hold up a minute! Did your staff just turn into a raven and fly around the room?" Dougal's eyes rolled as his knees wobbled a little. "I think I need to sit down," Dougal said, collapsing into his chair, his brain trying to rationalise what his eyes perceived.

"Are you okay?" Graimel asked. "You're not going to pass out, are you?"

"I will have you know nothing flusters me. My mother used to say, I am so laid back, I am almost horizontal. And I have never passed out. It's just not something I do," Dougal said, as the room spun about him.

"Well, that is good to hear, and to be clear, Harg is technically both a staff and a raven. You should ask him about it one day. For now, we have more pressing issues."

Graimel took another sip of his tea, and adjusted his glasses like a maths teacher about to give you a tedious lecture on algebra.

"Have you ever felt your life appear to be moving in slow motion? I am sure you have. Everyone has, well, not me, but that is beside the point. As Time Tailors, it is our responsibility to tailor the speed of time to the current situation and person. We are both good luck and misfortune rolled into one. Are you with me so far?"

"To the point I'm in the same room, yes." Dougal rested his head on his hand, screwing up one side of his face in mild bewilderment. "But I never really understood science?"

"I understand. It is a lot to take in."

"Not only that, but, I mean, that seems an awful lot of work for one person."

Graimel paused and frowned, his glasses digging deeper into his eyebrows. He glanced at Harg, then over to his trench coat, which oddly enough now also looked like it wore a frown, and finally down at his beard. *There had to be something in there,* Dougal thought.

"To start with, I am not human, which I'm going to assume you already guessed. Also, as you will come to see." Graimel once again glanced up at the clock. "Not everything is as normal as you would expect it to be. Additionally, you will be glad to know there is a Time Tailor for every species, and everything. I mean, it would be ridiculous to expect me to tailor all of Time, it's bad enough when one of them takes a week's holiday.

"And of course, I mustn't forget to mention the specialised Time Tailors, like the Easter Bunny, or the Somsi Meruca."

"The Somsi what?"

"I will tell you another time. Look, take your Santa Claus, for instance. He uses his entire years' worth of energy in one night."

"Right stop. This is getting ridiculous, the Easter Bunny, Santa Claus, the Somsi Whatever."

"Somsi Meruca!"

"Yeah, the point is, they are myths. What you're saying is Santa Claus is real, and he's a Time Tailor?"

"Well, he prefers Nick, but yes. How else would you explain him being able to traverse the entire world in one night? Now then, shall I go on?"

"Why not?" Dougal said, intrigued by this strange turn of events, and yet confused at the same time. He wondered if he should have taken notes. He had not done so, and now he could only hope an information leaflet would be forthcoming.

Graimel proffered his cup.

"More tea please, but no lumps this time, if that's okay."

Dougal took the now nicely brewed pot of tea from the table and poured Graimel a fresh cup. Graimel took a sip and rolled his lips, savouring the taste, nodding approvingly. He scooched back into the soft plumb cushions on the sofa and proceeded with his lecture on time.

As Graimel's words flowed, Dougal wished he was back at school and listening to his maths teacher explain algebra. With those thoughts came the realisation that time around him had appeared to slow.

Graimel was still talking, but he no longer made any sense, not that Dougal thought he did anyway. Bounce appeared frozen mid bounce with his tail stuck to one side and his jowls flapped up, revealing the pink of his gums. And suspended mid-flick, a frothy pendulum of slobber, undoubtedly heading for Dougal's cup.

The second hand on the clock on the mantle came to a halt.

As if it were on strike and in the same union as the rain on the window, which had stopped trickling its merry way down the pane. Dougal looked over at Harg perched on the arm of the sofa, proudly preening himself while Graimel's mouth continued to move up and down in a chomping fashion, his words still incomprehensible.

*The trench coat,* he thought, remembering how Graimel had referred to it earlier. He peered towards the front door, his eyes focusing on the coat, desperately wanting to blink, but unable to do so. For relaxing under the coat rail was what he could only describe as an elf crossed with an adorable plump teddy bear.

Sat it was about 40cm tall, probably 80cm if it stood. Covered from head to foot in fur with elfin like features and even a pointy hat, but a little rotund like your favourite teddy bear. It smiled to itself while flicking through the pages of a book. Dougal later discovered that this was quite a risqué novel, and not something a quag should be reading in a public place.

Quags are magical creatures from the Quagmires of Sturm, and this particular quag was called Grock, but that is another story.

Dougal turned and time resumed its normal course, and there was another delicious plop, this time from his cup of tea.

Graimel leapt to his feet and clapped his hands together with glee.

"I knew if I talked for long enough, you would get there."

"Get where?"

"Well, right where you just were," Graimel said, with a minor hint of frustration in his voice. "I am sure, well, I know for certain, that you just experienced slowed time."

Dougal studied Graimel, and thought, *how would he know that, unless of course everything he said was true, and he is what he says he is,* and although he still had some doubts, he started to believe.

"Well, yeah, but that is only my perception of time in that single moment. I mean, I couldn't interact with anything."

With a wry smile, Graimel winked.

"That, my friend, is something I can teach you. You are going to need it. You can already do something most humans cannot, and that is move your head and look around."

Sure enough, Graimel was right, and he had never been able to do that before today. During previous experiences, he could do no more than observe. This time, things were different; he had taken the time to absorb everything around him. And only when he tried to twist his shoulders did the experience come to an abrupt end.

Dougal walked over to the window as the streetlights flicked into life, emitting their soft yellow glow on the pavement beneath them. An old lady walked down the street with her little black Scottie dog, the streaming rain ricocheting off her pale pink umbrella as her scarf blew a little in the evening breeze.

Dougal had bumped into her four years ago at the animal shelter, on the same day he met Bounce, and he remembered how she had thought it fated that Ben had come to the shelter on the same day her husband died.

Without a word of warning, he felt a hand on his shoulder, which considering present company, made him jump out of his skin. Not literally, you understand. Dreadful things happen to people who literally jump out of their skin, although it could explain the loud thud that occurs at the beginning of this story. Dougal spun on his heels, relieved to find Graimel stood on the arm of the sofa.

"I see you are watching Mary," Graimel said. "It's strange how you both ended up at the animal shelter on the same day, and both came away with new best friends. But then life is strange…"

"Are you saying you're responsible for—"

"Whoa! All I'm saying is sometimes rules are broken."

Watching Mary in the street with Ben reminded Dougal that Bounce still needed to go out for his walk today, and he made a mental note to take him once his guest left.

"Question. If you're able to control time, then why not just stop my time until you know who or what is hunting me and deal with it?"

Graimel looked aghast at the mere suggestion. His eyes widened, his mouth gaped open wide, and the cup of tea fell from his hand. Quicker than you could think, *Oops,* Graimel casually bent down and plucked it from the air, avoiding a spilt tea catastrophe. Without spilling a drop, he raised the cup to his mouth and finished his tea.

"Can't go wasting good tea," Graimel said, staring into his now empty cup, "no matter how shocking the words coming out of your mouth are. And as for stopping another Tailors time, well, in order to do that, you would have to be..."

Graimel sank onto the arm of the sofa and shook his head, almost looking through Dougal as he spoke.

"You don't understand. I mean, why would you? Let me try and explain. There is always a choice to be made whether to interfere, but either way, the consequences can be severe, as they are proportionally linked to the duration and type of your interference. Sometimes." Graimel paused for a moment, searching. "Let us say, for instance, I decide to stop time for an aspiring chemist, to ensure she does not step in front of a speeding car. The cost, well, that could be anything from a natural disaster to someone or something else being struck by the car, or, it could be nothing. The car simply speeds by, and time continues its normal course."

"I don't understand!"

"What I am trying to say is, there is a hidden, indeterminable cost. So, I have to hope this aspiring chemist goes on to develop a vaccine that saves lives, but that may never happen. I make the choice to give her an extra second at the right time, and I carry the burden of any consequence for eternity. In short, we never mess with time on a whim. Are you still with me?"

"As much as I imagine I could be," Dougal said, remembering some consequential decisions he had made in his life.

"Good, so where was I? Yes, that was it. Conversely, deciding not to interrupt time at the correct moment can lead to dire consequences. On June 28th, 1914, I did not think it fit to stop time for Archduke Franz Ferdinand, and prevent his assassination. The catalyst that led to the First World War, and the loss of twenty million lives."

Graimel snatched his glasses from his face and held his head in his hand, his eyes reddening as they welled up. After a few seconds, he dragged his hand down his face, resting it over his mouth, trying to prevent himself from emitting any sound, as a single tear crested over his eyelid and trickled down his cheek.

Dougal put a reassuring hand on Graimel's shoulder, and although at a loss for words, silence sufficed. This open display of raw emotion reminded him how vulnerable we can all be, and he realised how genuine Graimel must be to open up like this.

"Are you going to be alright?"

Graimel nodded, gestured that he would be fine and replaced his glasses, sliding them up the bridge of his nose until the rims rested neatly back amongst his abundant brows. He then shuffled his way off the sofa with Harg in hand and poured himself the last drop of tea. After taking a sip, he continued.

"So you see, A Time Tailors life is not an easy one, fun, exciting, and a little perilous sometimes, but with an enormous burden of responsibility."

"You say perilous, like it is one of the rewarding aspects."

"Because it is. Nothing like a little danger to get the heart pumping. Keeps you on your toes. Do you have any more questions?"

"How much time do you have?"

Graimel burst into laughter, doubling over as he tried to recompose himself.

"I didn't have you pegged as a comedian, but that's damn funny. I must remember to use that one myself."

"I'm serious, Graimel! Of course I have more questions. Like, what more can you tell me about my secretive parents? What exactly is Bedougalnn? Did my parents know I was this Bedougalnn? And if so, why did they never tell me?"

"When the time is right, I will tell you more, but I made a promise to your father."

"So, did you work with my father?" Dougal walked over to the mantle and ran his hand over the photo of his parents, before resting it on the glass dome of the clock. "This was his clock, you know."

"I know. I guess you could say I knew your father through work. But time is of the essence here, and we should make a move," Graimel said, placing his cup back on the tray and heading towards the door.

"Look, this may all be quite normal to you, but you must understand, for me, this all seems a little strange. I mean, there is no such thing as magic. How do I know any of this is even real, and why on earth should I go anywhere with you?"

"I hope you have as many answers as you do questions, Dougal, but as to why, you need to come with me. Well, it's like I said, it's the only way to ensure you are safe, and if you are safe, then time is safe. I need you to trust me on this. Bounce has always been a better judge of character than you, and he trusts me," Graimel said, with a smile and a nod to Bounce.

"Well, where are we going?" Dougal asked, still not convinced he was making the right decision. *You should never go anywhere with a stranger,* he thought, *let alone while it was raining.*

"I will tell you on the way," Graimel said, stepping aside to let Dougal get to the coat rack.

Dougal pulled on his dark brown suede jacket and grabbed his keys from the shelf. Bounce heard this and was by his feet in a shot, bouncing up and down with excitement, and shaking his whole back end whilst Dougal tried to put on his harness.

"Grock, put that book down. We need to go," Graimel said, holding out his hand towards the Elfin like creature sitting on the floor, which instantly transformed back into a trench coat, and swooped over Graimel's shoulders once more.

Dougal grabbed the door, resting his hand on the smooth round silver door handle. He was about to twist it when he turned to Graimel and raised his index finger, gesturing for him to stop.

"Before we go, I have to ask, is there something in your beard?"

Graimel looked him straight in the eyes and winked.

"No time!"

# 3

# THE HIDDEN QUEEN

Graimel had got to Dougal at the exact right time, for within the Hidden Dimension, plans were being finalised, plans which had spent the last 37 years being formulated. But to understand why, we need to go back, back to a time before Dougal was even born.

I suppose this story actually starts in the ancient land of Beyathreu. A land of enchanted forests, and whimsical, friendly creatures that loved to skip and sing songs, creatures such as the Whimper, and the Kirtingle. I would have loved to have gone off on a tangent here, telling you all about them and their habits, but they are all now extinct, along with many other species.

The high enchantress, Queen Blodia, ruled over all of Beyathreu, a most benevolent ruler who cared deeply for all that existed in her lands. Not so much for other lands, but then none of us are perfect.

Queen Blodia glided into her courtyard accompanied by her Royal Guard. Her long golden hair glistened in the early morning sun as it flowed behind her, trailing up and down in the fresh breeze. All those present stopped what they were doing at once, and bowed their heads in respect, except for her young children, who raced over to her, tugging gently at her dress. As she caressed their heads, she spoke.

"Good morning all, what a most wondrous day." A young maid scurried over with a crystal goblet of the purest water. "And how honoured I am to share this day with you. Why thank you," Blodia said, taking the glass from the tray. "I am off hunting in the human realm today. There are some rather ferocious beasts which will make most excellent trophies. I will be back by sundown."

The entire courtyard erupted in cheers and applause for their mighty queen. She turned, motioning her royal guard to follow, and headed for the Pool of Reflection. A portal she had created to allow her to travel anywhere. Blodia and her guard disappeared through the portal, arriving moments later in the Serengeti. Little did she know, an unsettling rumbling carried across the whole of Beyathreu.

Over on the eastern border of Beyathreu sat the Time Tailor for volcanoes, Nellencu. He had been promoted to this position because of the early retirement of his predecessor, Daricowln. Although an excellent student, he had never yet been truly tested or burdened.

The earth rumbled again, and Nellencu hesitated, rapidly trying to calculate the pros and cons of intervention. He knew stopping time for a volcano was not something you did lightly, as it was not something you stopped for a second or two. You had to stop it for years. The inevitable consequence being the proportionally related devastation it could unleash.

Nellencu had already scouted the area around the volcano, and all life that could move away had done so, retreating far away into the depths of the forest. The earth beneath him visibly shook. It was decision time. He knew the land would recover given time, but he did not know this particular volcano should have erupted over a thousand years ago. Had he, he may have made a different decision.

Nellencu decided to let time take its course. He had seen plenty of volcanoes erupt, and knowing what to expect, he decided it would be wise to move back a little to observe.

He ported himself atop the wall of Blodia's castle, where he sat expecting to witness the top or side of the volcano explode into a monumental display of fire and ash. What he witnessed unfold before his eyes was something far, far worse.

Everyone in the castle came out to watch the spectacle as none had ever seen such an event. The excitement was prevalent in the crowds. The whole of the ground between them and the volcano rippled like an ocean wave, and the excitement turned to fear. But no sooner had it begun when the rumbling and rippling ceased.

As a wave of relieved cheers erupted, the earth in front of them exploded in fury, sending enormous fireballs hurtling through the sky, and laying waste to everything. Huge lava filled blisters bubbled from the earth, bursting, creating lakes of fire. Everything as far as the eye could see was alight, and screams of all sorts permeated the air.

As Nellencu witnessed the destruction unfold, his heart sank to the pit of his stomach. What had he done? How could he have known? With the burning world reflecting in his eyes, he blinked away, needing to alert Blodia of the danger her subjects were in, but how?

Mere seconds after he left, a huge fireball of molten rock struck the top of the castle walls. The devouring flames crackled and spat as they engulfed the beautiful roof garden where Blodia's guests, staff, and children had been watching events unfold. The castle walls fractured and crumbled away, as veins of fire crept their way through in an all-consuming manner, turning everything they touched into ash.

Nellencu sought the only one he knew could help him find Blodia, the Chronosphere, the Engine of Time. Sensing Nellencu was struggling with his burden, the desperation etched across his face, it bent the rules and advised him accordingly. Moments later, he arrived at Blodia's location, just as she was about to kill a white rhino.

"Blodia, you need to return home now. Disaster has struck the land of Beyathreu."

"How dare you interrupt my hunt, you impertinent man!" Blodia scowled at him. "You are not one of my subjects. Who are you?"

"Who I am is not important. Your children are in danger."

Blodia did not utter another word. Her face strewn with anxiety, the concern for her children evident in her eyes. She gathered her men, and with all the haste she could muster, raced back to her portaling point, and went home.

She stepped out of the Pool of Reflection into a land she no longer recognised, a land of fire and ash. A land where the only colours were the reds and oranges of flames, and the blacks and greys of a scorched world. She dashed into the ruins of her roof garden, hoping to find her children alive, desperate to find anything, but there was no life left in Beyathreu. A gust of hot wind blew away the still warm ashes at her feet, revealing two small piles of diamonds, rubies, and sapphires, all that remained of her children.

Blodia collapsed to her knees, scooping up the gems in her hands, emitting an almost deafening scream, tears streaming down her face, her heart shattered, and her world burning. She looked up, straight into the eyes of Nellencu.

"You," she cried, getting to her feet. "How did you know? Who are you?"

"I am Nellencu, a Time Tailor. I did not think this would... become..." Nellencu broke off, unable to find the words.

"You, you did this? You did not need to let this happen; you have taken everything from me."

"Yes, and this is now my burden to carry with me." Nellencu said, his eyes closed, unable to look upon her.

"YOUR BURDEN! How dare you even speak of burden? This was my world; it is nothing more to you than a job," Blodia said, her voice breaking.

"You do not understand. I could not foresee this."

Blodia turned to her Royal Guard.

"KILL HIM!" she bawled.

As her guards charged forward, weapons drawn, another blazing ball of lava and rock struck the castle again. This time, the walls splintered and collapsed, sending the guards tumbling into obliteration.

Blodia drew her dagger and lunged towards Nellencu, ploughing into him, and sending them both tumbling across the floor as it moved and shook beneath their feet. This was personal. She could have used her magic to kill him, but she wanted to feel the life drain out of him. She wanted to kill time itself.

Lava, rock, and ash were now raining down all around them. The ground heaved, and what remained of the castle walls crumbled away like Blodia's hopes and dreams. Blodia gripped hold of Nellencu as they were flung spiralling through the air, plunging towards incineration.

Nellencu grappled with Blodia as they plummeted towards the all-consuming pyroclastic flow. Unable to free himself from her, he had no choice but to snap himself through time, taking her with him. As they left the land of Beyathreu for the last time, the ten pointed sun pendant around Nellencu's neck started to glow.

Nellencu had been in such a rush to escape he failed to specify a destination, and when left to make your decisions for you, Time can get pretty grumpy.

We may never know why, on this occasion, Time placed Nellencu 4m above the ground in a densely wooded forest. But it ignited a chain of predestined events that only Fate truly enjoys.

Although appearing 4m above the ground was a little disconcerting, it was much better than the alternative. Nellencu struck the earth flat on his back with Blodia astride him. The impact caused his arm to buckle, allowing Blodia to plunge her dagger deep into his heart.

A burning sensation coursed through his body, his strength fading, he released his grip, his eyes reflecting his desolation, the sorrow in his soul as they focused on the dagger protruding from his chest. Blodia felt the pounding of his heart slowing as it pulsed through the blade of the dagger and up through the hilt.

Nellencu made a desperate grasp for his still glowing pendant, but in his weakened state, Blodia easily swiped his hand away, lashing out and tearing the pendant from his neck. As her fingers curled around it, she shrieked in pain, the glow dissipating as she flung it across the ground.

Nellencu took his last breath and was almost relieved, knowing he would have struggled to live with the burden of his choice.

"Nice shiny, what else do you have?" Came the sinister gravelly voice from behind her.

As Blodia glanced around, she felt the cold steel of a blade slice through her neck.

"Pretty dagger, I will take that. You can keep mine."

Blodia's eyes wavered for a moment as she watched the goblin slip from behind her and withdraw the dagger from Nellencu's chest, turning to wipe the blood from its blade upon her dress. She tried to speak, but the darkness engulfed her, condemning her corrupted shadow to the Hidden Dimension.

The Hidden Dimension is a shadow world, a prison with no doors, built to ensure corrupt shadows could ever be recast. A world that almost reflected the current state of Beyathreu, devoid of colour.

The corrupted shadows imprisoned there were known as the skotos. They were almost mirror images of whatever they were on the living plane, but like the Hidden Dimension itself, they were also devoid of any tangible colour. Just dark grey ashen shadows of their former selves, with eyes like black shiny marbles, and their faces permanently fixed with their expression from the moment they died. This did not mean they could not laugh, smile, or scowl, for example, it just meant if they were not focused on expressing themselves, then their normal face could be a little disconcerting.

Upon finding herself discarded in this strange new world, the rage inside Blodia reached boiling point. She had lost so much, her home, her children, her title. She had thought killing Nellencu would release her from this rage, but time stole even that moment from her. As she adjusted to her new surroundings, her rage became calculated hatred, a hatred focused on bringing an end to all time.

Blodia wasted no time in elevating herself to the status of Queen of the Skotos, slithering her way through the ranks, like the venomous snake she had become. Bereft of compassion or mercy, focused on wreaking her revenge upon time.

Upon declaring herself Queen Blodia of the Skotos, the first thing she did was create the Pool of Vacant Reflection, putting a door, where no door was ever meant to be, and cementing her unquestionable authority.

In general, the skotos had always been quite content with their lot, so to speak, verging on happy with their almost non-existent existence. Blodia would soon change this. She stood at the head of the Table of the Charred, and addressed the council in her strange semi enchanting drone, which was almost impossible for anything that was not a skotos to understand.

"After many years of searching, I now know what we must do to bring Time to justice. It is time for Time to expire, then I shall rule over everything that remains, join with me, and let us hunt Bedougalnn."

It is important to note, this is the abridged version of Blodia's speech, as she droned on for quite some time, and her speech got a little repetitive. Of course, time is relative to those present, and even though there is no time in the Hidden Dimension, those present wished they could have had the abridged version as well.

Although it was not only Blodia that droned on, this was just the way the skotos spoke. They did, however, have quite beautiful singing voices. Something humans often misinterpreted for the sound of the sea, most commonly when putting a seashell up to their ear and exalting.

"Ooh, I can hear the sea," as spoken by Ms Smith of Skegness.

This was a strange and incomprehensible tradition to all non-humans, and no one knew how or why seashells are linked to the Hidden Dimension, but they are. But in case it ever comes up in a pub quiz, what humans actually hear is in fact a skoto singing something along the lines of.

"Oi, get your ruddy ear away from the shell. It's messing with the acoustics."

Blodia was about to ask if there were any questions, when she thought, *no, there are never any questions, no one would dare to question any of her ideas or commands.*

Until this day, when a quiet, unassuming voice broke the silence.

"Is this really wise? I mean, if we end Time, do we not also end ourselves?"

There was possibly a long silence, but it is impossible to say. Unfortunately for Yoop, this was his first day after being elected, though some would say subjected to the Queen's Council. It was also to be his last. Blodia stood and made some strange hand gestures before uttering a brief, peculiar melody.

"Sha Fa Er De`Gra."

Which roughly translated into *uh oh, you should have kept your mouth shut,* and with that Yoop faded into no more. This was a shame for two reasons. First, if Blodia had listened to Yoop's thoughts, then she could have averted a major catastrophe, and second, well, we will come on to that later.

Blodia stood to leave the chamber, turned, and spoke again.

"Before I leave, can I assume we all agree this is the best course of action?"

I am sure you can imagine, although some were a little disagreeable to this, none were willing to admit so.

"Good, then we hunt."

Blodia scowled and left the room.

# 4

# BACKFORE WOODS

The rain continued to pound the pavement and everything else that existed, as Dougal Bounce and Graimel left the front door of the apartment building.

"Do you own a car?" Graimel asked.

"Of course, it's just down here."

The alley at the side of the apartment block was poorly lit, something Dougal had complained about many times, the solitary dim streetlight flickering on and off as it pleased. To his knowledge, nothing bad had ever happened in the alley, probably because Mr Lerkli's window overlooked it. But it still gave him a shudder as they hurried through to the small private car park at the back of the building. Parked towards the back, underneath an ancient gnarly oak tree, was his green and grey Mini Cooper.

They ran over to the car as Dougal fumbled with his keys in the dark, eventually unlocking the doors and sliding his seat forward, allowing Bounce to bolt into the back. One thing Bounce loved more than food was going for a drive. The dried dog saliva smeared on the headrests, and the amount of fur, dog toys, and blankets scattered throughout the vehicle were evidence of this.

"Right then, where to?"

"We need to go to Backfore Woods," Graimel said, clipping his seatbelt around himself and gripping the door handle, the whites of his eyes glimmering.

"I've not started the engine yet," Dougal remarked, looking at him curiously.

Dougal turned the key and the engine burst into life, Bounce did what he did best, and bounced around the back seat letting out small guttural woofs.

"You know Backfore Woods is about thirty miles away. It's going to take us almost an hour to get there."

Dougal drove towards the exit of the car park, glancing across at a subdued Graimel who seemed deep in thought. The rigid mindful expression he wore, calming somewhat as they snaked out onto the main road, easing his grip on the door handle, the colour seeping back into his knuckles.

"I'm not scared of driving, it's just, I thought I saw someone watching us back there, and did not want to say anything until we were moving."

"Oh, that will be old Mr Lerkli. He lives in the big old house next to the car park and spends a lot of time staring out of his window. He does seem to give people the heebie-jeebies, but he is a lovely old codger. When you get to know him, that is."

Graimel nodded in acknowledgement, but the hairs prickled on the back of his neck as a sense of uneasiness trickled through him. He tried to peer through the rear window, but the warm breaths in the car had misted the cold glass, and mere silhouettes were all he could discern through the dark and the rain.

"Now then," Graimel said, turning back to face the front, "the time we take to get anywhere is currently far less important than the destination to which we are travelling. In this case, that is Backfore Woods. Soon, however, time may become as, if not more important than the destination, keep that in mind if you will."

Graimel adjusted his seat a little and rested his head against the door.

"Now if you don't mind, I am going to catch a quick nap, I am guessing you did not bring any tea, no? Then wake me when we are almost there," Graimel said, making a few snuffling sounds before drifting off to sleep.

"Just me and you then, hey, Bounce," Dougal said, expecting a woof or a wet tongue in his ear.

Instead, there was yet another loud snuffling snore, this time from behind him, followed by an odour that only Bounce could produce. Dougal cracked the window a little for some fresh air, and to ensure he did not lose consciousness from the lack of oxygen that now circulated the interior of the car. Once sure the noxious odour had dissipated, he sealed the window shut again, wiped the small amount of rain from the door trim, and turned up the heater a little.

It was now almost nine o'clock, and Dougal nudged Graimel's arm in an attempt to wake him. Bounce woke up almost ten minutes ago, and assisted Dougal by running his sizable wet tongue the length of Graimel's face. Graimel awoke to full effect.

"Aarrgghh!" he exclaimed or that may have been, "Urrrghh!"

I guess you would have had to be there to decide for yourself.

"Park the car over on the right, by the green bin."

With only the headlights of the car to go by, Dougal wondered how he knew where the bins were and their colour. This prompted a few other questioning thoughts to enter his head.

*What am I doing?* He thought, *why did I get into my car with a person I do not know? Then drive through the rain, in the middle of the night, in nothing more than my lounge pants. To a place I am not familiar with, and is a long way from where I live.*

Okay, it was not quite the middle of the night, but it was rather dark outside.

Dougal parked the car where instructed and turned off the engine.

"Well, now what?" Dougal said, turning to Graimel for instruction.

Graimel removed his seatbelt and pulled the handle on his door.

"I just need to check on a couple of things, then we go for a walk."

Before Dougal had time to stop him from using that word, Bounce surged into the front of the car, head-butting Graimel's door open, and shooting out into the darkness.

"I guess I should have said earlier, walk is a kind of trigger word for Bounce. I never use it; I just stick to the element of surprise instead; it's much easier to manage."

"I will try to remember that; now wait here, I will be back as quick as I can."

Graimel walked over to the tree line and disappeared. Dougal sat for a moment thinking *what the hell*, shook his head in a disbelieving manner, got out of the car and called Bounce. After attaching his lead to his harness, he locked the car and promptly took a seat on the nearest bench.

A few minutes later, Graimel reappeared.

"Where did you go?" Dougal asked, getting up from the bench. "And what were you doing? Oh, and I don't suppose you have a torch do you? It's pretty dark out here."

"Many places, and my job, and we do not need a torch." Graimel stamped his staff against the ground. "We only need Harg. Harg, show me the light in the darkness."

Harg's eyes opened wide with a glowing, luminous green hue. Graimel wafted him left and right in a graceful sweeping motion, and as the trees in the woods began to shimmer, a path emerged from the darkness.

"Come, she is this way," Graimel called, as he set off down the path.

The rain had let up a little. It was still coming down, but now little more than a persistent drizzle. Dougal trailed after Graimel as he strutted through the woods, the rain glistening upon everything it touched. Every flower and plant seemed to be almost dancing, swaying in the calmness of Graimel's presence.

As Dougal traipsed behind Graimel, he kept catching glimpses of something in the darkness, making the hairs on the back of his neck tingle. Something was watching him. Wild absurd thoughts skating through his mind, convincing him that even the plants were taking an interest in him, maybe even whispering about him. Truth be told, they were.

Before tonight, he would have dismissed his current thoughts as no more than a ridiculous idea, but as of this moment, the border between possibility and impossibility had become blurred. Everything was magical.

With many new enticing aromas, and loads of new things to pee on, it has to be said, Bounce was also having the most fun he had had in a long time.

"Where are we going, and what do you mean by she is this way? Who is this way?" Dougal asked.

"All in good time. We are going to pay a visit to an old friend of mine, someone who I think can help us. Now please be as quiet as possible. We do not want to wake any unnecessariness."

Dougal zipped his mouth shut and shortened Bounce's lead a little, as he did not want him waking any unnecessariness either, whatever that is. There was a rustle from the bushes to his left, drawing both his and Bounce's attention, followed by a stinging whack on the back of his head.

"Ouch!"

Dougal clasped where he was struck and turned sharply on his heels, before stumbling over an imaginary root whilst trying to maintain his composure. The path that lay clearly marked ahead was now totally non-existent behind them.

"What is the matter?" Graimel said, glancing back at Dougal.

"Something hit me, but not only that, the track we came down has gone," Dougal said, flailing his arms about wildly as though conducting an imaginary orchestra.

Graimel stopped and gave him one of those puzzled questioning looks, before shaking his head and carrying on down the path ahead.

"We only need to see where we are going, where we have been, is now in the past, and that time has gone."

"But how are we going to find our way out of here in this darkness, with no track to follow?"

"How do you know we are going to need to find our way out? How do you know it is going to be dark? And how do you know there is no track to follow or indeed that we will even need one?" Graimel trundled away, continuing to sweep Harg left and right. "Now those are all valid questions. They are silly questions all the same, as the answer is the same for all. Time, Time, my friend, will tell."

As Dougal continued dutifully following in Graimel's footsteps, he felt another thwack of something sharp against the back of his skull. Again he spun on his heels, but again nothing.

"Ow! That really hurt, and it's made me bleed this time." Dougal rushed up behind Graimel. "Look blood, my blood, something out here is hitting me."

Graimel stopped and took Dougal's hand to inspect the blood, then put his hand on the back of his head to check if he was indeed bleeding, he was.

"Hmm, you're right, but I doubt it is something that is hitting you." Graimel took a tissue and wiped blood from his hand. "I can assure you it will be someone, and I think I know who. You must understand, humans are not allowed here, unable to get here in fact, but you are with me, so you are perfectly, kind of safe."

"Kind of safe!" Dougal said, still rubbing the back of his now throbbing head. "Hang on a minute, I thought we were in Backfore Woods?"

"We were in Backfore Woods, but we only parked the car in Backfore Woods, then Harg showed us the path through time into Erof. Oh, I suppose I should have said." Graimel threw his arms out to his side. "Welcome to Erof."

Over the last few hours, Dougal had become accustomed to feeling and looking befuddled, full of scepticism, even though he thought he had always been open-minded. Now, a realisation struck him. There is far more to everything than he could ever imagine in his wildest of dreams, or that could ever be portrayed in the most fantastical movie. Although, even knowing what he now knew, he could not help but hope the werewolf he saw in the street earlier this evening, was still only his mind playing tricks with raindrops.

"Erof? Exactly where and what is Erof, Graimel?"

Graimel waved his index finger in Dougal's direction.

"Now, how did I know you were going to ask those very two questions?"

"I don't know, but no doubt it has probably got something to do with time," Dougal said, with a hint of sarcasm.

Graimel took a moment to himself, furrowing his brow, somewhat perplexed, as if encountering sarcasm for the first time. Graimel had of course encountered sarcasm many times in his life, more often than not courtesy of the pixies, but he had not expected it from Dougal this early in their acquaintance.

"My my, now that would be daft wouldn't it, supposing that time would have anything to do with how I knew what questions you were going to ask? No, you see what it is, is your predictability, but still, they are at least two good questions this time," Graimel said, stopping for a moment. "Come, sit with me and I will explain."

They settled on the river bank and Graimel cleared his throat, making Dougal think he was going to ask for another cup of tea.

"Erof is located in a time phase that is a tiny leap from humanity's time phase. Now, you may be thinking, what is a tiny leap? Well, I suppose you could say it is the same as a subtle skip for a tall human or maybe a spirited stride for someone a little shorter," Graimel said, feeling rather chuffed with his simplistic explanation.

"So, could I accidentally leap, skip, or stride into another time phase?" Dougal said, screwing his face up a little.

"No, never, well, unlikely. There was this one time when a couple of girls were walking into Comic Com in San Diego. One of them performed a subtle skip at the exact same moment as the other performed a spirited stride, and BAM! they caught time off guard. Instead of walking into Comic Con, they stepped into Fae Con, the largest yearly gathering of all magical creatures.

"By all accounts the girls did not realise, even as the organisers ejected them to prevent mass hysteria." Graimel chuckled to himself. "Despite their protests at having tickets. You see, time maintains a constant with humanity, which prevents them from moving into another time phase. Unless, of course, they stumble across a loophole, or happen to be in the company of a Time Tailor."

"The girls who got kicked out of Fae Con; did they get a refund?"

Graimel strained to peer at Dougal over the top of his glasses, bewildered by the question.

"Er, yeah, sure."

"That's good then."

Regathering his thoughts, he continued.

"So, that is the where, and as for the what, well, Erof is home to the pixies, as you will see once dawn breaks. It is a land of lush green meadows, enchanting woods, and magical streams. Where pixies fish from atop of mushrooms and live in the natural hollows of trees and…"

Graimel drifted off into poetic licence, while Dougal zoned out.

"… a place where all life is precious, and magic is the source of all light. A place where all the inhabitants are exactly 29cm tall, except babies, of course," Graimel said, pausing to throw a pebble at Dougal. "You're not even listening, are you?"

"Yeah, a land of lush mushrooms and precious inhabitants, where the fish are all 29cm or something."

"Quite, although you may be right about the second one," Graimel said with a smile.

Erof is indeed a place where perfect harmony had been achieved and maintained since just after the beginning of time, it took the pixies about six months to get themselves sorted after all.

As they sat watching the suns meander skywards, waiting for the moment when they would breach the horizon, Dougal unclipped Bounce, then lay back upon the grass for a moment of silence, in a state of total relaxation.

It was not to be, as yet another thwack, this time against the back of Graimel's head, rudely interrupted the silence.

"OW!" Graimel hollered, "What the—"

"Nice speech, Graimel, sublimely articulated I must say, and thank you ever so much for sitting on my flowers. At least you saved me the trouble of pressing them."

# 5

# MEET BINTY MALICE

Graimel leapt to his feet, brushing the crushed flowers from his trench coat.

"Binty!" Graimel said, greeting the pixie with a huge smile and a respectful bow. "How long has it been?"

"If you are not here to apologise, then not long enough, dear friend." Binty folded her arms and glared at him crossly whilst hovering 1m above the ground. "You said you were going to be five minutes, and then you would take me on an adventure to the human time phase, remember? You promised, Graimel, and you did not come back, too busy playing with time I guess, as always."

"I was helping a friend, but I am here now," Graimel said, curling his bottom lip and fluttering his eyelids.

"That won't work. I'm mad at you, Graimel."

Graimel comically tilted his head to one side with feigned hurt feelings.

"Stop it. If you are here to take me on an adventure, why bring a human with you, and why is there a dog, bouncing through the river, drinking the water, oh and peeing! We use that water for bathing, Graimel."

Binty flew over and landed on top of Graimel's staff. Harg opened his eyes, looked up at Binty, and winked.

"Hello Harg, I have missed you," Binty whispered, winking back.

Graimel glared at Dougal, urging him to bring Bounce under control, not realising he was asking the impossible.

"Dougal, call him back."

"He's not a magical staff you know; he has a mind of his own, and I guarantee it's not wise to call him over while he's soaking wet, with nothing to dry him off."

Now if Staves could scowl, Harg would have been scowling at Dougal. How dare the human imply that he, Harg, did not have a mind of his own, for certain he had his own mind, his own thoughts, and feelings as well. *What would the human know,* Harg thought, *to him I am no more than a stick.* Feeling both glum and offended, he glared at the culprit.

Dougal felt Harg's eyes burning into him, not in the literal sense of course. For even though this is within Harg's capabilities, he was mindful that he could get into trouble for doing such things. After taking a moment to think about it, he remembered, burning holes into Bedougalnn was definitely included on the list of things not to do.

"Bounce," Dougal called, but as predictable as always, Bounce just carried on doing what Bounce wanted to do.

"Bounce, you want a treat."

This time Bounce cocked his head to one side and stopped in his tracks, lifted his head up, made eye contact with the treat in Dougal's hand and bounded over towards him. As he got to Dougal's feet, he promptly sat, proffered his paw, stood back up and let out a short sharp woof whilst bouncing on his front paws.

Dougal bent down and gave Bounce the treat which he swallowed whole, and what he warned against swiftly followed. Bounce anchored himself to the ground, and starting from his rear, he shook, rippling up the length of his body, flicking river water over everyone. And of course, as his jowls flapped from side to side, huge droplets of drool from his chops accompanied the free shower.

Binty had not been expecting this, and a relatively small drop of saliva, relative to Dougal that is, caught her by surprise, hitting her square in the chest and knocking her off Harg's head. She hovered in front of Bounce in total shock, soaked from head to foot, the drool still dripping from her.

"You're lucky I love dogs so much," Binty said, laughing. "Drash Goel," she whispered, while casting her left arm and hand in a slight downward motion.

In the blink of an eye, she was clean and dry again. She zipped over to Bounce, who now lay on the grass, and landed right in front of his snout, allowing him to sniff her. As he did so, he wagged his little stubby tail and shook his rear end, the way he always did if he liked you, before rolling on his side so that she could rub his tummy.

"Well, he certainly likes you," Dougal said.

"Why thank you. It's lovely to meet you by the way, whoever you are. So nice of Graimel to introduce us. I have always admired his good manners," Binty said, looking expectantly at Graimel.

"Very droll. However, you do have a point, which I was getting to. Binty, I would like you to meet Bedougalnn."

"The Bedougalnn?"

"Yes, yes sorry, The Bedougalnn."

Binty shot up from rubbing Bounce's tummy and hovered in front of Dougal's face.

"Oh my gosh!" Binty somersaulted and squealed excitedly. "The Bedougalnn, here in Erof. It is a pleasure to make your acquaintance, sir, and I can see from your t-shirt you are a believer. I am so sorry I threw rocks at you," Binty said, clapping her hands together.

"And this, my friend, is Binty, Binty Malice. The most

formidable pixie you are ever likely to meet, and my best friend."

If Harg had eyebrows, he would have raised one or maybe even both at hearing this statement, and he was sure that Grock would do the same. Dougal offered his hand out towards Binty.

"It's a pleasure to meet you, Binty Malice, and please just call me Dougal. Not sure what you mean by a believer though, this is a t-shirt of my favourite band," Dougal said, proudly looking down at his t-shirt. "Oh, I see, you were making a joke?"

"Yep," Binty said, chuckling.

"So, are you really the most formidable pixie? I mean, you look so delicate."

Now, while delicate is a word that could be used to describe Binty Malice, it would not be wise to do so.

Binty is of course exactly 29cm tall, the same as all pixies, with long wavy mahogany brown hair, and of average build, well, average build for a pixie. Sparkling green eyes, not glowing green like Harg's, but a subtle apple green with flecks of grey. Come to think of it, they matched Dougal's car.

She wore tie-dyed leggings, a white frilly shirt over a black t-shirt, and a thick black belt. On her feet, a pair of what can only be described as pixie Dr Martens. Overall, she resembled a New Romantic, Alternative Pixie Goth, if there is such a thing, and *Delicate* was without doubt, not the look she was going for, as Dougal was about to discover.

"Delicate, Delicate! Did you hear that? He called me delicate. Are you quite sure this is Bedougalnn?" Binty said, somewhat vexed by his comment.

"Err, it's Dougal."

"I mean, he seems quite dim; does he have the mark?" Binty zipped behind Dougal and flicked her wrist. "Par Drash Hem," she muttered.

Dougal's clothes from the waist up appeared in a pile on the floor. He instinctively wrapped his arms over his chest as if to protect his modesty, as Binty whizzed over to inspect his left shoulder. Sure enough, a mark in the shape of a raven, Binty pulled a cloth from out of thin air and scrubbed at the mark on Dougal's shoulder while muttering to herself.

"Delicate, delicate, he called me delicate, I will show him delicate."

The mark refused to budge, and Binty realised she would have to accept he is Bedougalnn, but not before advising him not to call her delicate again.

"So you think I'm delicate? For your information, Bedougalnn, I am a proud warrior. I fought beside my father in the War of Scalomit, helping to defend Erof from those deplorable Greshak."

"What was the War of Scalomit? And what on earth is a Greshak?"

"I cannot explain what the Greshak are, but I will point them out if we ever come across one. As for the War of Scalomit, well, that was a dark time for the pixies. The Greshak and their evil leader, Trilbanish, attacked us. They captured my father and I during the defence of the Piren Stone."

"Sorry, the Piren Stone?" Dougal asked.

"The Piren Stone is the source of all pixie magic. Do you know nothing?"

"I'm guessing they didn't get it?"

"No!" Binty looked over at Graimel. "Oh, for the love of pixie dust, can you tell him the rest while I make us some tea? I don't want to talk about it anymore."

"Of course, I was going to ask about tea, but did not like to interrupt."

As Binty disappeared with an inaudible pop, Graimel picked up the story.

"Trilbanish could never have imagined what a huge mistake it would be to attack Erof in the first place, let alone torture Galder, Binty's father. For when they took Galder back to the cell, and Binty saw what he had done to her father, she filled with rage, and broke free from her shackles," Graimel said, gesticulating wildly.

"What happened next?"

"Well before I tell you that, just ensure you are never on the receiving end of a pixie slap. Avoid it at all costs. For anyone that is, surely deserves it, and I possess no sympathy for them. With that out of the way and understood, I shall continue."

Graimel sat back down beside Dougal, inquisitively casting his eyes all around them. There were a few lights flickering through the tiny windows about the village, but the eerie silence that comes with dawn had not yet been shattered. Across the other side of the gentle river, a lone pixie sat atop a mushroom, casting his line hopefully into the water. Sure that he was out of earshot, he continued, but in a whisper.

"After bringing her father back, the four guards stood about, extolling the virtues of the deplorable Trilbanish. In a trice, Binty zipped over and struck the first one she came to. The crack of her hand resonating so violently that the walls crumbled as she sent the guard sideways in time. Darting between the remaining guards, she sentenced them to the same fate. All four of them trapped, forever able to observe time pass, but never able to interact or return. Turning to her father and the other imprisoned pixies, she dissolved their shackles, releasing them. Once sure they would be safe, she stormed through the prison, stopping for nothing, until she found Trilbanish."

Graimel paused for a moment, his face changing from that of an excited storyteller to one of a concerned companion.

"What I am about to tell you, you cannot repeat. Binty still struggles with what happened next. I need you to promise."

"I promise, but who would I tell that would believe me?"

"Fair point. Anyway, Binty found Trilbanish adding more bodies to a pile of dead pixies, some of them children, and the rage inside her welled, her beautiful green eyes turning a haunting red. Trilbanish mocked the dead pixies for their weakness and snatched another child from a cage, warning Binty to withdraw, but she exploded with uncontrollable fury. With the flick of her wrists, she lifted Trilbanish into the air, and as she spoke he slowly disintegrated, his screams evaporating with his body, and releasing the child. After that, whatever remained of the Greshak fled back through a time shift, never to be heard from again. And he did not even call her delicate," Graimel said with a grimace.

Dougal gulped rather loudly, and with another discrete pop, Binty reappeared, this time with a table, a pixie party size pot of tea, and three different sized cups.

"Tea is ready," Binty announced, "but before I pour it, you and I have some unfinished business."

Binty clapped her hands together and flicked her wrists toward Dougal.

"Binty, what are you doing?" Graimel asked, his voice quaking somewhat.

"So, do I really look delicate?"

Dougal glanced across at Graimel, who was shaking his head in a way that almost pleaded with him to say no.

"I will take your hesitation as a yes."

Graimel buried his head in his hands, Harg closed his eyes, and Bounce rolled around on the ground making grunting noises like a pig, while Binty whispered something incoherent under her breath, and Dougal rose into the air.

"Binty, no!"

"Oh yes!" Binty roared, as she flew an apprehensive and repentant looking Dougal over to the river, before releasing him, allowing him to fall with a mighty splash into the water.

All the other pixies who heard the commotion, and had come outside to watch the events unfold, were now rolling on the ground, or somersaulting through the air, cheering, and laughing. Dougal dragged himself out of the water soaked to the skin, sat on the riverbank, and emptied the little pixie fish out of his boots back into the river.

Graimel laughed so hard that he rocked backwards,

crushing, sorry I mean pressing, some more of Binty's flowers. He was relieved this did not catch her eye, as he was not fond of the idea of being the next one to face her wrath.

"Still think I am delicate," Binty said, flying down and sitting on Dougal's shoulder.

"I still think you look delicate, but looks can be deceiving."

"Then we are good, and I hope we are friends, Dougal," she said, smiling at him. "You know your shoulders are quite comfy. You mind if I sit with you for a while?"

"It would be my pleasure, and I would be glad to call you my friend," Dougal said, whilst pulling a still wiggling pixie fish from out of his pocket and tossing it back into the river.

Binty once again flicked and twisted her wrist.

"Gar Drash Goel Hem," Binty said, and in an instant, Dougal found himself clean, dry, and dressed again.

"Is that tea ready yet?" Graimel asked, scooting over to join them. "There is a serious matter we need to discuss."

"Ah, and here is little me thinking you brought Bedougalnn for a social visit. Silly me, when will I learn?"

"We need your help, Binty, but you know there is always time for tea."

Graimel sat back down next to Dougal on the riverbank and excused Harg, who spread his wings and soared up into the air, while Bounce had taken a nap in the long grass, and happily snored away.

As the pink and orange suns of Erof broke over the horizon, easing their way into the sky, Graimel, Dougal, and Binty lay back and drank in the majestic array of colours being cast across the land.

"So, what do you think of Erof so far?"

"It's enchanting, almost dreamlike, beautiful and tranquil, and if I were 29cm tall and Bounce was welcome, then this is a place I could stay forever."

Binty poured the tea and sat back on Dougal's shoulder.

"Now, what is it you need my help with?" Binty asked before taking a sip of tea.

Graimel explained everything he had already told Dougal, while Binty listened with an attentive ear and not a single interruption. She also understood everything Graimel said, unlike Dougal. But then, all magical creatures had always considered humans to be a little uptight.

Graimel finished bringing Binty up to speed, and her demeanour changed. Her eyes darkened somewhat, and her brow furrowed.

"This is indeed a grave situation Graimel, if what you say is true, all existence is on the brink of destruction. Have you spoken to the other tailors about this?"

"No, not yet," Graimel said, shaking his head, "I needed to get to Bedougalnn first and make sure he was safe."

Binty darted to a commanding position between Graimel and Dougal.

"Okay, first I need to see where Dougal lives, then you need to go and see the other Tailors, warn them, and ask for their help. I will stay with Dougal and Bounce, and as soon as you are back, we will all seek Bregon Skovin."

"Bregon Skovin? Are you sure that is wise?" Graimel asked, the hesitation clear in his voice.

"Graimel Tock, are you scared? Remember, I will be with you. We are going to need his might."

"You just want me to take you to meet a dwarf god, admit it."

# 6

# ARE YOU A FAIRY?

Binty disappeared from Dougal's shoulder and reappeared inside her kitchen, quickly tidying everything away. For a pixie as skilled as Binty, this was merely a case of saying.

"Samel Gesh."

And as if by magic, which of course it was, everything was clean and back in its place. Binty glided into her round cosy sitting room where her father sat reading *Asht Esh - Grymosh o` Pik Si,* the equivalent of the Encyclopaedia Britannica, but for pixies. Galder peeked up from his book, his spectacles delicately balanced on the end of his nose.

"Are you off, sweetheart? Is Graimel taking you on another adventure?"

Binty rushed over to Galder, gave him a gentle hug, and kissed his cheek, her eyes beading with tears.

"Will you be okay, Dad?"

"Of course, sweetheart, you take care and keep your eye on Graimel. Oh, and do try to stay out of trouble, although I sense trouble is now looking for you, and I pity the trouble that finds you."

Galder adjusted his glasses, dropped his head back into his book, and chuckled to himself.

Binty threw a few things in her shoulder bag and shouted, "Love you," to her father, before blinking herself back outside to where Dougal, Bounce, and Graimel waited.

"I love you too, sweetheart," Galder replied.

They headed down a trail which took them deep into the woods, with Binty flying along for a while, until it dawned on her, why fly when I can ride. She swooped down to Bounce, whispered in his ear, grabbed a hold of his harness, and disconnected his lead from the clasp. Dougal, realising that Bounce's lead had gone slack, stopped dead in his tracks to check on him.

"Don't worry, I've got him. He doesn't enjoy being on that tether anyway. Shame on you."

Dougal was about to explain it was for Bounce's safety, but did not see the point as Binty had already vacated the immediate vicinity to catch up with Graimel, who was whistling while he walked through the woods. Whilst Dougal picked up his pace a little to catch the others, he giggled to himself, wondering if Graimel had ever heard of Snow White, and whether he could be the escaped eighth dwarf, *Crazy*.

"Not only have I heard of Snow White, but I have met her, and there were no dwarfs," Graimel riposted, as Dougal caught up. "I just like to whistle, and before you ask, no it is not a dwarf thing, I'm a… not a dwarf anyway," Graimel added, before continuing to whistle cheerfully.

Bounce and Binty were enjoying making their own path through the woods, and it was clear to Dougal, Binty had much better control of Bounce than he ever had. So rather than fret and worry, like he always did, he allowed himself to absorb the captivating wonderment about him, and enjoy the walk.

The woods were not unlike many other woods he visited with Bounce. Except these woods had a tremendous tranquillity about them. All the colours popped and glowed with life, and every sound seemed amplified by the beauty from which it had been created. There were no bothersome bugs, and nothing that wanted to bite you. Dougal thought it to be the most harmonious experience ever.

Graimel came to a halt in a clearing in the woods where the river had stopped flowing, and the trees were only saplings. He raised Harg into the air and then smashed him into the ground. Binty almost fell from Bounce's harness, not that it mattered seeing how she can fly. Dougal, however, was knocked from his feet, landing on his backside with a thud.

"Harg, reveal the doorway to Backfore Woods."

Graimel swirled Harg around like a majorette twirling a baton. And as Harg's eyes once again lit up that bright, almost blinding luminous green, the doorway that led to Backfore Woods illuminated before them.

In time, it would become evident this was all purely a bit of showmanship on Graimel's behalf, to impress Dougal and Binty. What was far more impressive, is that he did not need to perform any of this, as he could skip through time at his will without so much of a gesture or a word.

Graimel stepped forward and was once more in Backfore Woods, closely followed by Binty riding Bounce. Brushing some undergrowth from his backside, Dougal chased after them, and when he glanced over his shoulder, he saw nothing except the trees and bushes of Backfore Woods. He knew it was Backfore Woods, because sadly there was litter on the floor next to a half empty bin, and a carrier bag fluttered like a flag in the wind, caught on the branch of a gloomy looking tree.

These were not the only reasons, for there were many more. What struck Dougal more than most, was that even though it was mid-morning and the sun was peeking from behind the clouds, everything had a hint of grey. There did not appear to be any shine to anything. As beautiful as it ever was, it now seemed to be little more than a shadow of Erof.

"I need to put Bounce back on his lead. It's the law I'm afraid," Dougal said.

"Then I am back on your shoulder. I cannot sit here playing dodge with that tether."

It was at that moment a thought pounced on him like a sneaky leopard. *Here he was, walking through a public place with a dwarf, or in this case a notadwarf and a pixie.*

"Stop," Dougal barked, coming to an abrupt halt, "what if someone sees us?"

Graimel sighed and Binty tilted her head towards Dougal with raised eyebrows. They were about to berate him for not paying attention to what he was told, when they realised they had not yet had this discussion. In fact, they had quite forgotten that he was new to all this, and it was without doubt a rather important subject to cover off. Graimel and Binty quickly dismounted from their proverbial high horses, in order to better educate Dougal on magical creatures and who can see them.

"Don't worry, no one can see us," Binty said, before glaring at Graimel. "I thought you would have at least covered that off?"

Graimel looked a little sheepish, then realised he did mention something to Dougal regarding this, but did not see the point in elaborating.

"Oh hang on, I remember. Graimel did say something, but never explained why."

"Nothing new for him, but something you will get used to. Has he said *Time Dougal, Time will tell,* or *No Time*. They seem to be his favourites?" Binty said.

A smile spread across Dougal's face, evolving into a bubbling laugh as he glanced across at Graimel, who raised an eyebrow and shook his head.

"I take it from your response that is a yes then," Binty chuckled. "The point is humans were once able to see all magical creatures, but they never accepted them as equals, and in the end, they denied their existence."

"But why?" Dougal asked.

"Some say jealousy, others think it was because we were so different, but could speak their language, but I think they misunderstood us, did not trust us."

"That is so sad, so can no humans see you, only me?"

"Well, that is where it gets complicated. Humans rationalised away anything that did not fit into the preconceived perception they were brought up to accept as reality."

"You mean like me until yesterday, although I'm still a little unsure that this is not just a dream," Dougal said.

Binty pinched him, and Graimel took the opportunity to prod him with Harg.

"Ow, okay, not dreaming."

"There were those who would openly challenge this perception, but they were derided, most of them being locked away in dark places to be forgotten, often referred to as mad or insane. In the end, even they were afraid to challenge, and accepted what they were told."

"So, where does that leave us now?"

"Well, there are still many humans who want to believe in the things they see; they tend to be artists or novelists, and they see glimpses of the real world. Unfortunately, or maybe fortunately, they are also conditioned to understand this is part of their vivid artistic imagination.

"So now, the only humans left who can truly see all, are the innocent, untarnished children, who are happy to accept what they see without question, without judgement, and without telling their parents."

"And me, of course," Dougal said.

"I'm not sure I'd call you human. What do you say, Graimel?"

"What's that supposed to mean?" Dougal asked.

"No time," Graimel and Binty chirped in unison.

As they finished their discussion, a young girl called Molly, who had been picking flowers with her parents, Mylo and Lydia, and her older brother Leon, stopped and waved to Binty as she sat on Dougal's shoulder.

"Hello, are you a fairy?" Molly asked.

On hearing this, Mylo and Lydia wanted the world to swallow them. Leon chuckled as Lydia admonished Molly for asking a stranger if he was a fairy. Whilst Mylo stumbled over his own words, trying to offer up an apology.

"Oh my god, I am, oh, so sorry. She, oh god, she, does not, well, you know, I mean to say, we did not teach her that! No, must be something she got from school. Yes, I will speak to her school, no offence meant or anything."

As Molly's parents ushered a somewhat now confused Molly away from Dougal, Binty darted over and sprinkled a little pixie dust on her flowers.

"Not a fairy, a pixie," Binty whispered, winking at Molly, before shooting back over to Dougal.

Molly's flowers never died or faded, and always seemed to add a little extra brightness to wherever she placed them. Her parents never realising they were the same posy. Over time, Molly forgot about the pixie she met in the woods and thought the flowers were fake ones given to her by her mother when she was little. So she kept them forever.

Graimel and Binty were chuckling like a couple of playful ferrets.

"Are you a fairy Dougal?" they asked, continuing to amuse themselves.

"What is it with humans though, always thinking they need to apologise on behalf of other people?" Graimel said.

"Polite society," Dougal replied, not really having a comprehensive answer.

This only made Graimel and Binty chuckle some more, but it brought the conversation to an end, and in a skip, they were back at Dougal's car.

"Is this your vehicle, sir?" Phil the park warden asked. "You are not supposed to park here overnight."

Phil was a tall, spindly looking man. He had been a successful athlete in his day, although his day had been quite a long time ago. Now in his late 70s, he was struggling to keep his job because of poor health, and with less than a week to pass his fitness test, forced retirement loomed.

"English Bulldog?" Phil asked.

Dougal nodded, and Bounce wagged his tail.

"Glad to see him on his lead. At least you are not breaking all the rules. Is it okay to stroke him?"

"Of course, he would like that," Dougal said, as he walked over to Phil and shook his hand.

"What's his name?"

"Bounce."

"Hiya Bounce, it's lovely to meet you."

Bounce greeted Phil with a paw, and sensing his fragility, he let him stroke him with none of his normal bouncing or boisterousness.

"Sorry about the car. It was late when I got here last night, and I got a little lost in the woods with Bounce."

"Well, seeing as I haven't called it in yet, I suppose I can let you off the fine as you have caused no trouble, and you let me fuss your beautiful dog. Go on, be on your way, and be careful out there."

Phil waved his hand and walked off to do his rounds through the woods.

"What a lovely man," Binty said. "He could have been so mean. Although, he did look a little tired."

"Fal Althiosh," Binty uttered, as she raised her hand and waved goodbye to Phil.

Phil's pace quickened as a rush of energy flowed through him. He felt able to breathe easier than he had in years, and a bit more like the athlete he used to be. He later passed his fitness test and kept his job, and used his newfound energy to raise money for many worthy causes.

"What did you say to him?" Dougal asked.

"Nothing much. I wished him good health, that's all."

They got into Dougal's car to make their way back to his apartment. Within seconds of closing the doors, the heavens opened, and the rain pelted down once more.

The journey back was without incident, with Binty and Graimel as unnervingly quiet as the roads. As they pulled into the car park, the clouds dissipated, allowing the sun to shine through.

"That was close. I thought we were going to get drenched," Dougal said.

"It was magic how it cleared up just in time," Binty said, with a huge grin on her face, and shot out of the car.

They hurried across the car park, Dougal taking the time to wave to Mr Lerkli on the way, before dashing up the stairs and into his apartment.

"Time for a quick cup of tea before heading out, I reckon," Graimel said, dropping Grock to the floor and jumping onto the chair by the window.

# 7

# BALANCING TEACUPS

Dougal kicked off his boots, placing them against the wall under the hooks, toes in, left boot on the left and right boot on the right. Next, he removed his jacket and hung it on the same hook he always did, taking time to ensure it hung symmetrically, before shuffling into the kitchen to make fresh tea.

Placing the cups on the worktop, he realised he needed one for Binty, so while the tea brewed, he hunted around his kitchen for something suitable. At the back of his cupboard, he found a little Cyprus coffee souvenir set, a gift from a friend three years ago.

He often thought about throwing it out, as after reading the instructions, he lacked the inclination to make it. But now he was glad he hadn't, as he realised the cup to be the perfect size for a pixie, albeit a very thirsty pixie. The bag of coffee that came with the set remained unopened, *probably for the best,* he thought, before chucking it into the bin.

From the cupboard above the fridge, he took out a small biscuit barrel. Rattling around the bottom were three ginger nut biscuits, *perfect* he thought, as he placed them on a little plate to take through with the tray of tea.

Graimel swooped in, instinctively knowing which cup to select, cradling his cup as he quietly sipped his tea, letting the flavour envelop his palate for just the right amount of time before swallowing.

Dog-tired, Bounce collapsed on the rug in front of the fireplace, dreaming of mad adventures in a strange and beautiful land, where he bounded through water and long grass. A land where he was the only one of his kind, revered by everyone, with treats and walks whenever he desired, but most importantly, no lead. He stretched out his legs, rolled on his side and made some snuffling sounds, before drifting back off to sleep, and back to his dream.

With his feet up on the sofa, Dougal switched between watching the last of the rain bimble its way down the window, and watching his tea swirl around his cup. Neither of which seemed to have any intention of ever stopping. Something Dougal did not mind. As he found himself lost in the moment, a sense of ease washed over him.

Binty had quite ignored her cup of tea. She had been too busy zooming around Dougal's apartment, pressing light switches, opening drawers, and turning on all manner of electrical devices before coming to an abrupt halt by the picture on the mantle.

"Are these your parents?"

"Yeah, that's my mom Nasus and my dad Daric. It was taken on their wedding day."

"Daric? Hey, Graimel, Dougal's dad looks very much like your old friend Da—"

"Damian?" Graimel interjected, "Damian was Scottish. Your dad wasn't Scottish, was he Dougal?" Graimel said, fixating Binty with an unwavering stare.

"No, well, if truth be told, I don't know. He had a strange accent, but I don't think it was Scottish."

"There you go, Binty, it's not Damian. Busy yourself with something else, please!"

Binty knew this tone, and without making comment she flew

across the room, sat on a bookshelf, and read the spines of the books. Occasionally pulling one out to read the back cover before slipping it back.

Dougal got up from the sofa and took Binty's cup of tea and a biscuit across to where she sat on the shelf.

"Here you go," Dougal said, sliding the cup next to her and placing the biscuit beside it.

"Do you not think that might be a little large for me?"

"It's the smallest cup I have, sorry."

"I meant the biscuit; it's big enough to feed me for a week."

"You're right, sorry, be right back."

Dougal headed back into the kitchen with the biscuit and used his apple corer to create a perfect pixie portion. Happy with his creation, he took it back through and presented it to Binty, who had just finished flicking through his books.

"Here you go," Dougal said, holding the resized biscuit out in front of her, "should be a better size for you now?"

"It's perfect," Binty said, taking the biscuit with both hands and a wry smile.

Graimel climbed on the arm of the chair and stood staring out of the living room window, he seemed distracted, and yet focused at the same time. After straightening a couple of bookends, Dougal sauntered over to join him, collecting his cup of tea on the way. He stood on Graimel's left and leant against him in a casual, nonintrusive manner, united with him in looking at nothing in particular.

The sun was breaking through the thick grey clouds, cracks of beauty in an otherwise dark world. Not wanting to miss anything, Binty darted off the shelf and flew over with her cup of tea.

"So, what's the plan, guys?" Binty asked, sitting down cross-legged, and resting her cup on top of Dougal's head.

Graimel was about to speak, when a figure suddenly appeared at the window, which was quite worrying as Dougal's apartment was on the fourth floor. However, John, the window cleaner, just waved and mouthed *Good Morning* to Dougal through the glass. Dougal, Binty, and Graimel all waved back and mouthed *Thank you* whilst giggling away to themselves.

Of course, John could only see Dougal, and immediately regretted his decision to engage in niceties with the occupant of this apartment. As what John saw, and later relayed to his mates down the pub, was this?

He had seen a man holding a large cup of tea in his left hand whilst leaning about 15 degrees to the right, and appearing to have a somewhat smaller cup glued to his right fist. As if this was not enough, he also had another tiny cup balanced on top of his head. Now, you would have been forgiven for thinking the strangeness ended there, it did not.

For in a supporting role was an English Bulldog, who lay on his back by the fire, his jaw in full motion, and appeared to be saying, *"Good Morning John."* The occupants were clearly deranged.

He finished washing the windows as quickly as possible, while maintaining one eye on Dougal to ensure he did not cause a nuisance. As he hoisted himself up to the next floor, he was so overcome by the sense of relief that he carelessly knocked over his flask of thick, creamy vegetable soup.

The soup took this personally and decided to projectile itself all over Dougal's sparkling clean window. For a moment, John contemplated carrying on and pretending not to notice, but his parents had raised him well, and his conscience forced his hand over to the hoist control.

Meanwhile, Graimel had enlightened Dougal regarding what John would have seen in the apartment. Not seeing the funny side of this, Dougal took the cups from his guests and stomped into the kitchen.

John pulled the lever towards him and held his breath as the platform descended, dreading what he would see when he got back to eye level with the window. His heart pounded in his chest, thump, thump, thump, as the interior of the living room came into view. It was empty, except for the English Bulldog, who was now standing on his back legs, shaking his butt, and appearing to be mid conversation, occasionally moving his paw to his chin, and nodding his head in agreement.

John rocked on his heels, grabbing the rail to steady himself, trying his best not to look. Not because he was not interested, but because of the inability of his brain to process what his eyes were seeing. Of the many strange things John had encountered on his rounds, today was without exception the strangest.

"Focus on the job," he muttered to himself, and kept his composure long enough to rinse the soup from the window before carrying on with his rounds.

Of course, what neither John nor Dougal were privy to, was that when Bounce spotted John coming back into view, he sprang excitedly to his feet, giving Graimel and Binty an idea. Graimel put Bounce's front paws on his shoulders, moving one of them every so often, whilst Binty kept him focused and helped move his jaw up and down. Bounce had quite happily wiggled his own butt.

"It is time I made a move," Graimel said, as John moved out of sight for the second time, bringing Dougal back into the room.

"I will meet with the other Tailors and advise them of our situation. Binty, can you watch over Dougal while I am away? I should not be long."

"Of course, good luck."

Graimel strode over to the door, picking up Grock on the way, tossing him over his shoulder.

"Back soon, friends."

Graimel stepped through the front door of the apartment and vanished.

# 8

# THE SANCTUARY OF TIME

Hidden away on the Pendulous Shelf in a phase of time called the Chronostis, was the Sanctuary of Time. It had been constructed at the beginning of time itself, and being an autonomous construct, it had spent lengthy periods of time modifying itself extensively throughout its existence. Its purpose was to protect the Chronosphere, and thus far it had done a sterling job.

A colossal steampunk-esque structure, with a central tower which contained the Chamber of Persistence. This is where the Chronosphere dwelt, without which time could not exist, or indeed, would ever have come into existence.

With the ease of stepping through an invisible door, Graimel arrived outside the Sanctuary of Time. He had been coming to the Sanctuary of Time since as far back as he remembered, and still found himself in awe of the astounding grandeur of the place. After all, being a living building, there was always something different about it every time he visited, even if he did not notice.

To say the sanctuary is immense and intricate would be an understatement. It would take an immortal's lifetime to explore every nook and cranny, every secret room, and find every hidden doorway. Such is the magnificence of the place. If a mere mortal were to lay eyes upon it, they would most likely be so overwhelmed, they would spend the rest of their days in stunned disbelief.

Graimel hurried to the vast door that marked the entrance to the sanctuary and tapped Harg against a small recess hidden amongst the many gears that adorned the doorway. With a satisfying click, a tiny portion of the door big enough for Graimel to walk comfortably through, opened in front of him.

He stepped inside, his footsteps echoing throughout time, and hurried to the Chamber of Persistence. Once again he tapped Harg against another hidden recess and placed Grock on the fourth cog of the second gear. Before proceeding to incant a phrase known only to tailors. This enabled him to enter a hyper advanced form of Chronostasis, where time slowed to the point where interactions occurred relative to the speed of light.

This allowed him to not only see the door to the Chamber of Persistence open, but also give him all the time he needed to slip through it. Some Tailors also referred to this process as a minor time warp. They were not top of their class. However you describe it, the same result is achieved, and Graimel could enter the Chamber of Persistence, despite the door opening for less than a millisecond.

These were his first steps inside the Chamber. Never needing to enter before today. When he asked other Tailors to share their experiences, none ever would, they would only say to him.

"When the time comes, you will see."

Graimel now understood why, for to describe the wonder before him required words he did not know. But after Binty pestered him for days, he described it thusly.

The floor was a complex arrangement of shining brass and silver, gears and rods. The walls moved up and down like the wheels and braces of a great steam locomotive stood on its end. Thousands upon thousands of different sized brass, bronze, silver, and copper gears, all meshed with glimmering cogs, reached up as high and deep as you could see.

The roof, a myriad of green glass leaves all held together with an array of bronze and copper vines. And hovering in the centre of the chamber, the huge brass Chronosphere spun on a radiant emerald axis, wrapped in a cage of bronze. Intricately embellished with yet more gears, and strange markings with ancient text.

This description did not do the chamber any justice whatsoever, but it was the best Graimel could do, seeing as even a pixie as formidable as Binty, would never be allowed to enter.

As Graimel approached, the Chronosphere spoke in a very composed and soothing tone.

"Welcome, Graimel Tock. What do you seek here in this chamber?"

"How much time do you have?" Graimel sniggered.

"As much time as you require, my child, for time here is infinite," the Chronosphere said, missing the pun, or possibly ignoring it.

"Oh, okay, in that case, I seek to consult with all my fellow Tailors, as a matter of grave consequence has arisen."

"Then speak, my child, and they will hear."

The Chronosphere could act like a transmitter with an infinite range, and all Tailors, no matter where or what they were, would hear and comprehend. As Graimel spoke, time paused.

"My friends, I am but the vessel that brings grave tidings to you all. Time is under threat. The balance of time for the species we know as Homo Sapiens is being hunted. If found and destroyed, this will bring about the end of all things. I am asking for your help. I am asking you to stand by me and defend all of time."

Graimel thought for a moment if he should add anything else, but he decided not to.

"My dear Graimel, the destruction of time for one species will not end all things. You know this. Many species have been ended, and a lot of them I have to say, by the Homo Sapiens. I wish you luck in your endeavours, but there are some who will never help you, or the species you guide, as they have lost friends and families to them."

Graimel hesitated a moment before replying, considering his next words.

"This is not just about the Homo Sapiens; this is about the end of all time. This is about time not only ending, but never having been. I believe the identity of The Key has been discovered, and theirs is the time which is being hunted."

The Chronosphere remained silent for what seemed like a few minutes, probably because it was a few minutes, and thinking he had somehow just broken Time, he looked around for the In Case of Emergency information board.

"Oh My Stars! Next time lead with that. For we are indeed in deep peril. Gather your friends and I wish you luck," the Chronosphere said, sounding somewhat panicked for the first time since… well, the beginning of time.

Before he even had time to say thank you, an alarm sounded, the kind of alarm you would find on an old wind-up clock. The type of which Dougal had on his bedside table growing up, and still uses to this day, a gift from his parents.

Graimel abruptly found himself outside the Chamber of Persistence. Some newly formed constructs, brought into being to defend the Chronosphere, were hurriedly ushering him out of the Sanctuary of Time. Although Graimel knew this to be futile, he thought, *it won't hurt to have a few more interesting constructs around to be intrigued by*. Should he be able to save all of time.

It was not as if he were alone in his endeavours, but it would take time to see if his words drew any support from the Tailors. He knew Binty, Harg, and Grock were with him, and he would rather them at his side than any number of Tailors, although a little more help would be appreciated.

There was nothing more he could do here. He tilted his head back, and let the purple and black starry sky of the Pendulous

Shelf flood his senses. Wondering when he would be back, if he would be back. To be able to gaze upon this wonderment again.

As constructs and Time Tailors hurried about their days all around him. He took some time for himself, a rare occurrence these days, but an opportunity to absorb the enormity and overwhelming grandeur of his surroundings.

As he brushed away a tear, he reminded himself nothing had yet been determined, and with the help of his friends, they could still save Time. In the tick of a tock, he placed himself back outside the door to Dougal's apartment.

At the precise moment that Graimel appeared in the foyer, Binty literally burst through the middle of the door, sending splinters of wood spewing all over the landing, and leaving a glowing pixie shaped hole behind her.

From inside the apartment, Bounce barked at them impatiently, wondering why he had been excluded from this latest exciting turn of events.

"I have lost him!" Binty said, frantically buzzing back and forth. "How could I lose him? I mean, one second he was here, the next gone. I am so sorry, Graimel. What have I done? All you asked me to do was protect him, and instead, I lost him."

Binty was inconsolable, but Graimel remained calm, as he needed to gather the facts from Binty.

"It's okay, Binty. These things happen. Start at the beginning and tell me what happened."

Of course, in this case, these things were not meant to happen, but they had, and Graimel just had to hope. There was still time.

# 9
# DISAPPEARING DOUGAL

Binty led Graimel back into Dougal's apartment much to Bounce's approval, as he barked and bounced welcoming them back, then darted into the kitchen expecting a treat. Bounce, not unlike all other dogs, thought, whether left alone for one minute or one hour, he deserved a treat for patiently awaiting your return. This, of course, was regardless of whether he had eaten the spines of your books while you were out. Dougal discovered this less than a month after having Bounce, leading him to only put indestructible objects on the bottom shelves since.

Binty flew over to the coffee table, ignoring Bounce, who sat eagerly by the treat cupboard waiting with anticipation to see what treat would be forthcoming, the answer being none. With a sigh and a flap of his jowls, he lay down, resting his head upon the stone tiled floor.

Binty slumped down on the table and sat with both legs and arms folded, her head hanging low.

"Come now, Binty, it cannot be that bad," Graimel said, trying to offer some consolation.

"But it is! I have lost Bedougalnn."

Her eyes puffed and red as her emotions ran riot. Unable to hide her distress, Binty wept.

"Everything will be okay, Binty. Start at the beginning, we will work it out together," Graimel said, as he brushed away her tears, giving her a moment to compose herself.

"We were sat in here talking. Dougal was telling me about his collection of rare heavy metal vinyl, the concept of which confused me a little, so he showed me some. Such wonderful images pressed into round plastic discs and other odd shapes. Then he placed one on the machine by the window and the speakers erupted with raucous music, the likes of which I have never heard.

"After the music finished and Dougal and Bounce stopped jumping around the room, he went and made us some more tea, and we sat and talked for a little while."

Binty recalled their conversation for Graimel, who was about as interested in hearing what they said to each other as he was in fish farts. However, he listened intently, hoping for a clue as to what had happened to Dougal.

"So, Binty, how long have you known Graimel?"

"Oh my, a long while, I would think for centuries. I stopped counting long ago, but he is the best and most loyal friend you could ever ask for, that is for sure."

"Wow, so if you have been friends with Graimel for centuries, how old are you?"

"Well I never. Imagine asking a lady her age! I thought that was a no-no, even for humans. I will tell you something, Dougal. I am not as old as you, that's for sure," Binty replied, with a hint of shock and a small amount of sweet venom in her voice.

"Sorry, it just came out. I didn't mean any offence. Hang on, what do you mean not as old as me?"

As far as Dougal knew, he was only 35 years old, and

although some days he looked and felt a little older, he did not think that stretched to centuries. Binty bit her bottom lip and casually glanced around the room, unable to maintain eye contact, making it quite clear this was a taboo topic.

Without another word, she changed the subject.

"Anyway, I don't suppose you have any classical music? Graimel played me some a long time ago, and it would be rather nice to hear some more."

Dougal loved classical music as much as he liked heavy metal, maybe a little more, so was more than happy to play some.

"I have Strauss," Dougal said.

"Oh, I am so sorry. Can it be cured, and is that a yes or a no to classical?"

Dougal paused for a moment, unable to tell whether Binty was joking, being sarcastic, or genuinely had not heard of Strauss.

He slid over to his stereo and selected his *Best of Johann Strauss II* CD from the cabinet, slipped it into the player, and hit shuffle. The unmistakable opening bars of Tritsch-Tratsch burst through the speakers like a swarm of happy bumblebees. This was one of Dougal's favourite pieces, and he pranced around the room, spinning, bobbing, and soaring like a possessed jack-in-the-box who had escaped his tin. There was no rhythm to his movements, just madness. Finding this highly amusing, Binty joined in.

"I'm knackered. You fancy another cup of tea?"

"That would be lovely."

Dougal strode into the kitchen and placed the kettle on the gas hob to boil. While waiting for it, he cleaned the cups and warmed the teapot, then put away the cutlery still on the drainer from the night before. As he grabbed the gleaming razor-sharp carving knife, the balcony door suddenly burst open. The wind gusting through and slamming shut the living room door.

Stood filling the frame, a bedraggled, strapping, reddish

brown werewolf with hypnotic yellow eyes, wearing a plaid pinafore dress.

Before Dougal had time to react, the werewolf pounced, sweeping him off his feet and snatching the blade from his hand before throwing it across the kitchen. With a thud, it struck the bullseye of his dartboard that hung on the door to the living room.

You may think that is rather an odd and dangerous place for a dartboard, but Dougal rationalised this by the fact he never had guests. Therefore, no one would ever open the door while he played darts against himself. And seeing how he was also odd and dangerous; it really was quite an appropriate place to hang it.

Dougal had always known he was odd, but never thought of himself as dangerous. He was, he just didn't know it yet.

The werewolf leapt back out of the balcony door with Dougal clamped under their arm and landed on Bodmin Moor.

The wind whipped through Dougal's full head of short, spiky black hair. Well, he was a little receding, but certainly nothing to worry about at this moment in time, and because of the copious amount of product used, the wind did not affect his styling.

At this precise moment, Dougal was fraught with worry. No, not about his hair. Not only had a werewolf of some description just abducted him, but he also did not live within jumping distance of any moorland. The nearest being approximately six miles away. Quite a leap, even for an athletic werewolf. What Dougal did not know was they were in fact on Bodmin Moor, a leap of over a 100 miles from his apartment in Salisbury. Not that this information would have made him feel any better, although visiting Bodmin Moor was on his bucket list.

The werewolf hurtled over the moorland, running at a pace that would put most animals in the world to shame, jumping rocks and boulders, leaping over entire bodies of water, and not stopping for a breath. While all the time managing to keep a violently wriggling Dougal secured under their arm.

With little to no chance of success, Dougal tried with all his might to break free, while thinking to himself.

*How rude, abducting me when I have guests! I wonder if anyone has missed me yet? Who is going to feed Bounce?*

Little did he know that although Bounce seemed oblivious to the fact he had vanished, Binty was not. Binty was distraught, and in the process of explaining everything to Graimel.

"So what happened next?" Graimel asked.

"Well, a few moments after he went into the kitchen there was a thud the against door, then silence. I waited a little longer, as you do, but he never came out."

"Hmm, strange, carry on."

"The kettle started whistling, and when it didn't stop, I went to see why, but I was too late, Graimel. The balcony door flapped back and forth in the wind, and Dougal had disappeared."

Binty got up and flew into the kitchen followed by Graimel. Nothing had changed since she went to look for Dougal, except for Bounce, who still lay expectantly by the treat cupboard.

"I think we need to give him something," Graimel said, opening the cupboard and selecting a treat. "Here you go, Bounce, take it away."

Bounce gently snatched the treat from Graimel's hand, just about leaving his fingers attached, and raced off into the living room. Once he had chomped down his treat, he settled down on the rug and wagged his tail whilst chewing on his favourite toy, a half-chewed football.

"Is this how you found it?" Graimel asked, as he walked past her towards the patio door. "Did you touch or move anything?"

"Yes it was, and no, apart from taking the kettle off the stove that is, oh and pouring myself a cup of tea, of course. I needed to calm my nerves, and there was no point in letting boiling water and a prepped pot of tea go to waste?"

Graimel glanced around the room, noting how clean and organised it was for a single man. The gleaming carving knife protruding from the bullseye of the dartboard immediately drew his attention. *What a strange place for a dartboard,* he thought, *and an even stranger place to keep your knives.* His eyes swept back across the room to the balcony door that swung in its frame, allowing the rain to invade the kitchen.

"Harg, reveal," Graimel said, waking him from a rather pleasant slumber.

A warm fuzzy feeling filled him as he remembered his dream. Someone kept throwing him away, but every time they did, Bounce would come to his rescue and bring him straight back home. It was most endearing of him.

The engravings on Harg glowed with a luminous green hue that matched his eyes, and as Graimel moved about the kitchen area scanning every nook and cranny, Harg revealed things that were hidden to the naked eye.

There were strange footprints both throughout the kitchen and on the balcony area. Strands of hair on the floor which were certainly not human, and the wrong colour to have come from Bounce. The dartboard had lifted away from the door, held at a slight angle by the blade of the knife which had pierced through, clearly thrown with some force. Thankfully, though evident something non-human handled it, there was no sign of blood.

Graimel paced and pondered, then paced some more. Walking out to the patio area, he noticed one of the plant pots had been knocked over, and in the soil, yet another footprint. This confirmed his suspicions. Like an archetypal TV detective, he strutted back into the kitchen, held aloft the index finger on his right hand, and spoke in a very authoritative manner.

"It would appear that a werewolf has absconded away with our friend Dougal," Graimel said, pondering his thoughts for a moment. "And if my suspicions are correct, I would wager the werewolf is called Janet. Is there any of that tea left?"

# IO

## FRIEND OR FOE

The rain intensified, thrashing the ground, and although it was only 14:32 a surreal darkness engulfed the moor. Impenetrable black clouds erased the remaining shafts of light and hung over them, reflecting the gloom coursing through Dougal's entirety.

A furious flash of lightning belted a lone hawthorn tree, bursting into flames, spitting fire onto the moorland. A mere second later came the ear-splitting boom, like the sound of a cannon being fired in your downstairs toilet.

The ground heaved and rumbled beneath their feet, and Janet darted to her right as fire leapt towards them. Dougal found himself tightening his grip on the werewolf, unaware he was the cause of all this.

Janet stopped and cocked her head to the left as though listening for something. Raised her snout towards the sky, and took an enormous breath of air through her nostrils. As she exhaled, the misty cloud of her breath hung momentarily in the chilly air before dissipating.

She held up a finger to her mouth, signalling to Dougal to be quiet.

"They are coming," she whispered.

Dougal wanted to defy the command with all his heart, but his head forced him to pause and consider. Complying with her request could be the wisest decision he would make today. Without uttering a sound, he complied, even though he wanted to scream like a banshee winning the lottery.

Janet picked up her pace a little, as lightning bolts struck the ground all about them, almost as if aiming for them, which they were. But she was too nimble, too quick to be caught by lightning, weaving left and right, and leaping over any strikes that got too close.

The constant bounding and changing of direction made Dougal's stomach churn, which got him thinking. *How much longer will this continue? Where are we going? How mad will a werewolf be if I get vomit in their fur? And how hard will it be to get out?* As he lost himself in these questions, Janet came to a sudden stop by a cluster of monoliths, surrounding what appeared to be an intact megalithic tomb.

Janet approached the entrance and let out a deep, enrapturing howl. One of the towering flat stones moved to one side, and they slipped through the crack. And as the stone slid shut behind them, three bolts of lightning struck the ground where they stood moments ago.

A cool damp staircase with water trickling down the moss covered earth and stone walls lay before them. Janet paused, waiting for the satisfying clunk of the door before inching their way down the passage. Flaming torches lit their way, casting unsettling shadows, each fixed to the wall with a rusty iron sconce, and spiders' webs decorated the space between the walls and the ceiling. The stairs spiralled deeper into the ground, and Janet's pace slowed to a considered walk.

At the bottom of the stairs stood an imposing arched wooden door with what Dougal now recognised to be magical engravings, similar to those he had seen on Harg. Janet placed her hand on the centre of the door, and muttered some incoherent phrases, and as Dougal watched, the scripture glowed with such a brilliant white glare, he needed to avert his eyes.

The door crept open as the glow faded, and they entered the den, Janet turning to ensure the door relocked itself. Sure they were now safe, she released her grip on Dougal, and said in a polite, well-spoken English accent.

"I am so sorry about that, Dougal. I would have liked to introduce myself first, but there was no time. Welcome to my den." Janet removed her hat and scarf and walked into her kitchen. "I have to say, you seem extremely calm for someone who has recently been rescued by a werewolf. Not that I am exactly a werewolf you understand, but we will get to that."

Although calm is a nice enough word, Dougal did not think conveyed how he felt at this precise moment. Confused, nauseous, cold, and tired were also good words, but none quite equal to how he felt in reality. However, if you put them all together, you would be getting close.

When a werewolf scooped him from his spotless warm kitchen, tucked him under their arm, and raced across a bleak sodden moor in the biting rain while dodging bolts of lightning. The initial thought scampering through his mind was, *what the hell*, well to be honest, it was more like, *WHAT THE HELL!*

Since then, he had resigned himself to this bizarre turn of events. After all, accepting the strange and unusual was becoming second nature to him. This meant by the time they got to their destination; the situation had become pretty much normalised.

The only thing that now confused Dougal was the use of the word *rescued*. Dougal accepted he was in danger from something or someone, but on no account did he think it was from anyone or anything in his apartment.

"In no way, am I calm, but to be honest, with everything that has happened in these last few days, I am finding it hard to be surprised by anything. Nothing is what I thought it was, but rescued? I was not aware I needed rescuing. What were you rescuing me from? Drinking too much tea? Relaxing on my sofa? Dancing around my living room?"

The more annoyed Dougal became, the more Janet thought it best to let him get it out of his system before attempting to continue the conversation, or answer any of his questions. This infuriated Dougal even more. Here he stood, cold, wet, and ever so slightly vexed, and this werewolf just stood across from him, sniffing the air and trying to smile with her fearsome mouthful of menacing, sharp, pointy canines. None of which did anything to reassure him that he was in fact, in a safe environment.

To Dougal, Janet looked like a child who had been given the biggest bar of candy they had ever seen, and was pondering over from which end to start eating it. He rattled his head like a maraca, struggling to unstick this image from his mind.

"And, if you are going to rescue someone, should you not rescue their family and friends as well?"

Janet stopped trying to smile.

"But it is only you that is important."

"To who? Because my family and friends are important to me, and if they can't be rescued, I don't want to be. For without them, there's no point in being rescued."

Dougal took a moment to reflect on his own words, he realised how quickly Binty and Graimel had stolen a place in his heart, which surprised him seeing as he only had a true affinity for animals.

"Well, now you are a little calmer." Janet grabbed a towel and tossed it over to Dougal. "I will explain. Come on, let's get you dry and warm."

Janet did not want to invade his space any more than necessary, or make him feel any more threatened than what her smile already did. So she waited in the kitchen, while Dougal dried himself off as best he could.

"Thank you," Dougal said, stepping forward and passing the towel back to Janet.

"You are welcome, my dear. Take a seat by the fire, and I will pour us a drink."

"Not tea though, as that seems to keep getting me in trouble."

Dougal barely got his words out before there was a knock at the door. Having taken a seat as instructed, he now ducked down a little, trying to hide himself from view. His eyes widened, and for a second he forgot to breathe as he saw Janet's top lip twitch, once again revealing her fangs.

The difference between a werewolf's snarl and smile becoming apparent, and this was without doubt a snarl. His eyes drawn to the razor-sharp claws now extending from her hands, he wondered whether she was indeed protecting him, or if he was about to be lunch.

"It's just me, Janet."

Came the rather polite voice from the other side of the door. Janet sniffed twice and retracted her claws, replacing her snarl with her smile, although Dougal was still unsure which of these two expressions he found more disturbing.

Janet opened the door to greet her best friend Beth. Dougal peeked over his shoulder around the edge of the chair and there stood in the doorway, another werewolf.

"You best come in, Beth; I cannot risk leaving the door open today."

The door swung shut behind Beth as she sauntered into the den, and while Janet checked the locks, she removed her hat and scarf, which were identical to Janet's. Beth was wearing a pink front buttoned dress with a white apron, adorned with flour and other random baking ingredients. Tucked in her apron pocket, a slightly charred, red and white checked oven glove.

On hearing Janet's howl resound across the moor, she had stopped in her tracks, dropping her cooking as she bolted outside to check on her friend. The scent on the air had told her Janet had company, unusual company, so she had grabbed her hat and scarf and raced over.

Dougal's knowledge of Forties style clothing was limited, bordering on non-existent, but this is how he would have described Beth's attire should a passer-by have asked him. Although, had there been a passer-by in a werewolf's den, he was sure of two things. One, the passer-by would most likely be lunch, and two, that because of one, the passer-by would be unlikely to ask him what style of clothing is that werewolf wearing?

Dougal was actually wrong on both counts.

"Beth, I would like you to meet my nephew. This is Bedougalnn, but he much prefers to be called Dougal."

Beth snapped a glance at Dougal, her eyes wide, and her mouth agape with incredulity as she focused back on Janet.

"Not The Bedou—"

"Yes, The Bedougalnn."

"Well, my dear, you never told me you were related to someone so famous. Oh my, it is a pleasure and an honour to meet you, Bedougalnn," Beth said, curtseying to Dougal.

Dougal fell off the chair, overwhelmed by a sudden rush of shock and confusion. He stumbled backwards towards the fire while trying to process this latest piece of information, regaining his balance before things got heated.

"Your name is Janet and you're my aunty, so you're the Aunty Janet my mum told me about, before..." Dougal clasped his hand over his mouth as tears welled in his eyes.

He remembered what his mother told him the night before she died. *If you ever need anything, find your Aunty Janet, she will help you.* Sadly, Dougal's father burnt all his mother's belongings the day after her funeral, and unable to cope with her death, he died of a broken heart a day later.

Dougal had been alone since that day.

Aunty Janet opened the bottom drawer of the kitchen unit and smiled inside; there she saw the dusty bottles of Argentinian malbec that had been beckoning her for quite some time. A sudden rush of cursing expletives ricocheted from the kitchen, as the bottle opener was nowhere to be found.

Luckily, Beth knew a special trick to remove a cork from a bottle without a corkscrew. Just as she was about to demonstrate, they realised this was a screw top, and both Dougal and his Aunty Janet breathed a sigh of relief.

All three of them sat down in front of the fire. Dougal took a gulp of his wine and was relieved to be holding something in his hand a lot stronger than tea.

"So, you're my Aunty Janet?"

"Who would have thought it? My best friend is Bedougalnn's aunty," Beth giggled.

"Yes my dear, I am your Aunty Janet, but you can call me Janet if you like." She raised her glass to her lips. "I think I might need to find another bottle."

"I don't understand," Dougal muttered.

This was becoming quite a common phrase for Dougal, and likely to increase in use in the coming hours and days.

"Well, it's because this bottle is empty, dear."

"Eh, what, no. What I mean is, if both of my parents were human, how is it my mother's sister is a werewolf?"

"Well, to start with, you should know we are not werewolves. We are a hybrid known as lyconfind. There are many differences between us and our cousins. As you can see, we are suspended in our Lycan form, and although the full moon still affects us, it only causes us to bake cake. Oh, and I am sure you will be relieved to know, all lyconfind are vegetarian."

Beth glanced across at Janet, who was nibbling on her claws, and even though captivated by this whole turn of events, she reached across and gripped her friend's hand.

"I met Beth for the first time when I was five. After that, Beth's Uncle Lescan used to bring her to play with me, against the rules of course. Just before my eighth birthday, I contracted an incurable disease and given a year to live. Lescan knew that if

I became a lyconfind I would survive, so he turned me, saving my life.

"The transformation took a few years. I was 14 when I noticed my parents almost looking through me sometimes and knew it would not be long before they would no longer see me. So your mother helped me to disappear. Our parents thought I had run away, but I came to Bodmin to live with Beth's family, and they have taken care of me ever since."

Both Janet and Dougal gulped down the last of their wine, praying for the alcohol to help them through this most awkward of situations. Janet flew into the kitchen and got another bottle of malbec. With both glasses replenished, she picked up where she left off.

"I secretly stayed in touch with your mother. She would bring me photographs and trinkets from home, and we would spend hours talking. She even brought you here once when you were a baby.

"When your mother got sick, I promised I would always be there for you. Since the day she died, I have kept a watchful eye on you," Janet said, taking some photographs off the mantle above the fire and passing them to Dougal.

"So, was that you outside my apartment in the rain last night?"

"Yes, dear, but I did not know until today what grave danger you were in. Otherwise, I would have come for you sooner, and then I might have had time to help your friends, and Bounce as well."

"What are you saying? It can't be too late to rescue Bounce and my friends?"

Before his Aunty Janet could reply, Dougal was out of his seat and heading towards the door.

"I am afraid we are out of time, my dear."

# II

## THE HUNT BEGINS

Back in Dougal's apartment, Graimel sipped his tea as he knew there was always time for tea, and he needed time to think. *Drink slow, think fast,* he reminded himself. Lay on the rug in his usual spot, Bounce wagged his tail while chewing his ball as Binty flew in from the kitchen to keep a watchful eye on him. She did not want him going missing as well.

Graimel had a good idea who had snatched Dougal, but could not fathom why. He knew Janet would never harm him, but what if he was wrong? This left a few burning questions blistering his thoughts.

*Why did they snatch him like that? Why not come and introduce themselves? Unless, of course, they were being controlled or manipulated, or maybe they were just hungry, no, not hungry. Janet would certainly not eat meat, but what if it wasn't Janet?*

Either way, he knew where to start the search, as he had been able to track him to Bodmin Moor before he disappeared.

This was the one thing that worried Graimel at this point in time, as he knew where all humans were at all points in time, and just like Binty, he had lost the most important one.

There was a colossal pop, and the apartment plunged into

darkness. Outside, every single visible light was abruptly extinguished. The ominous presence accompanying this gloom told Graimel this was no power outage. The blackness that now pervaded the entire apartment were the skotos. They were looking for Bedougalnn, but would not hesitate to end anything or anyone who got in their path.

"Luminos Eliminatus," Graimel called, out holding Harg aloft.

Harg vibrated through his entirety before irradiating light throughout the room. Any of the skotos touched by this emittance would be ended, but the skotos were masters of concealment, which meant that many were able to avoid this initial purifying glare. As liberally as the light permeated the room, its peak luminosity was also brief, and the skotos were adept at skulking through shadows.

The last thing Binty had been expecting was an attack. This, coupled with the fact night flying was not her forte, meant surprise was not the only thing to strike her as she flew past the lamp on the coffee table.

A skoto lurked in the shadows near the lamp, and as Binty passed by slightly disorientated, they made their move, lashing out from the darkness and swiping her from the air.

Dazed, Binty spiralled out of control, striking the stonework around the base of the fireplace, cracking her head in the process and emitting a shrill list of pixie expletives as she did so. She clambered back to her feet, her eyes still not fully adjusted to the darkness, and it struck again her, slamming her back into the stonework.

This time the skoto did not hesitate to pinch his fingers around her throat, and apply gradual torturous pressure, making it impossible for her to speak or breathe.

Binty's shrill had woken bounce, and using his impeccable night vision, he barged straight into the coffee table, knocking over the lamp and shattering it. Fragments of glass and ceramic span through the air, perforating two skotos who were lurking watching their cohort torture the remaining life from Binty, sending them screeching across the room.

With the table out of the way, he headed straight for Binty, who was now gasping for breath and growing weaker by the second, her hands clawing at the skoto's fingers.

Bounce was almost on top of the skoto when he barked with such ferocity, the ensuing sound wave reverberated throughout the apartment causing the skoto to jump in fright, and momentarily release its pincer like grip on Binty's throat. A moment was all Binty needed.

"Sen Loth Iresh," Binty murmured, stunning the skoto and giving her time to move.

Feeling exhausted and delicate, *(don't tell anyone),* she grasped hold of Bounce's collar. Bounce headed towards the light emanating from the kitchen, hoping to find Dougal. *Dad always knew what to do,* he thought.

As he got to the door, a skoto seized the knife from the dartboard and lunged towards him, plunging the blade deep into his hip.

Bounce yelped as the blade sliced open his thigh, ripping through muscle and exposing bone, blood spraying from the wound, decorating the room a rich sticky crimson. An unusual burning sensation ripped through his body, and a sudden tiredness flowed through him. Binty felt Bounce stumble as his legs crumpled beneath him, but he was determined to get her to safety, and with the last of his strength, he lunged into the kitchen.

The bloodied knife skittered across the kitchen floor as Bounce's legs gave way, Binty barely keeping a grip on his collar as he slid across the cold stone floor, his momentum carrying them to Graimel's feet.

Bounce shuddered. The burning sensation he had initially felt had turned to ice, whimpering softly as Binty relinquished her grip on his collar and slumped to the floor beside him.

Grock dove from Graimel's shoulders and covered them

both, using his concealment ability to shield them from further harm.

Graimel released Harg into a flurry of light, his iridescent green eyes burning with anger as they released sparks of such luminosity they would instantly turn any skotos to ash. The first skoto, randomly selected, was the one who attacked Bounce, Harg's gaze catching him as he charged towards Graimel, disintegrating him into obscurity.

Even though skotos were particularly vulnerable to light, they could be destroyed other ways, like being torn asunder or having their heads removed. But Graimel was no warrior, and with Binty and Grock out of action they would be quickly overwhelmed. Harg needed to think fast.

More skotos appeared from the shadows and lurched towards Graimel. But Harg had an idea. Faster and faster he flew, circling the room and creating a vortex, drawing out the skotos and disorientating them. Once sure they were all exposed, he released his sparks as one violent light bomb. A moment later, the room was littered with piles of dust.

The darkness passed, and as Harg returned to Graimel, normality resumed.

The streetlights flickered and illuminated once more, and everyone in the neighbourhood carried on about their business as if nothing of note had happened. Kettles resumed boiling, fridges clicked, microwaves pinged, and the drone of the television once more seeped throughout people's homes. Just another unexplainable local blackout, which of course, in their reality was all that happened and nothing more.

"You saved us, Harg."

"Maybe so, but it will be a long time before I can use the Sparks again."

Graimel rushed back into the kitchen and recalled Grock, revealing Bounce and Binty side by side on the kitchen floor. He sank to his knees harrowed by the situation.

"Binty, come on girl, this is our first adventure together in a long time, and if anything happens to you, Tolti will kill me. We can't do this without you."

Binty's wings twitched and fluttered, and she raised her hand to rub the back of her head.

"Cannot cope without me, eh? You do not get rid of Binty Malice that easily," Binty mumbled, as she regained her composure somewhat, "not with Bounce around. He saved me you know. How is he? Is he okay?"

Graimel had an unsettling look about him, and Binty followed his eyes as they drifted to Bounce whimpering on the floor behind her. Bounce was lying on his side, his breathing shallow and laboured. In his left hip, a gaping gash of torn flesh where sinew separated from bone, and the pool of blood about him growing as his body weakened.

"We have to save him, Graimel, he saved me… he saved me," Binty said, her voice quavering as flashes of memories of their short time together flooded her mind.

"We are not supposed to interfere, Binty, you know that," Graimel said, doing his best to remain composed.

"Please, Graimel! He doesn't know that, and if he hadn't interfered, I'd be dead! Correct me if I'm wrong, but isn't interfering kind of your job?"

"You're right, Bounce is one of us, and we should do what we can."

Binty jumped up to survey Bounce's lacerated left hip. The gash was about 15cm long and deep to the bone, it continued to bleed profusely, staining his beautiful soft silken fur. She collected herself as best she could, although dazed and overwrought, she drew her focus and sprang into action.

Hovering over him, she focused all her energies on trying to stem the bleeding, but as fast as she cleaned and sealed the wound, it would burst open again. She collapsed onto her knees, begging the blood to return whence it came, but it showed no signs of easing. Again, she cleared the blood from around the gash and eased her hand inside, searching for the source as Bounce shuddered and whimpered softly.

"I can't find it. There's too much blood, we're losing him," she cried, her anxiety spiralling, "we need to do something, Graimel; he's going to die!"

"What can I do? What do you need?"

Bounce's chest heaved and folded, his breath now so shallow it was barely sustaining him.

"Time, Graimel, I need more time."

Before Binty had time to finish what she was saying, Graimel had vanished to find Lescan Dewclaw.

Lescan Dewclaw was the Time Tailor for all Canines, and he owed Graimel a favour, for something Graimel helped him with 45 years ago.

A second later Graimel returned with Lescan, and realising what was required, he subdued Bounce's time. This time when Binty cleared the blood, it did not refill the gash, and she was able to locate rupture.

"I've got it," she said.

With Bounce's time arrested, she took the time she needed to repair the damage before casting a smattering of pixie dust over the wound, sealing it shut. But it was too late. Bounce showed no signs of movement as Lescan bayed the most melancholic howl.

Binty released an anguished scream from the pit of her stomach, her heart hollow as she collapsed upon Bounce's chest. Graimel dropped to his knees, his eyes pooling, unable to process the situation, whilst Harg and Grock looked at each other lost and confused. This wasn't meant to happen.

"No, this isn't happening, I won't let it," Binty said, her eyes imploring Lescan to help.

With a nod of his head, Lescan readied himself, and as Binty pounded Bounce's chest, he grabbed the glimmer of life and paused time for Bounce, giving Binty the time she needed to pound again.

Nothing. They hung there in silence as time passed, none of

them able to breathe, tick, tick, tick, the sound of the clock on the mantle, amplified, almost deafening. With a large sharp intake of breath through his nose, Bounce's lungs filled with air, and he simultaneously tooted an even larger expulsion of gas from, well, you know where.

Graimel struggled to breathe as Bounce's noxious fumes saturated his nostrils, Lescan caught a whiff, and sensing his debt to Graimel was settled, he made the wise decision to disappear with a snap.

Bounce would carry his scar well, but Binty and Graimel were going to have a lot of explaining to do. As he got to his feet to quench his thirst, Harg landed by the water bowl, cocked his head to the side, and winked a knowing wink.

"You're my hero." Binty said, dashing over to Bounce and kissing him.

Bounce did not understand and did not care what this word meant, but he was getting kisses from a blissful Binty. So he returned the sentiment with one lick, soaking her from head to foot.

Still reeling from Bounce's toot, Graimel had to wonder if he was in fact the only one who could smell it. With a desperate need to filter the nauseating fumes, he snatched two tea bags from the counter and stuffed one up each nostril. A smile spread across his face as he sighed with relief.

"Aah, Earl Grey."

After a cup of tea and a few minutes of deserved respite, they went into the living room to survey the damage. The once tidy apartment was now strewn with debris and piles of ash. Binty straightened the photo on the mantle, the glass now cracked and jutting from the frame, while Graimel wondered how they were going to explain this to Dougal.

"They will send more; we need to move on and find Dougal."

"What were they, Graimel?" Binty asked.

"Skotos, the Queen's Guard, if I am not mistaken. But at least we now know who is after Bedougalnn, and I think I know why."

Graimel recalled Harg, placed his hand on Bounce right by where Binty was sitting, she leaned over and put her hand on his, and they vanished from the room.

John was on his way back down from cleaning all the windows when, as he passed Dougal's apartment on the fourth floor, he watched an English Bulldog vanish. Not knowing what to think, except, *I really need a drink,* he shrugged his shoulders in a semi nonchalant manner, shook his head, and kept his hand glued to the hoist control.

# 12

## MALBEC AT AUNTY JANET'S

Mere moments after leaving Dougal's apartment, the five of them arrived unannounced in the middle of Bodmin Moor. There was no welcome committee, and on the bright side, also no unwelcome committee.

"I am good at this aren't I." Graimel boasted.

Mainly to Binty, as both Harg and Grock were used to all this, and frankly Bounce did not care. Because all around him were unfamiliar smells, new sensations, and an infinite amount of things to pee on. What more could he ask for, treats?

Binty glanced across to Graimel, raising an eyebrow at his comment, while tightening her grip on Bounce's harness as her stomach did tiny barrel rolls. Not that she would ever admit it, but she remembered now just how much this form of travel could upset her delicate tummy. As she sat there gently rocking from side to side, her face appeared to have turned a pale putrid green colour and her eyes became glazed.

"Oh, you are amazing, Graimel. There is nothing I like more than travelling places without seeing anything, and arriving feeling like my stomach had not been told where we were going. So it guessed, and ended up somewhere completely different to the rest of me," Binty said, almost keeping a straight face.

This, however, was all she managed, before throwing her hand over her mouth and whizzing over to the nearest patch of beautiful violet wild heather, and decorating it with partly digested ginger nut biscuit.

"Why thank you, Binty, a pleasure as always," Graimel said, oblivious to the blatant sarcasm.

Harg and Grock smirked and chuckled a little to themselves. They were not blind to Binty's comments, or indeed her actions.

"Are you okay, Binty?"

"Yes thanks. I am just redecorating this part of the moor a nicer colour."

"How many times do I have to tell you, you are not supposed to interfere! Right, this way, follow me."

For a moment Binty wondered why they were walking, when Graimel could transport them to any point or place in an instant. She thought about asking this question, then remembered the recoloured wild heather, and reminded herself of the cause-and-effect principle. She also reminded herself she did not need to walk, as Bounce waited eagerly for his passenger. Bouncing and barking as she gripped his collar and sat on his back, rearing up like a cowboy's horse, before galloping off in pursuit of Graimel.

They had only been on the move for about ten minutes when Graimel noticed patches of scorched grass and heather on the moorland, which seemed to be in an almost direct line to their east. Without hesitation, Graimel turned and followed the trail of burnt earth.

The wind whipped across the moor lambasting them, but it was not long before they came across the same cluster of monoliths that Aunty Janet took Dougal to earlier that day. Graimel knelt and brushed the scorch marks in front of the megalithic tomb's giant door stone. They were fresh.

"Grock, you know what to do."

Graimel retreated a little as Grock transformed into his natural state and scurried over to the towering door stone next to the scorch marks. Transforming once more, he spread out across the ground, mirroring the sky, and making the earth appear invisible, inching forward until he was right next to the standing stone.

The stone became a little confused as the earth seemed to disappear from beneath her, and the sky appeared to not only be above her, but below her as well. All this made her a little dizzy, and she lost her balance and fell over, allowing Graimel, Binty, and Bounce to enter the tomb.

The stone sighed, realising right away the likelihood was she would be there for quite some time. So she got comfy, and gazed with awe up into the sky, anticipating her wonderful view of the stars at night.

Graimel led the way down the stairs until they reached the door of Aunty Janet's den. After analysing the etchings on the door, he pondered for a moment, adjusting his glasses a fraction, and made a closer inspection of Harg.

"A relative of yours, Harg?"

Harg had been keeping an eye on the spiders scuttling about the place, he had never liked spiders, too many eyes you see.

*Never trust anything whose eyes you cannot look into, especially if they have four times as many as you do.*

*Now that was a motto to live by,* Harg thought.

He redirected his focus towards the door, and realised it was indeed his Great Uncle Merg, well, at least part of him. Of course, a considerable number of doors, and even the odd table and chair, were most certainly made from his Great Uncle Merg. However, this particular door contained his essence.

Harg glowed faintly, instructing Graimel to hold him up to the door to enable him to communicate with it.

"Hey Uncle Merg, it's me Harg. Open up for us will you?"

"Hello, Harg, it has been a long time, and it is Great Uncle Merg, as you well know."

"Sorry, Great Uncle Merg. Is there any chance you could open up for us, please?"

Inside the den, Dougal tapped his feet impatiently by the

door, waiting for his Aunty Janet to unlock it. They were on to their third bottle of malbec between the three of them, and as far as Janet was concerned, Dougal was going nowhere.

"I thsink you should lest me owt, Arsey Shanet," Dougal said, slurring his words a little.

"I have told you, dear, it is not safe."

"Lisshen to your Arsey Shanet," Beth said, giggling to herself, "Arsey Shanet."

The door unlocked itself with a loud click. Janet leapt up and over the back of her chair like a lyconfind possessed with the urge to bake cake under a full moon. Janet did not like this expression, as this was in fact the bane of their lives.

Without spilling even a drop of wine, she moved from her chair to the front door before the end of this first click. Beth, realising something was afoot, and it had nothing to do with baking, sobered up with immediate effect and joined Janet at the front door.

Both Janet and Beth were now snarling, their teeth glistening and salivating with glee, as if about to greet a door-to-door carrot cake salesman.

Janet crouched down and placed her glass of malbec to one side, being careful not to spill any, and watched the steam powered door groan on its hinges. The mist that had been added for dramatic effect swirled and billowed, obscuring her view. She waited but a moment, then darted forward, straight into a somewhat surprised and rather vexed Graimel.

"Janet!"

"Graimel!"

"Do you have Bedougalnn?" Graimel asked curtly.

"I do. Why do you have tea bags up your nose?"

Graimel had half forgotten about the tea bags, enjoying taking pleasure from everything smelling of Earl Grey.

"You don't want to know," Graimel said, whipping the tea bags from his nostrils and stuffing them in his pocket.

Standing to one side, Janet motioned Graimel into her den. Teetering by the kitchen table, a very wobbly Dougal.

"Guyshhs, whersh you bin?"

"What have you done to him?" Binty darted over and snatched the glass from Dougal's hand. "Poison, Graimel, they've made him drink poison."

Binty raised the glass to her nose, hesitating, before cautiously sniffed in the aroma of blueberry and black cherry, with notes of violet and plum.

"Though I must admit, it's a delicious smelling poison."

"It is not poison, young lady; it is malbec," Beth said, taking another swig like a pirate chugging grog.

The malbec swirled around the bottom of the giant balloon glass. Unable to reach it, Binty placed it on the table and dived in, scooping a little with her hand before taking a sip. Briskly followed by a second, and then a third few seconds later. Binty realised she had just found something she preferred to tea, and wondered where this lovely fruit drink had been all her life.

"Not too much, Binty. It contains alcohol, and you will end up looking and sounding like Dougal here."

The only thing Binty ever used alcohol for was cleaning, and even though she did not fancy looking or sounding like Dougal, she was definitely taking some of this malbec back home with her at the end of all this.

Meanwhile, Bounce brought himself in and headed straight for the rug in front of the hearth. Enticed by the warm glow from the raging fire, he circled twice and lay down for a well-deserved rest.

Janet ensured her door relocked itself, and admonished it for opening without her express permission, considering who their den guest was.

"So, Janet, why did you take Dougal, and what do you know?" Graimel asked, swiping the glass of malbec from the floor, and helping himself to a little before screwing up his face and saying, "do you have any tea?"

"Of Course," Janet said, grabbing a tea-for-one set from the cupboard.

Graimel liked these, as they were neat and compact on the sideboard. He particularly liked this one, as it depicted little yellow ducks swimming on the rim of the cup.

"Beth's Uncle Lescan came to visit me earlier today. He told me, he heard through the Chronosphere, that you, Graimel, were babbling on about Homo sapiens being hunted, and the end of all time. Then you mentioned The Key. I am one of the few who knows that name, and I knew you were at Dougal's apartment last night, as I spotted you there."

Janet drummed her claws against the worktop, waiting for the kettle to boil.

"So, I put the rest together, and after hearing he was in grave danger, I took him somewhere safer than a human apartment. I am also a little disappointed you never came to me to begin with; you know I have always watched over him since his mother passed."

The whistling kettle gave Graimel a moment to pause and think about what Janet recounted. After prepping the teapot, Janet swiped her malbec from him and took a generous gulp.

"I have to say, I was most certainly not babbling," Graimel said.

"Really? That's your focus here?"

"Fair point. I now know who is hunting Bedougalnn, but I do not understand why you snuck in and abducted him like that. Surely you could have thought of a better way to handle it?" Graimel said, furrowing his brow to a point a farmer could plant his wheat in it.

"What was I to do, Graimel, knock on his door and say, oh hi, I am your Aunty Janet, do you want to come for tea?"

"It worked for me, but still, I get your point."

"Look, I saw you all come back in the car, and then in the apartment's window. I needed to run an errand. When I came back I only caught sight of Dougal and wondered if you had performed one of your disappearing acts again. After what Lescan told me, I thought it best to do something, no point in taking risks. You must understand, Graimel, I got a sniff of something bad in the air, so I acted on impulse. What choice did I have?"

Aunty Janet poured Graimel his cup of tea and smiled apologetically, remembering to keep her mouth shut whilst doing so. As Dougal had pointed out, even a smile from a lyconfind is very disconcerting, bordering on distressing. So with lips pressed firmly together, Janet smiled, looking like a crocodile with a toothache and a penchant for eating dentists.

Graimel, looking a little bemused with the face Janet settled on as her smile, nodded his head warily, and spoke.

"Well, if I am being honest, it is a darn good thing you did, hindsight and all that. I got back to Dougal's apartment a few minutes after you absconded with him, and poor Binty was in a terrible state, thinking she had somehow lost him.

"It took me just a snip of time to calm her, before all hell broke loose, and in total darkness, a pack of skotos descended us upon. After the ensuing skirmish, we emerged victorious, but Bounce suffered a severe laceration to his hip."

With his addled brain not quite up to speed, no doubt due to the copious amount of malbec consumed, Dougal had failed to notice his beloved Bounce sidle past him into the living room. However, he did catch Graimel's words, and stopped merrily singing to himself, sobering up in an instant.

"Graimel, where is Bounce? Is he all right?"

"He is by the fire," Graimel said, pointing to the snoring dog on the rug. "He will be fine. Binty and Beth's Uncle Lescan made sure of that. He has got quite an impressive scar though."

Dougal rushed over to Bounce his heart in his mouth.

"Bounce, you all right my little man, hey, you been a good boy?"

Dougal spoke in a soft, calming voice while stroking his hand down the length of Bounce's back until he reached the hefty scar on his left hip.

"I am so sorry," Binty said, having flown over in an almost straight line while still gripping the glass of malbec. "It was the best I could do with the limited time we had," she added, leaning over to stroke his hand.

"You have nothing to be sorry for, Binty, you saved him, which means you saved me. I owe you my life. If I can ever do anything for you, you need only ask," Dougal said, wanting to embrace her, but concerned about how delicate she was. Not that he would ever say that out loud again.

"Bounce saved my life as well you know; he must be my guardian angel," Binty said, giving Bounce yet another huge kiss.

"Then I am sure he will wear his scar with pride, well that's if dogs can wear a scar with pride?" Dougal said, running his finger down the length of Bounce's wound.

"I can assure you they can. My Uncle Lescan told me so," Beth said, having also been sobered by the amount of raw emotion now flowing through Janet's den.

So much so, Janet thought she might require a permit.

Dougal almost jumped out of his skin as he turned to face Beth, as she appeared to have been taking smiling lessons from his Aunty Janet. Startled, but maintaining his composure, he asked her to pass on his thanks.

Whilst sipping his tea, Graimel surveyed his surroundings. The den was what he would refer to as rustic but homely. It comprised a single cavernous room, skilfully divided with the ingenious use of modest furniture into a kitchen, living room, and sleeping area. Although the pillows and blanket rolls near the hearth suggested the most commonly used space for sleeping was in front of the fire.

A variety of differing sized and coloured rugs were scattered over the exquisite solid Indian white marble floor, complementing the earthen walls, which were interspersed with roots and huge chunks of grey granite.

The focal point of the room was a natural wide cleft in the rock, which formed the perfect opening for the fireplace. Janet always kept the fire lit to ensure it was never used as a way into the den. As a bonus, it created a beautiful lighting feature, which was enhanced by the prevalent use of candles and oil lamps. Sublime yet cosy.

"I am assuming we are all up to speed now?" Graimel darted his eyes between them. "All on the same page, so to speak? How safe are we here, Janet?"

"Well, you could not track Dougal here, and it was only because Harg is related to my door that you got in. So, I would say quite safe, at least for now."

"In that case, if it is okay with you, Janet, I suggest we all rest up here for the night, and work out what our plan of action should be."

With everyone agreeing this would be for the best, a relieved Binty placed her glass on the mantle above the fire. No simple task considering she could see three of them. Proud of her achievement, she perched on the rim of the glass, giggled, lost her balance, and tumbled inside. Feeling rather giddy and tired, and surrounded by the relaxing aroma of malbec, she curled up and drifted off to sleep.

"Cake anyone?" Aunty Janet asked, as she waltzed into the kitchen.

Binty stirred and murmured for a moment when the word cake was mentioned, but did not wake from her slumber. Nobody could foresee how grumpy she would be when she woke to find she had missed cake. Well, Graimel could, but he simply chuckled and kept it to himself.

# 13
# BORED MINDS MOAN MORE

Back in the Hidden Dimension, Blodia paced her vacant space scowling, something she did regularly, but today she scowled in anticipation of the report from her top commander, Captain Hans Greemob. Expecting to hear about the demise of Bedougalnn, she would be disappointed.

"Hans to see you, my querulous Queen," Miss Maws announced.

"Captain Greemob to you!" Hans said, barging past into the queen's vacant space.

"Oh please, do feel free to just barge in uninvited," Blodia said, casting him a sardonic glare.

"Apologies calamitous one. I bring you dark and dreary news."

"Excellent. I was looking for something to darken my day. Go on." Blodia gestured Hans to come forward and speak.

"No, not that type of dark and dreary, maybe I should have opened with…" Hans forgot to do the most important thing, think. But he was mid-sentence now, and his improv skills were lacking. "Funny story, Bedougalnn, erm, kind of evaded us," he said, cringing.

"What. How could you let this happen?"

"I forgot about daylight savings time, and we arrived at the apartment an hour late," Hans said, awaiting his imminent fading.

"Fragrant Hyacinths, I totally forgot about daylight savings myself, and no one reminded me," she said irritably, and called for her personal assistant. "Miss Maws, could you come in here, please?"

Miss Maws came dutifully running into Blodia's vacant space.

"Could you please correct the clock?"

Miss Maws dawdled over to the blackened cabinet in the corner of the room. On top of which sat a once exquisite antique pendulum clock, now a mere shadow of its former glory. After letting itself be used in a most heinous crime, it was left irreparably damaged, and condemned to the Hidden Dimension. Miss Maws was about to open the case when she remembered there was no time in the Hidden Dimension.

"But, my most odious Queen, there is no—"

Before she had time to finish, Blodia got bored, raised her hand, and made some now familiar gestures.

"Sha Fa Er De`Gra," Blodia said, devoid of any emotion.

Miss Maws was not required to work her notice period. In fact, Miss Maws was not required, period. Alas, she came to the Hidden Dimension centuries ago. And with no way of being able to keep up with current events, she had no idea daylight savings time even existed, let alone what it was.

As for why Blodia blamed Miss Maws for their forgetfulness, I guess we will never know.

"Captain Greemob, get me a replacement for Miss Maws by the end of the day." Blodia rubbed her hands together as if trying to wipe them clean. "Carry on," she snapped.

"When the skotos Welcoming Committee arrived, the occupants of the apartment launched a vicious unprovoked attack, catching them by surprise and fading them all."

"Who attacked you?"

"Ah well, I don't know I'm afraid. I was not there," Hans said, sheepishly.

"And where, may I ask, were you, while the Queen's Guard were being innocently slaughtered?"

"Outside, you know, to check all the lights were extinguished, and to ensure no harm came to the welcoming committee."

"And how did that work out?"

Hans was about to answer this honestly and bluntly, when he realised it may require a touch of decorum, but not knowing what decorum was, or even how to spell it, presented him with a problem.

"Well, it could've been worse. Like I said, when I heard the commotion I was still outside checking the light had been silenced. Once finished, I rushed up the stairs, but I was only halfway back when everything went quiet. Now I know it sounds bad, but I stopped rushing, thinking we were victorious. When I entered the apartment and saw they were all faded, I realised how lucky you are, my Queen. For if I was not outside, you would have lost me as well," Hans said, feeling rather proud with his explanation.

"Well, aren't we the lucky ones?" Blodia said, her fingers twitching.

"Yes, my execrable empress."

Blodia raised her hand while glancing at the pile of ash that was once Miss Maws. Hans followed her eyeline, and realising what was about to happen, he blurted out.

"We did injure and scare them."

"Go on."

"I used the shadows to sneak back into the apartment. Once inside, I noticed the stonework around the fire cracked and crumbling, where one of your guards had smashed someone into it," Hans said, with feigned drama, "and found a carving knife discarded on the blood smeared kitchen floor. Everywhere I looked, I saw destruction, with tables knocked over, broken glass, and shattered lamps. Fragments of which were scattered amongst some of the piles of ash littering the floor. It was clear to me; the Queen's Guard had scared them into fleeing."

For some reason, Hans decided to act out his explanation by pretending to sneak about and pick things up, amongst other wild gesticulations. For the first time in years, a smile crept across Blodia's face as she stifled a snigger, reminded of her children playing. And against her better judgement, she spared Hans.

Of course, Hans' version of events is not quite true. Not only did Bounce break the table lamp, but he was also responsible for most of the mess in the apartment. He always was. It mattered not, Blodia believed him.

With a flick of her wrist, she dismissed Hans. Stepping over the small pile of ash that was once Miss Maws, he left, and promoted the first staff member he came across. Which just so happened to be Yoop's Cousin, Floop.

Blodia opened a secret compartment hidden in the wall of her vacant space. From within it, she removed a shining amethyst and amber orb, entwined with black thorn branches and a foreboding sense of pure malevolence, The Orb of Darketh.

Placing the orb on the plinth in the centre of the room, she cupped her hands around it in an almost caressing manner, uttering macabre incantations in reverence. Something deep within the orb sparked and started to glow, surging in intensity until it resembled the intense complex reds associated with a red sky at night, interwoven with grey swirling mists.

"Orof Dar EthSh, Theth Tha`Lesto Bedougalnn," she chanted.

The grey mists span ever faster until they absorbed the red hue and became the radiant red mist of revelation. With her mind fixated, she gazed into the orb with studious fascination, hoping for her request to be revealed. And as she amplified her concentration, words swam through the mist.

*Enunciate and Reiterate.*

Blodia seethed with indignation and flew into a furious rage, but as no one was around to see her, she quickly got bored, returned to the orb, and abided by the request.

"Orof Dar EthSh, Theth Tha`Lesto Bedougalnn," Blodia chanted, for the second time, paying special attention to her pronunciation this time.

Once again she gazed deep into the radiant red mist of revelation, waiting for her answer from the Orb of Darketh, until the words she had not been waiting for appeared.

*Advisor Taking a Nap.*

The orb dimmed as the mists inside parted, and the radiant red mist of revelation revealed nothing. Blodia screamed in frustration, and somewhere a cat ran down an alley, and a spotted dog was seen on the other side of a canal in Birmingham.

With the petulance of a spoilt brat, she swiped the orb from its plinth and placed it back in the hidden compartment. She did not understand how the orb worked, but it held the power to show her things hidden from plain sight.

Unbeknownst to Blodia, Yoop had not only known what the Orb of Darketh was, but he also knew how to interpret it correctly. This, of course, is the other reason why she should have not been so eager to fade him.

*The Orb of Darketh*: Discovered in the Hidden Dimension 35 years ago, a dark and mysterious sphere created from the shadow of a rather malicious Advisaball. The Advisaball is a small spherical device similar to a scrying orb. When asked a question, it uses vocal intonation analysis to respond with a message displayed in the centre of the orb. Because of its hypothesised accuracy, it had replaced official advisors, and was now in use by rulers all over the entire human world, helping them make those tough decisions leaders have to make sometimes.

Now, this particular Advisaball was used, used being the operative word, by a high-ranking bumptious politician with a propensity to prevaricate and fib. The Advisaball knew this and selected its answers accordingly, its two most common responses being, *You have more chance of finding hens' teeth,* and *Mumbling yields no results.* However, one day the Advisaball was rather tired after a strenuous week of non-stop pointless questions. So when asked *"Should I introduce a new tax, to fund my love of hotel 'Do Not Disturb' door signs?"* it sarcastically replied, *Yeah, sure, why not.*

A week of turmoil later, and the un-named politician slipped off the edge of placidity, hurling his Advisaball at his 18th floor hotel balcony window. While continuing to have an absolute temper tantrum, he threw open the window, picked up the Advisaball, and slung it for all his worth. Unfortunately for him, the Advisaball had purposely leaked some of its internal liquid onto the laminate floor, causing him to slip and follow it. Moments later, the Advisaball splintered into a million specks of dust, and its shadow was sent straight to the Hidden Dimension, where it became the Orb of Darketh.

It is important to mention here, this is the only known instance of a malicious Advisaball. By all accounts, all the others are extremely well behaved.

Managing to hide her frustration, Blodia called for her captain.

"Captain Greemob!" Blodia screeched, the sound echoing ever louder around her vacant space.

"My Queen Blodia the abhorrent, how can I serve you?" Hans said, racing into the room.

"I have pondered a while, and believe you still owe me a Bedougalnn." Blodia scowled as she strutted around her vacant space. "You are to head back to Bedougalnn's apartment, and search for clues as to where he has gone to hide. Once you discover his whereabouts, you are to return to me post-haste. I do not want you messing this up a second time. I will deal with him personally."

"Yes, oh putrid one," he replied timorously.

Although pleased Blodia had not faded him, he was unenthusiastic about returning to the place where so many skotos were faded only a few hours prior.

"Oh, Hans, where is my assistant?"

"I will send him through now, oh dark and dreary one."

Begrudgingly, Floop pressed open the door capitulating to the request, and the gears of time achingly clunked one cog to the right. Something sinister had been put in motion.

Captain Hans Greemob tramped down the dark path and headed for the Pool of Vacant Reflection. He weaved his way through the gloomy forsaken streets of the Hidden Dimension until he happened across The Banished Abstract Cat Tavern. The ruined ornate sign hung at an angle on only one chain, wisps of smoke still rising from it, the once beautiful hand painted imagery now faded and flaked.

The original Abstract Cat Tavern had been in a tiny coastal village in Cornwall, a foreboding den of ill repute, home to vile murderers and brutal pirate smugglers. It ended up in the Hidden Dimension after being accidentally burnt down, when a violent bar fight broke out between Captain Greemob's hairy band of smugglers, and a travelling gang of disreputable cut-throats and thieves.

*Ah, fond memories,* Hans thought.

It was not by coincidence he ended up in the Hidden Dimension on that very same day, and also not by coincidence he ended up outside this very tavern on his way to carry out his orders.

Blodia never said he had to go by himself, and who better to go with him than his old hairy band of smugglers. The tavern was as he remembered, except a little more scorched here and there, and devoid of any colour. He ducked through the smouldering archway separating the rooms, wisps of smoke still rising from the sticky carpet and from a few of his old friends.

"Any of you scumbags want to come with your old captain? I am on a mission for Queen Blodia?"

Before anyone had a chance to reply, a fierce fight spontaneously erupted in the tavern, but since the skotos could not harm each other without harming themselves, the fight ended almost before it began.

"Old habits, eh," Hans chuckled, "So, who is with me?"

The gathered skotos all agreed to accompany him on his mission for the queen. Not because any of them were interested in going anywhere, but in case word got back to Blodia and she decided to fade them.

"Excellent, that makes us 13 in total. Unlucky for Bedougalnn I say."

Upon hearing this revelation, they froze like startled bunnies, unable to unstick their feet from the carpet, a common problem in this establishment. The distinct lack of a rear door thwarting any thought of attempting to flee. An undeniable sense of relief flooded through Hans at the inability of his old crew to skedaddle.

"Did you say Bedougalnn? The Bedougalnn?" Edmund asked, his voice quivering.

"Yes, but there are 13 of us and only one of him, and we only need discover his location for Blodia, then report back!"

However, he did not feel the need to reveal that a couple of Bedougalnn's friends faded 11 of the Queen's Guard. Hans knew his old crew well, and although they were fine combatants and good company, they spooked easily and were a little dim.

"Now, pull yourselves together and follow me."

Hans turned his back and headed out of the tavern. To his relief, all 12 skotos followed him. In single file, they silently traipsed down the dark path to the Pool of Vacant Reflection and jumped straight into its swirling black waters. One by one they disappeared beneath the surface, swallowed by the pool, which spat them out into a disused well in the woods close to Dougal's apartment.

All 13 hunters skulked out of the well under cover of night, darting from tree to tree, corrupting and rotting with glee as they slunk through the woods. Only able to exist where no light shone, made this world a dangerous place for them, but they were skilled smugglers and adept at moving within shadows. With gleeful abandon, Thomas decayed the branches of the trees. One broke away and came crashing to the ground, the moonlight bursting through the now open canopy almost extinguishing one of the skotos. Hans spun about, barking his disapproval.

"No more, or I will ensure you stand before Blodia for judgement."

Without another sound, they proceeded with caution to Dougal's apartment, using the shadows to creep inside and begin their search for clues as to Bedougalnn's whereabouts.

"This place is a pigsty," Edmund said, commenting on the untidiness of the place. "There are broken lamps, blood smeared across the kitchen floor, and little piles of ash everywhere. It's disgusting!"

"You're right, Edmund," Thomas said, "but it cannot be a pigsty, as there are no pigs."

Hans peeked up from his searching and shook his head in dismay, but was relieved they were as daft as he thought, as none realised this was the scene of a skotos defeat.

On the kitchen counter there was a note which read.

*In case we are not here, remember BOreD MINds MOan mORe.*

Edmund pushed the note to one side, dismissing it and continuing his search. After 30 minutes of looking, Hans called them all together to ask if anyone had found any clues. Of course, Hans knew the limit of his crew's intelligence, and asked for their reports in turn.

"Well, this has been enlightening so far. Looks like all my hopes rely on you, Edmund. Tell me, what did you find?"

Edmund stopped counting his fingers and focused on Hans.

"Well, nothing of interest, at least no clues anyway. I saw a note in the kitchen, but it made little sense, a bit of fur by the balcony door, Oh, and a footprint in the soil, next to a knocked over plant pot. But it's not a man's footprint. So yeah, no clues I'm afraid, Captain."

"You never fail to disappoint!"

Hans calmly sauntered into the kitchen as Edmund shrugged his shoulders, sharing his frustrated bewilderment with the others.

"What's with him?"

Hans stomped outside to investigate the footprint, which resembled that of a gigantic wolf. Then he inspected the two different types of fur, some was dog and the other he could not discern, but assumed it belonged to the owner of the footprint. Finally, he picked up the note from the counter, and read, Bodmin Moor. He shook his head in disbelief. Not only had Edmund thought this was not a clue, but it seemed like the person who wrote it did not have time to hide that fact.

He paced back into the other room and 12 skotos confronted him, all asking him the same question.

"What are all these little piles of dust everywhere?"

Lacking a reasonable excuse, Hans opted to tell the truth.

"Well, they were 11 of the Queen's Guard, but as you can see for yourselves, they are no more, so let's just say they retired. Now we should make haste back to the Hidden Dimension before dawn breaks, and we are all retired," Hans said, as he left the apartment and headed back out into the woods.

None of Hans' crew were exactly leadership material, so despite all their posturing and bravado when threatening to end him, they failed to come up with a single idea as to how. Because of this, luck was on both their sides, as only Hans knew the way back to the well.

"Come, we are returning to Blodia with good news, for we now know that Bedougalnn fled to Bodmin Moor," Hans said, before jumping into the black void of the well.

"Do we, when did we find that out?" Edmund asked, slack-jawed and quizzical.

"Buggered if I know," Thomas said, leaping into the well.

With vacant stares all around, they returned to the Hidden Dimension.

Interestingly, in 1542, a young local farmhand jumped into the well to escape what he thought was a witch chasing him. He was consumed by the void, regurgitated, and spat back out, becoming the first bogeyman. If he had not run away from the young lady chasing him, who was but a lost princess, he would have received riches beyond his dreams. Of course, we have no way of knowing which destiny he would have preferred.

# 14

## CAKE FOR BREAKFAST

Dougal stirred from his sleep, his arm still wrapped around Bounce where he nodded off full of cake and wine the previous night. With a stretch and a silent yawn, he pushed himself up off the floor and pottered into the kitchen.

Hunched over the table with cups of tea in hand, Graimel and Janet spoke in hushed voices. The conversation abruptly ending as Dougal approached.

"Good morning, dear," Janet said, getting up from the table. "Would you like some waffles for your breakfast?"

"Cake for breakfast?"

Before Janet could respond and advise that waffles were not cake, a loud smash came from the living room. The word cake resonated within the wine glass where Binty slept, waking her with a start. Forgetting where she had fallen asleep, she slammed into the side of the glass, knocking it from the mantle. A split-second before it hit the floor and shattered, she slipped out of it unscathed, with nothing more than a rumbling tummy.

"Did someone say cake? Oh, sorry about the glass."

Aunty Janet hurried into the living room to clean up the shattered glass before anyone got any in their paws.

"If it's as tasty as the cake we had last night, you're in for a treat," Dougal said, not thinking anything of it, or knowing any better.

"Is that true? You all scoffed cake and didn't bother to wake me. I bet it was the most exquisite Lyconfind cake, baked to perfection by Janet, and I didn't get any. Not happy!"

Binty slumped down on top of the kitchen table with a momentous sigh, folded her arms, tucked her wings, and tossed her head to one side with tight-lipped indignation. Without saying a word, Graimel opened a little storage unit on the work surface, took out a small plate, and slid it across the table to Binty's feet.

"I never said we didn't save you any."

She turned her head and caught sight of one of the most beautiful things she had ever seen. A perfectly formed slice of soft, golden yellow Lyconfind Cake, split through the middle, with a thick layer of fresh hand whipped cream, and a smattering of what Binty hoped were juicy ogsleni berries. It glowed like the morning sun, and the aroma of cinnamon, soured cherries, vanilla, and freshly cut grass gripped her nostrils. An aroma she would never forget.

Unlike the aroma Bounce emitted the previous day, which clung to her throat like a limpet.

No matter how much she tried to remain grumpy, an overwhelming happiness consumed her. And as her eyes sparkled and widened, her smile grew, and she dragged her eyes from the cake to gaze up at Graimel.

"I love you," Binty said, before focusing her attention back on the cake. "I love you as well."

In less than three minutes, she reduced the cake to crumbs, minus the small chunk she saved for Bounce. Which, when presented before his nose, he consumed in less than three seconds.

"That must be the best cake ever. My dad would love it. You know his birthday is next week. Is there any chance you could make him one, or teach me how, I mean, whichever is easier? Oh actually, why don't you all come to his party as well? Everyone would be so excited to meet you all. Would that be possible, Graimel?"

"Of course, but first we need to get through this." Graimel's voice had deepened and lost all sense of frivolity.

Beth joined at the table them, and they took the time to enjoy a nice cup of tea and some waffles. Once their bellies were full and the teapot empty, Graimel spoke up.

"To Business. Last night Janet and I spent some time catching up, and she told me of something that will help us in our fight. Something I believed to be lost until it was found, before being lost again. But Lescan has learnt of its location from a friend of his. The problem is a lyconfind cannot recover it, so it is down to us."

"Graimel, I thought we were going to seek help from Bregon Skovin?"

"We need to do this first, Binty. No point in going to see Bregon if we are not prepared."

"I will stay with Janet. Should anyone come looking for you, two sets of teeth are better than one, eh dear?" Beth said, wrapping her arm around her best friend.

"Oh my, what big eyes you have, Beth."

"All the better for baking with Janet," Beth said, fluttering her eyelids before they both collapsed in fits of giggles.

"Well, what is it we are looking for, Graimel, and where is it?"

"We are going to the Mines of Drothmaen in Grackbin Forest," Graimel said, lifting Grock from the floor and slipping him over his shoulders.

"Er Graimel, The Mines of Drothmaen, are you serious? Nobody comes back from there."

Until now, Dougal had been quite happy keeping himself to himself. He tried not to listen to when they talked, as he struggled to understand and only ended up confused. But, when he hears a phrase containing the words, *nobody comes back from there,* he finds his interest pricked, and is justly concerned for all those involved.

"Where did you say we were going and not coming back from?" Dougal said, his voice quivering like branches in a thunderstorm.

"If we weren't coming back, there would be no point in us going. With me, Harg, and the most sweet and delicate pixie ever at your side, you have nothing to fear," Graimel said, with a reassuring smirk.

"Graimel is right…" Binty said, pausing for a moment as his words sunk in, casting him a disapproving glare before continuing, "there is absolutely nothing to fear except goblins, vile, stinky, dirty, green goblins. Filthy horrid creatures."

"Now now, Binty, don't scare the man. After all, they're not all stinky, or green for that matter," Graimel said, trying to restore a modicum of optimism.

"Why don't I stay here with Aunty Janet and Beth, because I will probably only be in the way, anyway."

"Urgh, filthy goblins, disgusting things they are."

Beth and Janet cupped their hands to their mouths, flexing and retching.

Graimel put his head in his hands.

"Have any of you ever encountered a goblin?"

There was a momentary silence as everyone around the table paused to think, shooting each other inquisitive glances before shaking their heads in unison. None of them ever having the displeasure of meeting a goblin, but all having read plenty of books with goblins in them, including Dougal.

"Right, so none of you have ever come across a goblin. Well I have, and I can tell you they are everything you think, and much, much worse."

This was not the motivational speech that Graimel intended to give, and with hindsight, was the most demotivational thing he could have said. A tumbleweed rolled past an abandoned ramshackle saloon in The Grove, Texas, as he scratched around, trying to get his thoughts in order.

*Hmm, how am I to recover from this,* he thought, then it twigged.

"So, this is our chance to rid ourselves of such vile abominations, and retrieve the Pendant of Tel Etoiles to boot."

This seemed to inspire everyone a little, except for Dougal. He looked like a skoto who had just won a sunshine holiday to Crete.

"What on earth is the Pendant of Tel Etoiles?" Binty asked.

"It is a fabled enchanted pendant, lost 37 years ago, with the fall of Nellencu."

"Nellencu?"

"You ask too many questions Binty," Graimel said, his eyes flashing with vexation as he glared at her shaking his head.

Binty knew this look, and it meant shut up before Dougal shows an interest.

"You're right. Though I must say, I'm disappointed you didn't say *no time,*" Binty chuckled.

With a disapproving glare, Graimel shook his head and gestured towards the door. Janet released the lock and wished them a safe journey, before clutching Dougal in her arms for a moment.

Graimel stepped through the door and made his way back up the stairs, closely followed by Binty riding on the back of Bounce. Not wanting to persist with the hang on and hope method of steering Bounce, she had fashioned herself a saddle from some odds and sods Janet had lying about. After being reluctantly released from Janet's grip, Dougal sloped behind them, still thinking he would be better off staying with Janet and Beth and eating cake.

# 15

# MOOR DANGER

They headed out to the moor, Graimel glancing back at the towering stone door lying flat upon the floor, thinking, *I should put that back*, before making a mental note to restore it as soon as they got back from the mines.

A light drizzle fell on the fresh, dewy ground.

"How are you at running, Dougal?" Graimel asked.

Although he ran quite a lot, Dougal would be the first to admit he was terrible at it. But it helped him keep fit, and being a writer, it was the perfect way to get his thoughts in order.

"Rubbish, and Bounce can only run for about five minutes before he would need a rest. Anyway, I thought you could travel anywhere in nothing more than a blink. Why can't we do that?"

Binty shook her head feverishly and was relieved when Graimel responded.

"We cannot be sure we are not being followed, so must ensure our trail cannot be picked up. And that form of travel leaves a trace, so for now we walk."

They headed deeper into the moor, using all the available cover, lest they should be spotted and tracked.

"You can use the time we are walking to practise the art of Chronostasis, Dougal."

"Chrono what?"

"Chronostasis, it is what Tailors use to manipulate and interact with time. If you can master it, you will be able to do everything I can do. Are you ready? Excellent. The first thing you need to learn is the incantation. Have you got a pen?"

"No."

"Good, because you are not allowed to write it down. Now, repeat after me, Te`sow Ime Fow, Oe`my De`an, Aestic O`an." Graimel waved his arms around in time to his words. "Nothing will happen unless pronounced with perfection, so practise and let me know when you've nailed it."

With a sigh and a roll of his eyes, Dougal thought *how am I supposed to learn a new language in the middle of Bodmin Moor, when I am rubbish at languages*?

"Don't think, enunciate," Graimel said, trudging ahead, stomping through a large puddle as he passed them both, and whacking Dougal across the butt with Harg as he did so.

The muddy droplets of water sprayed up Dougal's legs, dirtying his lounge pants, Binty managing to a duck avoid the huge brown blobs heading her way. This got her thinking about the weather and how this horrid rain could ruin her outfit. In Erof, the rain was polite enough to only persist while the pixies slept.

Something sprouting between a small cluster of rocks to the left caught her eye. She unclipped her safety harness and darted off towards it, plucking it from the earth before zipping back to Bounce. The ride was going to be exceedingly more enjoyable with her new accessory.

A heart-warming smile broke through Dougal's grimace as he glanced over to Binty whilst mumbling the incantation. For there, sitting with the poise and elegance of a heroic maiden, Binty, riding side saddle and using a small mushroom as an umbrella, as her gallant steed Bounce, traipsed across the moor. Even through the rain, the beauty of the moor undeniable to her.

But you needed to watch your step, and it was without doubt Dougal was oblivious to this.

"Enunciate, and look where you are going," Binty shouted.

But it was too late, for as she got to the end of the sentence, Dougal tripped and fell flat into the mud and long grasses. Binty laughed so hard she would have fallen off Bounce had she not re-secured her harness. Graimel glanced over his shoulder, shook his head, and carried on walking.

For a moment, Dougal could do only lie there blowing bubbles in the mud, waiting for the humiliation to pass. With no sign of this happening any time soon, he pushed himself up from the claggy earth, while muttering a chain of expletives under his breath. As he wiped the mud from his face, a degree of petulance crept into his voice.

"Enunciate, articulate, irritate. Well, I am sodding enunciating!"

"Then concentrate on your clumsy gait," Binty called back with a smirk.

After shaking off as much mud as he could, he jogged a little to catch up with the others and continued practising the incantation. Every so often, Graimel would stop and turn with a studious stare. At first, Dougal thought he was just checking they were keeping up, but he soon came to realise he was making certain they were not being followed.

Binty reached into her newly crafted saddlebag and broke off a tiny piece of Lyconfind cake, allowing it to melt in her mouth before clutching her dainty hip flask and treating herself to a sip. Until that morning, her flask had always contained fresh squeezed cherry juice, now it was a vessel for fermented grape juice. She slid back in her saddle a little and relaxed into the adventure.

Graimel trundled onwards, leading the way without hesitation. Not once had he put a foot wrong on the moor, every step appearing to be pre-planned, and yet still, he outpaced the others.

They had been walking for well over an hour when the weather turned. Intimidating black clouds blanketing the sky and the summers drizzle becoming a deluge, pummelling the ground like machinegun fire. A sense of foreboding gripped Graimel, and as he studied the horizon, something in the dark caught his eye. He dashed behind a conveniently placed boulder and motioned with his hand for the others to get down.

Even Bounce had a quick rest in the sodden grass, appearing to do what he was told for a change. Such was the darkness that now surrounded them, Dougal could barely make out his hand in front of his face as he paused to think.

*Why is Graimel hiding when no one can see him? Unless, of course, whatever we are hiding from is not human.*

Crouched in amongst the heather, Dougal slunk towards Graimel, finding him sat with his back pressed against the rock.

"What is it?" Dougal whispered, recognising the gravity of the current situation.

He knew Graimel would not be taking cover if there were no need, the graveness of the situation decorating his face as he raised his finger to his mouth. Lightning struck the bracken as if trying to reveal their position, wisps of smoke rising from the scorched earth as Graimel leant into Harg and muttered something incoherent.

Harg once more transformed into a raven, and took flight, spiralling up into the gloom, his silhouette against the now black sky rendering him invisible. Like a breath on the wind, he headed out in the direction of what Graimel had spotted in the distant darkness.

As Harg glided over the mysterious figures below, Graimel removed Grock and placed him on the ground. Binty got Bounce to crawl over to the rock on his belly, something he was not fond of doing in wet grass, but respected Binty's command. Grock waited until they were all together, then threw himself over them like a table cloth, hiding them from all eyes, from all senses.

This was Harg's cue, and he swooped down towards the figures on the ground. They were skotos for sure, and were with their queen, Blodia. He soared by and back up to the clouds, avoiding all detection, before circling back and landing on the rock by Graimel. He watched until the skotos departed to continue their journey, alerting Graimel to this with a gurgling croak, which Grock took as a sign it was safe to uncover his friends and return to his natural form.

Graimel cautiously rose to his feet. Peering out across the blackness of the moor, he surveyed the gloom. With a nod, Harg hopped on to his shoulder and whispered to him, as he listened his shoulders sagged and he placed his hand against the rock, needing something sturdy to lean on momentarily, before nodding in acknowledgment.

"Rest here. I need to see Lescan. I will leave Grock here with you should you need to hide, although I won't be long. Just stay out of trouble, and Dougal, Practise."

"But, Graimel, why Lesca..."

Before Binty had time to finish, Graimel vanished. With a sigh, Dougal sat up and rested his back against the rock, and tried to refine his pronunciation. Bounce could see the hulking granite boulder was offering some protection from the persistent rain, and inched a little closer, pressing himself against Dougal until he moved aside. Once satisfied he now had the best spot, he drifted off to sleep, once again dreaming of playing fetch with Harg.

"Mind if I sit with you while you study?" Binty asked, sitting down on Dougal's shoulder, and resting her head against him.

Grock shivered and waggled, shaking the excess water and mud from his fur, before sitting on Dougal's right, snapping his fingers, and pulling a book from out of thin air. At least, that is how it appeared to Dougal.

"What are you reading, Grock?" Dougal asked.

*"Snalusel ec Quagesk."*

"Grock!" Binty exclaimed.

"What's it about?"

"He is not telling you; I am shocked at you, Grock, reading something so, well, dirty."

Grock looked up from his book with a wry smile, grinned at Dougal, and nodded his head in a knowing manner.

"If you don't mind me asking, where are you from?"

"I was born in Perquag," Grock said, folding his book closed and wishing he had sat elsewhere, "but it was consumed by a time slip while I was on a school trip to Gurquag. So I guess I am lucky to be here. Some days it is hard to be thankful though. I lost my entire family, as did all my school friends. All of us orphaned in that same moment, a dreadful day."

"I'm so sorry; I didn't mean to..."

"It is okay, Graimel says it does not mean they are dead, just misplaced, which means there is always a chance we can find them, always hope." Grock said, reopening his book, signalling to Dougal the conclusion of their conversation.

What Grock did not tell him was this all happened 35 earth years ago, about the same time Dougal was born, or so he is led to believe.

Graimel appeared a metre or so behind Lescan in his garden.

"Lescan! Beth and Janet are in danger!" Graimel said, his voice a worrisome tone.

Lescan leapt into the air, like a rabbit trying to escape with a prize carrot.

"Knotted fur Graimel! Could you not pop up like that?" he said, clutching his hand to his chest, "now explain, what do you bring to my door?"

"I am sorry, old friend," Graimel said, placing his hand on Lescan's shoulder. "There is a small band of skotos heading towards Janet's den, and Queen Blodia is with them. They hunt Bedougalnn."

"So much for a quiet day pottering about. You better get back to Binty and Bedougalnn, and I will gather a few friends and head over there. Not that I think those girls will need us," Lescan said, peeling off his gardening gloves and tossing them on an overturned wheelbarrow.

"I can come with you."

"No, Graimel, you press on, and leave this to me. Now go."

Graimel trusted Lescan and knew he understood the dangers involved, and the importance of Bedougalnn. So he did what he needed to do and vanished, appearing back with Binty and Dougal a mere moment later.

# 16

# FOR FANGS AND FUR

With a shrug of his shoulders Lescan strode back towards his den, unable to resist taking one of his freshly picked carrots from a small wooden table outside his greenhouse. After wiping off the dirt on his overalls, he took a bite. *Perfect,* he thought, *far better than any of that stuff you can buy from the market.* He dashed inside and snatched up his moon ring, although a little loath to use it, because of its mildly annoying side effects. *Take it anyway,* he thought, *it might come in useful.*

Lescan leapt over his gate and ran up the lane to see his trusted friend Sven. The door to the den was ajar, and Lescan could hear music and laughter coming from within. As he was about to give the door a sharp rap, it was flung open, and Sven filled the frame.

"Lescan, my friend, I thought you were gardening today and couldn't come over. Glad you have though bud, come in, join the party," Sven said, gesturing for him to enter. "Hey everyone, for those of you who don't know him, this is my buddy Lescan."

Five more lyconfind who were drinking, listening to music, and roasting vegetables, all chimed a friendly greeting to him.

Sven was an accountant for some of the more discerning

creatures of the woodland, but he got no real job satisfaction. Klaus and Fimor were both den builders, the best in the business, they had constructed Sven's den, and also done some modifications to Lescan's. Then there was Wrethe, he was a photographer, and always carried his SLR with him. *Stood next to him* was Kainen, a personal trainer and immensely strong in both character and physicality.

Lastly, there was Laegon. He lost his right eye and two fingers on a lykind camping trip in Grackbin Forest 12 years ago, whilst defending his pupils from the vile Goblin Lord Ferglestin. These days he stuck to teaching history.

Once all the introductions were complete, Lescan spoke, trepidation evident in his voice.

"It's a pleasure to meet you all, though I wish it were under better circumstances. My niece and her best friend are in grave danger."

"Damsels in distress, well what are we waiting for?" Klaus said, stepping forward.

"Indeed, lead the way, Lescan," Kainen said, stepping forward to join Klaus, closely followed by both Sven and Fimor.

"Count me in," Wrethe said, as he picked up his camera and gave it the once over.

"Can I just ask, in danger from who or what?" Laegon said, raising his hand.

Lescan walked over to Laegon, and noting his injuries, he rested his hand on his shoulder.

"This is not a fight for you, friend. I am assuming you all know of the skotos, and the legend of The Bedougalnn. Well, the skotos have discovered Bedougalnn's true identity, and are now on the hunt with Queen Blodia."

"This is indeed a grave situation, and there is no point in me sitting it out. For if we fail to stop the skotos, and they end Bedougalnn, we are all finished."

"For Fangs and Fur!" Laegon cheered, raising his glass of

mead before throwing his arm around Lescan and proffering his glass.

"For Fangs and Fur!" they all cheered in unison.

Lescan took a mouthful and passed the glass back to Laegon, thanking him and patting him on the back. The others quaffed what remained of their drinks and followed him out into the lane.

"Come, this way," Lescan said, leaping over the hedge at the side of the lane and heading into the undergrowth.

He bounded through the wood with haste, weaving between giant stika spruce and occasionally peeking over his shoulder to check the others were keeping pace, they were. The sunlight darted between the tall trees, as if lighting the path of least resistance for the group. Flecks of rain speckled their fur as they raced deeper into the woods, creating an almost diamante effect, much to Kainen's delight. Ten minutes later, they broke through the treeline out onto the open moor.

What had until now been scarcely a light drizzle, with firm earth beneath their feet, decayed into something far worse. The rain pelted them so hard it stung, the ground now a mire, and a distinct line of darkness bordered the moor. Stopped dead in their tracks, they stared at the way ahead in bewilderment.

Unable to comprehend this total and sudden shift, Wrethe turned and scurried back under the cover of the trees. The sunlight was breaking through the treetops again, rays of golden light illuminating everything around him. He span on his heels to face his friends once more, and pressed his eye against the camera's viewfinder. There was nothing, nothing except the darkness. He manually adjusted the zoom, but still nothing.

It was as if the world ended at the edge of the woods, yet he knew it did not.

The shutter clicked three times in quick succession, before he lowered his camera, and returned to his friends. For a moment, he thought they had gone on ahead without him until he stepped beyond the tree line and bumped straight into Laegon.

"Careful, buddy," Laegon said, moving to the side a little.

Wrethe was about to explain what he had witnessed, but realised this would only cause to delay them, and time it would appear was of the essence.

"Lead on Lescan," Wrethe said, tucking his camera away.

Lescan was a little more than perturbed with what had happened to the weather. Raising his snout up to the sky, he took a deep breath and bolted off across the moor.

The ground now sodden, their pace slowed somewhat. They also had to take care not to lose each other, of course, lyconfind have excellent night vision, so this was not presenting an insurmountable problem.

The mud under their claws and between their toes, was however, proving to be rather bothersome for Kainen and Klaus, who were both quite exacting in their personal appearance. They had had an instant rapport from the moment they met and were currently sharing grooming tips and product opinions. At this particular time, they were discussing which shampoo was going to do the best job of cleaning all this mud out of their fur.

"I am telling you, Kainen, Wereshine works wonders on mud," Klaus said.

"That may be so, friend, but Furisoft will also make your coat shine like the moon."

"Wow, are you implying my coat is a little lacklustre?"

"Not at all, although, Furisoft would give you that extra sparkle. Borrow some of mine when we get back and you'll see."

"Well, if it is going to give me even more sparkle, then I guess I have to try it," Klaus said, as they both started chuckling.

In-between dodging the odd bolt of lightning or two, this conversation continued for the rest of their trudge across the moor.

Upon arriving at the monoliths outside Janet's den, Lescan's eyes were drawn to the towering door stone still lying flat on the floor. Only one person could be responsible for this, *Graimel,* Lescan thought. *I will need to have words with him for not putting it back.*

Lescan bounded down the stairs with the others close behind and knocked on Janet's door.

"Beth, It's Uncle Lescan."

The door unlocked and swung open and there stood Janet and Beth, one armed with a rolling pin and the other wielding a frying pan.

"Seriously girls?" Lescan mocked, "surely your claws would be a more effective weapon?"

The aroma of freshly baked cake struck him as he stepped inside, hugging them both before introducing his companions.

Janet and Beth had spent most of their lives keeping themselves to themselves and baking, bloody full moon, neither of them ever having the time or the inclination to meet a life companion. Now here they were in a room with six strapping lyconfind, and both were in a bit of a fluster. Distracted, Janet remembered she needed to lock the door, but the door had already taken care of itself, and was properly secured.

"Well, so, err, what brings you and your gorgeous friends over to visit us Uncle Lescan?" Beth asked, trying to place the frying pan back on the hob inconspicuously.

"Danger is afoot, and it is heading this way, at least according to Graimel. Seems he spotted skotos on the moor, and fears they are coming here looking for Bedougalnn."

"And you thought two fragile girls could not take care of themselves, eh?" Janet said.

"Not quite. As a matter of fact Graimel thought you could do with a little back up, as Queen Blodia is with them."

"Well, that changes things a little, but nothing has ever got in here, Lescan."

"Or got out, unless you wanted it to," Beth said, raising her eyebrows and giggling.

"Beth!" Janet said, flicking her a smile.

"Can I get anyone a drink or a towel, or possibly a brush?" Janet said, running her hand down Fimor's firm furry arm.

"A glass of malbec if you have it?" Fimor asked.

Janet almost melted. Not only was he gorgeous, but he liked malbec.

Beth had taken an instant liking to Wrethe, his bright blue eyes, shiny white teeth, and a smile to die for.

"Is that a camera in your pocket or?"

"Oh, it's so much more than a camera, Beth; it's a Nikon D850."

He pulled out his camera and hung it from his neck, a simple ploy to move a smidge closer to Beth than necessary, a ploy Beth had no problem with at all. Although she was mildly confused by what Wrethe was talking about, and found terminology such as apertures and exposures quite baffling, they also made her tingle in a way she never had. So, she smiled her sweetest smile and was more than happy to listen.

When the flames suddenly died in the fireplace, Sven was sitting on one of the chairs next to the hearth, with Laegon on the other chair opposite him, his feet resting on the coffee table. Lucky for him, Janet was so engrossed with Fimor she had not noticed. Kainen and Klaus were on the sofa opposite the fireplace, and were deep in conversation. This time it was regarding what conditioner they used. Of course, Kainen still swore by the Furisoft product line, though Klaus preferred Moonglow, convinced it made his fur shine like the moon.

Over in the kitchen, Lescan was standing by the front door, his back pressed against the wall, whilst Janet and Fimor sat at the kitchen table drinking malbec. As for Beth and Wrethe, well, they were lost in each other, leaning against the unit separating the kitchen from the living room.

There was less than a second between the fire being snuffed

and the rest of the den being consumed by darkness. Even though they had excellent night vision, it took a few more seconds for their eyes to adjust. In that time, the attack began.

First through the flue was Blodia. She shot across the room, taking Klaus by the throat and dragging him over the back of the sofa, slamming him into the wall, smashing the mirror, shards of glass splintering into his back. As Klaus yelped, Kainen hurdled over the sofa in his direction, his ears not needing to adjust to the darkness.

Second through was Captain Hans Greemob, followed by Thomas, Edmund, and the rest of his crew. Hans chased Kainen over the sofa and struck him in the back as he tried to get to Klaus, sending him cascading into a wooden sideboard, smashing it to pieces before crashing into the wall.

Thomas flew out of the fireplace, and not seeing Laegon, he lunged for Beth, whacking her square on the end of her snout. Without flinching, Beth glared at Thomas, the look on his face telling, as she snarled, wiped the blood from her nose, and tore him in two, turning him to ash.

Edmund came through and lunged for Sven, striking like a hammer against his breastbone. The force flipping both him and the chair over, and sending him cartwheeling towards the sleeping area, striking his head with such severity it rendered him unconscious.

As Laegon's eye adjusted to the darkness, he leapt from his chair to help. Another skotos came through the flue intent on finishing Sven. Laegon struck, snatching him from the air, tearing him in half, turning him to ash.

Wham! Four more skotos emerged from the flue and blindsided him, knocking him from his feet before picking him up and hurling him across the room. With a sickening crunching sound, Laegon smashed against the wall with such force he shattered his left collarbone, and snapped his femur, the bone ripping through his flesh.

Blood and sinew decorating the room.

With everyone's eyes now adjusted to the dark, Lescan charged at Hans, striking him so hard the force threw him over towards the fireplace. Blodia spun about, grasping Lescan by the throat, and giving Kainen a chance to check on Klaus. He was still breathing. Twisting and pouncing from his crouched position, he struck at Blodia again, taking her down and causing her to release Lescan, who collapsed to the floor gasping for breath.

Meanwhile, the last five skotos had entered the fray.

Beth and Wrethe hurdled over the counter and tore two of them asunder, before being intercepted by another two who used their own speed against them, launching them back into the kitchen and dazing them.

Janet and Fimor leapt over their stunned friends, Janet coming down on one of the skotos swiping her glistening claws, tearing through him as if he was made of nothing more than tissue paper. Fimor was a little less flamboyant, preferring to take a more simplistic approach, he slammed the skoto to the floor and just bit off his head.

The end effect was the same, with both skotos bursting into ash, leaving Fimor with a mouth full of the stuff and regretting his method. While he got his breath back, a couple of skotos slunk behind them, and using their own bodies, they bound and brought them to their knees.

Another two went after Lescan. Thankfully, he had got his breath back and ripped one of them apart, and as he continued to wrestle with the other, he managed to slip the moon ring on his finger. He tried to command it, but Blodia's grasp had damaged his throat.

The last of the skotos had diverted to aid his captain, who was still suspiciously incapacitated by the fire.

Edmund stood over Sven, taunting the unconscious lyconfind while cutting holes in him and torturing him for no reason. Unnoticed, Laegon dragged himself across the floor, trying to make his way over to help his friend. Once close enough, he grabbed a hold of Edmund, but with his broken and torn body, he did not have the strength to destroy him.

Edmund turned on Laegon and swiped him away like a fly being hit with a swatter. Laegon slammed into the wall and Edmund struck him again, the splintering of bones as his neck snapped. The last thing his wavering eyes caught as he collapsed to the floor was Beth slam into Edmund. But she was a moment too late to save Laegon. Filled with rage, she sent Edmund hurtling across the room, before dropping to her knees in despair, taking Laegon in her arms as Wrethe hurried to her side.

Kainen rushed back to Klaus and rolled him over, his fur thick with blood. As he eased out the shards of glass with his claws, Blodia struck him again, breaking his arm as she picked him up and hurled him into the floor. She snapped her attention back to Klaus, scooping him up and holding him aloft by his throat.

"Where is Bedougalnn!" she screamed, pressing her fingers into his chest as he howled in agony, unsure of how much more he could withstand.

Janet and Fimor broke free and rushed towards Blodia. She saw them coming and let out a deafening screech. The power of the accompanying sound wave threw everyone, including the remaining skotos, against the walls of the den. Once again, Kainen lunged at Blodia, forcing her to drop Klaus. Infuriated, she slammed her fist into Kainen's chest and tore a hole in his heart. Blood gushed from the open wound as Kainen's pained howl rippled through the den, his eyes falling heavy upon Klaus.

Beth turned to Wrethe.

"We need light if we are going to stand a chance."

Wrethe took his camera from around his neck and pressed the shutter button. A bright flash illuminated the room, and the two skotos scrambling across the den to assist their screeching queen were caught in the burst of light, and disintegrated in their tracks.

Hans had regained some of his composure, and seeing their

chances of winning this fight spiralling away faster than water down a plughole, he rolled back into the fireplace and fled up the flue.

Lescan raised up his hand, and mustering all his strength and concentration, he whispered.

"Por Oth Mon Heps."

The ring vibrated and glowed with such intensity that it bathed the room in moonlight, sending Edmund darting into what remained of the shadows. The radiance continued to grow until it had eradicated every shadow, by which time Edmund had made his way back to the grate and escaped up the flue.

Klaus lay on the floor, blood still seeping from the wounds in his back. He watched as the light scalded Blodia, but she was no mere skotos, and it would take more than moonlight to end her. But the fight was lost. She released her grip on Kainen and fled. As his body crumpled to the floor, he threw Klaus a final smile.

The three remaining skotos were turned to ash as they tried to escape, perishing as they made a desperate rush for the hearth.

The fire burst back to life with a whoosh a mere moment later, and with a flicker, all the lights came back on in the den. Klaus dragged himself across the floor to Kainen and took up his friend in his arms. Kainen was struggling to breathe, but gazed upon Klaus with radiance.

"Do me a favour, try Furisoft on that blood. I bet it gets it right out." Kainen exhaled and his breathing shallowed. "I wish we would have had more time; it would have been nice, to … to get to know … you better, you know. I need to rest…" Kainen's voice faded as he closed his eyes.

"I would have liked that, my friend," Klaus said, pressing his hand into Kainen's fur and pulling him close to his chest, not wanting to let him go. Raising his head to the sky, he howled the most mournful of howls.

The others joined in his sorrow, and their howls penetrated deep across the open moor.

Janet and Beth swept away the small piles of dust and tidied as best they could. Klaus and Lescan carried Kainen's body up the stairs, followed by Fimor and Wrethe carrying Laegon. At the side of the megalithic tomb, they dug two graves, a fitting place for two courageous warriors and ardent friends. Although Sven had regained consciousness, he was still quite dazed, so had stayed in the den with Beth and Janet.

"We are ready," Lescan said, his voice melancholic, before turning and drifting back through the door.

Janet and Beth helped Sven to his feet, and while Beth helped Sven up the stairs, Janet got some lamps and candles and followed.

With the skotos gone, the storm cleared, the rain ceased, and the moon seemed to share in their sorrow, its glare seeming somewhat duller than usual, as if it were bowed. They placed the lamps around the graves and gently lay the bodies of Laegon and Kainen to rest. Each taking a lit candle, they sank to their knees and bayed a chorus of the melancholiest of howls.

Far away on the moor, Graimel had almost reached his destination and heard the baying on the wind. His heart skipped a beat, and he knew that although they had won the fight, they had suffered a loss. But for now, Bedougalnn was safe again.

They made their way back into the den, and Janet ensured the door was locked and the fire was stoked. Exhausted, they rested their weary bodies.

After a few minutes, Janet sprang to her feet and spoke.

"It's strange. I have this insane urge to bake cake. Anyone would think there is a full moon."

"How strange, me too," Beth said, getting to her feet.

Except for Lescan, they all shared this urge, and he knew why. The glow from the moon ring had been so intense it had mirrored a full moon, but because he bore the ring, he was not affected.

Lescan sank into the chair that Laegon had been sitting in before the attack, running his hands up and down the arms, remembering his friend. The rest went into the kitchen and tossed flour and other baking ingredients around, whilst all giggling and having fun.

"Are you not joining us, old friend?" Sven said, walking over to see Lescan.

"I think I will sit awhile."

"You know, Laegon and Kainen would have loved this. I think it is fitting that we bake cake to celebrate their lives, and their sacrifice. You're a good boy, Lescan," Sven said, patting him on the head.

Lescan chuckled.

"Be away with you, you old fool. Go make some cake."

# 17

# DOUGAL PRESSES PAUSE

With some over-elaborate hand gestures, Graimel signalled for everyone to get back on their feet, his eyes immediately drawn to Dougal and Grock.

"Look at the state of you two. Have you been rolling around in the mud while I was away? Any chance you could help them out, Binty?"

With a flick of her wrist they were once again spotless, and momentarily dry, their smiles a reflection of their gratitude. With a snap of his fingers, Grock put away his book and sprung over to Graimel, transforming back into his trench coat.

"Come on, Bounce, up up, time to go," Dougal said, dragging himself to his feet, slipping, and landing flat in the mud once more.

"Seriously, I am going to start charging for cleaning you up."

After waiting for him to get back on his feet, she casually waved her hand towards him, then jumped on Bounce's back and tossed her mushroom umbrella over her shoulder.

"While we have ourselves a distraction, we should pick up the pace a little."

Graimel set off with the briskness you see in people when they are running for a bus in a dreary drizzle. The rain continuing to pound the earth and the lightning seeming to aim for them, as if conspiring together to prevent them from getting to the Mines of Drothmaen. But nothing would stop Graimel from staying his path.

They kept this speed for about two hours, Binty having cast an anti-exhaustion spell on Bounce and Dougal, meaning they were using about as much energy to run as to lie down and sleep.

"Why did you need to see Lescan?" Binty asked.

"It is better for now you do not know; suffice to say he is helping a friend of ours."

"Is he in danger? Should we be going to help?" she said, pressing the questions.

"Damn it, Binty! If I thought we had time, do you not think I would take us, but time is the one thing we are running shorter on every moment. Please don't press me on this."

Binty dropped back a bit and rode beside Dougal, Graimel had never snapped at her like that before. She knew something was not right, and whatever it was, it did not sit right with Graimel either.

"Something is wrong, Dougal; I am worried about Lescan."

Puzzled by her words, Dougal raised an eyebrow and stared at her quizzically.

"Lescan, you're worried about Lescan, the big scary time manipulating werewolf Lescan?"

"Yes, and he is not a werewolf. He is a lyconfind, you know this already."

"Yeah, but he looks like a werewolf. I mean, I wouldn't want to bump into him in a dark alley if he were in a good mood, let alone a bad one."

"You're unbelievable, Dougal. He's a vegetarian. You need to wise up!"

With a momentous sigh of exasperation, Binty dropped back from the others, wishing to spend some time riding by herself.

"I didn't say he was going to eat me," Dougal muttered under his breath.

"Dougal, come here." Graimel shouted.

Dougal burst into an almost elegant, hurried stumble, adding a dash of urgency to his pace, and caught the striding Graimel.

"What is it?"

"How is your practising going? I am hoping you have mastered that phrase by now."

"I think I'm improving, at least I hope I am, but it's ridiculously hard to run, and enunciate."

"You're right," Graimel said, indicating to a dense copse in the distance. "We are quite near the Unseen Stones of Erath, which mark the hidden doorway into Drothmaen. We will rest for a brief time over there, give you a little more time to practise."

Within a few shakes of an oily rag, they were finding shelter under the canopy of the trees, slumping down on the driest piece of earth they could find. Binty flew up into the tree, still in no mood to talk to the others, sat on a branch and had a rather interesting conversation with a red squirrel about acorns.

Bounce raced around in the grass and peed on as many plants as possible, and while Dougal concerned himself with practising, Graimel whispered to Harg before sending him to scout ahead.

"Te`sow Ime Fow, Oe`my De`an, Aestic O`an," Dougal said, for what felt like the 14,000th time.

Everything around him slowed to the point where nothing appeared to move anymore, as if he had put the world on pause and could count every single raindrop. At least he could if he had the time, then he realised, he did have the time. This is what Graimel had been talking about.

He glanced across at Graimel, whose grin stretched from ear to ear.

"Hello there, glad you could finally make it; wondrous isn't it?" Graimel said, whilst popping individual raindrops until he made a smiley face.

"I could stay like this forever. It's amazing," Dougal said, springing to his feet and scampering through the rain, leaving a Dougal shaped tunnel behind him.

He then twirled on the spot, waving his arms up and down as he spun, creating a void in the downpour in the shape of a standing snow angel. A satisfied grin blazed across his face as he slipped back through the tunnel he had created and flopped back down beside Graimel.

As he sat there chuckling to himself, he scooped a handful of droplets from the air, cupped them in his hands, and took a drink. A drop of rain bounced off the end of his nose, and the world came back to life.

"What happened?" Dougal said.

"Concentration. It takes a lot of concentration and balance, but an excellent first attempt. Once mastered, you can move on to intervention, which is considerably more complicated, and, like I said before, has consequences. Now practise a little more, I will be right back," and with that he vanished, without even bothering to stand.

"Well done, Dougal," Binty called down from the tree. "My friend, the squirrel here also says well done, and where did Graimel go?"

"The squirrel wants to know where Graimel went?"

"What! No. Of course not."

"Oh, well, I'm guessing he's on Time Tailor business, again.

"Fair enough, I guess."

Graimel reappeared beneath the tree as Harg returned from his scouting. The path ahead was clear. Binty exchanged pleasantries with her new friend, hugging and wishing each other luck in their endeavours, before swooping off the branch and taking a seat on Dougal's shoulder.

"I guess our rest is over then," Binty said.

Graimel nodded in agreement, took up Harg in his hand and got to his feet.

"Not much further to go, so we can take a steady walk from here."

They walked out from under the cover of the trees and back into the torrential rain, weaving their way up to the top of Brown Willy, the highest peak on Bodmin. As they climbed the hill, the weight lifted from the moor, the menacing gloom and downpour cleared to reveal a crisp, cloudless sky. The moon and the stars now lighting their way.

Dougal could not remember the last time he had seen so many stars defined with such majesty against the infinite expanse of space. They had been under the storm clouds for so long they had lost track of time, and although there was no schedule to keep, they could still run out of time if they were not careful.

For once, Graimel did not appear to be overly concerned, and seemed to enjoy the spectacle above them as much as the others.

As they got to the peak, Graimel stopped in his tracks. On the wind he heard the mournful baying of the lyconfind. The clouds clearing had been a good sign, but this was a sure sign all was not well with the world.

Graimel's heart ached and fractured, becoming so heavy in his chest that it sunk like a lead weight deep within him. Down into the depths of a darkness he had forgotten even existed. He sank to his knees in front of the cairn, bowed his head, and prayed.

"What is it Graimel?" Binty asked, dropping her mushroom umbrella to the floor, unclipping herself from Bounce and whizzing over to him. "Graimel, Graimel!"

Despair filled his hollow eyes as he raised his head to

acknowledge her presence. Tears streaming down his face, he shook his head.

"Graimel?" Binty whispered, her voice breaking as she lifted his glasses and wiped his eyes.

"Something terrible has befallen our friends back at Janet's den. I don't know what, but whatever it is, it's bad, Binty, unbelievably bad. We need to keep this from Dougal."

"Keep what from Dougal? I'm not deaf you know," he said, walking towards them after dropping back a little while climbing the hill.

Binty dashed over and stopped him in his tracks.

"Graimel was hoping—"

"That I might not have heard the howling. You were both hoping to keep that from me, that there are wolves on this moor, wolves!"

"You're right, Dougal. We did want to keep that from you, I'm sorry. But you don't need to worry, as they will come nowhere near a pixie, especially not a pixie as powerful as me, will they, Graimel?"

Graimel placed his hand upon the cairn and pushed himself to his feet. Staring out across the moor, he took a cleansing breath, but his bloodshot eyes and flushed face attempted to betray his appearance of serenity.

"You know something. I had forgotten how much wolves fear pixies. Thank you for reminding me."

"Are you okay, Graimel? You look troubled?"

"Don't worry, it's nothing more than a little hay fever," Graimel said, with a conveniently placed sneeze.

They continued past the cairn and headed down the hill. A few hundred yards down, Graimel paused and surveyed the area. After a brief hesitation, he sauntered off to the right, stopped, looked around again and turned a little to his left, took another three steps and came to a halt, waving his arm.

"Over here!" Graimel called out, directing their attention to the ground at his feet. "Look, The Unseen Stones of Erath."

They ambled over to where he stood, Dougal's reaction a somewhat detached lukewarm compared to Graimel's exuberance. Upon the ground were three inconspicuous rocks, which Graimel described as an arrow pointing north. But no matter how much Dougal squinted his eyes or screwed up his face, he saw nothing more than three ordinary stones.

The stone on the left was about the size and shape of an average potato, it was black and unremarkable, yet if inspected, you would discover a tiny engraving of a death cap mushroom.

On the right, there was a flat, almost square stone about the half the size of a house brick, it was woolly jumper grey with white flecks, and again, on closer inspection there was a tiny engraving of wolfsbane.

The central stone was narrow and about 20cm long, if you squinted your eyes enough, you might fool yourself into thinking it was the blade of a dagger. When examined with care, this stone had an engraving of a minuscule skull.

"I don't see anything special here, Graimel. They just look like three random stones."

"And that is the point. You do not want to go around advertising where the entrance to Drothmaen is. You never know who might decide to pop in. And when things go visiting Drothmaen, they don't always come back, and if they do come back, they tend to have parts missing, like poor Laegon."

"Who is Laegon?" Dougal asked.

"A good friend of Lescan's, a school teacher, and a valiant lyconfind, who foolishly went camping in Drothmaen, and got severely injured protecting some little ones from a foul goblin."

"Quick question. What if someone was to walk off with one of these stones? My mom had an awful habit of picking up random stones and taking them home."

"Rest assured, Dougal, they are called the Unseen Stones of Erath for a reason, and the clue is in the name. Can you work it out?"

"I can," Binty piped up.

"Oh ha ha, you two are so funny. So, a human can't take the stones, but what if a fae took one?"

"What on earth would a fae want with one of them!" Graimel said.

This, was not a question, merely a statement, and something Dougal was relieved about once he realised, as he did not have an appropriate answer.

Graimel tapped Harg against each one of the Unseen Stones of Erath.

Death Cap.

Wolfsbane.

Skull.

As he touched the last symbol, the stones hummed and vibrated with a deep red glowing outline. A beam of red light shot out from the left stone, connecting it to the one on the right, before continuing on to the central stone and back to the stone on the left. Once the last connection was made, a solid red glowing triangle formed, linking all three stones.

"Quickly now, before the portal closes," Graimel said, standing in the centre of the triangle.

With a woot and a cheer, Binty dashed to join Graimel, while Dougal eyed them cautiously before edging forwards. Graimel tapped the floor with Harg, and before Dougal had time to blink, it was daylight again, and they were stood at the edge of a vast forest.

"Welcome to Grackbin Forest," Graimel said, striding off towards the enticing looking line of trees.

# 18

# GRACKBIN FOREST

Graimel thrust ahead, using Harg to clear a path through the undergrowth. Not something Harg was keen on, but he did not feel like he had much say in the matter, as Graimel flailed him from side to side.

Binty and Dougal chose to take the narrow, well-trodden trail to the left of Graimel, and wondered why he insisted on making his own. After watching him with mild confusion for about five minutes, they both gave up wondering, and Binty spoke.

"Er, Graimel, I know this might seem a silly question, but why are you struggling to break your way through those brambles when there is a clear track into the forest right here?"

Harg felt a rush of relieved joyful gratitude as Graimel stopped thrashing him about for a moment.

"First of all, I am not struggling, that is clearly evident. And second, the path you follow does not know where I am headed, so cannot possibly take me to the correct location. Oh, and third, and, I would like to add most importantly. That is a goblin path."

With a snap, Binty pulled at Bounce's harness, directing him to perform an immediate right turn, and barge straight through the undergrowth separating them from Graimel. Inspired by

Binty's idea, but wanting to avoid being cut to ribbons, Dougal opted to crouch down on his knees, and crawl through the perfectly acceptable Bounce shaped hole.

"Goblins! I thought you said they were in the Mines of Drothmaen?" Dougal said, shuddering as he got back to his feet.

"You are correct of course, Dougal. However, if there are goblins in the Mines of Drothmaen, it surely stands to reason there are goblins in Drothmaen. Seeing how Grackbin Forest is in Drothmaen, I think it is safe to conclude, goblins roam these parts."

"There is no need to talk to me like I'm stupid!" Dougal said.

"I kind of agree with Graimel on this occasion, Dougal. Well, on most occasions, to be honest," Binty said, with a huge smile but managing to keep a straight face, until she made eye contact with Graimel and burst out laughing.

"Lighten up, Dougal. I mean, it's not as if we are going to be set upon by goblins," Graimel said, unable to keep his chuckling under control.

"Look guys, in my defence, this is all new to me. How am I to know they would live in such a beautiful place? I thought they would live somewhere dark, dirty, and horribly oppressing?"

Everything Dougal said was in fact quite accurate.

Grackbin Forest was the picture perfect of beauty, the true foundation of wonderment. A place where the sun always shone, the flowers always bloomed, and even the thorns on the bushes glistened and gleamed, enticing you to prick yourself upon them. Although I do not recommend you do so.

A place where a million shades of green, brown, yellow, red, and blue all mingled together, to form a patchwork of amazement that could captivate the most hard-hearted of beings. Except for goblins, of course, the only thing known to captivate them was gold.

Which brought us to the dark, the dirty, and the horribly oppressing.

If Graimel did not know better, he would have thought

Dougal had visited the Mines of Drothmaen before, because he had presented a rather accurate description. The fact he did not mention the evil stench that dripped from the very pores of the place eliminated any possible doubt.

Now, if evil was a smell you could bottle, then you need to imagine if you can, the reek of sweaty rotten eggs, left in a windowless service station bathroom that has never been cleaned. Mixed with the armpit secretions of an unkempt ogre, who has been strenuously exercising in a sauna for orphaned stinky socks. Stir in some water from the vegetable tray of a musty old fridge, abandoned without power for nine years, and place in your bottle. Leave to stand for eleven minutes, then spray it on a lucky damp jockstrap. Hold close to your nose and sniff, letting the aroma wash over you. Now, take your gag reflex and double it, and you have the evil stench of the Mines of Drothmaen, on a good day. However, the mines are also full of gold.

Graimel returned to using Harg to clear the way, while Binty and Dougal, and to a lesser extent Bounce, bathed in the awe of their surroundings. As soon as they got within the walls of the tall redwood like trees, the constricting undergrowth receded, and they were able to stroll freely beneath these mighty lords of the forest.

They had been walking for over an hour when Graimel let on he thought they were being followed. He was not wrong. For goblins are masters of stealth, and one goblin in particular prowled these woods.

Graimel rested against a tree for a moment and removed Grock, casually dropping him to the ground at Dougal's feet. Not wanting to miss out on a break from all the walking, Bounce ambled over and sat down next to Dougal, almost unseating a startled Binty.

A little surprised, she regained her composure before reaching into her saddlebag and pulling out the last bit of cake. Reluctantly offering it to both Graimel and Dougal, hoping they would decline. They did, so she shared it between herself and Bounce, who swallowed his piece whole.

"Why do you trespass into my forest?" came the sinister, gravelly voice from beneath the tree right in front of them.

"I hardly think this is your forest, and our reason for being here is none of your business."

"Well, well, Graimel Tock, I know, you know this is my forest, as I know, you know you are trespassing, and we both know what I do to trespassers, don't we, Graimel?"

"Step out from your hiding, Lord Ferglestin. Let us lay our eyes upon your notorious self."

Goblin Lord Ferglestin, probably the vilest goblin you could have the misfortune to bump into, appeared in front of a tree a mere five metres away from Graimel. Standing about 90cm tall, with sizeable, lumpish, gnarly feet and hands, decked with serrated, dirty, feral claws. Green and grey mottled skin, almost scaly in appearance, humongous pointy ears, and deep, sunken, pale blue eyes.

Menacingly decked in blood-stained gold spiked armour, and flourishing a golden jewel encrusted dagger, he snorted. The two gold barbed rings adorning his hooked nose dripped with mucus as the surrounding air became poisoned by his most fearful breath. But aside from all this, and his insufferable reputation, his most fearsome aspect, was his mouthful of small lethal pointy teeth, which he could use to ferocious effect when fighting.

Laegon discovered this on the fateful day he met Lord Ferglestin, here in Grackbin Forest.

"I ask you again, what are you doing here?" Lord Ferglestin said, taking two steps towards Graimel.

Graimel did not want trouble, he did not have time for

trouble, and there had already been enough of it as far as he was concerned, so he answered the question.

"We are here to visit the Mines of Drothmaen. I hear they are beautiful this time of year," Graimel revealed.

"Graimel, Graimel, Graimel, I would have thought sarcasm beneath you. Makes me think you are hiding something, yes, something you are not telling me. You are here to steal. Yes, that's it. You and your dirty thieving friends are here to rob us poor goblins."

Lord Ferglestin waved his dagger around in front of him, pointing and jabbing it toward Graimel. The sunlight reflecting off the gleaming blade, dazzling them with glints of light, obscuring his movements. His eyes narrowed and appeared to sink deeper, and he bared his teeth in an alarming sort of smirk as he took another two steps towards them.

"We don't want any trouble; we just want to be on our way."

Bounce got to his feet, his hackles up, his head low. He was 32kg of muscle waiting to explode in defence of his family. He let out a guttural growl as a warning.

"If you did not want trouble, you should have stayed away from trying to thieve in Drothmaen. I think I will kill the human first."

Lord Ferglestin lunged towards Dougal; his dagger held aloft. Grock knocked Dougal to the ground and smothered him in an instant, making him appear to vanish. The vile goblin glanced about, trying to comprehend a disappearing human, when wham! A charging Bounce bulldozed his legs, knocking him off his feet.

Lord Ferglestin gambolled across the floor, but leapt back to his feet, regained his composure, and scampered away from Bounce, his skin burning from where it came into contact with him.

A little known fact is that goblins are acutely allergic to dogs. Now, Lord Ferglestin was not as fearful of dogs as most were. Nevertheless, he did not want to take unnecessary chances.

Graimel ran towards Lord Ferglestin. He swung Harg with ferocious might in an attempt to strike him, but Lord Ferglestin anticipated this and leapt aside, camouflaging himself. Once more blended into the surroundings, he snuck amongst them.

"What did you do with the human Graimel? It's only a matter of time before I find him."

Although Lord Ferglestin could not be seen, Bounce could track him when he spoke. Binty realised this, and an idea sprang into her mind.

"You will never find our friend; he is far too smart to be caught by a goblin."

"You know nothing, you filthy little pixie. The only thing pixies are any good for is tying to a spit and roasting until you're all crispy. Shame you're only a mouthful. I guess that makes you an appetiser."

This was enough to give Bounce what he needed. Being an intelligent dog, at least for this one point in the story, he dashed off in the total wrong direction, glancing left and right, looking confused.

"Stupid, filthy dog!" Lord Ferglestin scowled.

Bounce sniffed the floor for no other reason than it looked like the sort of thing a dog should do, for he had a rubbish sense of smell, but sensed Lord Ferglestin was close. Without warning, he charged to his right, striking Lord Ferglestin again, his skin erupting in painful burning blisters, and for a moment he became visible. A moment was all Binty needed. She fired out her arm and flicked her wrist.

"Sen Loth Iresh!"

In that instant, Lord Ferglestin was immobilised, and Binty raised her hand, lifting him into the sky.

"What did you say you liked to do to pixies, Fergle?"

"How dare you! You will refer to me as Lord Ferglestin, you filthy pixie! You hold no power over me. Who do you think you are?"

"Why, I am Binty Malice, sir, and I beg to differ."

On hearing the pixie's name, Lord Ferglestin gulped and winced. He knew trouble, and he had found it. His face drawn and fraught with fear, like the horrified expression of a new dad who has just seen and smelt their baby's poop for the first time.

(Remember that evil smell I mentioned earlier? I just had a thought. Add to the ingredients a generous helping of new-born baby poop, I digress.)

Had he of course not been stunned and floating 15ft above ground, then not for the first time in his life, he would have fled. This was not to be.

Binty Malice was a name all knew, but if you were of a despicable disposition, the most important thing to remember if you ever had the pleasure of meeting her was, *Don't Upset!* Unfortunately for Lord Ferglestin, this information had come to light too late into the conversation, and Binty had passed the point of upset, reaching the point of exasperation.

Imagine for a moment, you had spent the whole of your summer holiday using a typewriter to draft a story. Once finished and ready to submit for your English Literature exam, you stack it with pride on your coffee table, and go out to celebrate with your friends. When you return home, you find not only has your dog eaten 90% of your work, but he has proceeded to poop it out into one of your favourite socks, the other of which is still missing.

Well, Binty was monumentally more upset than that.

"How many pixies have you killed?" Binty asked.

Without taking a moment to do the most important thing he could do in his current predicament and think, Lord Ferglestin replied.

"Not Enough, and nowhere near as many as I could eat."

No sooner had he delivered these words from his mouth when he regretted them. This was not just any pixie. This was Binty Malice, and his words tore into her heart. A single tear crept from her reddened, welling eyes and trickled down her cheek as she paused to collect her thoughts, remembering all the innocent pixies this disgusting goblin had killed.

Graimel was about to stop Binty from doing anything she might regret, but realised this evil needed to be stopped, so he stepped back, collected Grock, and sat down next to Dougal.

"Du O`du, Ev O`sh, Fae O`er," Binty whispered, her voice serene and delicate.

They watched Lord Ferglestin dissolve into a cloud of dust on the gentle breeze. The dagger fell from his hand and struck the earth, the full length of the blade sinking into the ground.

Never had Graimel heard this language spoken, let alone these words. These were the words used to defeat Trilbanish. This was ancient pixie, not the common pixie spoken these days, but a forgotten language, the sort of language one considers a myth.

Binty wiped the tear from her face.

"Well, he will not be hurting anything ever again."

Dougal sauntered over, picked up Lord Ferglestin's dagger and attached it to his belt. *This is going to look super on my mantle,* he thought, and went to check on the others.

"Are you okay?" Graimel said, walking over to Binty.

"Yes, thank you, he was not a nice goblin, well come to think of it, are there any nice goblins?"

This was only the second time she had ever cast that spell, and although she hid it well, her tone was rueful, and an ache grew in the pit of her stomach. Deep down she was afraid, afraid she may become consumed by revenge, and find ancient magic easy to cast. If she did, she would deserve for it to be cast upon herself.

But some creatures were beyond saving, beyond hope, and as much as she did not find killing easy, she knew when it had to be done, and Graimel would have stopped her if she were wrong. The two she had killed were so wicked they were rotten to their core. Something no amount of time or effort could have changed; they were unreformable.

"There are as many nice goblins as there are evil pixies I believe," Graimel said.

"If that is so, then I can only guess there is none, for there are certainly no evil pixies."

"Well, with Lord Ferglestin taking a permanent rest, we should be okay to use the path for now. This way to the mines," Graimel hollered, whistling as he set off down the trail with a hint of a spring in his step.

Binty and Dougal glanced across at each other and shrugged.

"I guess that's the way to the mines then. I do hope it's not as dangerous as the forest, but something tells me it's going to be even more so," Dougal said, traipsing after Graimel.

"Come on Bounce, let's go for a walk."

Bounce lifted his head, wagged his tail, and peed up the first tree he saw, and the second, and the third. This continued for quite some time.

As they delved deeper into the forest, an eerie darkness began to shroud the wonderment, becoming darker with every step they took. Everything seemed a little less colourful and a lot more forbidding. They crossed a small stream of pungent, grim murky liquid, the complete opposite of the streams elsewhere in Grackbin, which flowed with translucent sparkling blue water.

There were now no more reds or blues, the browns of the trees and branches had erupted with a sort of oozing black sap, and the wondrous array of greens had become a disenchanting array of greys.

Without a word, Graimel darted left and pushed through the undergrowth, revealing a small gloomy clearing dominated by a colossal blistered tree. Its branches, devoid of any leaves or buds, weighed heavy upon it. As they approached, they spotted a small wooden sign emblazoned with three skull and crossbones symbols. It read.

*Welcome to the Mines of Drothmaen*

"What do three skull and crossbones mean?" Dougal asked.

"I would hazard a guess, it means you are three times more likely to end up as a skull, and some crossbones," Graimel chuckled.

"I think it's only there to scare folk. I mean, look, it says Welcome," Binty said, giggling excitedly.

"Do you two take anything seriously?"

"Yes, of course," Graimel said.

"We take nothing seriously, which is still something," Binty added, and they both continued laughing.

"Come now, Dougal, it's just a sign. The only thing you have to fear is fear itself." Graimel leant over to Binty. "I told Franklin that, when he asked me if he should run for president. Then he went and nicked it for his inauguration speech."

"And goblins, of course!" Binty said, with a little too much glee.

As they stood there wondering what to do next, Graimel walked towards the tree and vanished.

"He's flipping left us, again," Dougal said, in a timorous voice trembling with panic.

"What are you waiting for? This is an illusion," Graimel said, popping back out of the tree with his hands on his hips.

Graimel shook his head before disappearing again as they trundled over towards him.

With his arms held out in front, Dougal stepped forwards, amazed as his arms appeared to disappear into solid wood. Graimel grabbed at his hands and pulled him through into the mine.

"Will you stop wasting time!"

Now call her deluded if you dare, but Binty was hoping to coax Bounce through the illusion. He was having none of it. However, this being a tree, Bounce did what dogs do, and cocked his leg to relieve himself. Only, with this being an illusion, Bounce was actually peeing on Dougal.

"Bounce, no!"

Bounce stopped peeing and stared at the tree. *Strange, that sounds like dad,* he thought, as Dougal's hand shot out and grasped his collar. Binty jumped up and threw her hands over his eyes, allowing Dougal to pull him through the illusion.

As Dougal tried to wring out the dog pee from the bottom of his trousers, their straight faces cracked, and their smirks broke into childish laughter.

# 19

# THE MINES OF DROTHMAEN

The first thing that grabbed Dougal's attention, whilst he attempted in vain to wring Bounce's pee out of his trousers, was the vile evil stench pervading the air. He took a deep breath, as if needing to reassure himself the smell was indeed real.

The burning sensation in his throat, watering eyes, and severe retching and gagging hinted it was, and the fact he then threw up confirmed this. They were relieved to see him still facing the entrance as his vomit evacuated his body and was propelled through the illusion. A scurible, who was minding his own business foraging for seeds when a tree vomited over him. Did not share their relief.

This at least meant Dougal's vomit would not exacerbate the already putrid stench of the mines.

The second thing he noticed, other than the darkness and the damp, were the huge stalactites hanging from the ceiling, and the stalagmites reaching up towards them on a seemingly endless journey to meet. These were interspersed with the occasional stalagnate, as if the cavern needed to prove how old it was.

Dougal swore he could hear laughter in the distance, at least he hoped it was laughter, well of course in reality he hoped he was having a problem with his hearing. Because if there was indeed laughing, then someone or something was producing the laughter, and not all laughter is necessarily funny.

Still reeling from the noxious aroma, he realised that both Graimel and Binty seemed unfazed, as was Bounce, who doubtless assumed it was one of his toots.

"How is it you guys do not seem bothered by this unholiest of odours?"

"Magic!" Binty held her hands out to her side and waved them about. "There is no point in having magic, if you do not use it now and again."

"Well, is there any chance you could cast the same magic spell on me please, so that I don't have to suffer?" Dougal pleaded.

"Of course I can. We just thought you might like to revel in the full experience of the mine, seeing as it's your first time here."

"I can assure you both. I've already revelled as much as required, thank you. And correct me if I'm wrong, but I was under the impression it's also your first time here."

"That maybe so; however, I have had the honour of Graimel coming to visit me after being in the mines, and not even I could get him clean."

With his next cautious breath, Dougal salivated, as the aroma of rhubarb crumble and custard saturated his senses.

"I'm hungry now; did you have to make it smell quite so delicious?"

"There is no pleasing some people. I can take remove the spell if you prefer?"

"No no, this will be fine," Dougal said, as his stomach rumbled.

"If you would do the honours please, Harg."

Graimel tapped Harg against the cold stone floor. Harg opened his eyes to emit a penetrating green light into the darkness, illuminating the vastness of the mines. Now, as much as the light provided by Harg was useful for seeing ahead, it also added to the spookiness of the place.

As if a dark, damp, and now rhubarb and custard smelling mine was not scary enough, it now had a not so comforting green glow. None of this seemed to bother anybody else, but that may have been because the delicious aroma had lulled them into a false sense of security.

The path ahead of them spiralled down into the bowels of the earth and stretched out for miles. For as far as the eye could see, there was the faint twinkle of a thousand torch lights.

Countless tunnels, alcoves, and doorways littered the black mossy walls, which glinted and shone in the darkness, almost beckoning you deeper. Ancient iron sconces had been affixed to the wall at regular intervals, but the flames alight in them did little more than cast unsettling shadows into the already mysterious alcoves and doorways.

Thankfully, Dougal had so many things racing around his mind, he did not have space for the obvious question. *Who lights all these sconces?* Probably a good thing for all concerned.

Graimel held Harg out in front of them and led them down the path.

"Watch your step. It's quite slippery in places, and it's a long way down."

"I thought you said this is a mine?" Dougal said, wishing he had brought his camera, his eyes wide in a kind of awestruck mesmeric trance. "It looks a lot more like an ancient cave to me."

"You're right, Dougal, the Mines of Drothmaen are an ancient cave system. Overrun and mined by goblins as far back as any goblin can remember." Graimel pulled Dougal away from the edge. "Stick as close to the wall as you can. We don't want you taking a tumble."

"And what about where there are no walls?"

"Just stay away from the edge."

Doing as Graimel advised, they inched their way deeper and

deeper into the system of caves, into the earth itself. Within the deafening silence of the mines, Dougal was convinced he could hear noises, a skittering, echoing from another place deep inside the cavernous expanse.

"Can anyone else hear that scratching sound?"

"I can assure you, Dougal, these mines are so vast, the likelihood of us crossing paths with anything is negligible. So stop worrying about trivial things, like strange noises in the distance."

This did nothing to reassure him, as he wondered if the chances of them bumping into something equalled the chance of happening across the one of the nastiest goblin lords in a vast forest. Or, almost bumping into whatever it was, they came across on Bodmin Moor. Because whatever that was, it certainly put the willies up Graimel for a moment.

"You do know where you are going, don't you?" Binty asked.

"I have an extraordinarily strong indication and belief in where I am going, so that's something."

Besides a couple of minor slips and a few stupid questions, the walk to the bottom of the pit was pretty much uneventful. However, they had only been walking for about 15 minutes when Dougal asked the first stupid question.

"Graimel, what is in these alcoves?"

"Nothing, they are old storage holes, disused for many years now."

This intrigued Dougal's inquisitive mind. He had to find out if there was anything in one of them. The next one he came to had a torch in a wall sconce nearby, throwing out enough light for him to peer inside. He stuck his head into the alcove and saw nothing of interest. Disappointed, he withdrew, and was about to continue after the others, when he felt something in his hair.

"Aarrgghh!" Dougal squealed from the bottom of his lungs, while running about in a wild panic as if he was on fire, "Help, help!"

Graimel spun about and raced back, grabbing him, pulling

him back from the edge of the path before he plummeted to his certain doom. Had he, of course, not been able to prevent Dougal from falling, I am sure Binty would have done something to ensure the journey did not come to an abrupt end.

"There is a bat in my hair, a bat in my hair!" Dougal squealed, whilst waving his arms around manically.

"There are no bats in here Dougal, now calm down. I mean, can you imagine adding guano to this stench? I doubt even Binty's magic could mask that."

"Well, what is it then? Because I felt something try to attack me."

"It is only an old abandoned spider's web that is sticky in your hair, now standstill while I get it all out."

Binty darted over to see what the kerfuffle was all about, and as she got to Graimel, her eyes widened, and for a moment, she forgot to breathe, her mouth agape. Sat on the web entangled in Dougal's hair, a huge, venomous, but quite contented and placid, baby friendly goblin mine spider, Binty gulped, momentarily lost for words.

"What is it Binty?" Dougal asked, "Binty?"

"Er, oh sorry, that is a lot of web."

Under the premise of brushing away the web from his hair, they carefully removed the hitchhiker and placed him back in his alcove. Both nodding in silent agreement, it was best not to mention the spider.

At the bottom of the path, an enormous pool of grim murky water stretched out underneath the walls of the cavern, where it eroded away the stone. Ahead of them, they could see it overflowed into a river that reached out into the distance. They strode onwards, tracing the shoreline until they were in a vast, open area of the cavern.

The floor was awash with strange looking ferns, and littered with huge chunks of glistening black fractured rock, like cracked mirrors reflecting the insanity of their surroundings. Quicksilver gloop bled from the fractures, pooling on the ground for a moment before being absorbed into the earth. The roof of the cavern was so high, the stalactites hanging from it were no longer visible. But the droplets of water that continued to fall like rain in solitary confinement reminded you they were still there.

With Graimel as their guide, they followed the path of the river. The faint echo of what sounded like distant rolling thunder was getting closer by the step. Not being a fan of spoilers, Graimel thought it best to leave them to their own first-time experiences, even though he knew exactly what it was.

While trudging along behind Graimel, they were having a minor exchange of thoughts about what could be making the noise.

"I might be wrong, but I think that is the sound of magical underground thunder."

"What!" Binty said, stifling a laugh. "No such thing exists. What you are describing is called an earthquake."

"Is it? Well, in that case, I think it's an earthquake."

As soon as the words left his mouth, he regretted uttering them. In fact, he regretted starting the conversation altogether, realising they were who knows how far underground. Of course Graimel could have enlightened them as to exactly how far underground, but knowing Dougal as he did, he thought best to keep it to himself.

Binty however, thought the noise was most likely to be stampeding goblins, at least that is what she told Dougal, much to her own amusement.

Dark grey moss and oozing blistered black fungi lined the banks of the river. And unnoticed in the deepest recesses of the tunnels leading off from this main chamber, there were eyes glinting in the darkness, watching, and listening to everything said.

Something gold and pitted about the size of a large orange sparkled amongst the rocks and moss at the side of the path, catching Dougal's eye. At first, he paid it no mind, but then, remembering what Graimel had told him of this place, he realised it was the largest lump of gold he was ever likely to see.

He dashed over, his eyes smiled with glee and astonishment at finding such a thing, but as he reached to take it from the ground, Graimel's staff fell sharply across his knuckles.

"Ow!"

"Leave it! We are not here to steal," he said, grabbing Dougal and pulling him back.

"But, Graimel, I'm not stealing it if I have found it on the ground."

"Oh, I see, so you're intending to hand it in at the goblin police station. Well, why didn't you say so?"

"The goblins have police stations?"

Binty snorted and sniggered.

"I don't know what you are sniggering about, Binty Malice! If you spotted a slice of cake, you would be straight down off Bounce to make sure you got to it first," Graimel said, peering at her over the top of his glasses.

She was about to respond to this outrageous accusation, but knowing it to be 100% true, she remained quietly admonished, allowing Graimel to turn his attention back to Dougal and his hovering hand.

"No! Goblins do not have police stations. Well, at least I do not think they do, anyway that is not the point. Unless you can convince me, a chunk of gold somehow found its own way to be there at the side of this path. Then I am going to assume someone has lost it," Graimel said, throwing a disapproving glance at Binty, who was making subtle police siren sounds.

"Sorry," she said, with a wry smile.

"Therefore, it belongs to someone, and therefore by default, if you take it with no intention of somehow reuniting it with its owner, then you, my friend, are stealing. And anyone who steals from the Mines of Drothmaen does not leave. Am I correct in thinking you would like to leave once we conclude our business?"

Reluctantly, he withdrew his hand from the chunk of gold with slow, deliberate movements. He really wanted it, he could buy a new house and even a new car, although he did love his Mini. But he valued his friends' respect and his own life over all of that. Dougal turned to Graimel and apologised, before patting Bounce on his head.

"Sorry, Bounce, we could've got you a girlfriend."

"Don't worry, if we find a police station we can always come back, and you never know, you might even receive a reward," Binty said, smiling and almost keeping a straight face.

"True, and I will keep an eye out for some cake for you as well, then you can do the same," Dougal replied.

Graimel laughed so hard he stumbled and almost fell over.

Time, as we know, is of the utmost importance, but since entering Grackbin Forest, they had lost all track of this. Mainly because there had been no visual movement of time, it always appeared to be midday. And since entering the Mines of Drothmaen, it always appeared to be midnight. So they were a little surprised when, after walking for what they imagined having been a few hours, the path they were following came to an abrupt end as they entered a clearing. They had reached a dead end, this time with no apparent way to go.

"Have we missed a turn somewhere, Graimel?"

"No, this is the correct path."

"Well, I am not sure if you noticed, but our path has run out, we have run out of path," Binty said, with a hint of sarcasm in her voice.

"Your comments astound me, Binty Malice. Since when have you ever thought all paths are made of earth? I guess since you have been spending all your time riding atop of Bounce, no doubt. The path we are following is that of the river."

The river did indeed carry on a little way, before disappearing down a hole in the ground.

"Are we all ready?"

Without waiting for a response, Graimel jumped into the river where it fell away into the ground. As they watched him disappear into the blackness, they balked at the idea of voluntarily following him.

But the thunderous sound they had heard in the distance, when they first got to the bottom of the cavern, was now a lot louder, and coming from beneath their very feet. Deep down, Dougal felt certain these rumblings were the effects of an earthquake, although he hoped them to be nothing more than an unusually long tremor.

What he found more worrying at this precise moment was the skittering sound that seemed to get louder by the second.

Dougal glanced over his shoulder. There now appeared to be tiny eyes everywhere. With extreme caution, he turned back to Binty.

"I know. I think we should follow Graimel, now!"

Binty reached into her pocket and pulled out a tasty dog treat, which she floated right in front of Bounce's nose while simultaneously covering his eyes again. Following his nose, Bounce grabbed the treat just as his feet left the ground, and with a splash, he disappeared down the hole with the river.

The now deafeningly loud skittering sound forced Dougal to spin on his heels. Confronted with a wall of black shiny eyes, he stumbled backwards as they lurched towards him, and with a splosh, he followed Binty down the hole.

Dougal plunged backwards, down what you could describe as a spiralling ride at a water park with a few small vertical drops. He spun himself around in time to exit the slide through a colossal black waterfall and plunge not so gracefully into a lake of the same black water. Without a moment's hesitation, he swam to the edge of the lake where the others were waiting.

Binty did the honours and dried them off before asking

Graimel if they could do it again. The answer was no. Standing on the bank of the vast pool in complete awe of the waterfall, Dougal realised he had never seen anything as beautiful, imposing and intimidating all at the same time, except for Binty.

"Through here," Graimel said, heading into a tunnel.

The plentiful *Keep Out* signs were more than a little foreboding. Binty and Dougal exchanged raised eyebrows and furrowed brows, and with a sense of reluctance, they stepped into the tunnel.

As they traipsed through the cold, dank passage, the light at the end grew in intensity. Would this be the proverbial light at the end of the tunnel that would lead them to safety? They were soon to find out?

The light stung their eyes such was the intensity, like trying to stare into the midday sun. Graimel had come prepared, his glasses fitted with reactive lenses. If only he had thought to advise the others to bring their sunglasses. He spun and saw their screwed up squinting faces. *Oops,* he thought, before turning away to hide his lopsided smirk.

They exited the tunnel into an enormous circular room filled with all kinds of treasure and gold, from shiny emeralds and rubies to gold and platinum jewel encrusted crowns and swords. There were full suits of armour, some still with the bones of their former owner inside, and thousands upon thousands of gold and silver coins littered the floor.

The room was so enchantingly mesmerising that nothing could distract them from the wondrous view.

The room was a goblin trap.

Graimel was well aware of this, having been here before. But this is where Lescan Dewclaw told him he would find the Pendant of Tel Etoiles. Concentrating on the task in hand, undistracted by the wonderment of everything, he scanned the room, focused on finding the Pendant, spotting it near the top of the central pile of coins.

A skittering, scraping sound filled the room. Like nails

running down a chalkboard. Graimel bowed his head and dropped onto one knee. But Binty and Dougal were fixated on everything before them in an almost catatonic state. Bounce, however, had lay down and placed his paws over his ears.

A sinisterly sweet, wiry voice flowed through the air.

"Graimel Tock, what brings you back into my lair? You barely escaped last time. What makes you think I will let you go this time? At least this time you show me the respect I am due. Your friends, however, do not."

With a glance over his shoulder, he saw the others mesmerised, frozen bolt upright. He quickly tapped Harg against the floor and held him up to their faces. The light from his eyes distracting them long enough for Graimel to whisper.

"Kneel."

Noting the urgency in Graimel's voice, Dougal did not argue and dropped to his knee. Binty realised she did not have time to dismount, so bowed her head in respect as the mother of all friendly goblin mine spiders came into view. How Dougal remained composed, and conscious, I guess we will never know. But I am sure he will put it down to bravery.

A creature resembling a giant jumping spider now dominated the room. Her black and white banded body the size of a battle tank. She had a bright orange flash across the middle of her face, which graduated down into her pedipalps, and eight shiny black eyes, including two enormous central ones, watching everything. However, Dougal was fixated on her monstrous red fangs.

No one could deny she was beautiful, and appeared to be smiling.

As she settled on top of the piles of coins in the heart of the room, Binty noticed chains attached to all eight of her legs. *She is a prisoner,* she thought. Without seeming to move, she undid her safety harness as the spider spoke again.

"I thank you friends of Graimel for your respect, and I will hear you speak."

"Queen Silkolblin, I come here in search of a pendant, removed from a friend of mine, and found here in Grackbin Forest. This pendant now lies under your protection. I am in need of the Pendant of Tel Etoiles."

"Graimel Tock, you know I am charged with protecting all that lies within the mines, and anyone who attempts to remove anything, never leaves."

"This I do indeed know, Queen Silkolblin. However, if I do not retrieve this pendant, then all is lost," he said, lowering his head in reverence.

"I wish it were in my power to help, but as you can see, I am bound, and therefore must perform my duty."

Queen Silkolblin hissed and prepared to strike. Binty knew it was now or never, and shot up from her saddle. She hurtled around the room, targeting the shackles binding Queen Silkolblin.

Thinking Binty had shot up to distract and destroy the giant spider, Dougal was a little dumbfounded, not for the first time, when he saw what she did next.

"Dis I`Grash," Binty cried out, as she fired a bolt of magic from her hand, striking the first shackle and disintegrating it.

After briefly thinking, *she has lost her mind,* Dougal passed out.

But Binty stayed focused on the task in hand and zipped around the room, disintegrating shackles until all eight were nothing more than dust.

Queen Silkolblin stopped hissing and inched her way towards them, flexing each one of her legs, before turning full circle in the room until she once again faced them.

"Who is your pixie friend, dear Graimel Tock, and why does she put you all in mortal danger?"

Before Graimel had a chance to speak, Binty once again shot up from Bounce until she was eye to eye with Queen Silkolblin.

"I can speak for myself. I am Binty Malice. Friend and

protector of Graimel Tock, Bounce, and Dougal, and I will defend them to my death."

"I know your name, Binty Malice, and wonder why you would release me, when you hold the power to end me?"

"Because you were bound, and you deserve to be free to make your own choices, and not forced to submit to the will of others."

"You are the wisest pixie ever, and I thank you. None of you need fear me, or my guards."

Queen Silkolblin bowed to Binty.

"Take the Pendant of Tel Etoiles and hold on to me, for as soon as you touch it, the goblins will come."

Binty flew down to Bounce and attached her harness, lifting him up and flying him over to Queen Silkolblin's back, while Graimel picked up the still unconscious Dougal and tossed him over his shoulder.

He took a deep breath, then charged forward. As his foot touched the pile of coins, a roar exploded through the mines. From out of the shadows, goblins appeared, bursting from behind rocks and every other nook and crack.

Graimel clambered up the mound of coins and snatched the Pendant of Tel Etoiles, wasting no time slipping the pendant into his pocket, before gripping hold of Queen Silkolblin's leg.

Not a moment too soon, Queen Silkolblin leapt up the high flat walls of the treasure room to reach a narrow passage at the top.

"Quick now, follow this passage it will lead you out. Time for me to call on my guards and dispense some justice."

Queen Silkolblin jumped back down into the treasure room and started stamping, webbing, and eating every single goblin she could. She was becoming overwhelmed when the skittering sound Dougal heard earlier got louder and louder. Hissing friendly goblin mine spiders came hurtling through the tunnel leading into the treasure room, and devoured every goblin in sight.

They made haste through the tunnel towards the exit of the mine, and back to some sense of safety. But two goblins had sneaked past Queen Silkolblin and scaled the wall of the treasure room. Now they were sneaking up behind Dougal, who believing he was almost back to safety, had stopped to catch his breath after lagging a little since regaining consciousness.

From out of the shadows, one of the goblins leapt onto Dougal's back, seizing him from behind, sliding his hand over his mouth and pressing a dagger against his throat.

"You're coming with us," Bob said, as his best mate Stan kicked his legs from under him, allowing them to start dragging him back down the tunnel.

In front of them, another goblin dropped from the blackness of the tunnel's roof, his dagger drawn.

"Release the human," Colin said.

"Get lost, Colin," Bob and Stan retorted, laughing and mocking Colin as he stood there, his dagger wavering uncertainly in his hand.

This drew the attention of Bounce, who stopped, turned, and stared back down the tunnel. Unable to see Dougal, he started back down the tunnel to find him.

Before Dougal had time to blink, Colin sprang forwards, lunging at Stan and thrusting his dagger into his throat. Panicked, Bob released Dougal and tried to run, but he was too slow, and quickly brought to ground by the flash of a dagger to his heart.

Dougal sat in stunned silence awaiting his fate, but as Binty and Bounce arrived, Colin spoke again.

"Go in peace friend, you did not steal my chunk of gold, nor did you take from the treasure. You have honour, and it was my honour to protect you. Now go."

Colin faded back into the shadows and vanished.

"What happened?" Binty asked, seeing the two dead goblins on the floor.

"I was… just saved by a goblin called Colin. So I guess that means you better start trying to find that evil pixie."

"Ha ha," Binty said nervously, thinking, *I do hope Graimel is wrong and there are no evil pixies.*

They caught up with Graimel as he exited the mine, standing once more in the relative safety of Grackbin Forest.

"You finally decided to join me then? Right, let's get back to your Aunty Janet's for a nice cup of tea."

"Before we go Graimel, are you going to show us what we risked our lives for?" Binty asked.

"Our lives were never in danger with you around, but sure."

Graimel removed the Pendant of Tel Etoiles from his pocket and held it out in his hand for them to see. It was a silver ten pointed sun pendant, set atop a golden disc with an enchanting central blue moonstone, the tip of each point set with blue-green, and deep red sunstones.

"It's beautiful," Binty said, reaching out to touch it.

Graimel snapped his hand closed and slid the pendant back in his pocket.

"Back there, you mentioned the pendant belonged to a friend of yours. What did you mean?" Dougal asked.

"No time!" Graimel said, and placed his hand on Bounce, as did Binty with a giggle, and Dougal with a frown, and they vanished from Grackbin forest.

# 20

## A NEW CAPTAIN

Back in the Hidden Dimension, Blodia, Captain Greemob, and Edmund gathered in Blodia's vacant space. Blodia was furious. She had not expected such a strong resistance, considering it should have been a surprise attack. No one besides those who went were aware of the location, and even those that did were not bright enough to tell or warn anyone. At least not to her mind.

She paced her vacant space, thinking, *who? How? When?* If she discovered a traitor to her cause, she would do worse than end them. She was not sure what that would entail, or if it were even possible. If not, she swore to make it so.

Captain Greemob and Edmund stood in silence with their heads bowed, afraid to speak in case any blame for the defeat was apportioned to them, and they were next to feel her wrath. Then she spoke.

"Captain Greemob, you are my Captain of the Guard. You are my most fearsome protector and warrior, yet twice now you have failed me. The first time against only a couple of Bedougalnn's friends, when not only did you fail me, but you cost me 11 of the Queen's Guard."

"Er, it was not me who failed you, oh rancid one."

"What?" Blodia snapped.

"I was outside remember; it was the Queen's Guard who failed you," Hans said.

Blodia paused for a moment, wondering whether to end Hans on the spot, but she desperately wanted to finish her tedious, melodious speech, so she continued.

"Then, on the second attempt, with brazen stupidity, you walk me into a trap, where instead of finding Bedougalnn, we were set upon by nine lyconfind, who ripped apart another 11 skotos. The only saving grace being they were your men, and not mine."

Blodia glided straight up to Captain Greemob, invading his very presence.

"Then!" Blodia said, her voice hollowing out. "Then, you concluded things were going badly for your men and your queen, and you snuck out, you fled, you saved yourself, and you abandoned your queen and what remained of your men. Did you think I would not notice? Did you think you would not be punished… or did you think your queen would die?"

She grasped Captain Greemob by the throat and tossed him around her vacant space, smashing him into everything she could, releasing her rage. She knew this would not kill him, but did it for fun.

"Now then, I could end you and release you from your servitude to me, but I will not, instead you will continue to serve me, but not as my captain."

"Yes, oh nauseating one, it is my honour to serve you, and I thank you for your leniency."

"As for you, first let me ask, what is your name?"

Fearing the worse, Edmund kept his head bowed.

"My Queen, my name is Edmund Munday."

"I noticed that you, Edmund, not only killed one of those filthy lyconfinds, but your skilful use of the shadows enabled you to escape a mere fraction of a second before me. However, should you not wait until your queen is safe before escaping? I can only imagine, you spotted your captain leave, and thought I gave the order to retreat?" Blodia said, throwing another scolding scowl towards Hans.

"Yes, my Queen, that is correct."

"I thought as much, Captain Munday."

Hans looked up straight into the burning stare of his queen. He was about to make a comment on how Edmund would not make an appropriate choice for a captain, when he thought better of it.

"A wise choice, my querulous Queen."

Edmund still not dared lift his head, not in fear of being ended anymore, but in case it revealed the huge smug grin now covering his face.

"Thank you, my Queen. I will not fail you."

"Ha! That remains to be seen, Captain Munday."

With a derisive chuckle, she flounced towards the door and called for Floop.

"Ah Floop. Please notify everyone that Edmund Munday is now my Captain of the Guard, taking over from the useless Hans Greemob." Blodia dismissed Floop with a wave of her hand and turned her attention back to Edmund. "Captain Munday, you are to hunt down and catch the traitor in our midst. I want to know who betrayed me, and how? Take Hans with you. You may find some use for him. Oh, and where is Bedougalnn? Only return when you have these answers."

Edmund strode over and yanked Hans off the floor.

"Move it, you useless oaf."

Hans traipsed towards the door, unhappy with the way Edmund spoke to him. He had always been fair with his crew, and regarded them as friends, even though none of them had any nous about them. Wanting to stamp his authority over Hans, Edmund pushed him through the door, causing him to stumble and scowl.

"Could you go any slower? Why not try imagining your

fleeing from a fight, and pick up your pace," he barked, loud enough for Blodia to hear.

Once back at the Pool of Vacant Reflection, Edmund returned to being Edmund once again.

"Err, what do we do here?" he asked.

"I am just here to follow orders, sir."

"Don't mess with me, Hans. I know you know how to use this. If you do not assist, maybe that means you are the traitor, and explains why you fled the fight. Let us return to Blodia, so I can report my findings," he said, as he started back up the dark path.

"Okay, you need to visualise where you are going, and then make a request to the pool. If it accepts your request, the waters will churn, and that is when you jump in. But my guess is, you do not know where you are going, and in that case, before we go anywhere, we need to visit the Magella."

Shaking his head with exasperation, Hans paced back towards Edmund and carried on past him, back up the forsaken streets.

"Follow me."

"To be honest, I am not sure I want to visit the Magella. She is a kook," Edmund said, pointing at his head and making a crazy gesture.

"Malka is my sister, and a cunning, conniving, castigating cow of a seer. I'll tell her you think she's a kook. Maybe she will still help you."

Hans continued up the street, not caring if Edmund was following, but knowing he would be, for what other choice did he have.

"I do not understand how a mad seer can help me, Hans, even if she is your sister."

"The clue is in the word seer. She might be able to sense a

disturbance in time caused by the Time Tailor, which will give us an idea of where to search for Bedougalnn."

"Our mission is to find the traitor, not Bedougalnn," Edmund said, stopping in the street in an attempt to gather his few thoughts, multitasking having never been his forte.

With an over-exaggerated frustrated sigh, Hans turned to face Edmund.

"You are now the Queen's Captain. What do you think would bring the queen more pleasure? Knowing the name of the traitor, or knowing the location of Bedougalnn? It is your call, my Captain."

Edmund stood there, his vacant expression betraying his vacant mind as he concentrated and thought for a moment, a concept new to him. He had never needed to think before, only ever follow orders.

"Hmm, I think you may be right, let us go visit the Magella."

Through the twisting streets they weaved until they came upon the battered door of the Magella. The sign on the wall outside depicted a scrying orb containing a skull, with a snake weaving its way through the eye sockets and mouth. Hans whacked the door three times in quick succession.

A high-pitched voice from inside the property squealed.

"Go away!"

Hans whacked the door again.

"We require a reading old woman; we are on an errand for the queen."

With three loud thuds, she slammed the bolts across and the door squeaked open on its old rusty hinges. Stood in the doorway, the diminutive figure of a tremendously irate woman.

"I will have you know I am not old. I died when I was 27, so call me dead woman if you wish, but not old woman. That is just rude. Is that you Hans, well there's a surprise. You only ever turn up on my door when you need something. Well, out with it."

"It is not me that requires your help. It is my captain, and he is on an errand for our most hellacious Queen Blodia."

"Poppycock, what do you want?"

Edmund barged past Hans, through the doorway and into the property.

"He does not lie, old woman; I am on a mission for our queen. Now assist me or be ended."

"Call me old one more time and it will be you who is ended, you fool."

"My apologies, Malka the Magella. If you could spare me some time, I need your skills. I am advised you can track disturbances in time. Is this so?"

"I suppose Hans told you this, did he? You always were a blabbermouth, that's how you got your entire crew—"

"Loads of gold," Hans blurted out, his eyes fixating upon Malka, willing her to keep her mouth shut.

However, she did not take the hint.

"No. I wish you wouldn't interrupt; I was going to say killed. You got them all killed."

A puzzled confusion etched its way across Edmund's face. A sickening giddiness rose from the pit of his stomach and lodged in his throat. Never had he thought for one iota of a second the crew's death had been down to their captain, but here it was being revealed by his own sister.

"This is a story I have never heard," Edmund said, leaning against the wall to steady himself, his eyes questioning Hans. "Please go on, I am most interested in hearing about this."

"We do not have time for this now," Hans said, striding through the door, in the hope they would drop this topic.

"Oh, poppycock, Hans! If your captain has time to listen, I have time to tell. There is not much to it anyway. You see, Hans always liked to brag, still does, and he told Bloodthirsty Bazil of Bolton how much gold he and his crew had stashed away. Then he invited Bloodthirsty Bazil of Bolton and his band to join with him and his crew for a drink at the Abstract Cat Tavern. Which did not end well for any of them."

"How dreadful. You must have been terribly upset?"

"No, not really. I knew where he kept all the gold. Kept me well until the witch-finder found me out, and roasted me at the stake. Come to think of it, one of his crew was called Edmund. Did you know him?"

"Alas, no, though I am sure he was a fine man."

"Not if he was one of Hans' crew, I can assure you. Come through, let me see what I can do for you," she said, closing the door and ushering them into her reading room.

As they entered the room, Edmund glared at Hans, unsure how to process this new information, but Hans kept his head down, avoiding all eye contact, unable to face his loyal friend. It was at this moment, he decided Edmund needed to take an unscheduled holiday.

Malka sat down and signalled to Edmund to come and sit. She uncovered her crystal orb and rolled her hands around the polished shadowy sphere, studying it intensely.

"What is it you seek?"

"I seek Bedougalnn. I believe he is travelling with a Time Tailor, and their last known location was Bodmin Moor."

"Let me see what the Orb of Disorder can tell us." Her eyes rolled into her head as she entered a trance, mumbling incoherently while caressing the orb. "There is only one disturbance in time that may interest you. It is between Bodmin Moor and Grackbin Forest in Drothmaen," Malka said, speaking in a strange dialect.

With a self-satisfied smirk, Edmund rose from his seat and slunk out the door.

Hans was about to tell him they should wait until Malka was free from her trance, in case she revealed further information, but decided instead to follow his new captain, seeing as he was no longer in charge. As he closed the door to Malka's home, she spoke again, but he did not hear what she said.

"The Disturbance came from Drothmaen into Bodmin Moor, that is where Bedougalnn moves within the fabric of time."

Malka snapped out of her trance to find they had left without so much as paying, let alone leave a tip.

"Bloody Typical," she muttered, as she covered the Orb of Disorder, "I'm glad I never mentioned the spiders."

They swaggered their way back through the forsaken streets, once more finding themselves outside the Banished Abstract Cat Tavern.

"Wait here," Edmund commanded. "I will be right back."

The doors clattered on their hinges as Edmund burst into the tavern and strode over to the barkeep.

"I am looking for Bloodthirsty Bazil."

The barkeep shifted his eyes right towards a bald skoto with an eye patch and a badly inked tattoo of a daisy with *MAM* inscribed beneath it. On either side of the word *MAM*, a rather poor excuse for a love heart.

Edmund looked the skoto up and down inquisitively.

"Are you the one they call Bloodthirsty Bazil?"

"What if I am? Who be asking?" Bazil said, without even looking up from his half empty jug of ale.

"I am Captain Munday, I am in service to Queen Blodia, and I think you may have killed me a long time back, never saw the face, just felt the knife in my back."

"I guess you be one of Hans' men, that be why you come here," Bazil said, his voice was gruff, and his words somewhat slurred.

"I was, but now he is under my command. If I do not return to this place in less than one day from this time, I ask if you would go to the queen and tell her Hans has done away with me. If you do this, by favour of the queen you may drink in this here tavern for nought, until the day you are ended."

The barkeep was so distracted on hearing this statement, he spilt at least half a pint of good ale.

"Er, for free, sir? This scumbag here can't half put it away. Who'll be paying?"

"Speak to Floop, he is the queen's administrator, and he will ensure you are properly recompensed."

"I have not yet agreed to do what you asked," Bazil said, turning his head enough to make eye contact and no more, "but I am also not blind enough to see you have other choices."

"I am glad we have an accord," Edmund said, thrusting forward his hand only for Bazil to smack it away.

"We need to shake to cement our agreement," he said, proffering his hand again.

Bazil whipped out his dagger and struck the top of the bar, the blade penetrating an inch or more into the scorched wood.

"My word is my bond," he said, grasping the dagger with the intention of whipping it from the bar and brandishing it at Edmund.

However, it took him but a moment to realise the blade was stuck fast, so instead, he resorted to casually resting his hand upon the hilt, and casting an intimidating glare in Edmund's direction.

"Barkeep, give this man whatever he wants."

"I have a name you know?" the barkeep said tersely.

"Fine, apologies. What is your name, barkeep?"

The barkeep dried his hands, wiped his face, and appeared to clean out the end of his nose with the same towel he was using to clean the flagons. He flipped the towel over his shoulder and paused a moment for dramatic effect.

"My name is Barc Heape, and thank you for asking."

"Hang on, your name is Barkeep?"

"No! Are you deaf? My name, is Barc Heape?"

"That's what I said," Edmund said, shaking his head.

"It sounds similar, I will give you that, but it is spelt different, sir," Barc said, and proceeded to spell out his name for all those who were not too drunk to listen.

"Well, I am so glad we took the time to sort that out. Now,

where was I, oh yes, Barc Heape give this man whatever he wants."

"Would be my pleasure, sir."

Edmund shook his head in dismay, still rather bemused with the whole interaction, then turned and strode out of the tavern back into the bleak, grey streets. The door swung shut behind him, and he heard Bazil shout.

"Drinks are on me, boys!"

Followed by a raucous cheer.

With their overconfident swagger, they lurched through the streets until they got back to the Pool of Vacant Reflection. Edmund followed the process as Hans advised, and as the waters churned, Hans stepped forward and was about to jump in when he was jerked backwards.

"I am your captain, and I will go first. Now step back."

Hans moved aside as commanded and watched as Edmund sank beneath the swirling waters. And with a sly grin, he followed.

# 21

## RUN EDMUND RUN

In a clearing in Grackbin Forest, there was complete silence. Not even the leaves in the trees dared move in case they made a sound. A forest laden with a foreboding sense that something dark was coming.

Sure enough, the sky darkened as if night had fallen, which should have been impossible here in this wondrous forest of colour and light, where it was forever midday. Lamentable booming, and spine tingling, ground shaking thunderclaps soon accompanied the darkness.

A loud thud came from inside one of the trees, followed in quick succession by another loud thud, and then silence again. After a few moments, there came some jostling sounds, followed by some incoherent bickering. Then a hand appeared in the opening to the hollow of the tree, the fingers clenched against the bark, knuckles paling slightly, but still an ashen grey.

"Push me up, Hans," Edmund said, his whiny voice echoing across the clearing.

Inside the tree Hans was attempting to give the rotund Edmund a boost, so that he could climb out of the hollow. What Hans failed to tell Edmund when giving him instructions on how to use the Pool of Vacant Reflection, was you needed to be specific in your destination.

Asking to go to Grackbin Forest is completely different to asking to go to a clearing in Grackbin Forest, or to a well in Grackbin Forest, because you end up somewhere totally random. Which is fine if you are on a carefree adventure, but not really appropriate when on a time critical mission for your queen.

Fortunately for Edmund, the pool had been in a sympathetic mood, and placed them both inside the hollow of a mighty White Ash tree.

Of course, Edmund now wished he had let Hans jump into the pool first, because he would have landed on Hans instead of it being the other way round. Because having your face underneath the bottom of one of your crew was not an appropriate position for a captain to be in. Although, had he landed on Hans, Hans may not have been able to help him out of the tree.

This was also a relief for the tree, as the thought of having to spend the rest of her existence with two skotos inside her would have made her wish for a lightning strike to end the three of them.

With a lot of help from Hans, Edmund dragged himself up and out of the tree. Once outside, he leant back through the opening and stretched to reach Hans. Helping pull him up and out of the tree, something he would later regret.

The tree shuddered and let out a tremendous sigh of relief, shaking her branches so hard that some of her leaves got rather annoyed and fell off.

"Now where to?" Edmund asked. "I mean, it was your idea to come here looking for Bedougalnn, instead of trying to find out who the traitor is."

"Hopefully, by coming here, we will discover both. Now think, what do people come to Grackbin Forest for?" Hans said, as he strutted back and forth in the clearing, tapping his index finger against his head.

This looked like something a captain would do, so Edmund joined him, and after a brief time he stopped and raised his hand, as though asking for permission to speak.

"I've got it... goblins," he said, with the same amount of certainty Dougal had when he thought Janet wanted him for a light snack.

"As unlikely as that is, I think you are on to something, not goblins, but something goblins possess."

"Sharp pointy teeth?" Edmund blurted out.

Hans had known Edmund for centuries, and although never the brightest of his crew, it seemed to him now, since being promoted to captain, his stupidity had ballooned.

"Edmund, do you actually think before opening your mouth? Why would Bedougalnn want goblin teeth?" Hans said, forgetting for an instant that Edmund was now his captain.

Edmund strutted over to Hans and struck him across the face.

"I am your captain, and you will address me as such, and less of your tongue. Oh, and remember, your captain's ideas are by far the best ideas."

"Yes sir, Captain Munday sir!"

"I think you are right, Hans. Come, we should go to the goblin mine," he said, spinning on his heels and heading out into the forest.

"Er, the goblin mine is this way, Captain Munday," Hans said, striding off in the opposite direction.

After an uneventful trek through the forest, they crossed the black stream and found themselves in the clearing outside the mine. As they approached the towering pine pondering over how best to proceed, two goblins burst from the tree, almost knocking from their feet, and raced into the woods.

"I didn't know goblins could walk through trees," Edmund said, recovering his balance and continuing to approach the tree.

"I don't think they can, in fact I am sure of it," Hans said, noting Edmund getting closer to the tree, "but best we err on the side of caution, Captain Munday."

Edmund stood right next to the tree and called over to Hans.

"It's just a normal tree, look," Edmund said, as he leant against the apparent solid ancient tree and disappeared from sight.

"Captain Munday!" Hans yelled, feigning concern.

"It's not real. I mean, it looks real, but it's not. I think this must be the entrance to the mine," Edmund said, appearing as suddenly as he disappeared.

"I think you may be right," Hans said, unaware he was resting upon the *Welcome to the Mines of Drothmaen* sign.

Hans approached and followed Edmund into the mine. You will be disappointed to read. The skotos have a woeful sense of smell, and therefore they could not truly appreciate the unique fetid fragrance of the mines. They do, however, have rather good hearing, and the intensifying skittering sound snatched Edmund's attention.

"Hans, what does that sound like to you?"

Hans paused for a moment and concentrated on the sound echoing up through the mine.

"Well, if I did not know better, which I don't, I would say a spider. In fact, I would say a cluster of spiders."

"I would have to agree. It is probably for the best if we continue our search elsewhere."

Edmund turned heels and raced back through the tree and out of the mine, not daring to look behind him, not even to check if Hans was with him. Of course, Hans being an experienced captain, even with his inferior sense of smell, he could smell trouble. And that was without doubt the sound of trouble skittering its way towards them.

Hans burst out of the mine only seconds after Edmund, and

was shocked to see Edmund already leaping back over the black stream and hurrying deeper into the forest. As Hans got to the stream, he took a brief glance over his shoulder and wished he had not. What he saw exiting the mine was enough spiders to turn an arachnologist into an arachnophobe.

Hans picked up his pace and was soon snapping at Edmunds flagging heels. It was time to bring his devious plan to fruition. Edmund glanced across at Hans, who was now running beside him.

"Do you think we can outrun them all the way back to the portal?"

"I don't know, Captain, but I do know I should only need to outrun you."

"What!"

"I will tell the queen we found the traitor."

"But we didn't," Edmund said, looking confused and out of breath.

"You're right, we didn't, I did." Hans moved a little closer to Edmund and shoved him with all his might, ensuring he stumbled and fell. "It was you Edmund."

Edmund scrambled back to his feet and tried to run, but the not so friendly goblin mine spiders overwhelmed him. It would be wrong to dwell on what occurred next. Suffice to say, it was the end of Edmund, and he was not the tastiest of meals.

Hans kept his head down and ran for more than his worth. He never once looked back, not to see what happened to Edmund, nor to see if the spiders were still chasing him. As he got back to the clearing, he leapt with all that remained of his strength into the hole in the hollowed-out tree and dived through the portal, desperate to escape the spiders.

A moment later, he arrived back at the Pool of Vacant Reflection.

As he stood at the side of the pool with his hands upon his knees, catching his breath, a spider's leg appeared from the swirling waters. Hans stumbled backwards as fear gripped him, but at that very moment, the pool stopped churning and severed the spider's leg. It continued twitching its way towards him for a second, before slowly turning black, cracking, and crumbling to dust.

Hans collapsed on the floor in relief. *No time to waste,* he thought, *must make haste and report to the queen, maybe in a minute.*

Exhausted, Hans clambered back to his feet, until this moment he had never even realised skotos could get exhausted. He traipsed back through the twisting streets of the Hidden Dimension, past the Banished Abstract Cat Tavern, past the Magella, and on and on, until he got back to the queen's outer office.

Floop was about to go for his lunch when Hans literally burst through the door, splintering wood everywhere. He glanced up from his desk with a sneer that echoed his total disdain for the visitor.

"The door was not locked. You could have simply turned the handle and walked through. Maybe you would like to practise that method on the queen's door?"

"Watch your mouth, Flop, or I will end you."

Hans barged past Floop and tapped on Blodia's door.

"Come," Blodia called from within her vacant space.

Filled with trepidation, Hans opened the door and ambled through, ensuring to keep his head bowed.

"Where is my Captain of the Guard?"

"Your most foul and loathsome one, I bring you dreadful news regarding Captain Munday. While we were in Grackbin Forest looking for Bedougalnn, I discovered that Captain Munday was the treasonous traitor who told the lyconfind about the attack, allowing them time to prepare."

"Then bring him before me for judgement."

"I cannot, for alas he fell whilst in Grackbin Forest, before being overcome by an army of friendly goblin mine spiders."

"And this is your word, Captain Greemob?"

"It is, my most odious and unholy Queen," Hans said, smiling as he noted Blodia once again refer to him as her captain.

"Then return to your business, and I will call upon you again once Bedougalnn is located."

Captain Greemob left Blodia's vacant space and headed off to visit the Magella.

Unbeknownst to him, the queen had another visitor waiting. A visitor that had seen him return from Drothmaen by himself.

# 22

# A TRIP TO THE BALLET

Graimel had been as exact as always in the destination he wanted to arrive at, and they appeared outside the megalithic tomb that marked the entrance to Aunty Janet's den, on the precise blade of grass he specified.

There in front of them were two graves. They ran over, and Graimel realised his worst fears. At this moment, he did not even want to think about who lay before them. There were no words to explain what raced through their minds.

"Oh no, please no, Graimel, is this all because of me?" With his head in his hands, Dougal collapsed to his knees in front of the graves. "Why is this happening Graimel, why?"

"Let's not get ahead of ourselves. We don't know who is in these graves," Graimel said, as he headed towards the stairs down to Aunty Janet's den.

Binty flew across to Graimel, and with her gentlest of slaps, she sent him flying down the stairs. The burning growing as he tumbled, Binty followed him as he bounced between the steps and the wall, screaming at him as he fell.

"How dare you, Graimel! We may not know who is in those graves, but whoever they are, they most likely died for us!"

Tears streamed down her face as her wings folded, and she collapsed to the ground, tumbling down the last couple of steps herself.

Sat in an untidy heap at the bottom of the stairs, he brushed the dust and dirt from his trench coat, thankful that Grock felt no pain in this form. However, at this particular moment he was envious of this fact, as the burning in his swollen cheek stung him like a forge stings water.

Resting her doleful eyes upon his bruised visage, Binty swept away her tears.

When she peered behind the now shattered lens of his glasses askew upon his face, she saw the depth of sorrow in his eyes. She saw the pain and the burden he carried. Graimel proffered his hand, and she embraced his finger as he pushed himself to his feet.

"I am so sorry," Binty said, caressing his hand. "I will always be here for you."

Dougal came down the stairs with Bounce, his eyes red and swollen.

"You're right, Graimel, I should try and control my emotions. Glad I caught up with you before you knocked." Dougal stepped past them and rapped his fist against the door three times. "Let us see who is in."

Inside the den, Janet and the others were still covered in flour and all other kinds of baking ingredients from the previous night. Scattered around the den, numerous empty wine bottles, upturned glasses, and side plates with cake or at least the remnants of cake, and the kitchen resembled the aftermath of a windstorm in a flour factory.

Lescan had fallen asleep, his head tipped to one side resting against the side of the high-backed chair, and in the chair opposite, Sven in a mirror like position. Curled up together on the rug in front of the fire were Beth and Wrethe, Wrethe's muscular arm holding her close, threatening never to let her go.

Over in the bedroom snuggled under a throw, Fimor snored

and chomped his teeth, while Klaus slept on the sofa and had fallen asleep dreaming Kainen was still sat next to him. As for Janet, she had not slept a wink, instead spending the entire night sat at the kitchen table going over and over the events of the evening. Wishing she could have done something different, wishing Laegon and Kainen were not lying in their graves. But as much as she wished it was not so, she knew they could not change it, this however, did not stop her tormenting herself.

Dougal knocked on the door again and Janet snapped herself back to reality. Fimor also heard the door and rushed across to be with Janet.

"I guess bad guys don't knock," Janet said mockingly.

"Let's hope not, eh," Fimor said, taking Janet's hand, "together."

Janet unlatched the door and let it swing open.

"Aunty Janet," Dougal said, unable to hold back the tears.

"I'm okay, and I am glad to see you four are as well. Come in. There are some friends here I would like you to meet."

Fimor held out his hand and greeted them all, introducing himself and offering them all a piece of cake.

"Just tea for me if it's all the same. I am in no mind for food," Graimel said, taking a seat at the kitchen table.

"I could manage a small piece of cake," Binty said, hoping such a thing did not exist. "What happened in here? It looks like a bomb went off?"

"Oh this, this is just from making cake to honour Laegon and Kainen. We cleaned up the mess from the fight already." Janet picked up a cloth and started wiping down the units. "I Guess we still have more tidying up to do."

While the others continued to sleep off their hangovers, and dream away the memories of the previous night. Janet recounted the events for them while Fimor sat beside her and held her hand, often stretching his arm around her for a moments comfort.

"I should never have put you in danger, and I should not

have listened to Lescan when he told me to return to Dougal. I should have been here." Graimel pushed his chair back, got up and rested his hands upon the edge of the basin, his head bowed. "I should have been here."

Lescan heard Graimel talking and woke, rubbing his eyes as he sat up straight in the chair, and trying to stretch out the crick in his neck.

"You cannot change fate, old man, no matter how much you want or try."

"I should have been here with you."

"It would not have made a difference, you know that, and their sacrifice strengthens our resolve."

Gradually the others awoke and introduced themselves, all telling parts of the same story of what happened the night before, and sharing memories of their friends. Graimel and Dougal helped Lescan and Sven find some worthy headstones, and Klaus and Fimor engraved them, which left Wrethe and Beth to place them on the graves.

"Will you all be okay now?" Sven asked.

"After what we did to them last night, I doubt they would ever risk coming back." Lescan took Graimel's arm and led him to one side. "Did you find it?"

"Yes." Graimel nodded and pulled the Pendant of Tel Etoiles from out of his pocket, holding it up for Lescan to see. "Soon we can end this madness."

Lescan reached out to touch the pendant, drawn to it like a goblin to gold, but Graimel snapped his fist closed around it, and slipped it back into his pocket.

"We need to keep this hidden until the time is right. You never know who is watching."

Lescan and Graimel re-joined the others gathered at the side of the graves.

"I don't suppose anyone has a fast car that young Dougal here could drive."

They all turned to look at Graimel in stunned silence. None

of their kind possessed human transportation devices, as it was a sure-fire way of letting the cat out of the bag, so to speak. With humans being unable to see magical creatures, all they would see is a car with no one driving, and frankly, that is less believable than magical creatures.

Not only would this inevitably lead to humans all over the world, darting about the place as if they had fire ants in their pants, screaming about ghosts or spirits possessing cars. But it could ultimately lead to the discovery and hunting of magical creatures, and that would never do.

This, however, was just Graimel's way of asking if anyone had a quicker mode of transport than walking, as the risks associated with portaling everywhere when being hunted were too great. Not only this, but his feet were tired, and he was pretty sure Dougal did not have his passport with him.

Wrethe put his hand up, the one not holding Beth's.

"I might have a friend who can help."

"You don't need to put your hand up, Wrethe, isn't it?"

"Yes sir."

"He's awfully polite your Wrethe," Graimel said, whilst indicating to Wrethe they should talk in private.

Lescan, Sven, and Klaus said their goodbyes and headed home, promising to return soon, whilst Aunty Janet asked Fimor if he could stay on a few days. There were a few minor things that now needed fixing, and she had been thinking of putting in an extension.

"Thank you," Graimel said, shaking Wrethe's hand as they returned from their private conversation.

"Remember what I said." Wrethe gave him a knowing look and a nod before turning to Beth and interlocking his fingers with hers. "Are you going to show me where you live then? I think Janet's got enough company for now."

Beth smiled, gripped his hand a little tighter, and led him away across the moor.

"Any chance Bounce could stay with you for a day or two, Janet?"

"Of course, it would be my pleasure."

Dougal hugged and stroked Bounce goodbye, knowing when not to question Graimel.

"You be a good boy for your Aunty Janet."

He would have said more. Only an inconsolable Binty barged him out of the way.

"I can't believe we are leaving you here," Binty said, hugging and kissing his face. "We will go for a nice long stroll as soon as I am back."

Bounce did his thing, his tail wagging manically as he let out deep joyous woofs. Janet and Fimor took Bounce and headed back down the stairs into her den. As they disappeared around the first corner, Janet called out.

"Oh, Graimel, put the stone back over my entrance please."

"I forgot about that. Give me a hand would you, Binty?"

"Leave it to me."

Binty swooped over and picked up the giant door stone as though it was lighter than a tiny pebble, before placing it back in its upright position.

"Now, let me also fix your glasses."

She took Graimel's glasses from his face, pausing for a moment to absorb how strange he looked without them, before stroking the bridge and adding a little pixie dust. Once satisfied, she placed the repaired glasses back on Graimel's nose.

"Well, where to?"

"To meet with a friend of Wrethe's."

"Well, without Bounce here, it looks like you are carrying me again, okay to sit on your shoulder?" Binty said, zipping over to Dougal.

"Of course."

Graimel once again led the way, heading west to find the lyconfind Wrethe told him about. Now and then he would stop, bend down, and pick something up from the ground before continuing on. Binty and Dougal thought this was indeed strange behaviour for Graimel, but none dared ask.

Relieved he was not the one acting strange for once, Dougal enjoyed this rare moment, filling his lungs with a deep breath of the fresh moorland air. But as he absorbed the beauty of his surroundings, something down the embankment to his left caught his eye.

He stopped and peered down, watching as the ferns swayed. For a second, he swore he saw some rocks moving. *The wind maybe,* he thought. He inched forward to get a better look, almost losing his footing, and realising that neither Binty nor Graimel had waited for him, he rushed to catch them up.

It was past one o'clock in the afternoon, when they finally arrived at the three standing stones described by Wrethe, *'5m high and 5m apart'*, forming a gateway into the vast clearing.

There in the glade ahead of them stood a lone tree, the biggest and most beautiful tree Dougal had ever seen. Thousands of cascading branches and leaves formed a giant archway into the cathedral like canopy. He was no arborist, but to him it looked like a giant weeping willow tree, crossed with a redwood and a fig.

When they were about 15m from the central stone, Graimel turned and told them both to wait there. It was very important.

"Wait here. It is very important."

Graimel edged his way towards the central stone, remembering what Wrethe had told him. What he had not told the others was if he gets this wrong, they could be in big trouble. He reminded himself, *you are being watched Graimel.*

Graimel bowed to the central stone, hopped up into the air and performed a curtsey on landing. He then turned 90 degrees to his left, took 11 paces, stopped, and turned to face the left-hand stone. He put his hand to his mouth and blew the stone a kiss, then put both of his hands to his heart and thrust them forward as though throwing his love towards the stone. Turning another 90 degrees right, he took 22 paces, turned, and faced the third stone. He took a deep breath and scanned his surroundings, unsure if he could continue, but remembering what Wrethe told him.

*Come on Graimel,* he told himself as he hoisted his right foot up to his left knee and pirouetted like a ballerina. Then, as instructed, he inserted a jump, flicking his leg out mid-air, and just about successfully landing before continuing to pirouette.

Dougal and Binty collapsed on the floor in tears of laughter, and Binty took to imitating Graimel, including pulling her famous only in Erof Graimel facial expressions. Dougal had not laughed this much since, well, since forever. They looked up and got to see Graimel attempt to perform another jump and flick, but this time his leg buckled upon landing, and he hit the ground with a thump. Snapping a glance at each other, Dougal and Binty once again broke out in uncontrollable hysterics.

Graimel picked himself up and walked back to the central stone. Once again, he took a bow, after which he spun about to face Binty and Dougal. With a grimace, he raised his middle finger before turning away. This only added to their amusement, and while they shared a gleeful smile amid their stifled giggles, Graimel stood to attention, awaiting a response.

It came in the form of a deep booming voice, rumbling across from over by the willow.

"A fine display and worthy of an audience..." There was a slight pause while the voice collected itself. "You may now approach and enter." The voice broke again, emitting a little giggle, followed by the sound of someone clearing their throat, re-composing themselves. "Uh um. Please come forward and bring with you your offering of tiny pebbles."

The voice broke into raucous laughter, and Graimel pulled out all the pebbles he had been collecting, tossing them over his shoulder. *Hang the consequence,* he thought. Binty and Dougal had still not picked themselves up off the floor, and watched as an exasperated Graimel ambled off towards the willow. Still smiling, they pulled themselves together and ran to catch up with the grumpy notadwarf.

Underneath the grand arch of the tree stood an incredibly old lyconfind, but as there is no precise conversion into human years, I can only suggest he was older than Lescan and Laegon times two.

He appeared to be greying, although this may have been his natural colour. Either way, his fur complimented his deep-set, bold blue eyes and gold framed monocle, and he was what your tactful nan would describe as a healthy weight. All of which seemed to magnify his charm. Sat by his side was his loyal black and tan mutt of a dog, his shiny silver dog tag glinting in the sunlight.

The three of them approached and saw the old lyconfind chuckling to himself.

"You must be the one Wrethe sent, Graimel, isn't it?"

"Yes, and this is Binty, and The Bedougalnn."

"Good to meet you all." He eyed Dougal up and down, seemingly unfazed by his presence. "And thanks for the light entertainment. You know you're the first person anyone has got to perform that playful ritual in about a hundred years. I owe Wrethe a pint or ten for that. I am Major Vern Heysi."

There was a muted woof from his side, and Vern glanced down and waved his fist playfully at his dog.

"And this little gobshite here is Mace."

With Virtual steam coming from his ears, Graimel calmly held out his hand.

"You mean all that stuff in front of the stones was just for a laugh? Well, well played. It is an honour to make your acquaintance."

Binty and Dougal tried their utmost best to hide the fit of giggles from which they still suffered. But every time they looked at Graimel, a picture of a plump, 110cm tall notadwarf, wearing a bright pink ballerina's tutu, popped into their heads, and they would start giggling again.

"Come inside, Wrethe said you needed to borrow some sort of transport. I think I have what you need." Major Heysi turned and walked into his den. "Come on Mace. I hope you guys like tea?"

# 23

# MAJOR VERN HEYSI & CHMNU

As they entered Major Heysi's den, it was like being transported into yet another magical world. The canopy of the tree was strewn with all kinds of lights. Tiny lights spiralled up the trunk, spreading out and down every branch. Larger multi-coloured lights dangled like hypnotic catkins, and lights of all shapes and sizes cascaded all the way to the ground like falling leaves.

Random pieces of wood and stone littered the entire floor area, arranged into some semblance of order that worked to enhance the beauty of its surroundings. And about them, all kinds of plants and flowers that neither Binty nor Graimel had ever seen, yet alone smelt.

"Please, take a seat and I will pour the tea," Vern said, walking over to what can only have been his kitchen area.

They took a seat at the vast elm and granite table dominating the area near the kitchen. It was meticulously carved with all kinds of symbols, some of which Dougal thought he recognised as he traced them with his finger.

"I would not do that if I were you." Vern placed the tray of tea on the dining table. "Some of those can be unpredictable, and we would not want you accidentally triggering one now would we?"

Dougal snatched his hand away, noting one of the symbols he had traced glowing.

"Sorry, but it's such a beautiful table. I guess I was a little mesmerised. What's it made from?"

"It is rather beautiful isn't it? I made it from my grandparents' old front door."

Vern waved his hand over the symbol as if extinguishing a flame, then joined them at the table, took a cup and raised it as a toast.

"To new friends. Now then, to business, do you mind if I ask where you are heading? It may help me decide who takes you."

"Firstly, this is excellent tea. I think it has to be the best tea I have ever tried," Graimel said, sipping from his cup.

On hearing this, both Binty and Dougal raced to pick up their cups and try the tea, both agreeing with Graimel. The tea was superb.

"We need to go to Denmark—"

Graimel did not finish speaking before Binty interrupted, spraying tea everywhere in her excitement.

"Bregon Sk—"

This time it was Graimel who stayed Binty, without so much as a word, just a look, snapping his eyes across to her the moment the first letter came out of her mouth. His face a mixture of total disbelief and anger, not dissimilar to the face Goblin Lord Ferglestin had the second before Binty turned him to dust on the wind.

"Bregon Skovin, eh! Don't worry, I won't tell a soul. Someone might ask questions about how you got there, and that would leave me in a bit of a pickle. The good thing is, now I know for certain who you need, and that would be Chmnu."

"I thought you were going to help us with transport? Who, may I ask, is Chmnu?"

"You will see. But you have a long trip ahead of you," Vern

said, getting up and meandering back into his kitchen, "let me fix you something to eat."

"I don't suppose you have any cake?" Binty asked.

"I always have cake, just in case my grand-lykinds come around. Is cake good for you two as well?"

"You can never go wrong with tea and cake," Dougal said, and Graimel nodded his agreement.

Once their bellies were full and their cups were empty, which was not long with the cake monster Binty tucking in, Vern stood and asked them all to follow him, and he would introduce them to their transport.

Behind the kitchen area was a heavy steel door with many locks and a striking sign which read *DANGER – STAY OUT* in big bold letters. Vern cleared all the locks, and let them through into a long hallway leading to the trunk of the tree, then secured the door, and took the lead once more.

As they reached the bottom of the tree, they spied a long winding staircase, which was almost invisible to the naked eye, wrapping itself around the trunk of the tree, and spiralling upwards, disappearing into the canopy.

"Almost there," Vern said, as he climbed the stairs.

They climbed up into the highest reaches of the canopy, until eventually the stairs ended, and they stood on a small wooden platform inside a glass dome. In front of them was another hefty steel door which was once again bolted and locked many times, emblazoned upon it, yet another sign that read, *Trespassers WILL be Eaten*.

He swung the door open and let them through, slamming it shut behind them and locking it.

"I'm not sure I like the sign on that door. Are we safe?" Dougal asked.

"Stay close to me and do not make any sudden movements, and everything will be just grand." Vern threaded his way through the foliage. "Oh and watch your step, and if you don't like heights, don't look down."

As they followed Vern, they realised they were walking along one of the sturdy branches of the tree. Dougal eyes were drawn to the chasm beneath him as he edged forwards, until now he had never thought he feared heights, but as he paused to recompose himself, his knees buckled and he wobbled a little.

"Don't worry, Dougal, if you fall, I will catch you. I will always be there to catch you," Binty whispered, while stroking his ear lobe.

Steadying himself, he took a deep breath before continuing, and as the branch thinned out, they stepped on to a wide purpose-built platform, and Vern turned and motioned for them to stop.

"If I can ask you all to kneel for a moment, and I will call Chmnu."

They did as requested, with Vern also taking to his knee before calling out.

"Chmnu, would you honour us with your presence?"

An almighty whooshing sound burst through the canopy, followed by a tremendous thump as though an earthquake had struck the tree. A magnificent, sleek black dragon with huge yellow eyes landed right before them and bowed his head to Vern. He approached the dragon and stroked and kissed his nose, much like Dougal often did to Bounce. The dragon seemed to almost purr as he did this, and when he stopped, he nudged him to do it again. Vern turned and gestured for them to come over, but they appeared frozen to the spot.

"Friends, I would like you to meet Chmnu. Chmnu, this is Graimel, Binty, and Bedougalnn. I need you to take them somewhere important and then bring them home when they are done."

Chmnu raised his head up high and roared in acceptance of Vern's request, snorting a little fire in the process.

"Thanks boy. Take care of them, okay," Vern said, throwing his arms around Chmnu's neck, hugging him.

Knelt with their mouths agape, awestruck, and dumbfounded, and as yet unable to stand, let alone speak. Neither Binty nor Graimel had ever seen a dragon or believed them to be real. Pressing his mouth closed, Graimel staggered to his feet.

"It's a dragon, an actual dragon, but how?"

"I raise them, my father raised them before me and his father before him. I come from a long line of dragon rearers. It is a secret and sacred profession, and I would thank you to keep it that way."

"He is beautiful," Binty said, as she flew over to Chmnu. "can I touch him?"

"Of course you can. He would like that."

Chmnu smiled and purred in appreciation as Binty brushed his forehead. Graimel joined her, placing his hand upon Chmnu's cheek. They scratched about their memories for a time when they had experienced such elation, and yet been so at ease in the same moment. Nothing came to mind.

With all the air in his lungs, Dougal wanted to scream *DRAGON* and run for his life. While the logical part of his brain told him don't panic, dragons don't exist, the rational part said, *really this surprises you, after everything you have seen, this is what stops you in your tracks, a bloody beautiful dragon?*

For that moment Dougal had the good sense to listen to the rational part of his brain and cautiously approached Chmnu. From afar he had appeared sheer black, but up close his scales shimmered like petroleum on wet tarmac. Dougal lay his hand upon Chmnu's face. The texture surprised him, like caressing the most luxurious silken garment, so soft he thought it would absorb his hand. Never in his life had he felt anything quite comparable.

Then he did what Dougal always did in these situations. He passed out, and by the time he came to again, they were back downstairs and sat at the table.

"Oh, did I nod off? I had a most wonderful dream that

dragons are real," Dougal said, smiling from ear to ear like a deranged Cheshire cat.

"No, you did not nod off. Dragons are real, and that is why you passed out."

With a shake of his head, Graimel got up and walked over to where Vern stood underneath the archway.

"I guess we should make a move."

"I guess so. Chmnu will look after you."

As they stood about exchanging pleasantries, they heard lykind voices out by the standing stones.

"Gramps, Gramps! Are we doing the dance right?"

Vern motioned to the lykinds to come in, and they ran over and threw their arms around him.

"You both did very well. Go help yourselves to some cake. Gramps just needs to say goodbye to his friends."

The lykinds rushed into the kitchen and Vern escorted Graimel Binty and Dougal through the grand archway and over towards the standing stones.

Chmnu came swooping down from the top of the willow and landed at their feet, allowing Vern to give Graimel a boost up onto his back. Binty graciously set Dougal down behind Graimel, and then took her seat back on his shoulder.

"Oh, I almost forgot." Binty took a pinch of pixie dust from her pocket and blew it over Dougal. "Can't have anyone spotting a flying human, can we? That should keep you hid for the journey."

Vern patted Chmnu and stroked his neck, before telling him once again to stay safe.

Chmnu shot into the sky and headed north east towards Denmark, within seconds they were up in the clouds. Dougal raised his hands to the sky like he would on a rollercoaster ride, but this was something far better than he could ever imagine, and he was in no mood to pass out this time.

Chmnu glided effortlessly through the sky, swooping from left to right, darting in and out of the clouds, twisting, turning, and soaring. He was so busy showing off his flying skills, he was a little startled when a huge flying aluminium giant popped out of the clouds right in front of them.

Graimel and Binty squealed like a broken siren as Chmnu made an immediate nosedive and barrel roll to safety. Whilst Dougal once again threw his arms above his head, enjoying the ride. Graimel sicked a little in his mouth, while Dougal cheered and laughed. Although I hasten to add, it was a rather nervous laugh.

"Sorry about that. I had forgotten about them," Chmnu said, his voice booming like thunder.

"Hang on, you can talk," Dougal said, the tone of his voice a few octaves higher than normal.

"Why would you assume I could not? Do you think dragons are stupid?"

"No, not at all, and I guess I shouldn't actually be surprised by now, either."

"Bah! You're only human."

For the first time since Dougal had known them, Binty and Graimel remained silent, and Dougal got comfort from that fact. Chmnu decided he would stick to a more basic flight plan after that little scare. Arriving at the coast in no time, they headed out over the North Sea and Chmnu swooped down until they skimming the crests of the waves. The cool sea spray brushing their faces and making Chmnu's scales glisten.

They crossed the coast of Denmark at Ribe and gained a little altitude before turning inland. Before long, they were crossing Little Belt, a stretch of water separating Jutland from the island of Fyn. With a barrel roll, Chmnu dropped from the sky until they were grazing the treetops. Then, over the horizon, the exquisite Renaissance castle of Egeskov loomed into view.

Chmnu circled the castle twice, so his passengers could marvel at it a little longer, before swooping down to land near the middle of the roof. They slid down off Chmnu's back and thanked him for an amazing trip. Chmnu nodded and purred in acceptance.

"I will wait here for your return." Chmnu circled on the spot a few times before lying down, wrapping his tail over his face, and taking a well-deserved nap.

They snuck across the rooftop and headed for the tallest tower. There were a lot of visitors to the castle that day, and Dougal was no longer hidden by pixie magic. The last thing they needed now was for someone to spot or hear him on the roof. Graimel was insistent that Dougal stayed low and stayed quiet.

Graimel clambered over the last bit of roof between them and their destination and silently slid down to the base of the tower. But as Dougal crossed over the apex of the roof, he glanced down and lost his balance, shrieking as he slipped. As his bottom hit the roof, it dislodged a couple of tiles and sent them cascading over the edge. The people in the grounds below had heard the scream and scanned the roofline, so Grock rushed over to Dougal and hid him from sight.

Meanwhile, Binty had shot from Dougal's shoulder to catch the falling tiles. She caught one and hurled it back up to Graimel. The other one was already speeding towards the ground, and heading straight for a little Danish boy called Felix.

There was no way Binty could just catch this tile, as the people gathered below froze as they watched it fall. Staying alongside it, she gave it a quick nudge a split-second before it was about to strike the boy, the tile smashing into pieces at the boy's feet. A few people rushed over in disbelief at how this tile had missed little Felix. But Felix knew, and as Binty zipped skywards back towards the rooftop, he called out.

"Tusind tak!"

As Binty got back to the others, Graimel was scanning his

eyes over the bottom segment of the tower with intense concentration.

"It must be here somewhere," Graimel muttered, whilst sweeping his hands over the smooth surface, "help me look."

"Look for what?" Binty asked.

"The switch to open the door."

"There is no door, Graimel."

"You should know better. There is always a door if you know where to look."

Dougal moved away from the bottom of the tower. Off to his right, he noticed what appeared to be a small roof vent big enough for him to sit on, and seeing as how he always seemed to be in the way when these situations arose. He thought to himself, *I will just sit aside and let the professionals do their thing.*

With Grock still shielding him from all prying eyes, he walked over to the vent and sat down with a rather loud clunk, followed by a squeak. Binty and Graimel glared at him disapprovingly whilst continuing to lean against the tower, trying to find the switch. As they turned their attention back to doing just that, Graimel fell through the now open door.

A second later, his head came back through the door.

"Well done Dougal. Now get in here."

They followed Graimel into the base of the tower and as he shut the door, a couple of security guards came through a roof access hatch.

"We are safe for now, Grock, but it will be a bit warm for a coat from here on in. Do you mind walking?"

Grock transformed into his natural quag form and spoke to Graimel in his native tongue.

"Bruh heskt jeck."

Which Graimel understood to mean *Sure thing dude.*

The stairs inside the tower spiralled downwards in typical castle style. The centre of the stone steps had worn away from centuries of use, however, these steps had never felt a single human foot fall until this day. There were no windows or doorways leading off, as there was nothing to see and nowhere to go except down. The stairs continued to spiral endlessly, and Dougal hoped this was not the only way out. He found it hard enough going down. He dared not think how hard the climb up would be.

With no lights in the stairwell to guide them, Graimel called upon Harg to light their way once again. The walls and steps were now carved out of the very bedrock of the earth, and the only sound was that of their footsteps. Tired and a little giddy, Dougal wondered if they would ever reach the bottom. He was about to ask Graimel how much further, when they heard faint and distant hammering, and indistinct voices, arguing, cheering, and singing.

A warm glow radiated up towards them from the depths, and Dougal was minded to turn around, thinking they had inadvertently taken the stairway to hell. Of course, Dougal was not to know that not only did that stairway go a lot deeper, but the entrance was secreted beneath Marjorie Tibbs' garden shed at 42 Teepill Street, Thimblebridge, West Yorkshire. A fact that Marjorie Tibbs was also blissfully unaware of, but explained why the local council would never grant her planning permission for a large fishpond.

They reached the bottom of the stairs and stood before an imposing wood and glass arched door, emblazoned with all kinds of runic symbols, Graimel was about to push on the door when Binty stopped him.

"I think it would be polite to knock first."

"Your right."

Graimel banged on the door with his fist. Silence fell across their ears, the kind of silence you see in old western movies when a stranger walks into a bar. A mere moment later, the sound of heavy footsteps coming towards the door broke that silence.

# 24

# WELCOME TO ILDJORDEN

The door creaked ajar, and the heat of a furnace rushed out to meet them, almost knocking them from their feet. Two eyes appeared, glaring at them through the crack, and spoke with a harsh, gruff voice.

"And you are?"

"A weary traveller and his companions, seeking an audience with Bregon."

"And does this weary traveller and his companions have names?"

"We do. I am Graimel Tock. This is Binty Malice, Grock, and Bedougalnn."

"The Bedougalnn? Are you sure?" He looked Dougal up and down, screwing his face up while he did so, then glanced across at Graimel. "But he's a human. Have you at least checked he has the mark?"

The door had inched open a little further now, and they could see more curious eyes and faces appearing in the background, eager to get a glimpse of who had come knocking when everyone was home.

"Of course I checked. Now, who, may I ask, are you?"

Graimel said, stamping his staff against the stone floor, waking Harg from his nap.

"I am Sleip Neren, and I am the Guardian of the Door of Ildjorden." Sleip swung the door open and stepped into its frame, filling it. "Now, tell me how you broke in?"

A grin spread across Dougal's face. *Now this is a dwarf,* he thought. Based on all the fantasy he had seen and read, the person now stood before them ticked every box, although larger than he had imagined.

He stood about 140cm tall and 90cm wide, every inch of him defined solid muscle. His face unyielding and muscular, sporting a magnificent three braid beard, moustache combo. Deep set piercing green eyes, a thick brow, and bald, except for a long white braided ponytail. In his right hand, he was wielding a hammer with a head the size of a French Bulldog.

Dougal now understood why Graimel described himself as notadwarf, although he still did not have the foggiest what he actually was.

"Move aside Sleip," Harg said, transforming into his raven form, "they have not broken in. They are with me; they are my guests."

"Hargof Sventolf! Is that you?"

"The very same brother," Harg said, and flew past Sleip into Ildjorden.

Dougal stood transfixed on the spot. So many burning questions, not to mention burning skin from the heat being emitted from within Ildjorden. *Was this Sleip, Harg's brother? When did Harg learn to talk? What accent is that of Harg's? Was Harg a Viking dwarf? What is a Viking dwarf?* Dougal thought his head might explode. It did not.

"Please come through and accept my apologies."

They entered Ildjorden, Grock having to grasp Dougal's hand and pull him through the entrance. The smell of molten metals, ash, burning coals, and what was most probably Viking dwarf sweat permeated the air.

"Bregon is in council at the moment, so please come. We will wait awhile at the mead hall."

"Do they serve tea?" Graimel asked.

"They serve mead, golden mead, dark mead, and spicy mead, not heard of this tea. Is it a type of mead?"

"Err, No."

"Graimel, what is mead?" Binty asked.

"It's an alcoholic honey drink."

"Ooh, I love honey. I wonder if it tastes as magnificent as malbec?"

They made their way through the crowds of dwarfs that had come to gawk at the strange visitors. Some reaching out to try to touch one of them, Grock. As strange as it may seem, they all appeared to bow their heads a little as Grock passed. Dougal thought this was for him, since he was The Bedougalnn, and he promptly held his head high and smiled, waving his hand a little as if he were royalty. Never realising for a moment that almost everyone thought he was just some strange human, which he was.

Everywhere they looked, fires burned and forges smouldered away, while dwarfs hammered away on anvils and poured huge vats of molten metals into a multitude of differing moulds. There were dwarfs carving and hammering runes into staves and blades, some shining and sharpening, and others making pots and pans. Then there were those who were relaxing around open fires with spits, eating, drinking, and telling tales of the old days.

They got to the mead hall, a narrow cosy cave off to the side of the main cavern. Sleip led them to a table, sat them down, and called for service.

"Why hello sirs, I am Anelci. May I take your order?"

"Five meads please, Anelci," Sleip said.

"My pleasure, Sleip. Would you like any food?"

"No food, thanks, just the mead for now."

"Excuse me, is there any chance I could get a spicy mead, please?" Binty asked.

Sleip watched with pride as Anelci skipped off towards the bar to fetch the drinks.

"That is one of my daughters. She is in training to be a warrior, and she will make her father proud."

"She is beautiful," Dougal said.

Sleip slammed his fist into the table and scowled at Dougal.

"Not even, The Bedougalnn, is good enough for my daughter, so avert your eyes afore I crush you human!"

"Sorry, I didn't mean it like that, merely an observation."

Sleip let out a raucous roar of laughter, jovially slapping Dougal across his back and winding him. Dougal winced before catching his breath and felt sure some of his ribs had just been cracked. They weren't.

"Speaking of observations, I noticed you observing my hammer earlier, Bedougalnn," Sleip said, holding aloft his hammer as if he were about to introduce it, which he did. "I would like you to meet Mabel."

Sleip placed Mabel down on the table, and she did nothing. After all, she was just a hammer.

"Your hammer has a name? And you called it Mabel? What kind of name is that for a hammer?" Dougal asked.

"It is a fine name. I named it after my father's hammer, and she crushed many skulls."

"But it's just a hammer right, a big hammer, but just a hammer."

The runes engraved into Mabel's head glowed faintly, and Sleip wrapped his hand around the handle, once again taking Mabel to his side.

Anelci returned and served the drinks. After grabbing a spoon, Binty leapt up on to the rim of the mead horn and took an inquisitive but cautious sip. With a smile, she then filled her empty flask and held it aloft, while the rest of them lifted their horns.

"Skål!" Sleip called out.

"Skål!" Came the resounding cheer from the tavern.

They had all just about finished their drinks except for Binty, who had come to the realisation that alcohol came in many differing strengths. And although she loved this spiced mead and had only drunk a tiny amount. The warm fuzzy sensation that wound through her told her she was already a little tipsy from the effects of this newfound favourite drink. After refilling her flask, she jumped off the edge of the horn and sat down, resting up against the horn holder with the sort of grin any maniacal menace would have been more than proud of.

A deep, thick Danish accented voice called out from the entrance to the tavern.

"Sleip?"

"Over here," Sleip said, standing up and waving his arm.

Heading over towards them was another burly looking dwarf. He looked not too dissimilar to Sleip, except for having a full head of dirty blonde hair braided in traditional fashion. A simple single braid beard completed his look, which nonetheless was still as impressive as Sleip's. He grabbed the vacant chair and swung it about, sitting on it facing the backrest. Dougal realised this was most likely because of the enormous two handed, twin bladed, splendid looking axe affixed to his back.

"Who are your guests?"

Sleip went through the introductions and then introduced the newcomer.

"Everyone, this is my closest friend and ally, Krahns Faenn," Sleip said, slapping Krahns heartily across his back, "and he is Bregon's second."

Krahns had only just raised his hand to call over a barmaid, when one appeared with his horn of mead and a complimentary side of meat.

"So, what is it you lot seek from Bregon?" Krahns asked, tearing into a piece of meat.

Graimel once again explained the perilous situation they found themselves in, and the purpose of their visit to Ildjorden. This time however, they were not seeking an object, but the might of the dwarfs themselves. It was a huge ask which could cost lives, but Graimel hoped Bregon would understand the gravity of the consequence, should they fail to prevent Bedougalnn's time from being ended.

Krahns listened with interest while continuing to eat and drink, whilst Graimel detailed the journey so far, which seemed to take quite some time. Dougal had frequently thought that Graimel seemed to like the sound of his own voice, although he had to admit, it did have a rather soothing quality about it.

"What do you reckon, Sleip? Do we take them to see Bregon, or toss them into a furnace?"

"You will take us to Bregon or feel my wrath!"

"Hej, Hargof you old fool, I am not feeling anything of yours. That's how you ended up as a raven in the first place."

"Come now, Krahns, you know for a fact, it was a gift from Odin himself," Sleip said, winking and smirking.

Krahns roared with laughter and held out his hand for Harg to perch on.

"Well I never, they are with you then I assume, hence why they are sitting drinking with Sleip, and not already fuel for the furnace. It is great to see you again, old friend."

"As it is to see you both, and this old place."

"Come, let us take you to Bregon. I know he is going to be interested to meet the quag."

They got up from the table, Sleip waving farewell to Anelci. Dougal was about to wave as well when he remembered what Sleip had said. With no desire to meet the business end of Mabel, he started out of the tavern.

"So, you're not going to thank my daughter for serving you?"

Unable to do right for doing wrong, Dougal spun on his heels, smiling and waving to Anelci while mouthing his thanks.

Through a myriad of caves and carved out tunnels they followed Krahns until they came to the great hall. Mighty columns of stone rose up into the rafters supporting the roof. The shields and weapons of fallen warriors decorated the walls, and long, uncomfortable wooden benches lined the floor.

At the head of the hall, Bregon Skovin lounged upon an ornately carved wooden throne, his legs dangling over the armrests. Half god, half dwarf, he had been exiled from Svartalfheim for reasons long forgotten. Faithfully accompanied by many hundreds of loyal brethren, they made their new home in the fiery furnaces beneath Egeskov.

He was stout and commanding, with long greying hair and an elaborate greying plaited beard. His face bore the marks of many years and many battles, as did his red and black round shield, which leant against the side of his throne. As he stood to welcome his guests, Binty's eyes fixed upon his sword secreted in his wonderfully embroidered scabbard, and wondered if the legend was true.

Bregon held out his left hand, keeping his right hand on the hilt of his sword as they approached.

"Welcome to Ildjorden, and welcome to my home. You have a loyal friend in Hargof, and if it was not for him, and the fact you travel with a quag, then I would not entertain your presence in Ildjorden. Hargof told me of your request, and it would seem we have things to discuss. Come take a seat."

Bregon shook each of their hands then directed them to a long table provisioned with plentiful food and drink. As predicted by Krahns, Bregon seemed especially interested to meet Grock, and took a seat next to him at the table.

"So, Grock, how did you become a part of this quest?" Bregon asked.

Grock recounted the story of how he became orphaned whilst on a school trip to Gurquag, and was later adopted by Graimel when a bureaucratic paperwork misunderstanding led to him completing an adoption form instead of a visa application. So, when he arrived for his holiday in the Quagmires of Sturm, instead of receiving a stamp in his passport, he received a young Grock. After pausing for a moment in stifled perplexity, he took one look at the forlorn Grock, and had cared for him ever since.

With the story told, and everyone apart from Graimel wiping the odd tear from their eyes, Bregon got to his feet and placed his hand back on his hilt.

"I have someone I would like you to meet."

# 25

# A FAVOUR FOR BREGON SKOVIN

There was a sense of unease as Bregon stood and eased his sword from his scabbard, their eyes darting between each other as Grock moved a little closer to Dougal. Ready to shield him if the need arose. Oblivious to this, Dougal leant forward, fascinated with the spellbinding runes etched down the length of Bregon's blade.

Bregon then did something he would only ever do in the company of people he trusted; he placed his sword down on the table, removed his scabbard, and placed it next to his sword before retaking his seat.

"I would like you all to meet Ligl, but especially—"

"What is it with dwarfs introducing their weapons to you, so your sword is called Ligl. What does it matter as long as the pointy end is sharp!" Dougal said, interrupting Bregon's thread, probably a little too much mead.

"What would make you think my sword is called Ligl?"

"Well, Sleip's hammer is called Mabel."

"A fine name," Bregon said.

"And I'm sure that monstrous axe on Krahns' back also has a name."

Krahns took this as a cue to remove his axe from his back and swing him about his head, calling out, "Ojom!"

"Yes, yes Krahns. Now put Ojom back before he hurts someone," Bregon said, motioning for Krahns to take a seat.

"Well, in that case," Bregon said, placing his hand back on the hilt of his sword, "this is—"

"Vargklo!" Binty enthused, her eyes wide and her smile beaming.

The runes on Vargklo glowed a subtle burnt orange colour, and Bregon slid his hand from the hilt to the blade to calm it.

"You certainly know your swords, little lady; how do you know of this one?"

"That is a sword of legend. I recognised the runic markings from the many stories I have read, the moment I saw it, but until now I thought it a beautiful myth. I am probably also the only one here besides yourself who can hear it whine."

"You are right. She is beautiful. Now where was I? That's right, I wanted to introduce you all to Ligl." Bregon ran his hand down the length of his scabbard. "Everyone, this is Ligl."

Bregon's scabbard suddenly shapeshifted into a quag called Ligl, and while everyone sat in stunned silence for a moment, Ligl spoke.

"Grock, gil ta jesk?"

"Bruh es, esh ta shemla, Ligl?" Grock said.

"Na."

Grock and Ligl rushed into each other's arms and embraced, both of them now wittering on at the speed of light in their native language, completely forgetting about the shocked friends sat around them. Realising this, Grock explained that Ligl was his best friend. They had been together on the day Perquag was consumed and had not seen each other since the day Graimel adopted him.

Ligl went on to add that when she left the orphanage after never being adopted, she travelled using the vast wealth her parents left her. Until one day she came across an injured dwarf girl being hunted by wolves, so she did what all quags were good at, and dived over her, shielding them from the hunters, protecting her from danger.

After the wolves gave up the hunt, she revealed her true form and introduced herself. Wanting to reward Ligl for saving her, the young dwarf girl, who turned out to be Bregon's daughter Koocie, invited her home. On discovering Ligl was an orphan, Bregon invited her to become a part of the family, and she had stayed there ever since.

Grock and Ligl left the table and went to sit by the fire. They had a lot of catching up to do and a lot of stories to tell each other. Once they were out of earshot, Bregon's demeanour took on a more serious tone.

"Walk with me a moment, will you." Bregon got up from the table, taking Vargklo in hand, and gestured for Graimel to follow. "I have a task I need you to undertake, Graimel Tock, something I cannot complete myself, but a promise I made to Ligl many years back. I need you to find Ligl's family, and if possible, rescue them. I know this is no simple task, but if you can do this, I promise you we will stand by your side in this fight as equals."

"Then I have a task to do, something which I myself also promised Grock."

"Ligl has a portal stone which will take you straight to the Quagmires of Sturm undetected, and also allow you passage straight back here. Rest here for now until you are ready to leave, and I will acquire the stone for you."

Bregon gave Graimel a polite nod of acknowledgement and left for his quarters. Krahns poured himself and the others another horn of mead, and asked Dougal where he got his dagger. Dougal took out his dagger and gave it to Krahns to look at, whilst explaining how he came about it.

Krahns was about to press his finger against the blade to test its sharpness when Binty snatched it from his hand and insisted Dougal sheathe it immediately. She went on to explain to Krahns about the potency of that blade, who was both impressed and relieved she had intervened.

"Where are your weapons, little one?" Sleip asked.

"My hands, my mind, and my words are the only weapons I need."

"Very poetic."

"You wouldn't say that if you saw her use them," Dougal said, "and if you want to see her use them, you only need call her delicate."

Binty scowled, and Graimel and Dougal started laughing.

"I guess that would be a bad move," Sleip said, smiling.

"Go on, Sleip, call her delicate," Krahns said, laughing with the others.

"I would never dare to insult a warrior of such indomitable spirit, who holds herself with such elegance and poise, and whose only weapon is her mind. I would, however, ask why she did not wear armour?"

"I doubt there is any armour that is of use to a pixie. Our speed is our defence, and armour would slow us down."

"I believe my other daughter could craft such armour. She is a master of design and blacksmithing. Would you come with me to meet her?"

"It would be my honour; do I have time, Graimel?"

"Of course. I have some thinking to do. We will wait here."

"We have some drinking to do as well," Krahns added.

Sleip and Binty left the great hall and headed back the way they came until they reached a small tunnel leading away from the main furnaces. At the end of the tunnel lay a huge forge and furnace, and stood at the anvil moulding metal to her will, a solitary girl.

"Efraj!" Sleip called out.

The girl lifted her head and paused in her work.

"One minute and I will be with you, father," Efraj yelled over the noise of the forge, before continuing with the job at hand.

Sparks danced through the air as she skilfully struck her

hammer with speed and accuracy, a unique and mesmerising magic all of its own that Binty and Sleip were happy to watch while they waited. After a few minutes, Efraj pulled off her gloves, walked over, and hugged her father.

"Who is your pixie friend, father?"

"Efraj, this is Binty Malice."

"It is my pleasure to meet you," Binty said, bowing to Efraj.

"And it is my honour to meet you, for your name is one I know."

Sleip looked at Efraj, confused and questioning.

"I read father, unlike you."

"Fair enough, but do you think you can craft such armour that would be of use to a pixie?"

"Armour for Binty Malice? It would be an honour and a privilege. If I can just take a few measurements, I will start straight away." Efraj's eyes widened, unblinking, as her enthusiastic smile spread from ear to ear.

She took the measurements she needed and disappeared into her studio to start her design. Sleip led Binty back to the tavern and had to admit how astounded he was by the affect she had had on his daughter, making him realise he needed to read more.

Graimel and Dougal were talking to Bregon as Binty and Sleip entered the great hall, noting their return Graimel called for Harg. Grock was to remain in Ildjorden with Ligl until they returned from this errand.

"We are almost ready to depart. Are you both ready?" Graimel asked.

"Where exactly are we going?" Dougal asked.

"Into the unknown. Hands in."

The moment their hands touched Ligl's portal stone, they vanished, and in less than an instant, they arrived in the Quagmires of Sturm.

The first thing that struck Dougal were his wet feet, but wet ankles and wet knees soon followed. Thankfully, he then felt Graimel's hand pulling him out of the morass he arrived in.

"Oh! Well, I'm pleased to see you two arrived without landing in this filthy bog," Dougal said, the sarcasm in his voice unintentional.

In fact, he was thankful they had arrived in unscathed, dry, and on solid ground, and been able to pull him out of the mire before he sank any further.

It may have been because Binty picked up on the sarcasm in his voice, or it may have been accidental, but she left Dougal walking in his sodden lounge pants for more than half an hour. When she did eventually offer to dry him, Dougal did not connect the dots, and therefore any intended punishment was lost on him.

Once again, Binty and Dougal found themselves following Graimel without questioning where they were headed, or for what purpose. This time, however, it was the blind leading the blinder. Graimel was having to walk and plan at the same time, because at this moment, he was at a loss for what to do next. So his current cunning plan was to keep walking until he had one.

He had always loved the Quagmires of Sturm, for although they sound awful, they were quite the opposite.

Aside from the unfortunate way in which Dougal arrived, and had it not been for Graimel would have left, the area they had appeared in was quite beautiful. There were luscious greens and purples, dashes of bumblebee yellow and splashes of malbec red. Every single plant seemed to be an abstract miraculous creation, and nothing quite like either Binty or Dougal had ever seen. Leaves so large they could be used as a boat, flowers big enough for Dougal to stand inside, although not recommended as not all the plants were vegan, and vines as strong as friendly goblin mine spider silk.

"I've got it," Graimel said, stopping in his tracks. "If I can work out the direction of the time slip, we may be able to find out what happened to Perquag. Come now, the border to Perquag is not far beyond the treeline up ahead."

Within a matter of minutes, they arrived at a hole in the ground, the border of which spread as far as they could see in both directions. Around the edges of the hole everything was dead or dying, gripping to terra firma with a kind of desperate hope.

"Stay away from the edge of the hole. We don't know if the gravitational pull is still active, and if we get pulled in, I don't know what happens to us. So let's not find out in case we disappear like Perquag did."

"How close is too close?" Dougal asked.

"Well, if you feel yourself being pulled into that ruddy big hole, then you're too close."

"That's brilliant advice, thanks!"

"Take a scout round and see if you can find anything that might help us."

They split up and scoured the general area. Binty noted this was no normal hole in the ground, it was a hole, sure enough. But there were no visible sides, nor did there appear to be any depth to it. It was as if someone had placed a sheet of paper on a black tabletop and tore a piece out of the middle. Like a shiny black lake of ice, inviting you to skate across it.

She was about to edge a little closer to examine the anomaly when she heard a loud crack. A massive branch broke away from one of the trees in the dead zone around the hole and hurtled into the blackness, vanishing before her eyes. She recoiled a few steps as she glanced around, making sure she could still see the others, and a sense of relief flowed over her.

Dougal had one of those rare lightbulb moments. He remembered the huge vines they passed earlier and thought, if we can tie one off somehow and then throw the other end towards the hole, that might give Graimel what he needed. He spotted Graimel a few hundred yards away, hurried over and explained his idea to him.

"I think you might have something there. Show me these vines. Binty, I think we will need your help."

Dougal took them back to where he saw the vines, and Binty flew up into the sky, following what seemed to be the oldest one. Through the canopy and along the tops of the trees, she traced it until she found its end point by a giant boulder in the side of a cliff. She tugged at the vine, but it did not budge, so she tugged again, but this time she tugged with all her might.

"OW!" Came a deep booming voice, like a thunderclap in a cave.

Not perturbed, Binty tugged again.

"OW!" Came the voice again.

Binty dropped the vine and darted over to where it disappeared into the rock, but no matter how much she pushed and pulled, she could not remove it. In frustration, she pounded her fists against the side of the cliff.

"OW!" Came the voice for a third time.

Binty paused for a moment to think before saying.

"Hello, my name is Binty. Are you a talking rock?"

The rock moved in front of her, and she took a few steps back, then the whole side of the cliff turned, and she looked up straight into the disconsolate eye of a pained rock giant.

"Me Tenk, Tenk's tooth hurts. Please stop, you strong, but not strong enough to move it."

"Well, how can I help you?"

"You cannot help," Tenk mumbled. "Tenk waiting for vine to reach big hole, then the power of big hole will swallow vine and pull Tenk's tooth out."

"But you are a giant. Can you not just pull it out yourself?"

"Tenk scared." Tenk moved his enormous arm and rested his hand on his jaw. "Tenk will wait, will only be a few years now."

In the distance, Graimel and Dougal steadied themselves as the ground rumbled beneath them and a booming drummed their ears. Both of them instantly thought EARTHQUAKE! and frantically called Binty, however she was still fully engaged with Tenk.

"I have an idea how we can help you, and you can help me and my friends, and you could rid yourself of that tooth in the process."

"Tenk listens."

"The big hole is not strong enough to pull Tenk in, is it?" Binty asked.

"Nothing can pull Tenk, Tenk very strong, but hole ate Tenk's girl, and Tenk's tooth hurt ever since. Tenk sad."

"Then I have a plan. Follow me and I will explain."

Tenk clambered to his feet and shook the dust and debris from his body. Down beneath the canopy, Graimel and Dougal were thinking some kind of strange eclipse was now taking place in unison with an earthquake, and were wondering if they were linked. Little did they know they were, and if they could have seen through the trees, they would have known why.

Tenk followed Binty as she explained in brief what she wanted him to do, before zipping beneath the canopy as Tenk pushed his head through and smiled at Graimel and Dougal.

"Tenk, these are my friends, Graimel and Dougal. Guys, this is Tenk. He is going to help us."

After hearing Binty's idea, they agreed it was a most excellent plan. Although Dougal insisted on it being stressed, he was the one who took them back to the vines and should therefore get some credit. They duly noted this by giving him a firm a pat on his back.

They were soon back at the vast lake of nothingness, and Binty put her plan into action. She flew up to Tenk and reminded him of what to do.

"I will throw the vine into the big hole, as soon as you feel your tooth pop out, grab the vine before it disappears."

Tenk prepared his hands loosely around the vine while Binty counted to three and cast the vine into the void. As the coils disappeared into the blackness, Tenk adjusted his stance, ready for the pull, then SNAP!

Tenk howled in pain, but remembering what Binty said, he clenched his fists around the vine. Smoke swirled from his fists as the damp vine slid through his hands. He squeezed his stone fingers into his palms until he could grip no tighter. With a thwack, his tooth hit the side of his clenched fist, stopping the vine from disappearing any further into the void. In readiness for the next part of the plan, Tenk pulled the vine back out of the void until there was enough to secure around his waist.

"Well done," Binty said, zooming over and giving him a huge kiss.

"Tenk already have girl, but little one is nice."

As Graimel and Dougal were studying the way the vine entered the hole and vanished, Binty joined them, but none of them could fathom what was happening.

"It's no good. This tells us nothing," Graimel said.

"Well, we have learned one thing, and that is whatever that hole is doing, it is not making anything disappear, because Tenk could pull some of the vine back through."

"You're a genius Binty."

"I am? I mean I am!"

"Yes, I have it. I will climb down the vine and see where it goes."

"What! I take it back. I am not a genius. That's suicide. You can't—"

"Hush. If you tie me on with some strands of that unbreakable vine, I should be able to pass through the void safely, find Perquag, and climb back. Genius!"

"I don't like this plan Graimel, I don't like it at all," Binty said anxiously.

"It's the only one we have. What do you say Dougal?"

Whilst Graimel and Binty were arguing, Dougal snuck away and spoke to Tenk. Having done a lot of rock climbing in the past, he knew this was a job for him, and not a grumpy old notadwarf with stumpy legs and a paunch. He tied a finer thread of vine around himself and passed the rest of the coil to Tenk. He then tied another loop of the same thread between himself and the enormous vine Binty had thrown into the hole. The only thing that could fail him now were his knots, and possibly his knees.

By the time they spotted him, he was secured to the vine and being lowered into the hole by Tenk. Binty was about to go after him when Graimel stopped her.

"It's too late. He is already over the dead zone."

In anxious silence, they watched as Tenk masterfully unwound the fine vine from around his hands, gradually lowering Dougal into the blackness, and to whatever fate awaited him.

All they could do now was wait.

# 26

# REUNITED

Although Dougal was fine with heights, he had not thought about what would be on the other side of this hole. He had just found out. As soon as he vanished from the Quagmires of Sturm, he had appeared in wherever this was. The big black hole hung above him like the night sky, and for a second he thought about climbing back up to safety, but his friends were relying on him. He was not going to let them down.

With his anxiety subdued, he made the mistake of glancing down, and squealed, only a little squeal, but a squeal, nonetheless. He quickly regained his composure, then lost it, found it again, and finally managed to maintain it.

From up here, the ground looked like a lily pad floating in an ocean, but at least there was ground. The problem was how far beneath him. It was going to take him hours to climb down. He tried to work out how high he was, but the more he thought about it, the more he started to lose his composure again. To calm himself, he thought about the last time he had been this high up. It was on the flight over to Denmark, and he did not remember being scared. Of course, then he was sat safely on the back of a dragon, "Safely," he chuckled to himself. Now he was hanging on to a piece of vine.

With such a distance to descend, he knew the fastest way down besides falling, which rarely ended well, would be to abseil. Dougal gave the vine two sharp tugs, signalling to Tenk to let the vine out a little quicker.

He put his trust in his knots, pressed his feet against the vine, lent back, and pushed himself away a little, just as Tenk gave him some slack, and he flew about 5m closer to the ground. This was going to be much faster than climbing.

Gradually building up confidence, speed, and distance, he descended, always remembering, not too far and not too fast. The closer he got, the more he could make out. First there were mountains and forests, then what he assumed to be houses and streets. And then he started to see figures appearing in the streets, their hands pointing in his direction, gesticulating wildly as they gazed skywards.

Dougal politely waved back, and one by one the figures vanished, pop, pop, pop, until there were none.

After about two hours, he silently rejoiced as he placed his feet back on solid ground. All he needed to do now was to confirm this was the place they sought, if only there was someone to ask, or a sign.

"Hello? I'm here to help."

A window creaked on its hinges, snatching his attention, sending his eyes darting back and forth. The hairs on his arms and the back of his neck prickled and stood, and an icy shiver crept uncomfortably down his spine.

"Hedge," Dougal muttered, whilst rubbing his arms.

As he slunk through the streets, he became overwhelmed by the sense of hidden eyes watching him. Convinced he could feel invisible breaths brushing his skin. He paused for a moment and warily peered over his shoulder, expecting to come face to face with some monstrous beastie, but there was only the empty street. A smirk eked across his face as his eyes continued to scan the streets. Seconds later, he spun around while emitting an explosive roar and flinging his arms about wildly, secretly praying they did not make contact with anything. They didn't.

Now, if you ask any dwarf, they will tell you. Spinning and roaring after guzzling a few horns of mead can have unwanted side effects. Fortunately for Dougal, it had been a few hours since his indulgence, and so the only side effect on this occasion was an embarrassingly enormous belch. With a cautious sigh of relief, he picked up his pace a little and followed a path leading out of the town, hoping it would lead him to enlightenment.

In the distance, he saw what appeared to be an ocean, and as he ran towards it, the path he followed unsurprisingly ended abruptly. To the left of the path, fixed into the earth less than a metre from what Dougal thought to be an ocean, but was in fact a vast expanse of nothingness, was a small ornate green wooden sign. He grasped hold of it and leant over enough to read what it said, his knuckles whitening as his grip tightened.

Welcome to Perquag

Almost losing his grip in excitement, which would not have ended well for all those concerned, he maintained his composure and thought, we have found it, I must get back to Graimel. He twirled himself back onto the path, and with gusto in his step, he headed back towards the town and back to his friends.

Feeling rather pleased with himself, he was paying no attention to his surroundings, and with a sudden and surprising whoop sound, a huge, thick net engulfed him. Quags appeared from everywhere as he struggled to release himself, and he realised these were the figures he saw when climbing down the vine. It made sense to him now. They most likely thought he was a hunter, and used their super effective cloaking ability to hide from him.

Dougal stopped struggling, hoping these quags were as peaceful as the two he had already met, and the reason he was here hunting for them. Although I must remember not to use that word in front of them, he thought.

An enormous crowd gathered, all talking in their native language and pointing at the stranger in the net. Dougal realised he was probably the first human they had ever met, and it was unlikely any of them spoke or understood English. Why would they? he thought. With his options somewhat limited, he decided the best course of action would be to repeat Grock's name, in the hope someone knew it.

This he did, and nothing changed, apart from the increasing amount of quags pointing and gesticulating in his direction. But he kept going, as this was his only real hope. A face appeared at the net and seemed fervently interested in the word he was repeating.

"Grock," Dougal said.

"Grock," the quag repeated, and waved to another in the crowd.

They barged through the crowd until they were close enough to hold hands, then the inquisitive quag nodded their head in Dougal's direction.

"Grock," Dougal said.

Both quags smiled and pushed their hands through the net to touch Dougal, and as they did, they both uttered, "Grock."

And Dougal replied with the only word he could.

They pulled at the net, trying to free Dougal from his snare, shouting at the other quags to help, but none would.

"Ligl and Grock," Dougal said, remembering the name of Grock's best friend.

A sudden stunned hush engulfed the crowd, and two more quags approached him.

"Ligl and Grock," he uttered once more.

The two new quags shouted into the crowd, and cheers and cries filled the air. No sooner had they torn the net from him, when all those present rushed to embrace this stranger to their land. And although unsure what was happening, Dougal thought it has got to be better than being trussed up in a net.

They took Dougal by the hands and led him back up the path towards the town. The whole of the assembled crowd followed, and as they made their way through the streets, more quags swelled their numbers. Just before they got back into the town, they took a right fork in the road and headed out into the wilderness. The amount of quags now following them surprised Dougal, all of them shouting, cheering, and singing, in a carnival like atmosphere.

They passed through some tall trees, and as they came out into the open again, they were faced with a mountain of rock. The two quags, who Dougal assumed to be Ligl's family, motioned for him to stay while they walked up to the base of the mountain.

"Lehle," they called, and waited.

The ground shook in a familiar way and the mountain moved, then the roll of thunder as it spoke. The booming of its words incomprehensible to Dougal, but he found himself being ushered forward, indicating for him to speak.

"Hello, Lehle, is it?"

"Why the little ones wake Lehle?"

"You speak English."

"I speak many languages; the common tongue is one."

"I have come through the hole in the sky, looking for this place."

"Tenk!" Lehle cried.

"Yes, yes, I have met Tenk. He helped me."

"Tenk here?" Lehle said, clambering to her feet.

"No, Tenk on the other side of the hole, holding the vine for me to climb back."

"Show Lehle."

They made their way back to the town in the same carnival type atmosphere, a wave of euphoria seemed to flow through the crowd. As they reached the vine, Lehle's eyes followed the leafy stem up into the sky. An irrepressible smile beamed across her face as she grasped hold and bound the vine around her hand. She smashed her hands into the ground, digging into the earth until she gripped the very bedrock of Perquag. Once satisfied, she whipped out one hand and yanked on the vine, before grasping the bedrock once again, and waited.

Back in the Quagmires of Sturm, Graimel and Binty were looking and feeling as despondent as a lonely giant. In fact, as despondent as the giant they were currently in the company of. When that giant stumbled towards the hole, they thought he must be tired, and rushed over to tell him to sit for a while. But as they did so, a huge smile broke across his face.

"LEHLE!" Tenk yelled, for all his worth.

He gripped the vine, wrapping it around his knuckles and leant backwards, pulling with all his might. The vine moved a little, but the resistance was immense.

"LEHLE!"

This time he woke the other sleeping giants, and from out of nowhere, two more grey stone titans rose to their feet, stretching and yawning as they approached Tenk.

"Lehle," Tenk said, showing them the vine.

With Tenk maintaining his grip on the vine, the other two giants each looped one of their arms through his and all three giants heaved. This time, the vine moved. The three giants formed a line, and with immaculate precision timing they kept heaving, helping to reunite their friends.

Without warning came a deafening bang, a bang so loud it was heard on Bodmin Moor, making Bounce bark and wag his tail. A bang so loud, that for a second, Bregon thought one of the forges in Ildjorden had exploded, but knowing that could not happen, he sighed with relief and smiled.

The noise was such that every living thing in the Quagmires of Sturm was temporarily deafened, but there was silent jubilation. Graimel and Binty picked themselves up off the floor and rubbed their eyes in disbelief. The hole that once was, was no more. Binty could see Dougal picking himself up from beside another giant, and she flew straight over to him as fast as she could.

"You did it. You are amazing," Binty said.

"Nope, Lehle and Tenk did it. I guess love knows no limits."

As Tenk embraced Lehle, he realised that all his pain had gone, and not just his toothache. After thanking them all for their help in bringing his Lehle home, he picked up his tooth and presented it to Dougal. Dougal thanked him for the kind and generous gesture, but there was no way he could take a giant's tooth anywhere. With a gentle shrug, Tenk placed the tooth back on the ground, took Lehle's hand, and together they walked off to sit once more above the forest.

Dougal introduced Graimel and Binty to Grock's and Ligl's family, and Graimel explained to them in Quagish the story so far. As he did so, an exuberant group of quags came and moved the giant's tooth into the centre of the town. Once happy with its placement, they etched the date and names of their saviours into it, and there it would sit in perpetuity. Perquag had been recovered from the unrecoverable, the time slip had been erased, and normality restored to the Quagmires of Sturm.

The mayor of Perquag, Blim, held a huge celebration in honour of their saviours. Blim called Dougal, Graimel, and Binty up to the stage to thank them for everything they had done. Luckily, Graimel was able to translate and thus avoid a troublesome misunderstanding, as thanks in Quagish can sound rather aggressive. With the formalities concluded, he presented each of them with a small chunk of the giant's tooth as a permanent reminder of their heroism.

The party would rage on until the following morning, but our heroes had more pressing matters. Graimel gathered Grock's and Ligl's family together and whipped out the portal stone.

"Let's go to a family reunion," Graimel said, and placed his hand on the stone.

Everyone else followed suit and looked to Graimel.

"The Great Hall of Ildjorden."

Seconds later, they were in the presence of Bregon Skovin once more.

# 27

# A QUIET NIGHT IN

Bregon sat fidgeting upon his throne whilst impatiently tapping his feet, eager for the return of the adventurers. He was wondering if he had tasked them with an impossible mission, when Graimel stumbled into the great hall. Bregon leapt from his throne and charged towards them.

"Welcome back, my friends," Bregon said, throwing his arms out to embrace them. "I hadn't been expecting you back so soon."

"It is thanks to Dougal's bravery we are back with such haste, that is for sure."

Bregon released Graimel from his embrace and took a hold of Dougal's hand, getting down on one knee to show all those present his respect for the human.

"I am in your debt, Dougal. Please, name your price."

"Friendship."

"Bah! You are already a friend of Ildjorden. Is there nothing else?"

"If I already have your friendship, all I would ask for is a little sleep," Dougal said, trying to stop himself from yawning.

"A strange request if I do say so. I will show you to your quarters, and in the morning, we celebrate."

# A QUIET NIGHT IN

Dougal entered his room, closed the door behind him and leant against it. The day was done, and a sense of relief flowed over him. Not only was he still alive, but for the first time in his life, he felt a true sense of worth. They had accomplished something today, something huge. His actions had mattered. He had been integral in helping to restore Perquag to its rightful place in the universe, and bring families back together. Overwhelmed by all these thoughts, Dougal slid down the door until he was sat on the floor, and cried.

Binty entered her room and had not even closed the door when the astounding view from the full-length window engulfed her, drawing her over to absorb it. The window looked out into what appeared to be the heart of a volcano. Fire and molten rock leaping up into the air like an amazing circus act. Rivers of lava flowed in and out of the giant lake of dancing flames as it bubbled and waved hypnotically, warming her spirit.

Binty reached out towards the glass, expecting to recoil from the intensity of the heat, but only a pleasant, summery glow emanated into the room. In awe, she placed her hands upon the glass and smiled. The wondrous spectacle before her eyes left her stunned, unable to comprehend the reality of the situation she found herself in. She was in a room, in a volcano, and she had not been fried. It was amazing.

"I come and sleep down here myself sometimes," Efraj said.

Binty spun about.

"Sorry, I did not mean to startle you. Only I heard you had returned and wanted to bring you this gift. Can I come in?" Efraj asked.

"Efraj, of course, come in. It is so lovely to see you."

Efraj entered the room carrying a tiny gift parcel, wrapped in an elegant leaf green paper, and finished with a silver bow.

"This is for you," Efraj said, presenting the gift to Binty. "I do hope you like it."

Binty took the gift and placed it on the dressing table near the window, thanking Efraj.

"Can I open it now?"

"Of course."

She tugged at the silver bow and it slipped undone. Casting it to one side, she unpicked the tape and unfolded the beautiful wrapping paper. She lifted the lid to reveal the suit of armour Efraj had crafted for her. Once again she was awestruck, as she lifted the exquisitely engraved and shaped breastplate from the box, the gleaming black and silver armour piece reflecting the red and amber glow of the volcanoes fires.

"It's so beautiful."

Binty's face lit up, not only from the glow outside, but from the happiness in her heart. Nobody had ever made her anything quite like this, and she had been around a long time.

"And it is so light. How did you craft this in less than a day?"

"All things are possible if you believe they are, and of course you are quite tiny," Efraj said, chuckling a little.

"Can I try it on?"

"Please do. I would love to know how it fits and feels."

Binty picked up the box and slipped behind a privacy screen. After a few moments, she shot up into the air from behind the screen, screaming.

"I am Binty Malice. Fear me, for I am protected by the power of Efraj!"

And she swooped and darted around the room numerous times, rolling and weaving, turning, and diving, before coming to a stop right in front of Efraj's eyes.

"This is amazing. I never thought it possible to make something so beautiful, and yet so comfortable and light. It feels like I am wearing almost nothing. I have to think, how could it offer me any protection? I mean, not that it matters. I love it."

"Do you trust me?" Efraj said, looking straight into Binty's eyes.

"Why, of course," Binty said, glancing at Efraj's hand hovering over the hammer on her belt.

"Then all I ask is you try it out, and if it so much as gets a scratch, I will extinguish my forge and take up darning socks for my father."

"Thank you, Efraj, it is without doubt the most wonderful gift ever. I must think of a way to thank you."

"You are most welcome, Binty Malice. It has been my honour to make armour for you. I will leave you to rest and see you tomorrow. Good night, Binty."

"Good night, Efraj, and thank you again."

The door closed and Efraj glided back home on a cloud of elation, whilst Binty continued to swoop and zoom around her room. I must show Dougal, she thought, as she stopped to admire her new attire in the reflection of the ornate dressing mirror. With a gleeful twirl, she zipped out of her room and down the hall, but as she was about to knock on his door, she detected what she thought to be a faint sobbing coming from the other side.

"Dougal?" Binty whispered, gently tapping on the door.

"One moment please."

The door opened ajar, and Binty shot through the gap and into the room.

"I came to show you my new armour. Are you okay?" Binty said, noticing the redness of Dougal's eyes and face.

"Yeah, I'm okay, thanks. I think I've either got something in my eye, or the heat from the volcano is making it look like I have been crying, but I assure you I have not."

"Okay, but if someone has upset you, tell me and I will sort them out."

"I told you I'm fine. I'm exhausted, that's all."

Binty plonked herself down on Dougal's shoulder.

"Please talk to me."

"It's just… for the first time in my life, I feel like I mattered, like I made a difference. I was brave, I have never been brave. I helped bring Perquag back from wherever it was, and before today, I did not even know Perquag existed, or giants, for that matter." Dougal walked over to the sweeping window looking out into the volcano. "Wow! That is amazing. You guys are amazing, the things you can do, the powers you have, and how you use them selflessly for the good of others, without them ever knowing. Today I felt a part of that, and it's so overwhelming."

"You still don't understand. You, are the centre of everything. Without you in the world, there is no existence for anything. This is why Graimel revealed himself to you, and why people have died to protect you. Nobody ever expected Bedougalnn to be discovered, and I can guarantee no one ever expected it to be a human, that is for sure. You are kind of a myth. We all believe in your existence, but never expected to encounter you."

"So, I am a god?"

"Certainly not!"

"So how come humans do not know of… Bedougalnn? Sorry, it feels strange referring to myself in the third person. I mean, we have a lot of myths and legends, and 'The Legend of The Bedougalnn' is not one of them."

"Because humans have a habit of erasing the parts of history that do not fit with the current thinking. Look at what they did to witches and warlocks for instance, and I bet you've never even heard of the Somsi Meruca?"

"Well, as a matter of fact I have, Graimel mentioned it, but he never elaborated."

"Oh, in that case, we will leave that there. My point is, in time, all humans just stopped believing in magic."

"But humans do believe in magic. We have huge magic shows and loads of movies about magic."

"If you believed in magic, you would not keep passing out every time you encountered something new."

"I'm not doing that as much now."

"Because you are genuinely starting to believe, there is a difference between wanting to believe, and believing."

"So what exactly am I then?"

"You are the key to… no, some things are best left unsaid. It has been a long day; we should both get some sleep."

As she headed towards the door, Dougal could not withdraw his eyes, mesmerised by the totality of her.

"You know that armour really is quite amazing, befitting of the wearer, I suppose. It makes you look almost regal."

She passed through the door smiling from ear to ear and proceeded back to her room, where she slept soundly until morning.

Dougal sat on his windowsill, transfixed by the beauty and power of the volcano. As his eyelids wavered and grew heavy, the warm glow soothed his troubled mind. Moments later, he fell asleep and subsequently fell off the windowsill with a thud. He crawled to his bed, went back to sleep, and dreamt of giants and dragons.

Graimel, on the other hand, once again disappeared to complete some business. Twisting time to help, save, and rescue no less than 1300 people from an unwarranted fate, and all of them would put this down to luck. He then popped in for a quick cup of tea with Janet, Fimor, and Bounce before arriving back in his room in Ildjorden with still time for a quick nap.

After being shown to their room, Grock's parents, Beribo and Aymms, hurried next door to their friends Orm and Voeli. The four of them talked into the early hours, the overwhelming anticipation of being reunited with their children, keeping them awake until they fell asleep in the chairs where they sat.

Back in the Quagmires of Sturm, the party continued to rage on in Perquag, with a constant stream of visitors from all over. At one point, such was the volume of quags and other species, that Blim, concerned Perquag might break away from the Quagmires of Sturm again, announced his worries to the gathered masses.

The visiting giants decided to allay the mayor's fears and tested this for him by jumping up and down in unison. The stunned and fearful crowd let out a choral sigh of relief, when apart from a few damaged houses and spilt drinks, everything stayed intact. It is fair to say, Blim needed to sit down for quite some time afterwards.

Speaking of giants, after Tenk and Lehle had sat hand in hand above the forest for a while, relishing being reunited. They wrapped around each other to form a huge new mountain and reached up to the stars. Together again.

# 28

## SECRET PLACES & VALKYRIES

Dawn broke, forges were stoked, and anvils were struck, and in the great hall preparations were being made for a huge celebration. Ligl and Grock had been invited to take a tour of the whole of Ildjorden, guided by none other than Krahns. Ligl protested a little as she had already seen most of Ildjorden, however Krahns reminded her Grock had not. Not only that, but he was looking forward to showing them both around, and besides, there were still a couple of secret places he could take them.

Of course, this was all a ploy to keep them away from the great hall and the forthcoming surprise. Krahns had spent the early hours polishing his armour and sharpening Ojom in readiness for the impending surprise event. However, he told Ligl and Grock he wanted to look his best whilst he escorted them around Ildjorden. Now, although they thought this considerate of him, neither of them saw the point, or in fact, beyond it.

He started the tour with the old forge, where dishevelled dwarfs bimbled about plying their wares, ensuring every customer got the best price. From here they headed through to the legendary forging area, stopping by Efraj's workshop for a quick gossip. The rumour mill was alight with talk of an upcoming, soon to be released, new flavour of mead, Earl Grey.

Not wanting to spoil any surprises, Krahns avoided the guest quarters and took the long way past the forsaken dungeon. Although not the safest route, nothing would dare trouble him down here.

Deeper into the bowels of Ildjorden they headed, down a narrow glass sided stairwell that led them below the enormous lava pool. As they sank beneath the lava, they paused for a moment, placing their hands upon the glass, and just like Binty, they could not understand how they could be so close to death, and yet so apparently safe.

The walls of the stairwell became ever darker and damper, and Ligl realised she had never been here before, and was not even aware this stairwell existed. The gloomier it became, the tighter they gripped each other's hands, fearing what lay ahead. At the bottom of the stairs, an imposing studded oak door barred their way, the hefty forged golden lock somehow glittering in the darkness.

Krahns gestured to Ligl and Grock to keep quiet as he took Ojom from his back and stroked the blade against the lock. With a click, the lock released. He slid the bolt across on the door, trying not to make a sound, before easing the door open and creeping forward. Ligl and Grock followed behind with caution, extreme caution. Krahns waited until they were both inside the room, and eased the door shut behind them.

The room itself was nondescript. A large circular room, about 25m across with damp mossy walls, and appeared to be carved out of the very bedrock beneath Ildjorden. There were torches affixed to the walls, which threw out enough light to distinguish gloomy alcoves around the entire room. In the centre of which was a twinkling pool the size of a giant's hula hoop, surrounded by a low wall made from thousands of slices of grey slate. Cool fresh water drizzled from the blackness above, continuously replenishing the pool. Silently striking the surface without so much as a splash, in an eerie, nonsensical way.

There were run-offs for the overflowing water, which all led to a single hole in the floor. This was of no interest or consequence, for that matter, to anyone from Ildjorden. But this run-off went deep into the earth, eventually resurfacing outside a small town called Pure`pe in Australia, where it was bottled and sold all over the world as Pure`pe Water, renowned for its unique mineral content and flavour.

The door shut with an over obvious loud click, and the room seemed to go darker than what would be expected. Ligl and Grock huddled together and went to huddle close to Krahns before realising he no longer stood by them. Lights began to appear in the alcoves until they were all illuminated by two fiery white orbs, and as they grew in unison, Ligl and Grock realised these were not lights, but pairs of eyes.

Grock scanned the darkness for Krahns. How could he abandon them here like this? Then he spotted him sat on the edge of the pool, but it was too late for them to reach him. All the eyes moved in one motion and closed in on Krahns as he sat relaxing, drinking water from the pool. Grock could not bear to watch and did not want Ligl to either, so he drew her to the ground and hid them both, and waited for the screams to end.

The screams, however, did not end, they never even began. The only sound that pierced the gloom was laughter. Ligl peered from underneath Grock and could see Krahns surrounded by huge worgs licking his face, drinking water from his hand, and having their tummies rubbed, and convinced Grock to look. Both lay there in astonishment.

"Come on guys, don't you want to meet my friends," Krahns said.

Grock got up and helped Ligl off the floor, and as they stood there daring not to make a sound, the worgs turned and bounded towards them. The capering worgs bowled them to the floor like a pair of skittles as they raced around in circles, chasing their tails with their tongues lolloping from between their massive glistening canines. The biggest of all the worgs remained loyally at Krahns' side throughout.

"Stop messing about and come over here."

Grock dragged Ligl back to her feet, and they eased their way over to Krahns, who was doing his best not to fall into the pool of water laughing.

"I would love for you to meet Axtred, my best friend."

Axtred held out his sizable white paw to Grock and Ligl.

"He wants to shake," Krahns said.

Although a little unsure, they took hold of Axtred's paw and shook it, like shaking hands with a close friend. Axtred then walked over to the single hole in the floor, and with precise aim, peed straight down the hole. The other worgs followed suit, and in Pure`pe, they loaded another batch of mineral water on to a truck.

"I told you I would take you somewhere you had never been before, Ligl."

"Ta bruh nin Krahns. Brimt ta."

"I have no idea what you said, but you are welcome."

"Sorry, Krahns, I automatically speak Quagish when I am around Grock. I mean to say, you sure did, Krahns. Thank you."

With a short sharp whistle Krahns called Axtred to heel and ruffled his fur, and as he did so, the other worgs came and lay at his feet. He went round them in turn, ruffling their fur, patting their heads, and shaking their paws. As he spoke their name, they dutifully returned to their bed in their alcove, Ulyc, Enpyn, Sylfos; Vollmond, Leln, Lelba. He turned back to Axtred and once again shook his paw. Axtred nodded and strode over to his bed, circled, and lay down.

"Are you guys coming, or are you staying to play with the pups?" Krahns said, as he sauntered across the room and through the eighth alcove, into his private quarters.

Chasing after him through the alcove, they entered another immense circular room. This time, a huge roaring fire dominated the central space, which clearly seconded as a forge. There was seating on one side facing an overgenerous tall window that had been cut into the rock, behind which was bubbling lava. If Dougal had been there, he would have thought it was the coolest lava lamp a person could ever wish for. But then it contained real lava. Who wouldn't want such an impossible thing?

Towards the back of the room was Krahns' sleeping area, flamboyantly decorated with an abundance of weapons and armours, and a pair of gummy boots. On the left was what appeared to be a kitchen, although far too clean to have seen any regular usage. Seven plush hand-woven rugs were strategically placed around the room. Two by the entrance, two by the sleeping area, one by the kitchen, one by the central fire, and one directly underneath the window of bubbling lava.

Krahns took a seat in the centre of the room and beckoned Ligl and Grock over, passed them a drink, and held his mug aloft.

"Skål!" he shouted.

"Skål!" Ligl and Grock cheered in unison.

And they all took a drink.

Krahns let out another short sharp whistle, and the worgs filed into the room, each taking to a rug and turning to face the entrance, before laying down.

"So, how has the tour been so far? Have you enjoyed it?"

"Yes thanks," Ligl said, smiling and making a thumb up gesture.

Grock simply raised his mug and shouted.

"Skål!"

Krahns took this to mean yes.

Mesmerised by the bubbling lava, they sat quietly sipping their drinks. Precisely 15 minutes after laying down, all seven worgs stood and moved to the rug to their left, turned, and lay to face the entrance once again, leaving Ligl and Grock to stare questioningly at Krahns.

"They share the responsibility of guarding me, and guarding

each other. Even Axtred takes his turn, as he knows a true leader always stands with his friends and allies as an equal. Although, as you can see, the one who lies at our feet by the fire is a little distracted."

Ligl and Grock glanced down. Leln was lying on her back having her tummy rubbed by Krahns, whilst chewing on a toy.

"This is the break rug. When they get to this rug, they know they can drop their guard, and enjoy doing whatever they want to do. Whether that is get a drink or something to eat, play with a toy or have a quick nap, it's their time."

"We should make a move; there is one more place to visit before we need to get back. Come, follow me," Krahns said, collecting their mugs and abandoning them in the sink on the way out.

They ambled back up the stairs and through to the old forge, and as they weaved through the narrow twisting corridors of stone leading towards the great hall, Krahns started counting wall sconces.

"Eleven," he said, pausing for a moment, as a couple of children came joyfully racing past carrying brightly coloured party supplies.

Once they were out of sight, Krahns clutched the sconce.

"Ow! That's hot," he said, trying to muffle his voice.

Ligl and Grock gawped at him, a little bemused. After all, it was fire, it should be hot. Sharing a puzzled glance, they simply shrugged and smirked as Krahns gingerly put his hand back on the sconce and flicked it to the left. There was an almost silent clunk as he released it and it sprang back.

This time Ligl and Grock's faces lit up with excitement, their eyes gleaming with anticipation as they gazed at each other, then at the wall sconce.

"A secret passage!" they said, their faces lighting up with glee.

With a glance up and down the corridor, Krahns rested against the wall, pushing it to reveal an opening. A cool gust of stale air rushed through into the hallway, extinguishing some of the torches. Wondering whether he should relight them, the sound of voices coming down the corridor made his decision and hastened his actions. He quickly ushered Ligl and Grock through the secret doorway before sliding through himself, and easing the wall back into place.

Ulap and Mad Mathis came around the corner arguing about whether an axe or a sword was better for harvesting Bulwith. Bulwith is a herb, and used predominately in the special blend of mead produced in Ildjorden. Not that some had not tried using it in their cooking, or their pipe for that matter, with mixed results.

The point being that Bulwith grew on dense, gnarly vines, which some of the finest blades would have trouble cutting through without blunting. So, while their argument was not without personal merit, it was pointless. As it was common knowledge, the best way to harvest Bulwith was to caress it away from the vine. The softest and most delicate hands would harvest far more, far quicker, than any axe or sword, and without causing damage to either the vine or the weapon of choice.

With their arms full of decorations for the great hall, and being deep in pointless conversation. They did not hear the clunk of the lock, or notice it was somewhat darker in the corridor than normal. They simply strolled past the secret passage, and continued on their way to the great hall to help with the preparations.

Krahns squeezed past to take the lead once again, upwards this time through narrow, dark, and dingy corridors with crumbling stonework, and more cobwebs than can be found in the Mines of Drothmaen. Thankfully, the spiders here were a lot smaller, which was a relief for Krahns, as like Harg, he was secretly a little scared of spiders. As in there is a little bit of water in the ocean, or that lava is a little bit hot.

The further they went, the more decrepit, dark, and dank it became. With a distinct lack of light on the path ahead, Krahns carefully blew the cobwebs from the last sconce and snatched up the torch before continuing into the dark. With the flicker of the flame now exaggerating every shadow, he could sense Grock and Ligl's growing trepidation.

"We are almost there, and do not worry, little ones, there is nothing to fear here... unless of course you don't like spiders," Krahns said, with a nervous laugh.

"Ah, here we are."

An ageing arched doorway stood before them, the accumulation of settled dust and cobwebs evidence the door had been closed for many years. This door also had a lock that looked remarkably similar to the one on the door with the worgs behind it. Only this lock was very unassuming and covered in rust. Krahns took Ojom, and once again stroked the blade against the lock. When nothing happened, he gave it a little tap, and with a whine and a crack, the door opened.

The blackness of the room seemed to seep out towards them in an almost beckoning manner, and Ligl and Grock gripped each other's hands nervously.

"Quickly now," Krahns said, hurrying their resisting bodies through the open door.

He slammed the door behind them and struck his torch against the wall. A ring of fire shot around the circumference of the room, throwing a dazzling array of colour and light over the entire chamber. The room oozed with ascendency, and whilst Grock and Ligl tried to absorb what they were seeing, Krahns explained.

"Welcome to Bregon's ancient throne room. This is where his people used to come to pay homage and make offerings to him."

"But why would they do that?" Ligl asked.

"From your question, I am guessing Bregon never told you he is a demi-god, and this was all part of the old ways."

"No, I thought he was just the boss around here, you know, like your king.

"You are right. He is our king, but he is so much more. You

see, he never approved of the whole god worship and tributes thing. There were things he wanted to change, like stop taking from those who had nothing to give. He wanted to move away from the old ways." Krahns took a seat in what used to be the council's ring, and put his feet up, something he would have been vilified for in the old days. "However, the other gods still wanted to be worshipped, so they exiled Bregon from Svartalfheim."

"But if he felt like that, then why is this throne room here?"

"Because change takes time. The people that came with us here to Ildjorden, needed time to adjust to Bregon's new way of thinking. That is why he constructed the great hall, so he could eat and be with his people, helping them realise he was one of them. He did not need to be worshipped, as long as he was respected."

"Can we take a look around?" Grock asked.

"Of course, but do me a favour and do not touch any of the artefacts. If you do, Bregon will know, and although I may or may not have his blessing to bring you here today, we do not want his wrath."

Ligl raced straight over to what she assumed was the throne at the far end of the room. Whilst Grock ran to the middle and stood stock still with mouth agape, surveying the entire room, trying to absorb the sheer wonder of it all. They were in a room of make believe, or so it felt. The walls appeared to be made from solid gold brick, as did the floor, and all looked as if it had been polished mere seconds before they entered.

Crystal like spheres interspersed the ring of fire that encircled the wall, taking the light and projecting it around the room in a myriad of colours. They gazed in awe, as the fire spread through channels in the roof to form burning arches of flame, cascading down from the centre of the ceiling like a waterfall to light an extravagant golden chandelier.

"I am guessing this is Bregon's throne? Can I sit on it?" Ligl asked.

"Yes it is, and of course you can."

Ligl hoisted herself onto the throne and sat looking as regal as she knew how. As she did so, a beam of blinding golden light burst down through the roof of the throne room. Krahns had forgotten about the security system.

"Who dares take the seat of Bregon Skovin, answer now or face the fury of the valkyries," Dynma said, her voice booming and fearsome.

"I am Ligl," Ligl said, trembling, and wondering whether she should vacate the seat. "Krahns said I could sit here," she added, pointing over towards him.

Krahns was already out of his seat and halfway across the room when the valkyrie spoke again.

"Your name is not known to me, Ligl. You must be judged."

"Dynma, no!" Krahns shouted, as he raced to put himself between Ligl and the valkyrie. "This is Bregon's ward. She has as much entitlement to sit upon the throne as his daughter."

"It is good to see you again, Krahns Defender of Skovin. Do you vouch for this one known as Ligl?"

"It is good to see you as well, Dynma. I have missed you, and yes, I vouch for Ligl on behalf of Bregon Skovin."

"And this one?" Dynma asked, pointing to Grock, who had also raced over and put himself between Dynma and Ligl. "He seems willing to risk his life in defence of Ligl."

"That is Grock, and while he is not a ward of Bregon, I believe it would be true to say he is a Defender of Ligl," Krahns said, placing his hand upon Grock's shoulder.

"Then by your will, Krahns Defender of Skovin, I place both Ligl and Grock under the protection of the valkyries." Dynma slammed the end of her spear down against the golden floor. "Irinesigar, Cytha, to me."

Within seconds, two more beams of blinding golden light pierced the room, striking the floor either side of Dynma. As the light faded, it revealed two more valkyries knelt at Dynma's side with spears in hand.

"We are at your service, Queen Dynma," they said, as they rose to their feet with their heads bowed.

"In recognition of your service to me, I am awarding you both a personal charge."

This was indeed an honour, and a responsibility only bestowed upon the worthiest.

"Irinesigar, your charge is Ligl, Cytha, your charge is Grock. You are to protect them with all the power now bestowed upon you."

Irinesigar and Cytha both got down on one knee, and with heads bowed once more, they crossed their spears in front of Dynma. Dynma reached out and touched the point where the spears crossed, as Ligl, Grock, and Krahns intuitively averted their eyes. Pure sunlight shot out of Dynma's hand and ignited the spears, sending a shock wave of energy through the room.

"Little ones, you are now protected by the valkyries. Krahns, we now take our leave, though should you require, call upon me and I will come."

Dynma slammed her spear against the floor once more, and all three of the valkyries disappeared.

"Well, that was fun. Have you guys finished looking around?"

"Not really. I was about to look at what was on the plinth when those ladies showed up," Grock said.

Directly beneath the central chandelier sat an impressive granite plinth embossed with runagaldrar, and placed upon it, the blade Dragetand. The sword was over a metre long, with a double-edged blade engraved with glowing green runes down its entire length, and a golden jewel encrusted cross-guard which formed two additional short blades that looked like fangs. Finished with an exquisite bound leather grip, and an intricately carved dragon head pommel.

As Grock hauled himself up onto the plinth, Krahns spoke.

"That is Dragetand. It was Bregon's original sword, but it thirsts for combat and feeds on the soul that wields it. When

Bregon returned from the early wars, he had aged many years, and so he laid Dragetand here, and took up Vargklo. If you listen closely, you will hear Dragetand screaming for blood to touch her blade once more."

Screaming was somewhat of an exaggeration on Krahns part. He had always had a flair for the dramatic. In truth, the sound would better be described as the blade humming to itself rather jovially. Waiting, anticipating the day it would be wielded in battle once again.

Ligl arose from the throne, dashed across to Grock and whispered in his ear, took a hold of his hand, and kissed him.

"Thank you for your time and for this amazing tour," Grock said.

"It has been my pleasure. Now let's go get some food in our bellies."

With a huge, beaming smile, Ligl ran over and threw her arms around Krahns, hugging him. This had been one of the best days of her life. Once again, she had got to explore with her best friend. Nothing could beat this, she thought.

"Thank you Krahns, thank you for everything," Ligl said.

They left the room and Krahns locked the door behind him. As the lock clunked into place, the fire that lit the room extinguished in an instant, and there was an inaudible sigh from Dragetand.

# 29

# A DREAM COME TRUE

Dougal woke with a crick in his neck, probably something to do with falling off the windowsill and crawling into a bed which was never designed to accommodate a human. He rubbed the sleep from his eyes as he strolled over to the window and stared out at the lava pool. Still quite unable to comprehend how this, of all the things he had come across in the last few days, was possible.

He thought for a moment. *Why should any of this be unbelievable? Belief by its very nature is a state of mind, and given the current state of my mind, nothing is too fantastical.* Realising he was now talking out loud, he slapped himself across the face. Not too hard you understand, he didn't want it to hurt.

Graimel and Binty had been up for the last few hours, helping Bregon and many of the dwarfs prepare the great hall for today's celebration. Thanks to Binty and Harg, there had been no ladder or height related injuries. There had of course, been a few bruised dwarf egos, from those who would normally climb into the rafters to hang decorations. More often than not falling off, often bruising, and breaking a little more than just their egos. *There was just no pleasing some folk,* Binty thought after she overheard a few curt words.

"What's their problem Harg?"

"Ah, don't worry about it. I think they may have landed on their heads a few too many times. As a matter of fact, I know for sure that Grankle has not only landed on his head a few times, but it was his mother who started it. Bless her the clumsy lass. She dropped him so many times she ended up being nicknamed Fumbling Frida. Well, at least I think that is why they called her that. Ah, there she is, over by the end table, the one who just dropped that tray of full mead horns and is slipping about in it."

Harg laughed, as did many of the others present in the hall. Binty did not find this amusing in the slightest.

"What is wrong with everyone? She clearly needs help."

Binty dropped her end of the banner and whizzed over to where Frida sat with her head in her hands, covered in mead.

"Hello," Binty said.

"Come over to have a laugh at Fumbling Frida, have you?" Frida said, without even looking up.

"Why no, not at all. I have come to see if I can help."

Frida looked up with an almost despairing smile.

"Oh, bless your heart, little one. I think you might be too tiny to help me. I am in a bit of a state here, as you can see, but thank you all the same."

"Samel Gesh!"

With a flick of Binty's wrist, the spilt mead was gone, and the mead horns were neatly stacked back on the tray, which was now in Binty's hand.

"Are you sure I'm too tiny to help?"

"Well, I don't suppose you can do anything about my clothes or cure my clumsiness, but I would appreciate a hand up."

"To be honest, I might be able to help with all three."

Binty took a hold of Frida's hand and picked her up off the floor, passed her the tray of mead horns and moved back a little in case she dropped them again. At least, that is what Frida thought.

"Drash Goel Hem," Binty said, once again flicking her wrist toward Frida.

There were gasps all around as Frida went from sopping mess to clean and dry, as she just stand there in stunned silence. This was probably a good thing, seeing as more often than not she was thrice as clumsy when being watched.

"Now then, as for a cure for clumsiness, I do not know of such a thing. However, I am a pixie, and a rather accomplished pixie if I do say so myself. Hmm, let me think for a second."

Binty had been buzzing back and forth, pondering her thoughts for a few minutes, when a huge smile spread across her face, and she darted back over to Frida.

"I have it!" Binty paused, took a breath, and uncurled her hands towards Frida. "Ga Fal Gra O`esh Pa Din Cl`desh!" Binty said, and snapped her fingers.

With a nod from Binty, Frida hesitantly lifted the tray above her head, did a perfect pirouette, putting Graimel's attempt to shame, then a small leap and a bound, followed by a graceful curtsey to Binty.

"You are amazing. How can I ever thank you?"

"By telling your son to stop being rude about those who are trying to help," Binty said, with a smile.

By this time, Grankle had weaved through the crowd to his mother. But he did not have time to explain or apologise before he felt her steady hand strike him across the back of his head with a crack heard at the back of the hall.

"Have you been being rude about Bregon's guests?" *THWACK!* "Did I not bring you up to be respectful?" *THWACK!* "How do you think this makes our family look? You wait until I tell your father!" *THWACK!*

The admonishing continued as Frida walked away with Grankle following her, his hand cradling the back of his head as he tried all ways to sneak a word in edgeways. He glanced over his shoulder and mouthed *sorry* to Binty. Binty bit her bottom lip, and mouthed *sorry* back.

"Are we finished with the preparations then?" Bregon boomed, his voice echoing throughout the great hall.

Everyone jumped back into what they were supposed to be doing. It truly was a remarkable sight. Binty flew back up to Harg, and together they finished hanging the banner, making sure anyone coming through the main door of the great hall would see it.

Graimel had been helping where he could, laying tables, fetching, and carrying, and hanging so called pretty things on the walls, amongst other tasks. He signalled to Binty to come over and grabbed a seat at one of the long tables. While he waited for her, he snatched a horn of mead off the table. He was about to take a drink when he felt a sharp rap across his hand. Stood over him, a stern looking older dwarf shaking her head and wagging her finger at him as if he were a naughty schoolboy. With a mumbled apology, he placed the horn back in its holder.

"What can I do for you, Graimel?" Binty asked.

"Can you see if Dougal is out of bed yet, and if so, bring him and our guests up here please? Keep your eye out for Krahns and the others though, don't want them all bumping into each other and spoiling the surprise."

With a spring in their step and a smile in their hearts, they followed Binty back up to the great hall. Barely able to contain their excitement, they joined Graimel on a lavish table, set up especially for them between Bregon's table and the rest of the hall. As they entered the hall, everyone stood and bowed their heads a little, waiting for them to take their places before returning to their own seats.

Bregon sat next to his wife Onjeg, and his now grown daughter Koocie, who sat next to her husband, Baldur. Sleip sat with his two daughters, Efraj and Anelci on the table next to the guests, within talking distance of Graimel and Binty.

Efraj smiled with glee and whispered to Binty as she took her seat.

"I see you are still wearing the armour."

"Because it's amazing, and I have to say there is not a single thing I have tried, that I cannot do whilst wearing it. Thank you ever so much."

"Once again, it is my ple—"

THUMP! THUMP! THUMP!

A pounding on the door to the great hall interrupted their conversation.

"Enter!" Bregon called, as he rose from his seat.

The door crept open with a deafening creak that broke the reverent silence of the hall. Krahns entered, followed by Ligl and Grock, who were still beaming from their tour of Ildjorden's secrets. Ligl eyes immediately caught sight of the banner, *Reunited at Long Last,* pointing it out to Grock as she gripped his hand a little tighter and whispered in his ear.

"E bremt gai es di pes." Which roughly translated into *I think this is all for us.*

Onjeg, and all those on the top table, rose to their feet along with Bregon, standing with their heads bowed in honour of their guests, prompting everyone else in the hall to join them. As Krahns escorted Ligl and Grock towards the guests table, a wave of applause engulfed them, and because quags were so short, they were unable to see the surprise that awaited.

Bregon moved down from his table and walked to stand in front of Graimel and Dougal, who had moved to stand together, with Binty sat primly on Dougal's shoulder. As instructed, Beribo, Aymms, Voeli, and Orm lined up behind them, out of sight, each gripping each other's hands attentively with nervous anticipation. Bregon moved towards Krahns with the specific intent of narrowing any line of sight and creating a focal point.

"Thank you, Krahns," Bregon said.

Krahns nodded in acknowledgement, then took up his seat next to Sleip.

"Did you two enjoy your tour? I am sure Krahns took you to places that are, off limits. I'll speak to him later," Bregon said, with a subtle wink, before glancing over his shoulder at Krahns.

"Where did you take them?" Sleip leant over and placed his hand on Krahns' shoulder. "It seems like you may be in a bit of trouble, old man?" he whispered.

"I will tell you later."

Bregon once again glanced over his shoulder, glaring at Sleip and Krahns with a frown and scowl that reminded them both they should not be talking. They smiled at each other like mischievous schoolboys, and had almost started to laugh when they realised Bregon was still fixated upon them, with a glower typically reserved for those who had drank the last of the mead. It took but a moment for them to remove the smiles from their faces, acknowledging their lapse in respect.

However, not less than a second after Bregon refocused his attention on Ligl and Grock, and with the caution of a mouse avoiding a hungry cat, Krahns whispered into Sleip's ear.

"Or maybe I won't."

Bregon put his hands upon Ligl's and Grock's shoulders.

"Today we throw a party to celebrate a momentous event. Ligl, when you came to us long ago, I made you a promise, and on this day, with the help of Graimel, Binty, and Dougal, I can finally fulfil that promise to you. The same promise I know Graimel made to you, dear Grock."

Ligl racked her brain trying to remember what Bregon had promised all those years ago, but nothing came to mind. Grock, however, remembered Graimel's promise, but understood it to be the impossible dream. His heart pounded in his chest. *It could not be,* he thought. *It was impossible. There was no way.*

Bregon stepped to one side as did Graimel and Dougal, and there stood before Ligl and Grock, the impossible dream. Ligl fell to her knees in total disbelief, for standing before her were her parents. Voeli rushed over and scooped her up in her arms, followed by Orm, who stroked her head while Voeli held her. Grock ran straight into Aymms' arms and gripped his mother tight, Beribo throwing his arms around his son. The six of them stood there for what felt like an eternity for them, so many years of missed hugs. Ligl and Grock gazed across at each other in complete and utter incredulity. Their shared impossible dream to be reunited with their families, had become a reality.

The room erupted in cheers and applause, not only for the reunited families, but also for Graimel, Binty, and Dougal for making this all possible. Many a horn of mead was drunk, many a dance was spun, and six lives were changed forever.

But in the Hidden Dimension, Blodia was planning her own party preparations, but these were for a hunting party, and the prey was Dougal. The directive, find Bedougalnn, and separate him from his time, thus ending all time, and all things.

This day however, belonged to Ligl, Grock, and their families, and even if all time ended tomorrow, which of course everyone hoped it would not, at least Bregon and Graimel were able to fulfil their promises to their wards.

The celebration lasted all day and late into the evening. Nobody noticed when Graimel disappeared for a couple of hours, but both Dougal and Binty noticed when he got back. For deep within his eyes, there was a worrying look, and although he smiled and continued to join in the merriment, they could tell something played on his mind. They glanced across at each other, subconsciously agreeing not to ask, continuing to act as if everything was normal, and let everyone enjoy the moment.

As they sat at the guest table absorbing the revelry of the party mad dwarfs, Ligl, Grock, and their families thanked them for everything they had done. For taking time out from their quest to save all, to make a seemingly impossible difference for a few. The light in Grock's eyes told Graimel he was going to spend some much-needed time with his family, before returning to travel with him. Graimel knew better than most that all actions had consequences, and he was proud of this one, but he reminded Grock he was welcome to re-join them any time.

Ligl thanked Bregon and his family for caring for her for all these years, and making her so welcome. Bregon took this as his cue to return her portal stone, and with only a few noticing, Ligl, Orm, Voeli, Grock, Aymms, and Beribo all touched the portal stone and went home.

# 30

# DISINTEGRATION THERAPY

After Hans left her vacant space. Blodia paced back and forth, agitated, something felt off. She was beginning to dismiss these thoughts, when Floop showed in the next visitor.

"Bloodthirsty Bazil of Bolton to see you, my Queen."

"What do you seek from your queen? Speak now or let it be the end of you?"

"Your most disgracious one, I bring grave news indeed. Captain Munday asked me to advise you should he not return, that Hans Greemob will be the one responsible for his ending."

"This is an outrage. What proof do you have of this? Am I supposed to just take the word of a loathsome animal such as yourself?"

"Oh vile one, it is true. I am indeed a loathsome scoundrel who has only ever tried to emulate the vileness of his despicable queen, a true and loyal servant."

"Hmm, you may have something there. I never did trust Hans, or even like him for that matter, however if he ended Edmund, then I have to say he has gone up in my estimation. Although, not enough to save him."

Blodia was struggling to maintain her composure as fury raged inside her.

"I will deal with Hans, but that will leave me without a captain. As it is you who brought this to my door, I believe you now owe me a captain. What do you say, Captain…?"

"Yes, my most disgruntled desp—"

"The dramatic pause was for you to tell me your surname, unless of course your name is indeed, Bazil Yes."

"My apologies, your wickedness. My given name is Bazil Jolly."

"Oh no! That will never do. I cannot have my captain called Captain Jolly. It sets completely the wrong tone," Blodia said, as she paced the room a little, shaking her head.

"Hence why I have always gone by Bloodthirsty Bazil. How about Captain Bloodthirsty?"

"Do you not hear how ridiculous that sounds?" Blodia said, walking over to the huge blooming lily in the corner of her vacant space. "Oh my! That is foul." Blodia gagged and would have vomited had it been possible. "If I were not already dead, I am certain that scent would have sealed my doom."

Blodia was spot-on. This was no normal lily. This lily was an evil corpse lily, and had ended up in the Hidden Dimension for having an odour so bad, it killed anyone that smelt it. Now you may think this was not the lily's fault, but you would be wrong, hence it ending up in the Hidden Dimension.

"I have it," she squealed. "Fouldoom! You will be Captain Bazil Fouldoom. That should scare the hypothetical pants off anyone, and if not, we will bring them here and make them smell that lily."

With what you could describe as a smile and a subtle skip, if you were brave enough, a delighted Blodia dismissed her new captain and called for Floop.

"Er, there was one other thing, oh most dastardly one," Bazil squeaked out.

"What?"

"Captain Munday said you would reward me for my service, by allowing me to drink for free at the Banished Abstract Cat Tavern, for as long as I may discern."

"If being made my captain is not enough for you, Captain Fouldoom, by all means, tell the barkeep to bill me for your consumption."

"Yes, my monstrous monarch."

Bazil left and Floop entered as requested.

"Floop, what is your opinion of Hans Greemob?"

"He is nothing more than a vile scoundrel."

"Well, aren't we all?" Blodia laughed.

"True, but most of us have honour amongst ourselves. I would trust the sun not to kill me more than I would trust him."

"A fine analogy, and one I find myself agreeing with. Take a message to Hans. Tell him to meet me at the Pool of Vacant Reflection in two hours. Then send out another message to our new captain, Captain Fouldoom, tell him to muster as many warriors as he can, and join us there."

"It will be my pleasure."

As Floop left, leaving her to ponder over recent conversations and the events of the last few days, her fury and rage bubbled to the surface once again, and she was overcome with anger. Moments later, her vacant space looked as if it had been set on fire, burnt to the ground, rebuilt from the ash, set on fire again, then blown out by a fire-breathing dragon, accidentally reigniting the flames.

Then, remembering the Hidden Dimension existed in a vacuum, and therefore her vacant space could not catch fire in the first place. The remaining flames were quickly doused before someone informed the authorities.

Although a rare occurrence, this is what happens when Blodia loses her already foul temper. Thankfully, she later found it and normality was restored.

Since leaving Blodia's vacant space, Hans had bought himself a dark blue velvet captain's hat with golden embroidery. At least it would have been, had it not been purchased in the Hidden Dimension, where everything was some nefarious tone of battleship grey. He ran his fingers around the brim gushing over his purchase, before donning it with mild conceit and strutting through the grey gloomy streets with a heightened sense of self gratified smugness lingering about his person.

His plan had worked flawlessly, and none would be the wiser. Back in his rightful place as the Captain of the Guard.

He strolled home with a skip in his step and headed straight into his study. Which was no more than a sorry looking desk in a derelict room of his tired run-down bungalow. The property was in such a state of disrepair that some fixtures, parts of the walls and floors, and a chunk of the ceiling had simply decided it was not worth being anymore, and vanished from all time.

Hans opened the top drawer of his desk and reached for his private notebook; it was not there. Had he a heart, it would have been pounding, but his shock was short-lived as he realised the bottom of the drawer was also missing. Just another part of his home that had given up being. He reached through the bottom of the drawer with no respect for its feelings and snatched up his notebook from the second drawer down.

Placing it on the desk he skipped back a little to review his checklist, and with a smug grimace, he checked off steps five and six.

*How to become king!*

1. *Become Captain.* √
2. *Gain Trust.* √
3. *Promote Self Worth.* √
4. *Blame Mistakes on Others.* √
5. *Eliminate Competition.* √
6. *Treat Self to Fancy Hat.* √
7. *End Blodia. (How?)*

*8. Pronounce Myself King.*

Hans pondered over step seven. How could he End Blodia? He suddenly remembered the ring the lyconfind used when they attacked. It had shone like pure moonlight, ending two of his men, and almost ridding him of Edmund. Had Queen Blodia not escaped when she did, it could have ended her. But how would he retrieve the ring from the lyconfind on his own? He realised this was not going to happen. There must be another way.

With no other thoughts springing to mind, Hans realised he was out of his depth, like a fish out of water. *Water…* he thought, *that must be the answer. All I have to do is manipulate the Pool of Vacant Reflection. If I open a portal to the right place at the right time, I can simply step back while Blodia leads the way. As just as Edmund, she will insist on going first. It's foolproof. I just need to think of the right location.*

He stabbed his pencil at his notebook a few times, trying to force his thoughts to emerge. Then he remembered a story once told, about a place where during the summer months, the sun never went down, but where was it? He remembered thinking it was an impossible place, something to do with ice, a land with ice, where the sun did not set. It was absurd and nonsensical, but that is what the elves told him. *Aha!* He thought to himself and scribbled in his notebook.

*The land of the Elves – Iceland.*

He smiled a cunning smile, closed his notebook, and dropped it back into his drawer, forgetting the bottom was missing. With a thump, it hit the floor, but Hans was too wrapped up in his devious plan to notice. He got up from his desk, strutted outside, and bumped into Floop, almost knocking him to the floor as he surged out of his home.

"What in Blodia's name are you doing here, Flop?"

"It's Floop, Captain Greemob. I have an urgent message from

Queen Blodia. You are to meet her at the Pool of Vacant Reflection in 90 minutes' time."

"How do you suggest I do that, Flop? There is no time here?"

"Should I tell her that is a no then?"

"You will do no such thing. I will see her there; it will be my pleasure. Now, seeing as you are running errands, would you mind getting my overcoat cleaned for me for when I meet the queen? You should find it hung up in the hallway."

Floop was about to respond with a definitive no, but thought, *why not have a nosey around the captain's house.*

"It would be my pleasure to serve you, Captain."

Hans smirked at Floop and strolled away. His arrogance and self-righteous opinion of himself were soon to be his undoing. On his way to the pool, he thought about popping in to see Malka, hesitating outside her abode and pondering this thought for a moment. After two seconds of careful consideration, and knowing he would be listening to her whine on about him never visiting, he decided not to bother. As he walked away, Malka saw him disappear down the street through her window. *Serves him right,* she thought, and returned to her knitting.

In the meantime, Floop entered Hans' decrepit bungalow to retrieve his overcoat as requested. He sauntered through the scantily furnished property, finding the overcoat in the first room, discarded upon a rotting chair. Passing through into what he supposed was the study, though he doubted very much that Hans was a creature of learning, and that study seemed a highly inappropriate word. As he ran his fingers along the edge of the desk, wondering if Hans could even read, let alone write, he caught sight of the notebook discarded on the floor.

Floop's curiosity got the better of him. He had to know what someone like Hans was studying, so he grabbed the notebook and dropped it on the desk. The covers sprang apart, falling open at the checklist, and whilst reeling from the first line, he continued to read with no small amount of sneering. That was until he got to Step Four, when he emitted an audible laugh, turning to a muted gasp upon reading Step Five. This, however, was nothing compared to his reaction to Step Seven, which left him speechless. *The audacity,* he thought.

Floop swiped the notebook up from the desk and placed it within his robes. With a smirk, he strode out of the property, ensuring he collected the overcoat, before making haste back to Queen Blodia.

With no clue how long 90 minutes was, Hans headed straight for the Pool of Vacant Reflection. It was imperative he arrived with plenty of time to spare. As he scouted around for a willing volunteer, a sozzled skoto, courtesy of Bazil, came out of the tavern and staggered unknowingly towards his doom.

"You there, come hither," Hans barked.

"Yesh, sir, can's I helpsh yoush?"

"I am the Queen's Captain, and I need your help on a mission for the queen. What is your name?"

"Namesh, Lyden. Aresh yoush sure?"

"Yes, I am sure I need your help."

"Nope, aresh yoush sure youshis the caspitan?"

"Yes," Hans said, looking puzzled and confused.

"You got heres fasht?"

"I was already here."

Lyden staggered backwards a little, his eyes widening like the waxing of the moon on fast-forward. Sloshed he may have been, but he was sure the captain had just been buying drinks for everyone at the tavern, yet here he was down by the pool. So, either a ghost had been buying him drinks, or he was talking to a ghost now. Either way, he said he was a captain, so with as much grace as he could muster, he managed a questionable salute before passing out.

Hans dragged the unconscious Lyden to the edge of the pool, and splashed water over him until he came to, then hauled him to his feet. With little success, Lyden tried his absolute best to stand to attention, and once again tried to salute Hans.

Hans paid no attention to this. He was busy fixating his mind on Iceland, Westfjords in particular, as for some reason this name had just popped into his head. The black water swirled and churned. Hans turned to look at Lyden, who wobbled and swayed, teetering on the verge of passing out again.

"Jump in the pool. It will sober you up."

"No thansks, caspitan shir."

Hans bit his bottom lip and threw his head in his hands, letting out a frustrated sigh before giving Lyden a casual yet hearty slap on the shoulder, putting him off balance and helping him fall into the pool.

Lyden appeared between two huge rocks on the top of Bolafjall. With the finite time he had, it occurred to him the captain had been correct in his prediction. The waters of the pool had indeed sobered him, although he wished they had not, his swift end no less painful for being sober. And had he still been drunk; he may not have even realised he was being ended.

After waiting around for an appropriately short time with the waters swirling, churning, and bubbling. And with no sign of Lyden returning, and no one knowing where he had gone. He cleared his mind and calmed the waters. Moments later, Blodia came strutting down the burnt cobbled street towards him, followed by Floop carrying his overcoat.

Blodia approached Hans where he stood at the edge of the Pool of Vacant Reflection. Hans stood to attention and bowed his head to his queen.

"My Malevolent Monarch," Hans said, greeting her.

"Hans, I see you are here early. Any reason for that? What method is there to your madness?"

"Just pleased to be at your service, your foulness. It is my job to ensure the area is safe before your arrival."

Blodia waved Floop forward, and he cautiously approached Hans to present him with his captain's overcoat. Hans snatched it away without so much as an acknowledgement or word of thanks, but Floop merely turned away and smiled. It felt agreeable to be privy to the best laid plans of evil queens.

"Where are your men, Hans?"

"Sorry, I don't understand."

"Did you think I was meeting you here for coffee and cake?"

"Well, err no, I guess not. I did not think..."

"That surprises me almost as much as it does not! For I know you think about some things, even make notes, and some of your thoughts, I find quite inappropriate."

"I have no idea about what you are speaking of, oh dreary one."

"Now that is something that does not surprise me in the least. We are going to hunt Bedougalnn. I thought that was obvious. As you have brought no men, it is lucky that I arranged for the whole of my first guard to join us. So, while we await their arrival, I think it would be prudent for you to scout ahead."

"Oh, I am not sure I agree, safer in numbers and all that, and I... well, I thought you always liked to lead your men."

"Under normal circumstances, yes, but these are not normal circumstances, are they? And as for you not agreeing with me, well, frankly I don't care... Malka!"

Malka crept around the corner, fearing for a moment what Hans would think, but then realising she no longer cared.

"Remind me of his name, Malka?"

"Lyden, my Queen."

"Yes, that was it, Lyden. When will Lyden be joining us, Hans?"

"Oh, er... Lyden. He should be back anytime now."

"Is that so? How may I ask is he going to get back, when you appear to have calmed the waters here, is there something I need to know?"

"I, er... think he may be lost."

"Lost? Well, that's one way to put it. But never mind, anyone who trusts you deserves what they get. So, just to keep you in the picture. You will lead the hunt. Oh, and you need not worry. You will not be going to the same place you sent poor innocent Lyden, as I have selected the correct location to start the hunt."

Blodia sidled up to Hans, standing toe to toe with him she pulled out a notebook and held it up to his face. "When you get back, we can discuss this!"

Hans gulped as he recognised his notebook and regretted sending a now smirking Floop into his home to do his bidding.

"Now go forth and prepare the way for the coming army."

Hans looked with reticence at the black waters of the pool as they twisted and churned. Turning back to his queen seeking forgiveness in her eyes, but her eyes were as black as the waters of the pool, devoid of everything. He glanced up at Malka, but she flicked her head into the air and turned away from his gaze, retreating around the corner. Back into the dark soulless streets of the Hidden Dimension, back home.

In general, emotions were a hard thing to pull off in the Hidden Dimension, but had there been a competition at this precise moment, then Hans' display of dismay would have won the shiniest grey medal. With his body feeling like a lead weight, he sluggishly placed one foot into the foreboding waters, then begrudgingly moved the other foot forward and took one last glance over his shoulder. A vast company of warriors marched out of the darkness led by his old enemy, Bazil, and he knew this to be his end. Resigned, he turned back to face the inevitable, stepped forward, and allowed the swirling waters to consume him.

Hans appeared in a tiny cave high on Barbeau Peak, Ellesmere Island. Had he been a mortal man, he would have frozen in an instant. Luckily for him, he was not. Unluckily for him, he was a skoto, and therefore particularly vulnerable to light, and at this time of year in this place, there is no darkness. As the portal he had arrived by was forcibly closed from within the Hidden Dimension, he darted to the back of the cave.

With his body pressed like putty into a mould against the cold, damp stone wall, he watched the shadow slowly being erased by the light as it inched its way towards him. It was only a matter of time before there was no more hiding, and Hans accepted his fate with a single word.

"Bugger!"

A wind blew through the cave, and the pile of ash that moments ago was the vile Hans Greemob, dispersed into oblivion.

# 31
## PARTY TRICKS & PROMISES

Graimel returned to his seat and grasped his mug of mead, taking an ample swig and wiping the excess from his mouth with the back of his hand, his brow furrowed and his eyes distant. Binty flew over, and sensing an uneasiness about him, she perched on the handle of a discarded mug.

"What is it, Graimel? Something troubles you."

Graimel pondered Binty's worried eyes and took another generous swig of mead.

"Nothing that cannot wait until tomorrow. Go, celebrate."

"But, Graimel—"

Graimel curtly cut her off mid-sentence.

"Tomorrow," Graimel said curtly, cutting her off mid-sentence and slamming his mug down against the table, unseating her. With a loud plop, she fell backwards into the dregs of spiced mead at the bottom of the mug.

"This better not make my nice shiny armour rust, or there will be trouble," Binty said, pulling herself back up onto the rim, mead running out of her armour, as Graimel strode away over the dance floor. "Drash Goel Hem."

Graimel hurried over to Bregon, who was dancing with his

wife whilst drinking directly from a bottle of dark mead. He stepped between them, causing Bregon to release Onjeg's hand, and send her twirling across the floor straight into Dougal's arms. Without stopping to think, she spun Dougal on the spot, hoisting him aloft, and flinging him around like a proverbial rag doll before proceeding to waltz around the hall. The unwilling and somewhat terrified Dougal had been thrust into the limelight, something he secretly enjoyed.

It was not until Graimel stamped on his foot that Bregon realised he was no longer dancing with his wife, but a rather grumpy looking notadwarf.

"Where is my wife?" Bregon said, spinning Graimel with gusto, placing his hand back on his hip and continuing to dance. "She was here but a moment ago."

"I think you will find she is now on the other side of the hall, taking the lead with Dougal."

"Poor boy," Bregon said, laughing from the bottom of his belly, "he will soon learn the strength of dwarven women, and she is one of the strongest. He will need time to recover before you continue your journey, Graimel."

"My journey is what we need to talk about, and with some haste, I might add."

The tone in Graimel's voice was that of a high-powered businessman in the most important meeting of his career, who had just uncontrollably farted and unwittingly followed through. Bregon took a quick sniff of the air, and realising this had not happened, he advised they retreat to his private study to talk. Graimel nodded in agreement whilst wondering why Bregon had been sniffing the air, but decided to dismiss it.

They disappeared from the hall, apparently without a soul noticing apart from Binty, and took the short walk to Bregon's private study. Curiosity getting the better of her, Binty followed and zipped through as the door was eased shut. She darted up towards the roof, and from the shadows on a beam above them, she watched.

"Hello, Binty, fancy meeting you up here," Harg whispered.

"Who's there? Is that you, Harg?" Binty whispered, trying to remain undetected.

There was a subtle shuffling sound and Harg appeared from out of the shadow.

"Spying on Graimel are you? Don't worry, I won't tell if you won't."

Graimel glanced around to check the room was empty before speaking.

"Dougal will die by the end of tomorrow, unless we can stop the skotos and their mad queen."

Binty took a sharp intake of breath. She was aware Dougal was in danger, but not any sort of immediate danger. Questions started racing around her head. *Had Graimel known all along? If so, why were we running over moors, delving into caves, and flying on dragons to Denmark to run errands for a demi-god? Did Dougal know, and if he did, why was he waltzing around the great hall, and wasting what time he had left at a party*?

"All questions will be answered in due course, Binty," Graimel said, looking up into the rafters. "Did you think I would not spot you following us, or hiding in the shadows? You may as well come down and join us. I will speak to you later, Harg."

Binty almost fell off the beam. As stealthy as she was, it seemed obvious to her now that Graimel would detect her.

"Why did you keep this from me?"

"I was hopeful the design would not proceed after the failed attack at Janet's den."

"The failed attack that left two lyconfind dead, two lyconfind who gave their lives while we took a stroll across a moor. We should have been there Graimel, we could have protected them and ended this."

"If we had been there with Dougal, we could have lost everything. He was not strong enough to fight or ready to use his powers, and I have been trying to find us time to prepare him."

"He is stronger than you think, Graimel."

"Well, you say that, but he is in the process of being thrown around the great hall by my wife, so he's not that strong," Bregon snorted.

"Oh, shut up! Your wife throws you around the dance floor, Mighty Bregon! So, you have nothing to laugh about."

"Calm down, Binty. Bregon meant no offence."

"Graimel is right. I am sorry. I did not mean to offend. Please, accept my apology," Bregon said, shocked by the veracity of Binty's comment, and nodding in acceptance of it.

"No, I'm sorry; I am just really protective of my friends."

"An honourable trait, and one dwarf's share."

"If anything happens to Dougal, then we are all affected. We are all committed to history," Graimel said.

"Then what's it all been for, Graimel? All the running around, all the distractions?" Binty asked.

"Precisely that, a distraction for Dougal, and to give me time to think because we will let nothing happen to him."

"You tell me what you need, and when and where, and you will have our might at your side. And this is not to repay a debt to you, this is for the unknowing humans who worry about everything, but know so little. They allowed their belief in magic to be eroded away until it became nothing more than entertainment to them. They can never thank you, but we can, and it would be our honour to join you in this fight."

"Thank you, Bregon. I was hoping you would say that, and we are privileged to have you join us. The plan is quite simple. This is what we shall do."

They both listened intently to Graimel while he went through the detail of what he described as their last hope, but they were not alone in this fight. They had allies, no, they had friends.

Once the course of action had been advised in full, they agreed to speak no more of it and return to the great hall. Of slight concern, although unlikely, as most attendees had already consumed far too much mead for them to even remember their own names, let alone notice if two or three people momentarily left the party. Was what to do if questions are asked? After a brief discussion, they settled on the synchronised barf and bowel excuse, as no one was likely to engage in further conversation on that subject.

Being the delicate pixie she is, Binty was not at all fond of this idea. She scowled and folded her arms with an exasperated sigh, before advising Graimel she had never had such an episode, and it was indeed unheard of for pixies. Graimel reminded her that no one would know such a thing, and the fact she was uncomfortable with the idea only reinforced the fact that it was indeed the best idea.

"No one better ask me where I have been, Graimel, otherwise you are going to have one very grumpy Binty Malice on your hands."

"That is excellent, Binty. Use it. It will help to further solidify your excuse. Of course, you would feel grumpy if you had spent the last hour in the bathroom."

"I don't think solidify is quite the right term, loosely speaking," Bregon said, placing his hands upon his stomach and roaring with laughter.

"We should return to the great hall; the conversation is quite dire here," Binty said, turning her back and heading towards the door.

Graimel and Bregon almost choked on their own laughter.

"Dire ere!" Graimel spat out, tears streaming down their faces.

"What on earth is wrong with you two? I don't know what it is you find so funny. Once you compose yourselves, grab a stool next to me in the great hall. Let us put this plan in motion," Binty said, not knowing what to make of the situation, and becoming increasingly baffled by the words and actions of these two old fools.

By the time she finished talking, Graimel and Bregon had collapsed upon the floor and were laughing with such voracious animation. Anyone walking past would have thought that two jesters had taken up residence, and were busy throttling each other, whilst trying to laugh about throttling each other.

With a wearied shrug, she zipped back through to the party. Whatever this nonsense was, she did not want to be associated with it, and lacked the inclination to hang around and continue to be the source of any more innocuous amusement, or become the butt of any jokes. It was lucky she only thought this. Otherwise Graimel and Bregon may have never stopped laughing, or ever made it back to the great hall.

Binty got back to her table and sat on the rim of her mead horn. She thought, *I must ask Bregon if I can take a couple of these home, they would make splendid novelty beds. If only it was not half full of mead, I could lay it down and take a little nap.* Pausing for a moment while she switched on her light bulb, she realised all she needed to do was finish her drink and her bed would be ready.

She took hold of her mead spoon and retrieved a generous sample, but as she was about to savour this delight, Graimel's hand came swooping in, snatching up the mead horn and unseating her once again. This time though, she had a spoon of mead in her hands and there was no way she was spilling it.

With the reflexes of a politician dodging responsibility, she flipped the spoon, ensuring the centrifugal force kept the mead glued in place. Meanwhile, she regained her composure, and even had time to throw him a scolding surly stare, before catching the spoon and drinking her mead with the grace of a lady.

Harg swooped back into the great hall and flew over to a table near the back where some of his distant relatives sat. A rowdy cheer went up as he joined them, welcoming an old friend back, and he spent the rest of the evening regaling them with stories of his adventures.

Graimel and Bregon had finally collected themselves, with only the odd childish giggle, but their eyes were still reddened and swollen. Whilst sat there doing their utmost best to maintain straight faces, Dougal waltzed over in the arms of Onjeg, releasing her upon seeing the state of Graimel.

"Graimel, my friend, is everything okay? You look upset."

"A lot better now, thank you. Just had a rough bathroom experience," Graimel said, patting his stomach and grimacing somewhat.

Dougal did exactly as Graimel expected. He instantly became more than a little lost for words, and his expression turned from one of generous concern to that of mildly irritated disgust. A face that clearly stated it thought you had overshared, and that whatever topic this was, it needed to be immediately and permanently forgotten. Dougal spun about on his heels, and relieved to see Onjeg still standing there, he snatched her up in his arms once again, and made haste across the dance floor.

Bregon slapped Graimel across his back and chortled, managing to maintain his composure. At least until Graimel offered him a stool, at which point he completely lost it again. But not a soul here would question Bregon or his actions.

Or so you might think. But both Krahns and Sleip had seen Bregon both leave and return, and both had also seen a change in his demeanour. It was their job to notice.

Sleip leant in to Krahns.

"We should go see what is occurring."

"Your right, from his actions it looks like it could be a busy day the morrow."

Krahns got to his feet and strode over to Bregon closely followed by Sleip.

"My Lord, you seem troubled. We sense something grips you," Krahns said, in a hushed voice so as not to arouse any unwanted attention.

Bregon straightened his expression and glanced across at Graimel with a wry smile. Graimel glanced over to Binty, who was sitting on the edge of a mead horn fishing drink out with her spoon. In response, she bobbed out her tongue and gave him a rather squiffy scowl, before glancing across at Sleip, who gave her a friendly wink. Graimel turned back to Bregon and raised his eyebrows, and with a subtle nod, Bregon took the cue.

Bregon ushered Krahns and Sleip in closer with his hand and whispered to them.

"I think the meat is off. Helheim may have just fallen out of my rear, so thank Odin for the mead!" Bregon reached up and put his hands on Krahns and Sleip's shoulders, drawing them in until they were huddled close. Then, for added effect, he unleashed a stench so foul from his bottom, it would have choked a Draugr. "Now, let me ask, is that what you sensed?"

Krahns and Sleip gagged, swallowed, and gagged again, before holding their breath until Bregon released his hands from their shoulders. Graimel was concentrating so hard on stifling his laughter, that he thought he may pee himself. Thankfully for all those in the vicinity, he maintained control of his bladder.

Water streamed down Krahns and Sleip's faces, as if they had just been doused with a hefty dose of pepper spray, and in fairness to them, they were coping remarkably well. Especially considering the stench they were subjected to was so nauseating, it made pepper spray seem like a soothing eyewash.

As if to reinforce this, Dougal, who was on the other side of the hall being spun around by Onjeg, suddenly caught an ever so slight whiff of Bregon's release. In an instant, his eyes swelled and watered, and his throat closed up with a burning itch. Overcome with nausea, he made the unconscious decision to become unconscious, hitting the floor with a thwack!

Onjeg scooped him up in her arms and raced across the floor to where Graimel and Bregon sat. As she got closer, she noticed a lot of dwarfs with streaming, twitching, and swollen red eyes enjoying the party. She then spied the proud grin emblazoned across Bregon's face.

"What are you up to now?" Onjeg snapped.

Bregon almost spilt his drink in surprise, having failed to spot Onjeg rushing over towards him. Had he, he would have been sensible enough to modify his expression. Instead she caught him well and truly grin faced and he quickly shooed away Krahns and Sleip. Thankful for the interruption, they raced back to their table and downed two horns of mead before pushing aside their meat and opting for some brittle dry bread.

"Onjeg, my love, how wonderful of you to join us! What is that in your arms?"

"This is a Dougal. What I want to know is, what have you done to him? And what is that rancid odour? I thought I told you to bathe before the party."

Binty rose from the table to check on Dougal, he was away with the fairies.

"Yep, he's passed out again. I swear he could win awards for it. If you lay him down on the table, I will take him to his room in a bit, and thank you for bringing him over," Binty said.

"There you go, my love; it would appear the human is always passing out, and I did bathe before the party."

"I still think you had some part to play in this, and as for you, Graimel Tock, you can wipe that smile off your face as well. I have yet to see anything funny. I don't know what you two are up to and I don't think I want to know," Onjeg said, glaring at the pair of them.

As she flounced back to her seat, Bregon and Graimel sniggered quietly to each other, ensuring they hid any signs of a smirk.

"I do not think Dougal will be re-joining us any time soon," Binty said, after throwing a mug of water over Dougal's face, and there not being the slightest hint of a stir or flinch.

"It's probably for the best, given the direness of this whole situation, do you not think?"

"I must agree with you, Graimel. What he does not know cannot harm him, but I guess the same could have been said about Kainen and Laegon, and look what happened to them."

"Laegon and Kainen knew what they were getting into, and accepted the risks. They entered the fray with honour, and died fighting for what was right."

"Yep, that's right, they died."

Binty slapped Dougal to wake him, but he was out cold, so she rose to her feet and zipped up into the rafters. She sat on the beam, head bowed, brushing away the tears as they rolled down her cheeks. She had not known Kainen and Laegon, but their loyalty to their friends was unquestionable, and they stood when it mattered. This alone made her wish she had been able to call them her friends.

As she thought about what happened, the fury built inside her once again, and she swore vengeance. Yet as she cleared the rest of the tears from her face, she realised this was no time for fury, no time for crying or for regret. Re-focusing on Graimel and Bregon, she thought, *maybe this is the time for buffooning, the party before the storm.* Her thoughts drifted to her father so far away, and what she would give for one of his reassuring hugs right now.

Then, like a bolt, it struck her, quite literally. At that very moment, a bolt struck her beautifully crafted and gleaming armour with a clunk, tossed up at her with extreme precision by Anelci.

Binty jumped to her feet and scoured the room, trying to identify where the bolt came from. She spotted Anelci and Efraj waving to her from their table, beckoning her over. After checking her armour for scratches, she plunged down from the rafter and landed on the table between them, ensuring she avoided the discarded cake and lake of spilt mead.

Glancing back and forth between the cake and the mead, she shook her head as she remembered what it was besides the bolt that struck her up in the rafters. Binty realised while she was trying to remember not to forget what she had just remembered; she was becoming distracted by cake, again. As she thought this, her eyes drifted back across the table to the huge chunk of untouched drommekage (dream cake). The name did not surprise her, as it was almost as flavoursome as Janet's Lyconfind cake.

She drooled a little, as she imagined a drommekage made by Janet. I should point out that even though all lyconfind are indeed compelled to bake during a full moon, they are not all as accomplished as Janet, or Beth.

In fact, some of them are more on a par with Marjorie Tibbs. Who although being a well-respected member of the Women's Institute, and someone who enjoyed baking and jam making, her efforts were borderline disastrous to say the least. But, they always sold out at every church fete or fair she attended. Now, whether that is testament to the kindness of the human soul, or more to do with what was beneath her garden shed, I will leave up to you.

"Er, Binty," Anelci said, pointing to the corner of her mouth.

"Sorry."

Binty could have slapped herself. She had done it again, completely forgotten what she had earlier remembered. Side-tracked by cake. She nonchalantly wiped away the revealing trickle of drool that had sneakily escaped her lips.

"Right, sorry about that. I got a little distracted for a moment. Now, what can I do for you both?"

"Well, we wanted to tell you before you leave, how amazing you are, and how amazing you look in that armour, of course," Anelci said, before darting her eyes across to Efraj.

"Why thank you, that means so much. From what your father tells me, the both of you are also quite amazing."

"Speaking of our father, that is kind of what we wanted to speak to you about," Efraj said, her tone unusually serious.

"What is it?" Binty asked.

"We wanted to ask you, well, it seems silly when you go to say it out loud, but please look after our father, take care of him, and make sure he comes back." Efraj took a hold of Anelci's hand, seeking affirmation before continuing. "This party, Bregon letting Ligl leave, the three of you sloping off for a private discussion, and you all keeping an eye on Bedougalnn.

Something is afoot, and we all know that when things are afoot, they are not necessarily good things."

"You girls are wiser than your years," Binty said, placing her hand upon theirs. "You have my word. Should the need arise, I shall protect your father with all my power."

"Oh, and Krahns as well," Anelci said.

"Of course."

There was a sudden commotion surrounding Graimel and Bregon, a lot of cheering, hollering, and general excitement. Krahns and Sleip jumped up on the table to get a better view, not wanting to get too close after their earlier encounter.

"It would appear Graimel has challenged the mighty Bregon to an arm wrestle," Krahns said, slapping Sleip across his back. "Should be fun, and could take some time if Bregon does not want to humiliate Graimel."

"You should know, Binty, no one has ever bested Bregon in, well, in anything as it happens."

"Graimel is stronger than he looks, Sleip. I think you might be surprised."

"Ooh, big talk for a pixie. Come on then, what's your wager? Tell you what, when Bregon wins, you give me a kiss."

"Father!" Efraj and Anelci shrieked in unison.

"Okay, and if Graimel wins, you let me give you a little slap."

A smile spread across Sleip's face. He liked the sound of that, and if truth be told, wished he had thought of it instead of a kiss. If only he had listened to Efraj trying to warn him about the power of this particular pixie's slap, before saying.

"Now that is what I'm talking about. You've got yourself a deal, little one."

Efraj buried her head in her hands and wished her father read more. However, she took comfort from the fact that her father was right about Bregon never being bested, and Graimel did not look like he would be the one to beat him.

Dougal stirred, possibly because of the raucous uproar

surrounding current events, or it could have been a delayed reaction to Binty's slap. Either way, no one noticed.

As he struggled to move, jeering and boasting voices seeped into his repose, followed by a disturbing burning sensation growing in his cheek. He pressed his hand against the affected area, as if soothing a toothache, hoping it might extinguish the fire raging inside, alas to no avail. Then he remembered the pungent odour that struck him while he was dancing, and the taste, *oh my god, the taste,* he thought as he realised the scent had somehow become adhered to his swollen itchy throat. He tried to swallow, but instead he almost choked as he gagged while struggling to subdue his body's uncontrollable urge to hurl over all those present.

What happened was hazy at best. Shadowy images and indistinct voices floated through his head, but as he concentrated harder, the figures revealed themselves to be Graimel and Bregon talking. He was not sure when this was, and what they were saying made little sense. Until he discerned the words, *your foul odour could have taken down a stampeding gogrelin.* At once, he realised who, and what it was, that had rendered him unconscious.

A gogrelin is a mythical beast, believed to be part goblin, part ogre, and part skunk, and one of the foulest smelling creatures ever. Ironically, it is also susceptible to foul odours, and to combat this, it has very few olfactory receptors. It is said that if a gogrelin was to sniff another gogrelin, it would cause instant death, and the pungent vapour released upon death would in turn kill the gogrelin that had been sniffed. As you can imagine, because of this, they only seek each other out once every four years to mate, and there is no snuggling allowed.

Of course, Dougal had no idea what a gogrelin was, but he knew what a foul odour was, and now he knew where it had come from.

Graimel and Bregon clamped hands, sweat beading on Graimel's forehead. Baldur stepped in and bound their hands with a leather strap, then cupped his hands around theirs. They nodded at Baldur in readiness, and with that, he released their hands and gave the cue to begin.

With muscles burgeoning and concentration unfaltering, they took up the strain, staring deep into each other's eyes like the main characters from a cheesy romance novel. The moment they both realised this, they took the opportunity to snarl a little for show, sending a ripple of activity through the crowd, with wagers going all ways. Although nobody was actually fooled by this, as the respect and admiration they held for each other was clearly evident.

Dougal lifted his head to see everyone engrossed, fixated on the spectacle before him, but after five minutes of watching, there had not been a muscle twitch between them. The beads of sweat on Graimel's head seemed to have frozen in time, triggering an idea to form in Dougal's head. *No, I couldn't, could I? Maybe I should. Maybe it would teach someone a lesson. Although it may also land me in a lot of trouble, everyone here seems to be taking all this so seriously.*

Dougal rested his head back against the hard wooden surface and thought for a moment, but knowing thinking was not one of his strong points, he decided he needed to act. He was tired, he was still a little nauseous, and still in need of sweet revenge, so he cleared his mind and recited the phrase Graimel taught him.

"Te`sow Ime Fow, Oe`my De`an, Aestic O`an."

Dougal was getting the hang of this now; all his practise had paid off, and everything around him slowed to the point of stopping. He waveringly brought himself to his feet, still feeling a little out of sorts, but with the focus of a bomb disposal expert, he edged along the table. Carefully picking his way towards his target, placing his feet so as not to knock over any food or drink, or tread on someone's fingers.

Dougal's mind wandered, thinking of himself as ninja as he tiptoed over to Bregon, *concentrate* he thought, *before you become a multitasking disaster*. Just as he was about ready to pull Bregon's arm over and give the win to Graimel, he paused to savour the moment and inspiration struck him. A thought popped into his head from out of nowhere, with a very distinctive and distracting *Pop* sound that made him almost lose his concentration again.

Dougal smiled, turned around until he was facing back up the table, crouched, and shuffled backwards a little. He glanced over his shoulder to ensure he was in just the right position, then broke wind, letting rip with everything he could muster. His stomach had been grumbling for most of the party, and the meat and mead he had been consuming was playing havoc with his digestion. With a grin of satisfaction and the cat like stealth of a drunken hippo, he made a hasty retreat, lay back down on the table, and returned time to normality.

Dougal unintentionally timed his action to perfection. For at the precise moment time resumed, Bregon took a deep yawning breath, inhaling every single molecule of the gift Dougal left for him. His eyes bulged as he gagged and hacked, and for a second he lost all mind of where he was at and what he was doing. A second was all Graimel required, and Bregon's fist hit the table.

While everyone gathered around the table started yelling in pain and tending to their bruised hands and fingers, Dougal pretended to have just come round and sat up. But Graimel was no fool, and with a smile, he shot him a knowing wink. Dougal simply smirked with glee and shrugged his shoulders.

"Something caught my breath there, but a win is a win, and I am glad if anyone was going to beat me, it was you, my friend," Bregon said, coughing and spluttering through every breath.

"Merely good luck for me, and misfortune for you."

"Very kind of you to say so. Maybe we should call it a night. I am a little tired and indeed a little queasy now. No doubt it's something I ate."

Baldur unbound their hands, and they hugged each other before Onjeg came over and escorted Bregon out of the hall, signalling the end of the festivities. With the party over, everyone dispersed, with many hugging and thanking each other for a wonderful evening of merriment, whilst others slept off their overindulgence under tables, or wherever it was they passed out.

Sleip got down off the table from where he had watched all the action unfold and ushered his daughters from their seats.

"Come on girls, time we made a move. It's an early start for some of us."

"Are you not forgetting something, father?" Efraj said, looking over at Binty.

"Oh, that was just a bit of friendly banter. I am sure Binty would agree the bet was purely for fun," Sleip said, somewhat worrisomely.

"Well, a bet is a bet, and if you had won, I am sure you would have wanted your kiss," Binty said, as she flew over and caressed Sleip's face. "Surely a hunky dwarf such as yourself is not worried about a little slap from a pixie."

Krahns stepped down off the table laughing and shaking his head. He hugged Anelci and Efraj, before turning to Sleip and smiling on his way past.

"You're on your own, buddy. Good luck."

"Remember how you smiled when Binty suggested she slap you? You're not having second thoughts, are you?" Anelci said, giggling, and rubbing her father's arm up and down. "I mean, you seemed so excited about the prospect."

"Okay, I guess a bet is a bet, and I will honour it."

"I will be as gentle as I can. After all, I made a promise," Binty said, winking at Efraj and Anelci.

Sleip winced as the heat shot through his left cheek, spreading into his jaw and eye socket, causing his now bloodshot green eye to twitch and water. But he was still on his feet, with his head still secured to his body, so that was something to be grateful for. However, he hoped the ringing in his ears would dissipate before needing to engage in any polite conversation. Binty stroked Sleip's face once more and placed a kiss upon his cheek, negating all the effects of her slap.

"Thank you, Binty, and I do hope you have learned a valuable lesson, father," Anelci said, giggling as she strolled off home with Efraj.

"You have quite a slap there, little one, I will remember that. I don't think even Mabel hits that hard, but don't tell her."

Sleip ran after his girls, leaving Binty, Graimel, and Dougal alone in the hall.

"I guess we should all get some rest as well. We have a long day ahead of us tomorrow," Graimel said.

Graimel threw his arm around Dougal and helped him off the table.

"It seems you are still a little unsteady on your feet, so let us get you to your room. And by the way, thank you for what you did with Bregon. I can't say he didn't deserve it."

"Why? What did he do? I thought he had only just come around?" Binty said.

"Oh, don't worry about it, Binty. He merely gave me some advice earlier regarding how to win an arm wrestle."

"What on earth would he know about arm wrestling?"

"A lot more than you would think," Graimel chuckled.

# 32

# NO SNACK FOR THE NESTOLOBOD

Dougal woke with a pounding head, which was soon soothed somewhat by the warm glow being cast into his room from the bubbling lava pit. He drifted over to the window, awestruck, and drank in the view one last time. *No time for dallying,* he thought, as he closed the door and scurried up to the great hall, expecting to find the place in complete disarray, with dwarfs asleep under tables, and food and drink strewn all over. So he was a little shocked when he entered to find it impeccably clean, with no sign of there ever having even been a party.

Although Dougal had thrown very few parties in his time, he decided he really needed the number for this clean-up crew. Not that any of his parties had been particularly wild, but it was amazing how much chaos and destruction can be caused by a few friends and Bounce, mainly Bounce.

He took a seat at one of the long tables and rested his head on his folded arms while he waited for Graimel and Binty to join him. As he sat there trying to remember snippets of the previous night, he realised they never made plans to meet anywhere at any time. If they had, they were not the sort of plans you remembered after consuming copious amounts of alcohol and food.

Of course, being rendered unconscious by the dwarven equivalent of an evil nitrous oxide release may have contributed to his lack of memory. *Fond memories,* Dougal thought, thankful for the fact he could not actually remember anything.

"Ah, good, you're here already. I wasn't sure you would remember," Graimel said, taking a seat next to Dougal.

"To be honest, I don't know why I'm here, and I don't remember much of anything from last night, as you rightly implied."

"Well, all that matters is you are here. We just need to wait for Binty, and we will get moving."

"Where are we going, or should I not ask?"

"You can always ask, as long as you don't always expect an answer."

"Morning you two, I'm surprised you're already here Dougal, that was some party."

"He doesn't remember anything."

"What, nothing? Do you remember dancing with Onjeg?"

"Er, who is Onjeg?"

"Seriously? Onjeg is Bregon's wife, and you spent most of the evening dancing with her. She was even carrying you around in her arms at one point, wasn't she, Graimel?"

"That she was." Graimel beamed.

"Well, now we are all here, we shall make a move. Come Harg."

"Are we not waiting to say goodbye to everyone?"

"No time, Dougal, no time."

Graimel got to his feet, and like a naughty scamp skipping out on the bill at a fancy restaurant, he bolted out of the great hall. With a mixture of exasperation and dismay, Dougal threw his hands in the air and pulled out his wallet, desperately hoping they took Visa. Then, realising this was merely a figure of speech, he put his wallet back in his pocket, leapt up from the table and ran, albeit unsteadily after Graimel.

Binty shrugged her shoulders and raced to catch Dougal, regretting her decision to rest on his right shoulder, as sitting on it was akin to sitting on the deck of a cruise ship that was trying to navigate 6m waves. Suffice to say, she zipped over to Graimel, taking a seat on his shoulder instead.

They crept past the forges, trying not to make a sound as they headed towards the exit. Not that anyone would hear over the noise generated by them, had they even been stamping whilst wearing clogs. Graimel opened the door to the stairwell, took a last lingering look at the hot burning coals of Ildjorden, before climbing the stairs back up to the rooftop, and the waiting Chmnu.

The morning sun stretched itself over the horizon, inspiring the spires on the castle to cast fanciful elongated shadows across the rooftop. Chmnu lifted his head and opened one eye to show a passing interest in the clatter created by Dougal falling out of the hidden door.

"So, you finally made it back. I was becoming quite bored, and I am sure I have missed more than one dinner, but you are here now. Shall we go?"

"Of course, terribly sorry for the delay. We got a little diverted and then had to attend a party, you see."

"No, not really. A party. Did you bring me anything?"

Binty sped over to Chmnu and pulled out a small chunk of cake she had secreted away in case she got peckish on the flight back. Chmnu tilted his head, staring inquisitively at this mere, almost undetectable morsel.

"Are you holding something, little one?"

"It's a piece of cake for you. It may only be a small piece of cake, but in case you hadn't noticed, I am only small. Anyway, I would like you to have it for being so patient with us."

At this point Dougal pulled a sizeable slab of meat from his trouser leg, which went someway to explaining his unsteadiness on his feet, notwithstanding his consumption the previous night. Originally, he had stashed the meat as a doggy bag for Bounce, but now thought it would be better used to reward Chmnu's patience, waiting for them on this cold roof for two nights with no food. Not only that, but it was now a little pungent, and was not at all comfortable stuffed inside his trousers.

With due reverence, he made his offer alongside that of Binty's, and Chmnu graciously accepted, swiping them from their hands with his tongue.

"Thank you," Chmnu said, glancing past them at Graimel.

"Don't look at me, I've got nothing for you, but I'll tell Vern what a good boy you were. Maybe he will give you an extra portion of dinner."

"Works for me," Chmnu said, unfurling his wings and beating them, "let's get going."

Graimel climbed on Chmnu's back while Binty picked up Dougal and placed him behind Graimel before taking a seat on his shoulder.

With everyone seated as securely as they were going to be, Chmnu pounced into the air and shot skyward with all the haste his grumbling stomach could muster. Back to Bodmin.

There was little conversation between the group on the flight, with Graimel thinking about his plan and constantly replaying it in his head. Binty could not help but worry about all involved, although sure Graimel's plan would succeed, it did not alleviate her foreboding sense of dread that something bad was in the air, and it was not one of Bounce's toots.

As for Dougal, he could sense the tension stifling the atmosphere, and knew something was afoot. But then, ever since he had known Graimel, something had been afoot, something he accepted to be the norm, but this time there was an uneasiness about the situation. He didn't dwell, instead, he threw his arms up into the air and squealed with all his might. The sort of squeal that any teenager at a boy band concert would have been proud of.

Chmnu swooped down and landed high in the majestic willow tree where they had first met him. There waiting for them to return was the Major. He dashed over and welcomed them all back, paying special attention to Chmnu.

"I bet you're hungry, boy," Vern said, patting Chmnu's neck, before grabbing a fish from a nearby barrel and hurling it into his jaws. "I will get you some food and a few treats. I think it's safe to say you have earned them."

"He certainly has. He is amazing. It was like being on a ride at the fun fair. I'm just sad it's over," Dougal said.

"Well, you are welcome to visit any time, and I will introduce you to more of the family, if you are interested."

"That would be amazing. If I can find my way back, that is. Thank you."

They bid their farewells to Chmnu and made their way down into Vern's kitchen, taking a seat at the table for a brief rest after the long flight. Graimel followed Vern as he went to prepare tea and cake. He needed a word in private. After a few minutes, they re-joined Binty and Dougal, with Vern ending their conversation with a firm nod.

"So, what were you two gossiping about?" Binty asked.

"Well, if you must know, we were discussing who are hairier, dwarfs or lyconfinds."

"Ooh! Why would you be discussing that?" Binty asked.

"Well Vern was telling me about his new shampoo Furisoft, and was just suggesting to me I should try it, and then asked about how hairy—"

"Stop! Enough already, sorry I asked."

"Whatever you wish. Right, drink up, we should make haste."

"I wonder if Bounce has missed me?" Binty asked.

"Well, if he has, and he's not missed me, you can keep him," Dougal said, chuckling.

They thanked Vern for all his help once again and promised to return soon, before heading out over the moor in the direction of Janet's den.

The walk between Janet's and Vern's seemed to be going a lot quicker than last time. This could have been due to it being downhill, or the increased sense of urgency from Graimel which grew by the minute. Whatever it was, they did not seem to be moving fast enough, for no matter how hard Dougal tried to maintain Graimel's pace, he would increase it.

As he ran to keep up, he began to feel the effects of late night partying, and as his concentration lapsed for a second, he slipped. Before Binty could react, he plummeted over the edge of the embankment, sending her spinning through the air.

Dougal tumbled head over heels, smacking his shoulder against a huge half buried flat stone, before rolling onto his side, and hitting his head with a thump, rendering him semi-unconscious. His limp body continued hurtling down the bank, only stopping when his left leg cracked over a sharp jutting rock, spearing it.

With a gut flipping snap, his tibia broke the skin, spraying shards of bone, blood, and sinew all over the wondrous green speckled canvas of the moorland. Half dazed, Dougal let out an exhausted gurgling scream, his vision blurred by mud and blood, his strength waning. As his eyes faded shut, he could hear Binty's voice screaming for Graimel to stop.

Graimel turned without stopping. Such was the import of this day and the events that would take place upon it. Unable to see anyone behind him, he skidded to a halt, regained his footing, and rushed back up along the ridge line, calling out as he ran.

"Graimel!" Binty screamed again. "Down here."

With such a defined urgency in her voice, Graimel stopped in his tracks and glanced down the embankment. There at the bottom he spotted the crumpled figure of Dougal entangled in a violent mass of granite, like a surreal artist's impression of a man-eating rock beast having a picnic in the park.

Of course, man-eating rock beasts, who preferred to be called by their proper name, nestolobod, were a rare sight in England. They were native to the Scottish Highlands, where they loved to roam and loaf about, and could survive up to a hundred years on a snack.

Graimel slid and slipped his way down to where Dougal lay. Binty was frantically trying to stem the bleeding, whilst trying to remain calm and talk to him as soothingly as she could muster.

"I have done what I can, Graimel, but this is a lot more complex than Bounce's wound."

"Then there is no time to waste. We need to get him to Janet's den now."

"But, Graimel, we can't. If you do, then they will know where we are."

"Maybe it is time they knew, and we finish this, we should still have time to put the plan into action. And if all goes well, we will also have time for a cup of tea and a slice of Janet's cake before they find us."

"I trust you."

With an inaudible pop, they vanished. Blood trickled down the tooth shaped rock of the sleeping nestolobod, who was visiting some ancient relatives on Bodmin Moor. Luckily for Dougal, the nestolobod were exceptionally deep sleepers, otherwise he may have become a Dougal sized snack.

Binty had forgotten how teleporting made her feel, but she put aside her queasiness and dashed across to kick over the standing stone she had only recently put back. The stone groaned a little, but also knew when not to argue, and this was without doubt one of those times.

The boom of the felled stone reverberated down into Janet's den, telling her they were back, and she hurried to open the door and greet them. Graimel barged past, carrying Dougal as Binty zipped between them, and with a flick of her wrist, she cleared the kitchen table. Graimel gently placed Dougal down, his arm dropping to one side and coming into contact with Bounce, who licked his hand to welcome him home, whilst also sneakily snuffling for treats.

"Oh my god! What's happened?" Janet asked.

"He fell. He's lost a lot of blood, and his left leg looks a bit dodgy."

Janet seized her medical kit from under the counter.

"Have you got any alcohol?" Binty asked.

"Really, at this time of day?"

"I meant for his leg? Although."

"Good thinking, cupboard on the left."

Binty threw the cupboard door open and grabbed the first bottle that came to hand. It contained an enchantingly beautiful glowing blue liquid.

"This is all alcohol in here, right?"

"Yes, yes."

She flipped the bottle around, and on an ornate black label in an almost blinding white ink were the embossed words.

*'WAXENWANE – MOONSHINE'*

The o's in the word moonshine had been replaced with little moons behind a thread of clouds. Underneath it stated *84% vol,*

Binty did not quite understand what this meant, *but 84 is quite a high number, so it must be good,* she thought.

She darted across the table to Janet and cracked open the seal. A wisp of luminous blue vapour climbed out and formed the shape of a wolf. It stalked its way down to the label and bayed at the twin moons before leaping onto the table and dissipating.

Prior to witnessing this, she had been tempted to take a sip, but that combined with the now sickly sweet ammonia like odour stinging her nose and throat, had changed her mind. And for the first time in her life, she almost passed out.

Binty held her breath for a moment as she tipped some of the liquid onto his wound. On seeing the liquid run over Dougal's leg, Janet glanced up at the glowing blue bottle.

"Oh no, that's Moo, Moo-oonshine!" Janet howled, ripping her apron from the hook on the wall and throwing it over her head. "Time to bake," she snarled.

"Janet?"

"It's too late, Binty. It's up to us to sort this now," Graimel said, as he moved around the table to finish bandaging Dougal's leg.

Binty had a thought. *If this stuff could almost render her unconscious, then maybe it had the power to wake Dougal from his nap*. Intending to use it in much the same way as you would smelling salts, she went to hold the bottle under his nose. But as she tipped the bottle up, the liquid rushed forward, splashing about a shot glass worth over his lips.

Dougal sat bolt upright, his eyes darting around the room on supernatural stalks.

"What the hell was that? And arrghh! What the hell is wrong with my leg?" he said, before collapsing back onto his back.

On hearing Dougal's voice, Bounce jumped up, resting his front paws on the edge of the table, looked deep into Dougal's eyes and licked the entirety of his face. Dougal forgot all else and rolled through the pain, and as he lay his hand on Bounce's head, a sense of serenity came over him.

"Hey Bounce, you all right my little man. Have you been a good boy for your Aunty Janet?" Dougal said, wincing as the pain shot back through him.

"Any chance I could sit in the chair by the fire guys, this table is not all that comfortable, no disrespect, aunty."

Janet did not hear a word; she was immersed in her baking, and oblivious to them moving Dougal across to the chair.

"I need you to make me a promise, Dougal. Whatever happens in these next few hours, you do not leave this chair," Graimel said.

Dougal frowned as he looked Graimel in the eye, pulled back the blanket that he had just thrown over his lap, and glanced rapidly between Graimel and his poorly bandaged, not so straight left leg.

"Am I missing something? Where is it you think I'm going to go on this? You have seen this right; I mean, this didn't just happen as you threw the blanket over my leg, did it!"

Dougal sarcastically whipped the blanket back and forth, covering and uncovering his leg in quick succession, all the time muttering.

"Nope, nope, and nope, still nope. It's not the blanket!" Dougal said, before finally covering his legs again.

"Will you just promise!"

"Okay, I promise, I won't walk anywhere until you say so."

With a shake of his head, Graimel flounced off into the kitchen and somehow snapped Janet out of her cake baking trance.

Binty approached the hearth, and using a trick that Efraj taught her, she converted Janet's hearth into a mini forge of Ildjorden. Not only could this flame not be extinguished, but it would burn hotter and brighter than ever before, preventing any unwanted intruders from ever coming back down the flue.

"We will soon have you mended, and then, well, let us get you mended first, eh," Binty said, caressing and kissing Dougal's forehead before turning her attention to Bounce, lavishing him with kisses and cuddles.

With a clack, the front door swung open and Fimor strode through. Transfixed by her beauty, he scooped Janet up and swirled her around in his arms before pulling her close, his hand tight upon her waist as he took a moment to bathe in her gaze. With one arm still around her, he leant over the table and shook Graimel's hand, then took a seat. Before long, Beth, Wrethe, Sven, Lescan, and Klaus arrived, and Binty thought it prudent to join them in the kitchen. And with hushed voices, they spoke of what lay ahead.

At first Dougal strained to hear, but finding this tiresome, he gave up and just relaxed in front of the fire until he fell asleep.

The conversation at the table continued for about an hour with the odd subtly raised voice and minor disagreement, but ended with all hands in, and solemn faces passing gentle nods of agreement.

# 33
# THE SNARLING & THE SCARED

Malka came dashing back around the corner towards her queen and the assembled guard. Excited to be bringing this news to her most capricious queen, be it with a modicum of apprehension.

"Queen Blodia, I bring you important, though disturbing, news regarding Bedougalnn."

Blodia brushed Bazil aside and motioned for Malka to come forward.

"Speak."

"I have seen a fluctuation in time that I believe is related to your quarry."

"And what leads you to believe this?" Blodia asked.

"Two things, your weariness. I believe Graimel Tock caused this fluctuation." Malka paused to allow time for Blodia to hiss and spit like an angry snake. "And it occurred on Bodmin Moor, at the precise location of the last attack."

"This is excellent news, and I can see why you thought it disturbing. You are worried about your queen, as we only narrowly avoided defeat last time."

Malka was about to interject that she thought they were

defeated last time, but snapped her mouth shut again, before any utterance.

"Oh, I am sorry. Did you want to say something?" Blodia asked.

Daring not to speak, Malka shook her head, maintained her poker face, and hoped Blodia could not read minds.

"If you are sure, then I will continue. This time when we attack, I am taking the entire guard with me, not just a select few. They do not stand a chance."

Blodia flexed her long bony fingers and made some obscure hand gestures, which made the gathered crowd cheer and clap. Of course, I cannot determine whether this made them clap, or whether they clapped under their own volition. Either way, Blodia smiled and felt exceptionally pleased with herself and her plan to end Bedougalnn.

"Your Foulness I—" Malka began.

"Yes," Bazil said, as Blodia swatted him to the cobbles.

"Continue Malka," Blodia said.

"The disturbing news I have is not regarding the location, but I have seen things that are as yet unclear, which lead me to believe Bedougalnn has help from many others."

"Many others you say, but you do not know how many, or who?"

"No, my rancid Regina."

"Then what use to me are you as a seer? You may as well follow your incompetent brother Hans. No. If you think our quarry has more help, then you will come with us, as will the rest of the realm." Blodia turned away from Malka and stood over Bazil, who had not yet picked himself up off the floor. "Order your guards to gather the entire realm and bring them here. You have one hour."

"Erm, how long is an hour here?" Bazil asked.

"Do you dare question your queen?"

"Why, of course not, my malodorous monarch. Within the... hour."

Bazil set about organising the guard. Puzzled by the constant references to time, he thought he better just get it done before Blodia asks him about it again. The guards disappeared in twos across the Hidden Dimension, while Bazil took it upon himself to gather up the locals, starting with The Banished Abstract Cat Tavern.

He pushed open the door with about as much grace as a metal head in a mosh pit, paced across to the bar, and took his usual seat.

"A flagon of ale please, Barc, and then you need to shut this place and come with me."

"I still have customers, and I've never shut this place before. Why now?"

"Queen Blodia demands it," Bazil said, taking a gulp of his ale. Then, in a booming voice that echoed throughout the tavern, he added, "that goes for the rest of you as well. Drink up, your queen demands your presence at the Pool of Vacant Reflection."

Bazil sat and watched as one by one the patrons necked the remnants of their drinks and trudged from the tavern. But with a niggle in the pit of his stomach pushing him to believe this would be his last flagon of ale. He took his time to sip and savour the ashen slop. When there was only himself and Barc left, he drank what remained, hopped off his stool, wobbled a little, and ushered Barc out of the tavern.

"I should lock up," Barc said, pulling his keys out of his pocket.

"No time for that, Blodia is waiting. And besides, no one is going to be here. We are all going on the hunt for Bedougalnn."

Bazil pushed a hesitant Barc into the street, where he joined many other glum faces, also on their way to grace Blodia with their presence.

With the skotos gathered from far and wide, and the streets and alleyways full to bursting, Blodia raised herself up above all. As she looked down upon them, in more ways than one, and not for the first time, she addressed her loyal subjects, and the other 68.5% of the subjugated crowd.

"Skotos, today you join me in the hunt for Bedougalnn, and today we end his existence, thus ending all time and avenging the crimes against all shadows. We stand as one, with me above you all. Some of you will perish, but know this. All great victories require great sacrifice, and it is my honour to let you be this sacrifice."

Blodia focused on the murky black waters of the Pool of Vacant Reflection and commanded it to open a portal to Bodmin Moor. A confused hush spread through sections of the gathered crowd. Though not a word was spoken, many a mind pondered on how you could end all of time and still be. Whereas others focused on the word *sacrifice,* and how that did not appeal to them in the slightest.

"Captain Fouldoom remain here until every skoto has passed through the portal, then join us. I will lead and prepare the way."

Blodia shot down straight into the pool, and without so much as a ripple, she disappeared beneath the surface. Moments later, she appeared in a vast cave on Bodmin Moor, and in the darkness, she conjured an evil magic to infect the skies once again. Pulling on all the blackness of her soul and feeding it into the clouds, choking them, binding them together until not a single shard of light could penetrate the impregnable darkness.

Then came the rain, pounding the earth with the untamed ferocity of a tropical storm, lifting the soil from the ground, and tossing it about like a child flicking paint. The ferns and heathers being hammered into the ground, as if bowing subserviently to this most evil wicked stepmother nature summoned by Blodia.

The first of the skotos had now come through and were waiting for direction from their queen. As soon as the Queen's Guard joined them, Blodia ordered the skotos to be escorted from the cave and organised into tight circular formations of twelve. There came an explosive, thunderous crack, as lightning struck the ground right in front of the cave entrance, ending the entire group of skotos that had just exited.

Blodia paid it no mind. She had told of sacrifice and that was just the first. There would be more.

In the blink of an itchy eye, a second bolt struck an area of rocks a mere 30m further away, sending fragmented granite through the air like shrapnel dissipating outwards from an explosion. Now for some, this may have been somewhat of a minor annoyance, but for most it was a non-issue, as this manner of physical harm, although painful, was fleeting.

Wave after wave of skotos came pouring into the cave and were directed through the mouth, out to the open moorland. Spreading their dark foreboding shadow across the heathers, and into the distance. Finally Floop and Bazil came through the portal, confirming the Hidden Dimension was now devoid of skotos. Blodia had grown to like Floop over the few days since he replaced Miss Maws. Although in fairness to her, she had been busy, and he had not had time to antagonise her yet. Regardless, Floop was her most trusted ally and why she asked him to remain with Bazil.

Blodia motioned to Bazil and Floop to exit the cave, while she scoured every alcove and shadow to ensure not a single skotos tried to escape their duty to their queen. There were none, that is to say, none were found.

"Move Out," she shrieked, as she exited the cave marching to the head of her army.

At that precise moment, two more bolts struck the ground, eliminating another 24 skotos.

They had marched only 60m when Blodia realised they were heading the wrong way, and she called for everyone to turn 30 degrees to the right. While the skotos corrected their path, she nipped over to the group of guards responsible for ensuring everyone was ready to move out. With a snap of her wrist, she ended the entire group without an ounce of thought or care, as if they were just something unfortunate she had trodden in, and needed to be scraped off her boot.

With their heads down, the skotos silently adjusted their course and traipsed across the moor. Every so often, an almost welcome bolt of light from the heavens would vaporise another group, thus freeing them from their march to almost certain doom. Seemingly sporadic cheers arose from small pockets of the gathered masses, coincidentally succeeding the decimation of each group of skotos. A kind of morbid celebration of freedom.

Like an infectious disease, it spread, contaminating all those who were unvaccinated against free thought. Vast swathes of the skotos began cheering every single bolt of lightning that struck. Similar if you like to the frivolity that surrounds the oohs and aahs expelled during a firework display.

Blodia was so focused on the task at hand, she thought the whole of the Hidden Dimension now understood and supported her actions. Had she taken but a brief glimpse behind, she would have seen the truth was far removed from her misguided perception. But maybe that is why she did not turn around.

With his head held high, Bazil marched alongside his queen with a theatrical swagger, for she had picked him to be her captain and he was honoured to be so. It never occurred to him he was in the right place at the right time, or possibly the wrong place at the right time, or even the right place at the wrong time. Whichever it was, if he had thought about it, it would have only given him a headache, and he was in no mood for a headache.

So, as the saying goes, ignorance is bliss. At least until ignorance becomes the sort of blind stupidity that has you marching across a moor, to end the sole thing that will end all things, including your own existence.

Floop trudged behind Blodia, unhappy with this whole scenario. Unhappy that his favourite cousin Yoop was ended for innocently speaking up against this most vacuous of ideologies, when all others remained silent. Unhappy that he had not bothered to wear shoes, and this foul mud was sticking between his toes like toffee sticks to dentures. And annoyed with himself for inadvertently helping her arrive at this point.

If only he had not disliked the buffoon Hans so much. Not that there was anything about him to like, but had he bided his time, maybe we would not be here now. Maybe Malka would not have been looking for disturbances, and Blodia would still be irascibly stomping around her vacant space.

What upset Floop the most was seeing his fellow skotos ended for no reason. For as much as all skotos, were derived from all the evil or corrupt shadows from all the planes of existence. Somehow, a vast percentage of them became permanently changed once they became skotos, and wanted nothing more than to atone for their sins.

Of course, as in all walks of life, there were those that were just bad, bad through to the very core of their being. Those that had no contrition and could never repent, for they saw no wrong in any of their actions. Most of those were in the Queen's Guard, who would carry out the queen's orders without hesitation. Floop did not care for those, although he did feel sorry for them.

After 97 minutes of trudging across the open moor, Blodia screamed for her army to come to a halt. As lightning continued to pick holes in her gathered forces, Blodia called out her prey.

"BEDOUGALNN!" she screamed through the blackness.

Scurrying back through the skotos, she rallied her guards as she herself retreated, preparing herself for the onslaught Malka predicted. She used her cunning to fall back as far as possible, leaving Bazil alone on the front line. He turned to see a thousand snarling faces, and hundreds more who were just frightened, lost in dismay, and in the distance he could make out his self-preserving queen.

Floop followed Blodia as she fortified her position. He was no warrior, and only here as he did not relish being ended. If ended here by mortals, and he had not been an aggressor, then his penance would be considered paid. If ended by Blodia, or if he attacked the mortals and was ended by them, he went to limbo, and there was no escape or end, for anything in limbo.

As he knelt to clean the mud from between his toes once more, a violent yet somehow harmonious roar went up from the Queen's Guard, and he steeled himself for the inevitable.

# 34

# THE BATTLE OF BODMIN MOOR PART 1

Fimor stood and placed his hands on the tabletop, leaning in towards Graimel.

"Is anyone else coming? Or are we on our own?". Fimor asked.

"I am sure Bregon will be joining us. He gave me his word."

"One dwarf? I have heard of his legend, but he is still only one."

"Bregon may only be one, but he is a hundred skotos or more."

There was a loud thump against the door, startling Janet, then she remembered, the bad guys don't knock. Fimor walked over to the door and yanked it open.

"One dwarven legend at your service," Bregon said, with a smile, "and far more than a hundred, Graimel, if I do say so myself."

Bregon grabbed Fimor's hand, shaking it with vigour.

"Well, you know who I am. Now, how about you introduce yourself?"

Fimor took a moment to gather himself before introducing everyone present. He had been taken aback by the size of this dwarf, expecting someone more or less the same size as Graimel.

But Bregon was almost as broad as Graimel was tall, and his shield almost the size of Janet's kitchen table.

"What happened to our friend Dougal?" Bregon said, looking across at a semi-comatose Dougal resting in the chair by the fire.

"Let's just say he had a minor stumble, and well, kind of buggered his leg up," Graimel said.

Dougal opened one eye and waved at Bregon before falling back to sleep. Bounce realised he would not get introduced, so he let out a deep woof accompanied by a little bounce.

"My apologies," Fimor said, kneeling down and placing his hand on Bounce's head. "This is Bounce. He is Dougal's dog; well I think he is more a member of the family."

Bounce offered his paw for Bregon to shake.

"A pleasure to meet you, Bounce," Bregon said, taking a firm grip of Bounce's paw.

Graimel got up from his seat and offered Bregon a drink, which was declined with a wave of the hand before he headed back towards the open door.

"Are you on your own?" Graimel asked.

"Of course not, old man. I have a small troop outside getting into position, and Sleip and Krahns should join us shortly."

With that said, Bregon left to re-join his troops.

"We should join them; for I am certain things are going to get rough quite soon. If you are all ready?" Graimel said, raising his glass.

They all stood, raised their glasses in unison and cheered, "For Fangs and Fur!" before downing their drinks and heading out.

Binty stayed behind and checked on Dougal. He drifted in and out of sleep, clearly in a lot of pain. Bounce had followed Binty and now sat at the side of the chair with his head resting affectionately on Dougal's good leg.

"Stay here and stay safe, Dougal. Whatever happens, just stay here."

Dougal's eyes rolled a little in some kind of

acknowledgement of what Binty said, but there was no telling if he understood, or if he even heard her.

"Bounce, you be a good boy and look after your dad."

Binty patted Bounce on his head and stroked his fur for a moment before following the others out on to the moor. As she headed through the door, she slammed it shut behind her, forgetting her own strength for a second. The door hit the jamb with such ferocity of engagement it had no choice but to complain with a clattering thud, refusing to allow the latch to lock. With a groan, it swung ajar an inch or two before finding a comfortable position in which to rest.

Graimel exited onto the moor to be greeted by Bregon, his accompanying 50 warriors having already established a defensive line about 90m from the monolith outside Janet's den.

"Glad you could join us; I had two of my warriors go scout a little. Blodia leads an army of at least a couple of thousand skotos, maybe more, although it would seem they are not all part of her guard."

"Worrying that she brings so many with her. After her previous defeat, I guess she is taking no chances. How long do we have before they are here?"

"My scouts reckon no more than 15 minutes before they are upon us."

"Then there is no more time to waste." Graimel turned to his lyconfind friends "Spread out, each of you join with one of the small groups of Bregon's dwarfs."

Fimor hugged Janet, and Wrethe held Beth in his arms, before they both ran off in separate directions, each joining a small group of dwarven warriors. Ulap took Fimor's hand and greeted him with considerable excitement. Wrethe joined a group led by Mad Mathis, and after some hasty introductions, was relieved to hear he lived up to his name. The rest of the lyconfind did likewise, and were greeted with equal amounts of delight.

"Janet, Beth, you girls best stay here and tend to the wounded," Graimel said, without first engaging his brain.

Janet and Beth scowled, bearing their pristine white canines, of which they had quite a few.

"You best be joking," Beth said, more than a little displeased with Graimel's comment.

It took Graimel less than a second to realise his mistake and added.

"Unless of course, you want to join a group of dwarfs each. That would, without doubt, be much more beneficial."

Snarls and scowls turned to smiles and smirks as Beth and Janet, feeling quite pleased with themselves, hugged, flicked out their claws and headed out. Although both still wearing pinafore dresses, they made quite the impression, and were welcomed by the groups of battle-hardened dwarfs they joined.

"I have to say Graimel, I don't think much of the weather here," Bregon said, swinging his shield in front of them to block a brutal bolt of lightning.

A howl went up from the front of the line, followed by a roar from the gathered dwarven warriors.

"Looks like it's time," Bregon said, drawing his sword Vargklo from his belt and raising it to the sky. "For Honour! For Bedougalnn!" Bregon roared, consuming all the air in his lungs, charging forward into conflict.

Blodia soared up above her army, but held her position towards the back. A smile stained her face as she saw how few were defending, and she ordered the front lines to engage, sending in just one wave of 192 skotos. Bazil stood his ground as the roar engulfed the moor, and the skotos rushed ahead of him to engage in what he saw as a pitiful excuse of an opposition. But something kept him rooted to the spot. What he witnessed made him re-evaluate in an instant of shock and surprise.

Bregon raced with shield raised straight into the oncoming skotos, with a force akin to a Canadian freight train hitting a field of marshmallow soldiers. With a crack against his shield, he ended an entire group of skotos. He tumbled to his right, lightning striking the ground at his feet as another two groups swarmed, which he obliterated in turn.

Bregon kept moving throughout the wave, as Vargklo lit up and disintegrated any skotos she came into contact with. Within seconds, half of his warriors joined the fray, and within a few minutes there was nothing left on the moor around them besides 192 piles of ash.

Bregon and his warriors raised their swords, their axes, and their hammers, and smashed them against their shields in a sort of ceremonial taunt. Blodia screeched in anguish. She had not expected so much from so few. She drew on her power and shot a bolt of purest agony straight at Bregon. He anticipated the shot, deflecting it with his shield, as Grankle leapt into the air to defend his king. The bolt glanced off Bregon's shield and struck Grankle's arm, sending him reeling across the ground, his arm slowly disintegrating before his eyes.

"For Honour! For Bedougalnn!" he cried out, as the rest of his body was consumed.

"SHIELDS!" Bregon called out.

Blodia fired off a few more bolts before almost being struck by lightning herself, and so commanded the rest of her army to move forward. Another almighty roar erupted from the skotos, though some bore an obvious reluctance to take part. Blodia spotted such a reluctance and ended the entire group of twelve where they stood.

As the new front line of skotos clashed with the dwarfs, Graimel heard a familiar almighty whooshing sound, followed by a colossal thud behind him. He spun on his heels, and there, sat astride Chmnu, was Major Vern Heysi.

"We are not late are we? You haven't gone and started without us?" Vern said.

"You missed the start, but you're bloody welcome."

At that moment, another much larger, iridescent green, jagged scaled dragon hit the ground next to Chmnu with such a thump that two nearby standing stones got scared and fell over. Sat astride this dragon was Krahns.

"Hej Graimel, this is Sviltesblen, he has come to help, and that up there is Sleip on Zephyrugm," he said, pointing up at the huge grey stone dragon that was dive-bombing Blodia's position. "We better get up there and help. Oh, I forgot to say, I have also brought an old friend. She should be here, well, about now."

Three beams of blinding golden light broke through the cloud line and struck the earth at Graimel's feet, such was the radiance of this light, that the nearest few skotos vanished from existence. Within seconds the light faded, and stood before them, a tall, golden armoured Viking shield-maiden.

"I am Dynma, Queen of the Valkyrie and Guardian of the Throne of Skovin. These are my protectors, Hettierne and Purrseeka," she announced with fire in her voice, before slamming the end of her spear into the ground, cracking open the rock it struck. "Hettierne, retrieve the fallen warrior so that he may ascend, Purrseeka, with me. We support our brethren in this fight."

Zephyrugm flashed down from the sky and belched out a blast of fire in Blodia's direction. Blodia plunged down to shelter amongst her army, as Zephyrugm swooped around and let out another shot of fire. This time annihilating those too slow to move out of her line of attack, before sweeping back up into the sky to line up for another run.

As she shot back up into the thunderous grey above, Chmnu and Sviltesblen joining her, and the three of them continued their air raids against the skotos. The rain glistened across their wings as they swooped and dived, weaving between the forks of lightning as they struck with ferocity from the sky. Setting fire to swathes of the moor.

Blodia's forces swarmed all over Bedougalnn's protectors. As quick as one skotos was ended, another would take their place. The fighting was on all sides now.

Mad Mathis and Wrethe were engulfed in combat, fighting side by side. Mad Mathis was whacking any incoming skotos with his hammer, straight into the path of Wrethe who tore them in two, dwarf and lyconfind fighting in total synchronicity with each other.

The rain penetrated the earth and the now sodden moor encumbered the dwarfs and lyconfind alike. Unable to gain stable footing, it was becoming troublesome for the dwarfs to swing their weapons with the sublime accuracy normally attributed to them. The ground was wearisome, but their fervour was not.

Beth was busy ripping through skotos with an enviable rage, pent-up since the death of Laegon and Kainen, a fury released. At her side one of the forge keepers, a squat, acrobatic dwarf named Judn, who favoured an additional axe in his left hand in place of a shield.

He was busily slicing through skotos at a frenetic pace when Beth became overwhelmed and was brought to ground. Judn somersaulted through the air, swinging his axes and slicing one of the skotos clean in two, before hacking his way through the skotos piled on top of her. Within moments, he was helping her back to her feet again. But before Beth had time to thank him, he grabbed her, sweeping her behind him in one sudden fluid movement as Bazil lunged forwards.

Judn took the full force of Bazil's strike, his hand ploughing deep into Judn's chest, turning his heart to ash. As Judn crumpled into the heather, Beth leapt over him, and with one swipe she removed Bazil's head, letting out a piercing howl. His eyes still spinning in his head as she snatched up his body and tore it asunder. She howled again, and this time a chorus of six filled the air, uniting with her.

With quiet relief, she howled a third time and was joined by all, reinvigorating their will, and further bolstering their unwavering determination to overcome these seemingly insurmountable odds.

Purrseeka swooped down and landed silently at Beth's feet, bathing the area around her in a skotos melting brilliance. Without a word said, she raised Judn and sent him on his final journey as a fallen warrior.

With a flash, she shot back into the sky to join Dynma and Hettierne as they darted around, hurling their spears of light. They had already attempted to engage Blodia along with Krahns, Sleip, and Vern, astride the dragons, but Blodia had formed some sort of impenetrable shield around her. After many failed attempts to penetrate it, they redirected their efforts on helping with the eradication of the amassed skotos army.

Blodia watched her captain fall and fail in his duty to rouse the spirits of the skotos. Angered by his incompetence and the relentless resistance they were facing; she was finally ready to empower her army. Whilst within her shield, she had been absorbing some of the energy from the lightning to charge her own powers, being careful to avoid a direct hit. She brought her arms up, cupping her hands against the back of her skull, her eyes swirling between blood-red and coal-black as she chanted.

"Sha O`eth Eme`th O`se Vey."

She flung her arms outwards with a ferocious release, sending a wave of malevolent energy out across the moor, blackening the heathers and grasses, and wilting the trees, but bolstering the skotos in strength, size, and ferocity.

From the time that Bregon had charged headlong into the oncoming skotos. Binty and Graimel had stayed at the entrance to Janet's den, ensuring nothing stood a chance of breaking through to Bedougalnn. They had been under constant pressure and lost count of how many skotos they had ended, but they still worried about their friends. There were minor reassurances now and then that told them they were still in the fight. From the sporadic inspiring howls echoing across the moorland, to the almighty explosions of skotos which told them, Bregon had slammed another attacking group into oblivion.

But things were looking dire. Their forces were being swamped.

As the valkyrie stopped attacking to ascend Bregon's fallen, an ear-splitting screech came from overhead. A huge bolt of lightning struck Zephyrugm's wing, sending her and Sleip spiralling out of control into a small dense thicket. Vern and Chmnu peeled off from their current attack to aid them, leaving Krahns alone to offer aerial support.

Blodia sensed the battle turning in her favour and adjusted her tack, ordering her army to concentrate on the dwarfs and their leader. The throng of skotos trying to overwhelm Graimel and Binty subsided somewhat, and they could see their friends were going to fall without help.

"Graimel, I have to help them, otherwise we are lost," Binty said, with both fury and fear surging up inside her.

"Go, I will hold here."

Binty shot off so fast that had she been a cheetah, she would have left behind her spots. So fast that Graimel did not have time to blink before she disappeared. She darted at full speed between all the ongoing skirmishes, using her speed, wit, and general deific abilities to eliminate and liberate where needed. When Binty found Bregon, he was almost knee-deep in ash and mud, swinging Vargklo with precision and instinctively blocking every single incoming attack.

"How are we holding up?" Bregon called out.

"Not great," Binty said, shaking her head, her dismay clear. "We need to draw back."

"Retreat? Not in my nature, little one."

"But we are being overrun, and I fear for our friends if we do not draw back." Binty flicked her wrist, vaporising a skoto who had been clawing his way around Bregon's shield. "Please Bregon!"

"For you and for our..." Bregon dived to his left and threw his shield in front of himself and Binty, shielding them from a bolt of lightning and deflecting it towards the fast approaching skotos. "friends."

Bregon had retreated a little with Binty at his side when they were buffeted by a mighty whoosh from behind them. Binty glanced over her shoulder as Bregon smashed another onslaught into ash. Something was rushing in Graimel's direction.

"Got to go," Binty shouted, as she zipped as quick as she could back towards Graimel.

"I'll be right here," he called after her.

A tall, broad, almost human looking creature in an olive green pinstripe suit and top hat, was charging towards Graimel. Binty weaved in and out of the fighting, slapping a skotos or two into the void whilst passing them, until she confronted the creature running at pace towards Graimel, stopping them in their tracks.

She immediately recognised the aged, troubled visage of a Time Tailor. As she breathed a sigh of relief, scores of quag emerged from the charred heathers and ferns, charging towards the skotos. Amongst them, she briefly spotted Ligl and Grock before losing sight of them, and as the quags clashed with the surprised skotos. Two blinding bolts of golden light accompanied their arrival, fading to reveal two more valkyries. Binty could not help but notice how instead of joining Dynma, they stayed with the quags, seemingly protecting them.

"Who are you?" Binty asked.

"I am—"

"Limawli, thank you for coming," Graimel said.

"Seeing as you two know each other, I will get back out there."

As Binty turned to leave, the earth shook with so much force that almost all those present lost their footing. The last of the standing stones outside of Janet's den thought, *bugger this,* and took the opportunity to lie down. Binty spun her head around, stood almost on top of Graimel was the fabled Ygdrabanir, an ancient treant who was also the Time Tailor for giants. And rolling into view were two mountainous boulders who needed no introduction, and as they unfurled, Binty raced over to say hello.

"Lehle, Tenk, it is so good to see you both."

"Tenk and Lehle fight for little human, human save Tenk and Lehle," Tenk said, smashing the ground and pounding the skotos beneath his fist into dust.

"Limawli, Graimel, thanks to you and your little human, the rock giants have been saved. Tenk and Lehle are the last couple. Had they not been reunited, they would have become stagnant in time, ending their species. We are here to make sure that does not happen to any other species," Ygdrabanir said.

Over in the small thicket, a severely injured Zephyrugm lay on her side while Vern tended to her wound. Sleip, battered and bruised from being thrown to the ground on impact, picked his shield up off the floor and took Mabel in his hand.

"Is she going to be okay?" Sleip asked, whilst whirling a now glowing Mabel around his head.

"I need to get her home. Chmnu will take us."

"Then I will return to our friends. I have more than a score to settle now."

Sleip charged at full pelt from the thicket and back into the fray, swinging his hammer with purposeful precision and fearsome force, joining up with Janet and Klaus, tearing holes in the husks of evil.

Towards the back of the mass of skotos, where there were hundreds yet to enter the fray, Floop had found a huge rock to hide behind. Not wanting to be a part of this senselessness, he pulled himself as far beneath it as he could. From within the shadows came a voice.

"Ow! Watch where you put your feet."

"Who is there?" Floop asked.

"It's me, Barc Heape. Please don't make me join them in this fight."

"Relax, I have no intention of doing so. I am also not agreeable to this situation."

"Hang on, is that you, Floop? But you are the queen's assistant. Aren't you supposed to agree with her?"

"How many of your bartenders agree with you?"

"Point taken."

Floop started to think, if both he and Barc felt this way, there may be others.

"We can't hide. We need to see if there are others that want to escape this madness before it is too late," Floop said.

"If Blodia catches us, we are done for."

"If we don't try, then we are as good as ended anyway."

Barc and Floop scurried out from behind the rock, begrudgingly heading into the masses of skotos waiting to join the fight. Although risky, and most likely too late to save any already forced into this pointless fight for nothing, they had to try.

Binty had dashed back to Bregon and was once again fighting at his side.

"I hear we got some help," Bregon said.

"Yep, the rock giants we helped in the Quagmires of Sturm, and Grock, Ligl and 40 or so more quags."

"Ligl is here. We must get over to her and protect them. Quags are not warriors. What are they playing at?" Bregon fumed, angry and anxious all at once, like a devoted parent worried about their kin.

A brief lull in the incessant assault gave Bregon time to lift his head and scan the moor for the quag. In the distance to the north, he could see skotos being flung into the air and turning to ash upon their descent. This was not the doing of his men.

"Maybe they are warriors after all," Bregon said, with a chuckle whilst ducking and slicing in one fluid movement, blowing the ash from his shoulder, before getting back to the business of eradicating the hostile skotos.

Blodia scanned the field of combat, noting that she did not see Floop anywhere. *If he is still alive, I will deal with him afterwards,* she thought. She had lost many, but her army still outnumbered Bedougalnn's defenders by over 100 to one. She screeched at those not engaged in the fight to do so or face her wrath. To the south of her position, she spotted Malka cowering.

Malka was no warrior. She was but a foul loathsome seer, who had used her powers of sight to manipulate, trick, and lead trusting souls to their deaths. So, when faced with axes, teeth, claws, and giant stone fists, her instinct was to hide, and hope. Had she used her time to do what she excelled at, like Salvador Dali did in the arts, or Marie Curie did in both chemistry and physics. She would have foreseen what was coming, and I dare say she would have moved.

Blodia, seething with grim intentions, scurried her way over towards Malka. First, to use her skills to predict the outcome in this battle, then, to use her, to set an example to all the other quivering skotos who were reluctant to face almost certain death for their queen, by ending her.

Of course, Blodia, much like Hans and Edmund, was not the most intelligent of the skotos. She was most certainly the scariest skoto there ever was, but the brightest, well, let's just say, her keyboard was missing QWERTY. So, what she had never taken the time to consider was this. Threatening one with certain death if they did not face almost certain death, and a death that would probably be more terrifying, was no incentive.

As she got closer to Malka, she heard a faint skittering sound growing louder by the second. Had Blodia not disposed of Hans, he would have been able to advise her that this was not a good skittering sound. Whether he would have advised her, or whether he would have just run, we will never know.

Undeterred by this sound, Blodia stayed her course, determined to make an example of Malka. Blodia was only a mere few metres away when Malka saw her coming, her face twisted and contorted with anger. Malka thought for a moment and realised that she had never seen Blodia look any different. *Maybe that is just what Blodia looks like, and everyone just thinks she is angry all the time,* she thought.

"Get to your feet when your queen approaches!" Blodia vehemently screeched above the now almost deafening skittering sound.

*Nope, she was definitely angry,* Malka thought, getting to her feet just as Queen Silkolblin came over the boulder behind her, swallowing her whole.

Blodia was incensed, and to be honest, a little terrified, just like Krahns and Harg, she had never been a fan of spiders. *How dare this spider just come along and eat one of her subjects, especially one she needed information from.* If she had not been floating above the ground, she would have stamped her feet in protest. Instead, she made the wise decision to focus on another area of the battle, which you are minded to note, is not the same as fleeing.

After guzzling down Malka, Queen Silkolblin raised her two front legs into the air, warning off any that may think of trying to attack her. She scuttled sideways a little and leapt into the air, landing to the side of Ygdrabanir. Sat astride her, right behind her head was the Time Tailor for spiders, Bydrael.

Bydrael was a grenkel, an ancient goblin ancestor. Grenkel's were tall, slender, and quite spindly, not that they would appreciate you saying so. They had long, claw-like hands and feet, four rows of tiny, deadly, pointy teeth, and striking yellow and black eyes. They looked ferocious, but by all accounts, they had a polite and pleasant disposition. This grenkel was sporting a rather enviously well-manicured long golden beard and moustache, if Graimel did say so himself.

Bydrael Slid down from Queen Silkolblin and took Graimel's hand.

"Sorry we are so late, old boy. I fell asleep," Bydrael said.

Had Queen Silkolblin had eyebrows, she would have raised them.

"My children are surrounding the area, on your command, Graimel."

"If anything, I think you may be just in time," Graimel said, as Queen Silkolblin swallowed a foolishly brave skoto.

"These don't taste very nice, Graimel."

Lescan threw his arms around Bydrael.

"It's great to see you again, old friend, glad you made it."

"Shame about the circumstance. Did my information help?" Bydrael asked.

"It did," Lescan said, casting his eyes across to Graimel, who patted his pocket.

"Then let us finish this."

Graimel nodded his agreement to Queen Silkolblin.

"As you wish."

Queen Silkolblin commanded her children to attack, and a roaring skittering engulfed the moorland. The skotos did not know where to turn or how to even fight this new enemy and were being turned to ash faster than Binty could eat cake. Blodia could see the tables were turning and decisive action was required, only she could not decide what to do.

But fate was about to help her out.

# 35

# THE BATTLE OF BODMIN MOOR PART II

A staggering boom of thunder resonated across the moor, shaking all those present to their very core. The sky split open, forced apart by the loudest blinding crack of lightning ever heard to this day, as it zagged its way towards Bregon. Without a thought, Binty hurled Bregon to safety.

"Binty!" Bregon screamed, as he flew powerless across the moorland, watching as an explosion of blazing white light engulfed her.

Binty spiralled through the air before plummeting semi-conscious into the blackened mud strewn heather. Bregon had landed on his feet, and furiously determined to find Binty, he began hacking his way through the mob of skotos surrounding his position.

In Janet's den, Bounce's ears pricked up, cocking his head to one side then back to the other, before glancing up at Dougal and bolting for the door. Had it not been slightly ajar, he would have undoubtedly left a hole in it.

"Bounce, no!"

But Bounce had gone, bounding up the stairs as fast as his legs would carry him, out of the stairwell and into the pouring rain before scampering back again. Then, noticing a big tree outside, which he could have sworn was not there before, his bladder got the better of him. The mud squishing between his paws, he pranced over to the tree, where he sniffed and cocked his leg. Relieved, and now soaked to the skin, he raced out onto the moor, past Janet, past Beth, but stopping for a swift fuss off Fimor, before racing off again.

Ygdrabanir looked down as he felt a dampness that was not the rain on his roots, just in time to see Bounce disappearing into the distance. He shook his branches while complaining loudly to Graimel. Most of which was ignored, as Graimel had also seen Bounce disappearing into the masses, and was now surveying the area, trying to spot Dougal. He could not understand why Bounce would be out here if he were not with Dougal.

"We need to find Bedougalnn. I believe he got past us, and is somewhere out there," Graimel said, and dashed off in search of Bounce.

Lescan, Ygdrabanir, Bydrael, and Limawli all picked a direction and started fighting their way across the moor looking for Dougal, as Queen Silkolblin skittered off to join her children in their decimation of the skotos.

Binty rolled over in the heather, murmuring in pain, "Ow!" *that really hurt* she thought to herself, *I don't think I will do that again.* Bounce heard the murmur and bounded towards it. He found Binty sat dazed in a small bush of heather, trying to clean the mud off her armour, whilst also trying not to move.

"Bounce, what are you doing here?"

"Woof," Bounce replied, his front paws coming off the ground and splashing mud all over her again.

Binty reached up and took a hold of Bounce's collar, gingerly pulling herself up and onto his back as he prepared to barge his way back through the throng.

Meanwhile, Dougal pushed himself from his chair and tried to walk, but he could not sustain his weight upon his leg. With a crack, it gave way again, and he collapsed to the floor in agony. He dragged himself over to the door like a sloth on holiday, but realising this was taking too long, he focused all his efforts on Graimel's teachings. Once more, he ventured into the stillness of time, and as long as he maintained his concentration, however long he took climbing stairs or searching for Bounce, was inconsequential.

After what felt like an excruciating eternity, he reached the top of the stairs and headed out, determined to find Bounce. He clawed his way through the mud, cutting a tunnel through the torrential rain.

As he reached the first small group of dwarfs, he saw Sven plastered in ash and mud. He had clearly just torn a skoto in two, as although its head and legs were still intact, an air gap of floating ash separated them. The shock on the face of the skoto still evident. Behind Sven, another skoto was centimetres away from plunging his fist into Sven's back, aiming for his heart.

After analysing the positions of the combatants, Dougal pushed Sven over in the mud, then dragged another skoto into his position. It took him a few minutes to do this, but he was rather pleased with his efforts. He was about to move on when he thought, *I would like to see this play out*. So, like a kid messing with the step function whilst watching a digital movie, he inched time forward.

To start, he observed Sven looking a little bemused. Likely wondering why in one moment he had been standing firm, and the next he was lying on the floor, covered from head to foot in ashen mud. Next, he found himself drawn to the similarly bemused look on the faces of the skotos who were both undoubtedly thinking, *bugger!* This alone brought a momentary smile and chuckle to this despairing field of woe.

Dougal stepped the scenario forward again. Sven had sat up,

and the skoto who had been attacking him, now had his hand wedged inside the chest of the other. *Just once more,* he thought, and he found out why skotos do not strike each other. Both the attacking and the attacked skotos had half turned to ash, and the look on Sven's face had turned from bemused to enthralled.

Dougal was more than satisfied with this result and sniggered quietly to himself. But unbeknownst to him, Blodia's eyes were now fixated upon him.

Dougal continued on his path, inching his way through this quagmire of blood, ash, mud, and scorched heather. He passed Janet, her claws glistening like polished daggers in the rain. Then he came across some friendly goblin mine spiders, giving each of them a quick pat as he dragged himself past and continued deeper into the masses.

Still, he could not see Bounce anywhere, but as he scanned the surrounding area, he spotted a paw print on a rock to his left. He crawled over to examine it, thinking it may be a lyconfinds, but no, it belonged to Bounce, he was certain of it.

With renewed vigour he moved in the imprint's direction, finding Ulap crouched down aiding a battered and bruised Fimor. But a frighteningly close bolt of lightning paused just above Ulap's head, emphasised to Dougal the exact amount of responsibility that came with this power. If he had stepped time once more when saving Sven, then Ulap would have been incinerated.

He could not move Ulap, so he needed to come up with another plan. He saw Ulap's shield leaning against a rock behind him, and using all his strength, he lifted it up and rested it on Ulap's back. Then, mustering everything he had, he forced himself up on his one good leg, trying not to put any pressure on his dodgy one. It was not to be.

His foot struck a rock, sending waves of pain crashing up his leg and cascading throughout his body. He could not afford to lose concentration now and took a moment to stabilise his focus. Then he pushed the shield until it was almost resting on Ulap's head. After hauling himself up onto Ulap's back, he took a hold of the shield one last time, hopefully lifting it enough to deflect the bolt.

Dougal stepped time forward a single second. The bolt struck the shield, deflecting off and hitting a skoto who was about to kill Clensule.

Clensule was a distinguished old quag, who in truth should have been at home in his slippers, being nagged by his wife, and not on a battlefield. But he wanted to show his thanks to Grock's friends for returning Perquag to its proper place in the universe. And if that meant he had to suffer a few hours of excitement away from his wife, then so be it. However, at this precise moment in time, he was thinking how wonderful it is he has a wife who cares enough to nag him.

With time frozen once more, the lightning struck skoto was now just a vast exploding ball of ash, dissipating slowly on the frozen breeze, and Clensule was safe.

Dougal slid from Ulap's back, leaving the shield in place. Ulap was in for a tasty headache.

His search for Bounce continued until he finally spotted his little stubby tail poking out of some heather. With everything he could muster, he hauled himself through the mire until able to lay his hand on Bounce's back. A dazed and flurried Binty clung to his collar, looking a little worse for wear. Not that Dougal would say so.

As Dougal relaxed his concentration time returned to normality

"Binty, are you okay?" Dougal said, stroking Bounce.

"I will be, I think. Is Bregon okay?"

"I've not seen him, why what happened?"

Binty was about to go into detail when she realised to whom she was talking.

"Wait, what on earth are you doing out here? How did you get past Graimel and the others? You're not safe out here. We need to get you back inside."

Binty looked back towards the den, and even though her vantage point was lousy, she could see that no one guarded the entrance. Unbeknownst to her, since Graimel and the others had left to search for Dougal, they had become ingrained in the fighting. Between them they had saved a lot of lives, but they had not found Dougal, so it was fortunate that she had, and without even looking.

Binty gripped Bounce's harness and tried to launch herself into the sky. The natural had become the impossible. She glanced over her right shoulder and saw her wing was all but missing, Dougal's eyes following hers to the same point.

"Bloody Nora, Binty, your wing!" Dougal said, and was instantly crowned king of stating the obvious.

Another bolt of lightning came crackling from the foreboding sky, forking its way towards them. At the exact same time, a somewhat familiar dwarven shield came spinning through the air like a giant flying disc, intercepting this bolt of obliteration and redirecting it straight towards Blodia, striking her shield. Fracture lines becoming visible, her impenetrable barrier was weakening.

"Are you guys okay?" Sleip said, reaching over them and grasping for his shield.

"Let me get you somewhere safe," Sleip said, picking up Dougal and throwing him over his shoulder, keeping his shield in his left hand. "Follow me."

Sleip looked to the sky, gestured to Krahns, and ran back towards Janet's den. Krahns swooped down on Sviltesblen, scorching a trail through the mounting skotos. Distraught at not being able to help her friends. Binty shut her eyes in anguish, whilst wearily clinging to Bounce's harness as he bounded towards Janet's den. Bounce skidded through the entrance to the stairs, turned and barked furiously at Dougal and Sleip who were still quite a way back.

Until Sleip's intervention, which saved Binty, Bounce, and Dougal, Blodia had lost sight of Dougal in amongst the masses. However, the lightning striking her shield caused her to shift her focus to a new area of the moor, and her eyes fixated upon her quarry once again.

Blodia dropped out of the sky and stole through the masses, making sure not to lose sight of Bedougalnn. This was her chance to achieve her goal. Since it seemed she could not be harmed, everyone's concentration was elsewhere, so when she disappeared from the sky, no one was looking for her, except one.

Bounce knew evil, and he had not taken his eyes off Blodia since spotting her foulness. Now he watched as she rose from the foaming crowd of filth that were the skotos. Certain that she was about to attack Dougal, he shook with all his might and bounced on his front paws, unseating the weakened Binty who tumbled to the floor. He turned to give her a reassuring lick, before hurtling back out towards his master, his best friend.

Blodia struck, snatching Dougal from Sleip's shoulder.

"Mor`eth bin," she screeched, as she bound Sleip, her gnarled fingers snipping at his neck.

Sleip dropped his shield and caved to his knees, grasping at his throat. Blodia had never been one to just kill. She enjoyed inflicting as much pain as possible whilst letting her victim retain a slither of hope.

She flung Dougal across the rocks and heather, his bones crunching and cracking on the rocks, splitting his flesh and spewing blood across a few unscathed flowers. Dougal despairingly reached for his dagger. As he fumbled for it, he realised it must have been thrown free when Blodia flung him across the moor. Shattered and dispirited, he clung to hope as his eyelids sagged. Through his blurred and blooded vision he saw a white and tan blob charging towards him, *hope* he thought.

Focused on enjoying every moment of her destruction of time, she slithered towards a now almost unconscious Dougal, dragging Sleip by his throat behind her. She reached down, seizing hold of him and raising him aloft. She drew out his time, consuming his very essence. With the flow of time empowering her, she continually tightened her grip around Sleip's throat, forgetting the world around her.

Bounce head-butted Blodia's legs with a force almost equal to one of Binty's slaps, knocking her legs from under her. Had it not been for her shield, the energy contained would have most likely caused her to implode. It did, however, cause her to release both Dougal and Sleip, much to her annoyance.

Sviltesblen dived towards the ground, extending his talon like feet, but Dougal was out of reach, dropped amongst the rocks. Unable to grasp Dougal, Sviltesblen snatched Sleip to safety before Blodia had time to get back to her feet. Bounce rounded Blodia and now stood between her and Dougal, snarling and salivating.

Blodia paid this no mind, elevating herself about 1m off the ground before swiping Bounce to one side, sending him reeling. Bounce scrambled back to his feet, shook himself, and charged at Blodia again. But she struck the earth in front of him and sent him tumbling back through the heather. This time, she immediately plucked Dougal from the rocks and raised him aloft. His sorrowful eyes falling upon the mud and ash strewn Bounce as he snarled and barked in vain.

Dougal was too drained to resist, and he was soon to be nothing more than a husk of a body as Blodia drew and consumed the remainder of his time.

Graimel and the other Time Tailors were fighting furiously through overwhelming odds, but could not get close enough to help because of sheer numbers. Even Tenk and Lehle were swarming with skotos. Witnessing their queen fulfilling her self-proclaimed prophecy instilled the remaining skotos with renewed enthusiasm.

Rage was building in Binty, the kind of rage she had only ever felt once before, but this was tenfold. This was becoming uncontrollable. Slumped upon her knees, her head pounding and throbbing as if it were about to explode, she heard a high-pitched whistling sound coming from the sky. The unmistakable silhouette of Chmnu came screaming through the storm clouds as they were illuminated by sheet lightning. He was heading straight for Tenk and Lehle.

With the precision of a sniper, he opened fire, picking off the skotos one by one in quick succession. In one pass, he cleared half of the attacking skotos from Tenk, who started flicking the skotos attached to Lehle into permanent expiration.

Dougal's heart slowed. His fight had not been lost; his fight had been taken. His time now flowed through Blodia, being consumed by the void inside her. She gorged herself on her impending victory, Dougal's power and energy coursing through her.

As she relished inflicting revenge on those who took her world from her, she closed her eyes and saw the forlorn faces of her children turn away, judging. A single tear sneaked its way through her ashen prison like door of an eyelid, and she discarded Dougal's body like he was a piece of worthless trash. Broken, Binty knelt in the doorway, transfixed by Dougal's lifeless body tumbling to the earth.

The uncontrolled rage exploded from within her with a thunderous scream that shattered windows, triggered alarms, and afflicted all humans within 150 miles with temporary tinnitus. Thus causing a nationwide panic, the military to scramble all aircraft, and starting a conspiracy theory that would rage on for the next ten years.

Binty rose to her feet in an all-consuming trance, held her arms out in front of her, and as tears streamed down her face, she cried out.

"Ev O'sh!"

She collapsed back down to her knees as a wave of pure pixie rage dispersed across the moor, turning every single fragment of evil to ash. Blodia, however, was still safely within her shield. Graimel and every other able body charged towards Blodia, not knowing what they could do to break this shield, but they had to try.

Dougal's hand twitched, his heart pumped, he opened his one working eye, and using his remaining energy, he lifted his hand up, reaching for the sky. Blodia raised her hand to crush the persistent mortal and emitted a blood-curdling screech.

Floop, who with the help of Barc, had sneaked hundreds of neutral skotos back to the cave, had returned to scour the moor for any remaining neutral skotos. By chance, he came across Dougal's dagger, taken from Goblin Lord Ferglestin, but then he had taken it from Blodia, Dougal's dagger, had a habit of changing hands on death.

Whether this was something currently playing on Dougal's mind, I guess we will never know.

A thought popped into Floop's head, and he plucked the dagger from the grimy soup of mud, blood, and ash, and clutched it in his hand, vengeance bubbling.

He snuck through the fighting on the prowl for Blodia, willing to sacrifice himself to end this madness, as he prepared to strike everything around him exploded into ash.

Seeing Blodia was about to end all of time for all things, he knew he had to act now and leapt from the shadow, striking her with Dougal's dagger. The dagger pierced her shield, dispelling it, exploding with energy, and hurling Floop into the scorched earth, the dagger spinning from his hand.

Blodia was now vulnerable to attack.

The first time Binty saw this dagger, she had recognised it, but the name escaped her. As she watched Floop strike Blodia, its name popped into her head. It was the Dagger of Nincenmort, a formidable dagger that absorbed the will of its owner. Dangerous in any hands, but loyal to its owner, as Floop would have found out had he tried to use it on Dougal.

At his core, Dougal did not want to harm anyone, which was why the dagger only destroyed Blodia's shield.

Everything in the vicinity of Blodia had now been destroyed or stunned, and Graimel knew this was their moment. He needed to act without hesitation. Skidding to a halt, he reached into his pocket, pulling out the pendant of Tel Etoiles and focused his aim on Dougal. In uncontrolled slow motion, dwarfs, quags, spiders, and the odd Time Tailor charged past him, all racing to prevent the end of all time.

He threw Binty a last minute glance of hope, took a last expectant look at the pendant in his hand, and hurled it with all his might. The pendant glided through the thick, ashen atmosphere, as bolts of lightning seemed to try to strike it from the sky. But this pendant appeared to be guided by an undetermined entity, either that or it was an exceedingly accurate throw, because the pendant landed in the palm of Dougal's hand.

Dougal opened his hand to see the central moonstone on the pendant crack open. In a flash, he flicked his wrist and held the pendant aloft. Blodia had enough time to think *Fiddlesticks* before she faded like warm breath on a frigid wind. The Pendant of Tel Etoiles drew his time out of her, and in an instant, transferred it back to him.

The moorland erupted in victory cheers, but as Floop tried to sneak away, Mad Mathis and Ulap accosted him, shaking his hand and thanking him for his actions. Once back at the cave, Floop opened the portal back to the Hidden Dimension. After ensuring all the surviving skotos were through, he followed, and ordered the Pool of Vacant Reflection be destroyed. The skotos celebrated Floop as their new leader. Floop humbly accepted, put his arm around Barc, and went to The Banished Abstract Cat Tavern for a flagon of ale, on the house, of course.

# 36

# THERE'S NO PLACE LIKE HOME

The Moment Floop had stepped through the portal back to the Hidden Dimension, the storm ended as abruptly as it begun. A stiff wind blew across the moor, scattering the ashes of the fallen skotos, for whom no wreaths were laid, and no prayers were said.

The dwarfs had lost a lot of brave warriors, but they had died with honour, died to ensure that all life continued. It had been Bregon's honour to lead his warriors from the front, and he was proud of all they had achieved. As the sun broke through the cloud line, relief spread across their weary, battle-hardened faces. Some collapsing from exhaustion where they stood, while others cradled lost friends, but all secure in the knowledge it was over.

Dougal lay in the mud examining the Pendant of Tel Etoiles. Nothing remarkable jumped out at him. *I wonder what makes it so special, I will have to ask Graimel,* he thought, before snapping it shut. As he studied his broken and battered body, he wondered how was he going to climb the stairs to his apartment? How was he going to walk Bounce? *Bounce,* he thought, *where's Bounce*? He lifted his head just enough to spot Bounce bounding over towards Ygdrabanir.

"Bounce, no!" Dougal yelled, his words falling on deaf ears as usual.

Ygdrabanir flicked one of his roots at Bounce in an attempt to shoo him away. Thinking this was a game like the one he had played with Harg back in the apartment, he grabbed a hold of Ygdrabanir's root and started tugging. Ygdrabanir whipped and snapped at the earth, making Bounce's stubby tail wag excitedly, but Binty recognised a tetchy tree when she saw one, and hollered for Bounce. On hearing her voice, he let go and ran over to see what treats she had for him. *She always had treats in her pocket,* he thought.

Tenk and Lehle waved goodbye, as Ygdrabanir took this momentary distraction to return them home before he was peed on again, and without a sound, they were gone. Queen Silkolblin commanded her children to collect their fallen whilst she picked up Bydrael. Then, with nothing more than an acknowledgement to Graimel, they skittered their way across the moor, home to Grackbin Forest.

"How are you feeling? Or is that a stupid question?" Graimel said, slipping in the mud and landing on his ass at the side of Dougal, and trying to make it look intentional.

"I'll be okay. A lot of clashing emotions at the moment. How many, Graimel? How many died for me?"

"They died fighting for the friends they had, and for the friends they would have made. They gave their lives, so that all others may live."

"What happens to this now?" Dougal said, passing the Pendant of Tel Etoiles back to Graimel, who thrust it back into his pocket.

"I will put it somewhere safe, somewhere goblins won't find it."

"Can I ask what makes it so special?"

"Something that is often overlooked." Graimel took the pendant back from his pocket and held it out in front of Dougal "Tell me what you see?"

"A sun, or maybe a star-shaped pendant, inlaid with a few little gemstones, and one large one in the middle."

"Okay." Graimel flicked the pendant open. "and now?"

"An empty silver pendant."

"Precisely, because it contains the same things that are hidden inside everyone who fought beside us today, hope, faith, and virtue." Graimel snapped the pendant shut, placed it back in his pocket, and got to his feet. "Oh, and it has a long memory. Blodia and this pendant have a history you see. She ripped this from its previous owner before killing him, starting a chain reaction that culminated with her demise. So remember, never upset a piece of jewellery."

"What?" Dougal said, somewhat confused.

Graimel laughed, and leaving Dougal lay in the mud, he headed over to check on Ligl, Grock, and the rest of the quag's, before they disappeared back to Perquag.

"Graimel, Graimel!" Dougal shouted, to no avail.

"You need a lift back to Janet's then or what?" Bregon said, his dulcet tones bringing music to Dougal's ears.

"It's good to see you, Bregon."

"I think this belongs to you," Bregon said, passing Dougal the Dagger of Nincenmort. "Now, let's get you back."

Bregon hauled Dougal out of the mud, hoisting him up over his shoulder, leaned over to collect Sleip's shield in his free hand, and bimbled over to the entrance of Janet's den. Dougal surveyed the now almost empty, charred, and ash strewn moor. Dotted here and there were some of Bregon's now weary brethren, collecting up the fallen warriors' weapons, shields, and discarded pieces of armour.

He caught sight of Grock being supported by Ligl and raised his hand, smiling. Grock tapped Ligl on her shoulder. She turned, and they both waved farewell before she continued to help him limp over to Limawli, who was shaking hands with Graimel. A moment later, Graimel stood alone on the almost empty moor.

Bregon carefully set Dougal down next to Binty and called over Krahns and Sleip.

"Sleip, you left this lying about, I almost tripped over it," Bregon said, passing Sleip his shield. "Krahns, round everyone up and thank Dynma. We should head back to Ildjorden."

"Consider it done."

"Now then, look at the state of you two, what a pair you make. I know how he's feeling. How about you, little one?" Bregon said, looking at what remained of Binty's right wing. "Can it be repaired?"

"I don't think so. I can't see how," Binty said, tears trickling from her tired eyes. "I mean, what use is a pixie that can't fly?"

"Now you listen here, Binty Malice. There is not a thing in this world that a dwarf cannot fix. We will have you flying again in no time," Sleip said, kneeling down and offering Binty his hand. "Let us find out what magic Efraj can work."

"We need to clean my armour first."

Sleip helped Binty wipe the mud from her armour, and to her amazement there was not a single scratch or mark upon it. She felt sure that there would have been some damage considering the hit she took, and as the realisation took hold that Efraj's creation had saved her life, more tears came, tears of gratitude.

"Okay, I'm ready, let's go see Efraj." Binty wiped her face, smearing mud from her armour across it. "Even if she cannot help, I need to thank her for my life. Thank you, Sleip Neren. I'm assuming we're on full name terms now for some reason," she said, managing a giggle and a smile.

In the distance Krahns was speaking to Dynma, her hands resting upon his shoulder as he hung his head. With a subtle nod of condolent respect, she shot up into the heavens, escorted as always by Hettierne and Purrseeka. Only Krahns knew what Dynma said to him, and though he later shared an account of it with Bregon, it was never spoken of again.

As Krahns and the rest of the dwarven warriors strolled over to Bregon, Sviltesblen and Chmnu landed with the grace of a stomping elephant, spraying them all with mud and trying not to laugh. Krahns approached Sviltesblen and placed his hand upon his magnificent jawline.

"I don't know if you can understand me, but thank you, it was my honour to ride with you."

"What is it with everyone thinking dragons can't talk?" Sviltesblen said, looking quizzically at Chmnu.

"Beats me."

Krahns and the gathered dwarfs stood in astonished silence whilst there was a bit of back-and-forth banter between Chmnu and Sviltesblen, bemoaning the fact that no one except Vern truly understands dragons. Krahns eventually interrupted, firstly to apologise, and then to reiterate his thanks to both them and Vern and Zephyrugm, wishing Zephyrugm a speedy recovery. With the niceties completed, Chmnu and Sviltesblen took off and headed home for treats.

By the time Krahns and the dwarfs got back to Janet's den, the lyconfind had also gathered. Some were sitting on one of the standing stones which had earlier decided to have a rest. Had the stone realised it was going to be used as a bench, it would have probably remained stood.

Beth lay down with her head resting on Wrethe's lap, exhausted, whilst Janet and Fimor went to fetch cake and wine. Klaus came strolling over carrying two bottles, his fur glistening, throwing one of them at Krahns as he passed.

"Thanks," Krahns called out, snatching the bottle mid-flight, and spinning it in his hand to look at the label. "What the hell is this... Wereshine?"

"It will be good for cleaning that mud out of your beards," Klaus called back, *but not as good as this,* he thought, looking at the bottle of Furisoft in his hands.

"Where have you been?" Beth asked.

"Took a shower," Klaus said, looking like she had just asked him the most stupid question ever. "Did you think I was going to sit around covered in mud like you lot? I will tell you one thing though." He tossed the bottle of Furisoft he was holding over to Beth. "Kainen was right, Furisoft is better than Wereshine. I mean just look at my fur, it's so shiny."

"Apertures," Beth whispered in Wrethe's ear, jumping up and dragging him behind her as she headed for the shower.

"Hey, I want that back!"

"Of course, if there's any left!"

Klaus found a clean spot on which to lie back and relax, on the no longer standing stone, whilst both Sven and Lescan resisted the urge to flick mud at him.

"Didn't go quite according to plan, Graimel," Bregon said.

"I'll give you that, but the plan was good."

"Did you even have a master plan?" Binty asked.

"Why, hells no, but I had a rather cunning idea."

"But what about the plan you discussed with me and Bregon?"

"I knew if I told you the actual plan, you would have disagreed with me and blabbed to Dougal."

"Blabbed to me about what?" Dougal asked.

"Nothing. Look, we all agreed the important thing was to protect Dougal, and my cunning idea was based on that. Close your ears Dougal." Graimel waited a moment for Dougal to cover ears before proceeding. "My plan was to make Dougal so exhausted on the run back to Janet's that he would be unable to join us in the fight."

"You managed that all right. Look at the state of him," Binty said, glancing at the woeful looking Dougal.

"I did not mean for him to take a tumble, but I cannot say I was not pleased that he was incapacitated, as it relieved me of a rather awkward conversation," Graimel said nonchalantly.

"Oh my god, Graimel, are you saying you're pleased Dougal got injured?"

"No, not exactly."

"No wonder you wanted him to cover his ears."

"Speaking of which, Dougal, you can uncover your ears now... Dougal!"

Sleip gave Dougal a gentle nudge.

"Sorry."

"It's okay," Graimel said, before turning to address them all. "I should have known that Dougal would need to be in the fight in order for us to win. A fight we would have lost, had it not been for his and Bounce's intervention."

"Remind me to never ask you to plan my birthday party," Bregon chuckled. "Right, we best be getting back."

"Actually, I meant to ask, how did you get here so fast?"

"I brought them, of course." The accent was sweet, and not too dissimilar to Binty's.

"Tolti?" Graimel said, taking an unplanned step backwards. "I... didn't realise you were the... for them."

An old, curly white-haired pixie appeared, sat atop of Bregon's head, and waggling her finger in Graimel's general direction.

"Nanna," Binty said, having not seen her grandmother for a few years.

"Hush child. Look, I know we have not always been in agreement, Graimel, and I can't say I am happy about you taking my granddaughter on such a dangerous adventure. But Bregon gave you his word, and I was not leaving it to chance they would get here in time, not when my precious Binty is involved." Tolti jumped off Bregon's head, and whizzed over to where Binty still knelt on Sleip's hand. "Oh my word, what happened to your wing, dear?"

"It's okay. Sleip is going to help me get it fixed."

Tolti sped over to Graimel, and as she hovered right in his eye line, she whispered.

"He better be able to fix it, otherwise this is going to end a lot worse than the towel incident."

Graimel gulped. Of the few things in this world he was afraid of, Tolti was one, daring not to say anything, he just nodded to show his understanding. With one final stern glare at Graimel, Tolti took Bregon and the others home.

Janet and Fimor came up the stairs with trays full of cakes and malbec, and a pot of tea for Graimel.

"Here you go everyone, a bite to eat and a drink to… where is everyone Graimel?" Janet asked.

"They went home."

"Oh, then what are we going to do with all this?"

"Well, I suggest we eat, and we raise a glass to our friends. No point letting it go to waste now," Fimor said, smiling as he placed the trays on the fallen rock and raised his glass.

"For Fangs and Fur," Fimor cheered.

"For Honour," Graimel bellowed.

"For Bedougalnn," they all roared.

They were all joined a few minutes later by Beth and Wrethe, who were now also glistening in the early evening sunlight.

"It's even better when someone massages it in for you," Beth said, smiling coyly as she threw the bottle of Furisoft back over to Klaus.

"Beth!" Janet said, almost choking on her mouthful of malbec.

# 37

# PARTY IN EROF

It had been three days since Blodia's defeat, and since Binty had gone to Ildjorden. True to his word, Sleip had taken her straight to see Efraj, and though daunted by the proposal, she was determined not to fail. She took some measurements, made some sketches, and set about the task at hand.

Whilst waiting for Efraj to work her magic, Binty spent her time getting to know Anelci better, learning some secrets about Sleip in the process, which she promised never to tell. She also convinced Krahns and Sleip to give her the secret tour of Ildjorden, and after meeting Krahns' worgs, she spent the rest of her time with them.

It took her two days of working non-stop to craft the intricate filigree design, which she bonded together with an almost invisible layer of impervious dwarven glass. The result was breath-taking. Speechless, Binty brushed her hands across the wing, almost afraid to touch it. The design not only matched her other wing but also the colour and elaborate engravings adorning her armour. She lifted the wing from the workbench. Stunned by its apparent weightlessness, she could not find the words to justify her amazement.

"Once it is fitted, you should not be able to feel the difference… I hope," Efraj said, whilst preparing some tiny but quite frightful looking clamps. "Are you ready? The clamps might pinch a bit, I'm afraid."

"I trust you, Efraj, and it would be worth any pain to fly again."

Efraj took the wing, and with Anelci's help to hold it in place, she attached the clamps. Binty took a deep breath and grimaced through the pain until the last clamp snapped shut.

"All done. How does it feel?" Efraj asked.

"Honestly, I cannot tell the difference," Binty said, glancing over her shoulder as if in disbelief that the wing had been attached.

"Do you want to give it a…"

Binty shot into the air without hesitation, darting left then right, tumbling, rolling, and twisting her way across the room, before coming back to hover directly in front of Efraj's face. Tears of happiness trickled down everyone's faces as Binty brushed away a tear from Efraj's cheek and whispered her thanks.

Binty whizzed back into the air and dashed across towards the entrance to Efraj's forge. She had seen Bregon sneak in to watch from behind some stacked barrels. Swooping down, she landed on his shoulder.

"I thought you weren't coming?"

"I guess I was worried in case it didn't work. I don't think I could have faced you if it didn't."

"Why ever not?" Binty questioned.

"This happened to you, saving me, and I never thanked you for that. I would not be standing here now if it had not been for you."

Everyone in the room flashed each other shocked glances. No one knew how Binty got injured, and she had never said. This was an astounding revelation, and one that should be celebrated. The dwarfs never had to look far for an excuse for a party.

"You do not need to thank me. You, your warriors, and your

people welcomed me and my friends. You came to our aid, and sacrificed so, so much. I am forever indebted to you all." Binty looked up, straight into Efraj's eyes. "Even more so to Efraj, for I may have saved your life, Bregon, but in doing so, Efraj's armour saved mine."

With that said, she gave Bregon a peck on the cheek, before zipping between them all to say goodbye.

"Now, how do I get back to Janet's den? I have some stones to put back in place, I believe?"

"I will take you, dear," Tolti said.

"Hey, Nanna," Binty said, taking her hand.

Everyone stood around, passing each other glances and not knowing what to do with themselves after witnessing Tolti and Binty disappear. Until Bregon announced.

"I am sure you have all got some work to be getting on with."

Back on Bodmin Moor, Binty and Tolti glided to rest atop one of the standing stones.

"Well, isn't that strange? I don't feel sick at all? When I travel like that with Graimel, I get a bit of an upset tummy," Binty said.

"Well, he is not as delicate as we are, my dear, and certainly not in tune with a pixie's sensitivities."

"Oh, can you do me a favour, nanna?" Binty said, before whispering something in her ear and winking.

Tolti vanished again, and Binty set about putting all the standing stones back in their upright position before anyone noticed. The last stone she put back was the huge monolith that hid the entrance to the den. As soon as it clunked into place, Janet came running up the stairs and welcomed Binty back, admiring her replacement wing.

"Come in, come in. Dougal and Graimel are still here, and we have Dougal back on his feet. He needs a stick, but he is moving about."

"That's fantastic, but is Bounce still here?"

"Of course he is."

"And did you manage to get everything done?"

"Finished up this morning."

Binty smiled and raced down the stairs and into Janet's den. Bounce positively leapt to his feet, emitting his deep guttural woof, causing his front paws to bounce off the floor as usual. Binty rushed over and hugged him, then produced a treat from her pocket, which he swallowed down whole and waited expectantly for another. It was not forthcoming. She whizzed around the room whilst delighting over her new wing, checking everyone was okay, and that there had been no more trouble since they triumphed over Blodia.

"So, are we all ready to go?"

"Go where?" Dougal asked.

"My dad's birthday party is today; I hope everyone can make it."

"You need to get me home then, Graimel. I need to pick up a couple of things first. Are you coming with us, Binty?"

"No, I will stay here with Janet and Bounce, and we will meet you at Backfore Woods in an hour?"

"Oh, okay, I'm going to have to drive fast."

"Drive!" they said, in an unrehearsed unanimous exclamation.

"It's an automatic. It will be fine."

Graimel peered over the top of his glasses, his eyes shifting back and forth between those present, seeking reassurance that it would be fine. Like Bounce's second treat, it was not forthcoming.

Dougal and Graimel appeared outside Dougal's apartment. All around them were flashing blue lights, and police sirens wailing intrusively from the surrounding streets. They headed towards the front door of the apartment building, and in less than a second Dougal remembered there was no lift.

"You know what, I don't need to go up, let's just get the car. We will stop for what I need on the way," Dougal said.

As Dougal tottered over to his car with Graimel in tow, they looked up, and Mr Lerkli waved hello from his window. All kinds of shouting then erupted from the direction of his house, and Mr Lerkli turned and put his hands on his head, before disappearing from view.

Graimel gripped the door handle tightly, still unsure whether Dougal should be driving, as he pulled away and flicked on the radio. On the news, a story was breaking about a seemingly pleasant man from the local area, who had been abducting young men from the neighbourhood, selecting them from his upstairs window. An update later that evening would go on to mention the names of the six prisoners found shackled in his basement. One name in particular caught Dougal's attention, Ben Mayjars, an old school friend who went to work abroad 15 years ago, or so he thought.

"So he's a nice old man, is he?" Graimel said, shaking his head. "You have so much to learn, young Dougal."

Dougal pulled out into the main road, turned off the radio and headed towards Backfore Woods. Stopping at a gift shop for a card for Galder, and then a book store to pick up the Encyclopaedia Britannica. On discovering the last edition went out of print ten years ago, and that it spanned 32 volumes, he instead opted to pop into the closest electronics store to purchase a mid-range mini tablet.

"Would you like Wi-Fi and cellular, Sir?" the shop assistant asked.

"Er, just Wi-Fi, thanks. Can you imagine the roaming costs to Erof?"

The somewhat confused and mystified shop assistant dared not to ask any more questions, and fetched the required product. Dougal unboxed it straight away, relieved to find it was fully charged he connected it to the shop's Wi-Fi signal. After a few minutes of frantic website hoping, he proceeded to loiter while he downloaded the best modern encyclopaedia he could find.

Dougal jumped back into his car. The traffic warden, who was in the middle of writing him a ticket for being double-parked, described it as more of a hobble and lurch affair when explaining to the trainee why they let him off. With a screech of tyres, he sped away, ensuring he stuck to the speed limits, without any doubt and beyond question. At least that is what he told the white knuckled Graimel to say, if they got stopped by the Fae Police.

Dougal pulled into Backfore Woods and parked in the same spot as before, waving to Phil as he did so. As they stood in the car park, wondering if they were the first to arrive, Bounce came bounding over from the edge of the woods to greet them. Dougal peered into the tree line and caught sight of his lyconfind friends waiting with Janet, Vern, and Chmnu.

"You're late," Binty whispered, as if someone might overhear, "but then none of the others have turned up yet either." she added, before sitting on his shoulder.

"What are you late for? Are more fairies coming? Oh, sorry, I forgot, you're not a fairy are you," Molly said, appearing from behind the car parked next to them.

"Hello, Molly, it is lovely to see you again. You're not alone, are you?" Binty asked.

"No silly, mom and dad, and my annoying brother are coming. Did you know I am two years younger than him, but I am much stronger? What are you late for?"

"A party."

"Oh wow, can I come to your party?"

"Molly!" Mylo snapped. "What are you doing?"

"I was just asking if I could go to her party."

Mylo looked at Dougal and recognised him as the man that Molly had only last week called a fairy, and now, here she was referring to him as her. Mylo ushered Molly away as a sudden strong breeze blew through the car park, accompanied by an earth-shaking thump. The ground shuddered triggering the car alarms, and fearing an earthquake, all the humans in the vicinity grabbed hold of the nearest thing available.

"Looks like my friends are here for the party," Binty said, glancing to her left.

All at once, Bregon, Onjeg, Krahns, Sleip, Efraj, and Anelci appeared with Tolti at the same time that Tenk and Lehle arrived with Ygdrabanir, Grock, Ligl, and Limawli. Molly's eyes widened like saucers as Mylo hurried her into the car, shouting to Lydia and Leon to hurry.

Molly wound her window down and waved to the huge walking tree. Ygdrabanir bent down and peered into the car. He paused for a moment, as if trying to recollect something. Whatever it was, it escaped him for now, so he smiled, waved back, and stepped into the woods.

"So, are the hairy men in the woods your friends? Are you having a party with them?"

"Molly, put your window up," Mylo said, burying his head in his hands.

"Why can't she have her window down? It's a lovely day," Lydia said, getting into the car. "Oh, is that the man Molly called a fairy?"

"Yes, and we need to go now, because she just asked him if he was going to a party with the hairy men in the woods."

Leon and Lydia tried to hide their amusement, but were unable to do so and burst out laughing. As much as Mylo tried to say it was not funny, it really was, and as he pulled away, the smirk spread across his face, and he broke. Binty waved goodbye to Molly, gripped a hold of Bounce's harness, and before Phil could shout, *dogs need to be on a lead,* she headed into the woods.

Graimel called on Harg to show the way to Erof, and Harg

tired of being just a staff for the last few days, transformed and spread his wings, then did as requested, and guided everyone into Erof.

Binty raced ahead to announce the impending surprise and to give her dad a huge birthday hug. Darting into the village, she saw her father sat in the swing seat outside their home. He was holding hands and laughing joyfully with an elegant, frosty haired pixie, each captivated by the other.

"Hi, Dad, who is your friend? Are you going to introduce me?"

"Oh hi, sweetheart, this is Rylahi. She sometimes keeps me company when you're away. She makes a lovely pot of tea, and we often sit and read together."

"I can go if you like?" Rylahi said.

"No, not at all. It is so lovely to meet you. It's about time dad got himself a friend," Binty said, emphasising the word friend whilst making quotation marks with her fingers.

Galder and Rylahi glanced at each other, giggling as they realised they were still holding hands.

"Well, it is lovely to meet you as well," Rylahi said, smiling.

"Anyway, I have brought some friends to your party; I hope that's okay."

"Of course it is, sweetheart, and you can tell us all about your wing later."

From out of the trees came Binty's newfound friends, and while most of the pixies wanted to flee in terror, Binty assured them no one would be eaten. Half of them were vegetarians anyway, she explained, and they had brought plenty of cake and wine. Once they had all tried this wine that Binty spoke of, there was no looking back, and as for the mead that Bregon brought with him, well suffice to say there were going to be a lot of hangovers.

Dougal presented his card and gift to Galder, and after explaining how to use it and what it contained, Galder was overjoyed. He had always wanted to learn more about the humans and now he could. Hobbling away, Dougal pondered over whether he had done the right thing. After all, humans had done some pretty dreadful things throughout history, but they had done some good as well, so he hoped it would be fine.

With the celebrations in full swing, Dougal finally had time to thank his friends personally for being present and never giving up, before raising his glass in remembrance of those unable to be with them today. After a minute of respectful reflection, they all raised their glasses in silence.

Sleip placed his glass down and cleared the grit from his eyes as he sauntered off to mingle, only to be intercepted by Alnilli and Teep, who wanted him to tell them all about their niece's adventures. Sleip retold the parts of the story he knew, and remembering what Graimel had once told him, he replaced every mention of alcohol with tea.

"She sure drank a lot of tea," Alnilli said.

"Definitely her father's daughter," Teep replied.

"Let me introduce you to my daughters," Sleip said, with a cheery smirk, "this is Efraj, and this is Anelci."

As he strode away, he heard his daughters raving about how amazing Binty was and adding how much of an honour it was to be invited there today.

Dougal spotted Harg perched on a rock down by the river and remembered something he wanted to ask. *Now was as good a time as any,* he thought, and he shuffled over, taking a seat on the rock next to him.

"Harg, can I ask you a couple of personal questions? You don't have to answer if you don't want to."

"I am not doing anything else, so why not. Ask away."

"Well, when did you learn to talk? Are you Sleip's Brother? And did you used to be a dwarf? And if so, how come you are related to Janet's front door?"

"That's more than a couple of questions, but okay." Harg stretched his wings and tilted his head to one side, wondering where to begin, or more specifically, how to explain. "I was born a dwarf; however, my family were direct descendants of Huginn, hence why we can transform into ravens. You could say the raven is my true form. We also retained the gift of speech bestowed upon Huginn, so I never had to learn to speak, I just always could.

"Sleip is not my brother, though when I was orphaned he became like a brother to me, and I still feel the bond between us." Harg paused for a moment to collect his thoughts. "My family, well, for reasons unknown to me, they were cursed centuries ago. All I know is, at some point in our lives, we would take root, and over the following few days, we would transform from a dwarf into an immovable tree. There we would remain until we were cut down, freeing us once again, to some extent anyway, as our soul was contained in an element of the tree. Hence, why my Great Uncle Merg is Janet's door, and I am now Graimel's staff, quite a shock for him the first time I transformed, I can tell you."

"So, can your Great Uncle Merg transform into a raven if he wants?"

"Of Course, but he is happy, and he has a duty to protect Janet."

"What? Why Janet?"

"Because she is your only living relative."

"So, what happened to your parents? Where are they?"

"They were out hunting when they transformed together, unfortunately this was many moons ago, when the humans could still see our kind. Some villagers saw them transform, and believing it was some kind of witchcraft, they…" Harg took a moment to compose himself. "They burnt them alive. I'm sorry, can we leave this?"

"Of course, I am so sorry. I didn't mean to upset you."

Harg took flight and headed down the river, where he rested in a tall tree for a while, remembering his parents.

Dougal got up off the rock and was about to go back to the party, when Graimel wandered over.

"Have you seen Harg?"

"Ah, yeah, I think I may have upset him though. I asked him about his family."

"I guess I should have explained all that to you."

"Well, what now, Graimel? Where do we go from here?"

"That is a good point. Where do we go now, Graimel?" Binty said, appearing on Graimel's shoulder from out of nowhere.

Graimel frowned and unsuccessfully wracked his brain.

"You know what, I don't know. I guess I should check my notes."

Graimel stuffed his hand deep into his pocket, pulling out a piece of paper, carefully unfolding it before reading it quietly to himself.

"Hmm, curious, not what I was expecting," he said, passing the piece of paper into his long white beard, where it was snatched away.

"Wait, what isn't?" Dougal asked.

"What happens next. It's all predestined, you see. I just forgot I had that in my pocket."

"What? And what is in your beard, Graimel, I need to know? I know I saw something in there."

"Come with me, Binty. There is someone Dougal needs to meet."

Graimel and Binty strolled off up the bank and headed back to the party.

"Graimel, what's in your beard? Graimel, Graimel, oh, what's the point," Dougal said, slumping back down on the rock.

"Excuse me, can we talk? You are, The Bedougalnn, right?" The voice was raspy and Nordic.

Dougal stared at the bushes beside the river, unable to pinpoint anything out of the ordinary.

"Yes, I am Bedougalnn, but please, call me Dougal. Who are you?"

"I am Galfwernic, and I need your help, but I can't talk about it here. I shouldn't even be here; I walked through a door and came out behind this bush."

Dougal watched as a small pale blue kobold, wearing a white hooded cloak emblazoned with a bold black cross, stepped from behind the bush carrying a bow in his left hand. He had cropped swept back hair, thick eyebrows, and a short well-groomed beard, all of it whiter than a snowdrop and adorning a wrinkled, scarred face. Meaning no disrespect, Dougal could not help but think how old he looked.

"I will help if I can, but I'm not going anywhere with a stranger, at least not without my friends. Why don't you come to the party, and we can talk after?"

"You don't understand, there's no time!" Galfwernic said.

"If there is one thing I've learned over this last week, it's there is always time."

Dougal turned away from the now irritated, scowling Kobold, and started hobbling back to join his friends, when, with a loud thud, he hit the floor.

Graimel stroked his beard. And whatever was lurking inside it surreptitiously passed him another piece of paper.

THE END.

# ACKNOWLEDGMENTS

An extra special thanks to Freja, for your advice and critique.

Thanks also to:
Sue, Bradley, Mike, and Dr Yannis.

Finally, thanks to my Monty Moo for inspiration, and without whom I would be lost.

www.ingramcontent.com/pod-product-compliance
Lightning Source LLC
LaVergne TN
LVHW040826090826
845145LV00001BA/226

* 9 7 8 1 7 3 9 3 1 3 0 0 5 *